D0275645

The Dark

Emma Haughton

The Dark

HODDER &
STOUGHTON

First published in Great Britain in 2021 by Hodder & Stoughton
An Hachette UK company

1

Copyright © Emma Haughton 2021

The right of Emma Haughton to be identified as the Author of the Work has been
asserted by her in accordance with the Copyright, Designs and Patents Act 1988.

A CIP catalogue record for this title is available from the British Library

Hardback ISBN 978 1 529 35660 1
Trade Paperback ISBN 978 1 529 35661 8
eBook ISBN 978 1 529 35662 5

Typeset in Sabon MT by Palimpsest Book Production Limited, Falkirk, Stirlingshire

Printed and bound in Great Britain by Clays Ltd, Elcograf S.p.A.

Hodder & Stoughton policy is to use papers that are natural,
renewable and recyclable products and made from wood grown in sustainable
forests. The logging and manufacturing processes are expected to conform
to the environmental regulations of the country of origin.

Hodder & Stoughton Ltd
Carmelite House
50 Victoria Embankment
London EC4Y 0DZ

www.hodder.co.uk

For those I love most – you know who you are.

I

12 February

White. Endless, featureless, mind-numbing white. A white so bright it hurts your eyes, at once beautiful and dreadful. I've arrived, finally, at the end of the earth – or rather its southernmost tip.

And there's absolutely nothing here.

'You okay?'

Jim's voice is barely audible over the drone of the Basler's engines. I nod, though it's far from true. I'm exhausted. Bone-achingly, brain-crushingly tired. Three days into my journey, and everything is beginning to feel surreal.

It *is* surreal, I decide, as we fly deeper into the heart of the continent, peaks and glaciers giving way to bizarre ice formations that eventually subside into the vast plain of Dome C, an endless expanse of snow, ridged like a frozen sea, the same in every direction. No wonder it's nicknamed White Mars – this is the coldest place in the world, and the most deserted.

My new home for the next twelve months.

For the first time since leaving Heathrow for Christchurch in New Zealand, I feel a niggle of doubt. A dent in my excitement.

This had seemed a good idea, back in the warmth and safety of my Bristol flat, reading the job application. A year as the doctor in an Antarctic ice station had the ring of adventure about it, and I could tick all the boxes: broad experience in emergency medicine; basic surgical training; no disqualifying health conditions. Plus, the clincher – available immediately.

Even so, I hadn't expected to end up in this little plane, flying over mile upon mile of ice. The position in the new research base was open to anyone in the world. What were the chances they'd pick me?

Yet here I am, against all the odds.

Excited. And terrified.

'A couple more hours and we'll be there.'

Jim reaches behind my seat and retrieves the sandwiches, handing a packet to me. I unwrap it without enthusiasm. Though fresh when we left New Zealand two days ago, the lettuce and tomato have turned limp, the bread unappealingly soggy.

Suck it up, Kate, I tell myself as I force them down. They're some of the last fresh vegetables I'll eat in many months, once those stacked in the crates behind us are gone. This is the penultimate flight to the United Nations Antarctica station – more affectionately known as UNA; when the final plane carries away the last of the summer team next week, no one can reach us again for over half a year.

My stomach tightens at the thought. Will I be able to cope? For that matter, will the other twelve members of the winter team? While it all seemed manageable – academic, almost – during the four-week crash course in Geneva, here, now, faced with this vast Antarctic wilderness, the chilling reality of what I've let myself in for is hitting home.

After all, I've heard the stories. Rumours of people going off the rails, destabilised by the isolation and constant darkness, the strain of being trapped in such a small social group. A cook at McMurdo, the large US base, who attacked a colleague with a claw hammer. An Australian staffer who became so violent he had to be locked in a storeroom for months. A drunken Russian welder who stabbed an electrical engineer in a fit of rage.

No wonder some stations don't let new staff meet the outgoing winterers.

Shit!

The plane gives a mechanical cough and suddenly dips. Despite the dampening effect of the pills I took before boarding, my breath stops in my throat, and for a second or two of pure horror I'm certain we're about to plunge into the unforgiving ice.

Moments later we're flying steadily again.

'Hey, relax.' Jim reaches across to squeeze my arm. 'She does that once in a while. Touch of cold in the engines.'

I smile at the Aussie understatement – it's minus forty out there. 'Sorry. I'm not exactly the world's best flyer.'

'No worries.' He grins. 'You're in good company. Had one guy last year – an engineer, so you'd think he'd understand aeronautics – sobbing for most of the return flight. You're doing fine.'

I flash him a grateful look, but my heart is still pounding. If anything goes wrong, if we crash or we're forced to make an emergency landing, the chances of rescue are vanishingly small. We could freeze to death within minutes.

I shove my hands under my thighs, trying to hide the trembling, but my body rebels with a rising tide of nausea. Oh God, please don't let me be sick. I squeeze my eyes shut against the relentless dazzle of sun on ice, breathing slowly and deeply.

Fox eyes glint at me in the glare of headlights, and my world begins to spiral.

Stop it, Kate, I hiss under my breath, pushing the image away.

Just stop.

* * *

3

'Want to take a look at your new home?'

I wake at the sound of Jim's voice, surprised I'd fallen into a doze. Pressing my face to the window, I squint in the direction he's pointing. At first, see nothing except that ubiquitous white, the deep blue dome of sky above. But gradually, as my eyes adjust to the light, I make out a little huddle of buildings in the vast, flat plain below. Beyond them, some distance away, a tall silver tower.

We're here, I realise, with a tremor of anticipation.

The ice station.

A tiny oasis in all this emptiness.

As we draw closer, two taller pale-grey buildings loom into view. Several small, squat structures are dotted around, trails criss-crossing the snow between them.

Beside me, Jim has an air of focused attention, adjusting dials and switches on the dashboard as we begin our descent towards the runway. If you can call it that. As we line up for the approach, I see it's nothing more than a long strip of compacted snow. Fear erupts again, squeezing into my throat. I grip my seat tightly as the ground rushes up to meet us.

'Don't worry.' Jim glances at me and grins. 'I've done this a thousand times.'

The little plane bucks and shakes as the wheels hit the ice. I exhale, relief flooding my body as we rapidly decelerate, coming to a halt several hundred metres away from the main buildings. The two largest, I can see now, are three storeys high, raised on massive steel legs to keep them clear of the drifting snow. A couple of figures are descending the steps and making their way towards us.

'There you go.' Jim sits back and rubs his neck. 'Home sweet home.'

My smile is weak, my heart still racing from the adrenaline of the landing.

'You ready?' He zips up his thick parka.

'For what?'

A moment later I have my answer. As Jim opens the plane door, impossibly cold air rushes in and my lungs contract with shock. Despite my goose-down jacket and salopettes it's like an assault, a collision with something solid. I try to breathe steadily, but inhaling is painful. As I ease myself out of my seat, longing for firm ground beneath my feet, I feel the moisture around my nose, my eyes, my lips instantly freeze. Even with goggles, the sunlight bouncing off the snow is blinding.

The next thing that hits me is the silence. Thick, almost cloying.

The sound of pure emptiness.

I take a few steps then stumble, dizzy, disoriented. A hand grabs my arm. 'Steady there. Takes a minute or two to adjust.'

I look up at the face gazing down at me. Or rather, I catch a glimpse of stubble on a small section of his exposed skin. The rest of him is covered head to foot in cold weather gear, huge reflective goggles obscuring his eyes. Even so, I can tell he's good-looking; something in his tone, the confident way he holds himself.

'Andrew.' He extends a gloved hand towards mine. 'But everyone calls me Drew.'

I shake it weakly. 'Kate.'

'Welcome to the bottom of the world,' he says in a soft American accent, then turns to introduce his companion. 'This is Alex.'

Alex gives me a brief nod, then goes to help Jim unload the crates from the back of the plane. I push away a little pang of something I identify as disappointment.

But what did I expect? A welcome parade?

'Let's get you inside,' Drew says, before turning to the pilot. 'You staying for a while?'

Jim nods. 'I'll be there in a minute. Put the kettle on. '

Drew picks up my heavy bags as if they're weightless, and heads towards the nearest building. I trail after him. Walking feels strange, the snow nothing like the soft, slushy stuff that occasionally appears back home. This is an altogether different beast: hard, crystalline, squeaking and groaning beneath my boots. Though it rarely snows up here – Dome C has so little rainfall it's technically a desert – when it does snow, it stays, amassing over thousands of years into ice several kilometres deep.

As we approach the station, the silence cedes to an array of hums and beeps, testament to the activity inside. The sound of life. Generators, instruments, everything we need to sustain ourselves in such a hostile environment – without these machines, we'd quickly die.

'Good journey?' Drew stops, waiting for me to catch up. I'm gasping with the effort of this short walk. The altitude, I remind myself; we're 3,800 metres above sea level, and the air is thin as well as fiercely cold.

'You've come all the way from London, right?'

I nod.

'Your first time in Antarctica?'

I nod again, too breathless to speak.

'You get used to it.'

As we reach the closest building, Drew pauses to show me the Union Jack in an array of flags strung above the door. 'You're sharing it with Alice, but I'm sure you won't mind that.'

'So that one's for you?' I point to the stars and stripes at the end.

'Yup. Midwest born and bred.'

On impulse, I dig my phone out of my pocket, pulling off my gloves to swipe the camera icon, wanting to record the moment of my arrival. But before I can take a picture, the screen freezes – literally – the surface covering with a light dusting of frost.

'Hell.' I peer at it in disbelief before stuffing it back into my jacket, fingers already aching with cold.

'Yeah, cell phones can be temperamental in these temperatures,' Drew says. 'Don't worry, it'll be fine.'

We climb the dozen aluminium stairs to the main door, the effort making me dizzy. Seconds later I find myself in a sizeable room packed with an assortment of outdoor gear: coats and parkas draped across pegs, various sizes of snow boots lined up beneath. Goggles and safety hats stacked on shelves.

In the corner, a snowboard and several pairs of skis. I frown at them, puzzled. Surely it's way too flat out here?

Drew follows my gaze. 'A couple of the guys like to get towed around behind the skidoos. You should try it some time.' He hands me a pair of navy Crocs. 'These look about your size.'

I sit on an empty bench and remove my coat and boots, teeth chattering as I slip the Crocs onto my feet. 'Thanks. I'll give them back when I've unpacked.'

'Keep them. One of the summer crew left them behind. We've got a whole room full of stuff nobody wants any more. Anything you need, just ask Rajiv – as well as cooking our meals he's in charge of supplies, which makes him pretty much the station equivalent of God.'

This makes me smile, and I try not to stare at Drew. Now he's removed his outdoor gear, I can see my intuition was correct; he is disconcertingly handsome. Tall, with short muddy-blond hair. Deep brown eyes and the sort of honed features that wouldn't look out of place in a glossy magazine.

I feel instantly self-conscious and instinctively turn my cheek from his gaze. Then stop myself. Why hide it? It's not as if he won't notice.

'C'mon, let's get you a nice cup of tea,' Drew says, in a terrible imitation of a Cockney accent.

'That would be wonderful.' I'm shivering so hard my voice quivers like someone in shock.

'You can warm up and meet everyone. Caro baked a cake in your honour.'

I follow him out of the boot room, through a network of corridors painted in a bland institutional blue that reminds me of the hospital. I'm feeling unaccountably nervous at meeting the people I'll be cooped up with for the next year.

What if they don't like me?

Don't be ridiculous, Kate. This isn't school. Why on earth wouldn't they like you?

Drew leads me to a large room which I'm guessing is the communal lounge. Big picture windows face out over an empty expanse of ice – the relative warmth and comfort inside, the scattering of sofas and armchairs, the lamps and bookshelves piled with paperbacks and well-thumbed magazines, all providing a stark contrast to the lethal cold just beyond the glass.

A dozen or so people look up as we arrive, and my features freeze into a rictus smile as Drew reels off introductions. I try to fix each name and job title to a face as one-by-one they get to their feet to hug or shake my hand. Rajiv Sharma, the chef, easy to remember with his close-clipped beard and neat blue turban. Sonya Obeng, a Canadian meteorologist with a warm welcome that immediately takes the edge off my nerves. Luuk de Wees, the Dutch station electrician, so tall that if he stretched up an arm he could touch the ceiling. The Kiwi plumber, Caro Hinds, and Alice Munro, an atmospheric scientist from Edinburgh. Tom Weber, the shy-seeming data manager from Munich, whose gaze barely meets mine – the only person, I notice, wearing glasses. Rob Huang, our Australian comms manager, who looks like a fashion designer with his tight-fitting black clothes and bleached blond hair. Plus Arkady Vasiliev, a big bearish Russian in his forties who maintains the generators. Not to mention the motley remains of the summer crew, due to leave next week.

No sign of Sandrine Martin, the station leader, I realise. Nor Alex, the guy I met outside.

There's an awkward silence once the introductions are over. Everyone is being careful not to stare at my left cheek.

'How about that tea?' offers Drew, as I sink into an unoccupied chair. 'How'd you take it?'

'Milk. No sugar. Thanks.'

'I'm afraid it's powdered milk,' says Alice, her eyes darting towards my scar then away again. 'But you'll get used to it.' With her dark-blonde hair and pale blue eyes, she and Drew could be brother and sister. She's astonishingly pretty: slim, with delicate features and a soft Scottish accent.

'I bet you're knackered,' she adds, and I grimace. I can only imagine how gruesome I look. I've barely slept since leaving Heathrow, and lacked the energy to apply any make-up before the final flight with Jim. Anyway, what was the point? There's no disguising the damage to my face.

Now, however, I wish I'd made more effort. I feel dirty and sweaty, my hair greasy after three days without a wash. More than anything, I want to escape into the oblivion of a long, hot bath.

But that's impossible now. With water and power in limited supply, baths are out of the question – the base rations showers to just two minutes, every other day.

Yet another thing to get used to.

'You okay?' Caro hands me a slice of the chocolate cake she baked in my honour.

'I'm pretty shattered,' I admit.

'I'm not surprised.' She plonks herself down on the sofa opposite my chair. 'I passed out for fifteen hours when I arrived, and I only came from Christchurch.'

No chance of that, I think. I can't remember the last time I got a solid eight hours. Partly from the rigours of working in A&E; partly because I haven't slept well since the accident.

'Are you from that part of New Zealand?' I ask, examining her short punky hair and the piercings in her ears and nose; not as stunning as Alice, but pretty in her own, more casual way. In contrast to Alice's floral top and pale blue leggings, she's wearing a pair of large baggy dungarees and a faded orange T-shirt.

Caro shakes her head. 'Near Dunedin. Parents had a cattle farm there. But I've been living in Wellington for five years.'

Luuk flops next to her, spreading his long legs so wide Caro is forced to the edge of the sofa. 'Where are you from?' he asks between mouthfuls of cake, making no effort now to hide his scrutiny of my face.

'Bristol, in the south-west of England. But I grew up in Surrey.'

He nods, though I'm guessing this means nothing to him. 'Amsterdam,' he says before I can ask. 'But my mother's English.'

I smile, unable to think of a response that isn't utterly banal. My brain feels sluggish and I have the beginnings of a serious headache. I'm desperate to dose myself up, crawl into bed, and fall unconscious – or at least try. Instead I sip tea from the mug Drew hands me and nibble at Caro's cake, though I'm too tired for hunger.

Make an effort, I urge myself. First impressions and all that.

Thankfully I'm saved from further small talk by the arrival of a dark-haired man, along with a smartly dressed woman in her fifties, an air of authority in her demeanour. This must be Sandrine, the station leader.

I stand to offer my hand. 'Hi, I'm Kate.'

'I know,' she says with a clipped French accent that somehow makes her more intimidating. 'Welcome to UNA.' She stares unabashed at the scar on my cheek for a few seconds, then introduces the man behind her. 'This is Raffaelo de Marco – the doctor you're replacing.'

Raffaelo gives me a wide smile. 'Nice to meet you,' he says in perfect English, 'however briefly. My apologies for rushing off like this.'

'What do you mean?' I'm confused. He isn't due to leave until the last plane next week.

The doctor looks visibly embarrassed. He glances at Sandrine, but she doesn't comment. 'Did no one tell you?' he asks. 'I'm departing today.'

I gaze at him blankly, unable to take this in. *He's leaving?* Raffaelo was supposed to spend the next week handing over, helping me find my feet. 'No, no one told me.'

'Raff's son is ill.' Sandrine's tone is matter-of-fact. She studies my reaction dispassionately. Almost critically – or so it feels.

'Oh, I'm sorry,' I stammer, trying to cover my consternation.

'It's not serious.' Raffaelo offers another apologetic smile. 'But he has to have an operation and my wife needs me at home.'

'Okay.' I know I sound insincere, but I'm too shocked to appear more sympathetic. How on earth will I manage without him to show me the ropes?

Suddenly Jim arrives, gulping down his tea. 'Sorry, mate.' He slaps the doctor on the back. 'We need to set off right away. Just had a report of bad weather coming in.'

Raffaelo quickly says his goodbyes in a flurry of hugs and handshakes. Then picks up his rucksack and turns to me. 'I've left a file on your desk, along with instructions on where to find everything. You'll be fine – Jean-Luc made meticulous notes.'

Jean-Luc Bernas. The French doctor who died out on the ice two months ago. The reason I'm here.

'Thanks,' I say, automatically. 'I hope everything goes well with your son.'

Raffaelo nods, then disappears. Sandrine turns and walks off without another word.

I stand there, mood spiralling. I'd been relying on having someone here to show me how to manage all the medical experiments and generally bring me up to speed. I feel stupidly let down. Abandoned. Though of course it's no one's fault.

For a crazy second or two I fight the impulse to run after the pair of them and tell them I've changed my mind, that I want to go back home. I stare into the distance, trying to pull myself together, then notice Drew watching me carefully.

My cheeks flush. I sense he knows exactly what I'm thinking.

'C'mon, Kate,' he says gently, collecting my bags from the corner of the room. 'Let's get you settled in.'

2

12 February

'This is you.'

Drew opens the door to a cabin at the far end of the corridor and gestures me inside the diminutive bedroom. Two bunks, both neatly made up, are crammed into the corner, a wardrobe of thick, dark plywood, with a plain desk and chair tucked behind. The walls painted in the same bland grey-blue as everywhere outside.

'You're in luck.' Drew dumps my bags on the desk. 'Your room-mate left last week, so you've got the place to yourself.'

I stare at the tiny space, as small and sparse as a prison cell, and imagine sharing it with another human being. How on earth would you have any privacy?

'I'll leave you to unpack,' Drew says, retreating. 'Then maybe show you around the base before supper?'

I nod. 'Thanks.'

'Shall I come back in, say, an hour?'

I glance at my watch. Three fifteen local time – getting on for midnight at home. 'That'd be great.'

As I raise my head, his eyes flick away from my face. I can't blame him; everyone does it, their attention inexorably drawn to the jagged silver line running down the left side of my cheek. I wish I could say I'm used to it, but like a scar, the sting of self-consciousness never entirely fades.

'You've been rather thrown in the deep end, haven't you?' Drew says. 'Raff leaving so suddenly.'

Tears prick my eyes, followed by a twinge of irritation. I hate sympathy, hate people feeling sorry for me.

I don't deserve it.

'I'll manage,' I reply, a little too brusquely, bending to heave my over-stuffed rucksack onto the bottom bunk.

'Bathroom's two doors down on the left if you want a shower. Remember, no conditioner – it screws up the water recycling.'

With that, he's gone. I stand there, too exhausted to think or move, fighting the urge to collapse on the bottom bunk. Suddenly my mind is full of Ben and I'm missing him like it was yesterday. The way he twitched the tip of his nose when he was amused – or annoyed. The long, smooth curve of his spine. The feel of him inside me, pressing down, keeping me warm and safe and protected from everything bad in the world.

Shit. This isn't helping.

Fresh start, remember?

I unpack the contents of my rucksack and dry swallow a couple of pills. Stash the rest, concealed in a large innocuous-looking vitamin bottle, at the back of my wardrobe, then pause to examine the view outside. The cabin is at the rear of the station, so there are no outbuildings to interrupt the vista of . . . well, nothing. Mile upon flat mile of ice, the horizon a clean incision line against the bright blue sky, the surface of the snow carved by the wind into long horizontal waves – in shadow, the effect is uncannily like an ocean.

Enjoy it while you can, I remind myself; in a few short months, the sun will disappear entirely. When it sets for the final time, there'll be nothing but darkness for weeks on end. I shiver at the thought. I never mentioned to UNA my long-standing fear of the dark.

Among other things.

Back when I'd accepted the job, my anxieties had seemed remote, manageable. But now, standing here, the prospect of that endless night ignites another flare of misgiving.

Have I made the right decision in coming here?

Part of it was altruism, wanting to do my bit. UNA, barely three years old, was established to bring together scientists across the world to further research on climate change and the crucial role of Antarctica in global weather systems. And it needs staff of every stripe, not just scientists: plumbers, electricians, engineers, mechanics, chefs and, of course, doctors.

Underneath, though, my reasons were more selfish. I desperately needed to escape the daily reminders of Ben's absence, the ever-watchful gaze of those around me – my sister and mother, colleagues, nurses, even the ancillary staff. The constant air of concern and sympathy only made things worse. This vast continent, with its promise of splendid isolation, seemed the ideal place to hide.

But was I mistaken? Is this place simply a mirror, reflecting back my broken, frozen heart?

Enough, I tell myself, lowering the blind to cut out the worst of the glare. You're exhausted – everything will feel different tomorrow. Unzipping my carry-all, I unload clothes and possessions into the wardrobe. It seems an absurd amount of stuff, much of it issued by UNA: two jumpsuits, down jackets and leggings, all bright tomato-red for maximum visibility against the snow. Several sets of thermal underwear, six pairs of gloves and mitts in different thicknesses, three fleeces and a wool sweater, seven pairs of socks, three pairs of cotton trousers. Not to mention polar boots, inner liners, extra soles, goggles, hat, and sunglasses.

I cram as much as I can into the wardrobe, but it's way too small. So I arrange the rest neatly on the top bunk, wondering again how on earth two people could coexist in this cabin –

there'd barely be room to breathe. Then I strip off, wrapping up in the thick fleece dressing gown that seemed a good idea back in my chilly Victorian flat, but now, ironically, feels far too warm – it might be minus thirty outside, but the station itself is sweltering.

I shower quickly, towelling my hair dry before returning to my cabin. Moments later, there's a knock on the door.

'You decent?' calls Drew.

Jesus. Has an hour passed already? 'One sec.' I pull on the first fresh clothes I lay my hands on. 'Come in.'

His head appears around the door. 'Want that tour now?'

I nod, trying to appear enthusiastic. A few more hours, I tell myself, then I can go to bed.

Though I've seen plans of the layout, the base is bigger than I imagined, and far more disorienting. Drew walks me around a maze of corridors, some so narrow two people can barely pass, others with low ceilings that make them feel more like tunnels. Everything has been packed in to maximise space, Drew explains, as well as insulation – the outside walls have to be thick enough to cope with a 100-degree difference between the inside and 'out there'.

We explore Alpha first, the living quarters that form the main building. Drew shows me all of it: twenty bedrooms and four bathrooms; the kitchen and dining area; the sizeable lounge and next-door games room, with pool table and table football; the library that doubles as a mini cinema; the small but well-equipped gym; a launderette with an array of washers and tumble dryers; and finally my clinic and adjacent surgery.

Next up is Beta, the neighbouring tech building, reached via an enclosed corridor. Accompanied by the constant hum of machinery, we tour the radio and comms labs, the Skype room, and various scientific laboratories. Underneath, on the ground floor, Drew guides me around the garages, workshops, and food storage areas, the generators, and water recycling system.

In contrast to the relative orderliness of Alpha, Beta is all very industrial: steel floor beneath a chaos of pipes and trunking, and large twisted cables, some strung along the walls, others suspended from the ceiling. The corridors are littered with a mess of message boards and maps, hooks hung with outdoor gear, myriad racks of shelving crammed with folders and manuals, and boxes full of various bits of hardware and equipment.

I follow Drew around what feels like a labyrinth; God knows how people manage not to get lost. 'These are the hydraulic rams,' he explains as we pick our way across one of the workshops to the edge of the building. 'They keep the whole structure from being buried under the ice. Without them, we'd be underground in a decade or two.'

I recall a picture of an old metal hut somewhere in the South Pole, a wooden support all that was preventing its collapse from the accumulated snow. How on earth did those early explorers endure such hostile conditions with so few resources? With every passing minute in the station, I'm ever more aware how dependent we are on the technology around us to stay alive. How vulnerable we would be if any of it failed.

'Not enough time today, but tomorrow we can take a look outside, if you like,' Drew says, after filling me in on the water recycling. 'There's some pretty interesting stuff out there. Plus we store emergency medical supplies over in the summer camp in case this place burns down – you should know where they all are.'

'That'd be great.' I'm praying this is the end of the tour and I can have a few minutes of rest in my cabin before supper. But on returning to Alpha, Drew pauses outside a closed door just down the corridor from my clinic. Station Leader, according to the sign.

Drew knocks, sticks his head inside. 'You want a word with Kate?'

I hear Sandrine answer in the affirmative, so follow Drew inside. She's sitting at her desk, writing in a large notebook. Everything around her as neat and orderly as her perfectly applied make-up and immaculate clothes. More Paris, somehow, than Antarctica.

'You settling in okay?' she asks, her tone curiously flat.

'Yes. Thanks.'

'Good.'

There's a moment's silence I'm unsure how to fill. 'Do I need keys?' I prompt, aware that Drew is witnessing every word of this exchange. Very few rooms on the base have doors that lock, I've noticed, including the sleeping cabins – the exceptions being my clinic, the comms room, and Sandrine's own office.

'Oh, yes.' Sandrine gets up and opens a sturdy wooden cupboard mounted behind her desk. Hands me a set of keys. 'Let me know if there's anything else you need.'

I withdraw, feeling deflated again. I hadn't expected a fanfare, sure, but I suppose I'd counted on something warmer than this.

'Don't worry.' Drew catches my expression as we head down the hallway. 'She grows on you.'

I muster a half-smile, hoping he's right.

'And hang on to those keys. Sandrine lost hers a few months ago and they were hell to replace.'

'I will,' I say, desperately hoping that's it. I'm so tired I can hardly stand. The pills are beginning to wear off and I can feel an edginess creeping into my mood.

'Anyhow,' Drew continues, 'I've saved the best till last.'

Oh God. I force myself to look keen and follow him along another rabbit warren of corridors. We arrive at a room at the far end of the station, a small narrow space overhung with a dense array of bright LED lights.

'Ta-dah!' Drew grins, gesturing towards a few sparse plants hunkered beneath the glare. 'My babies.'

I survey the forlorn-looking salad leaves: several types of lettuce, rocket, kale. All bizarrely out of place in this stark white room in the middle of this stark white continent.

'The only green stuff you'll set eyes on all winter,' he says proudly, flashing me a perfectly aligned smile. With his short hair and two-day stubble, Drew really does resemble a male model, the kind that might advertise sports gear or outdoor clothing. 'Sowed them a month ago. Should have the first crop in a few weeks.'

Barely enough for a meal, I imagine, but try to look appreciative.

'So that's pretty much it,' he concludes, checking his watch. 'Thirty minutes to supper. I'll see you in the dining room.'

I reach out and touch his arm as he turns to go. 'Thanks, Drew. It was nice of you to take the time.'

'No trouble at all.' His gaze is friendly, warmly professional. 'It's really good to have you here.'

By the time I arrive in the canteen, half a dozen people are already spread along the four neat rows of tables. No sign of Drew yet, but Caro waves as she gets up to greet me, her spiky hair giving her a cute, elfin look.

'Enjoy your tour?' she asks, guiding me to the serving hatch.

I nod. 'It's a lot to take in.'

'No kidding. I got lost about a dozen times when I arrived. But you'll get the hang of it.'

I survey all the food on the counter. 'Do I serve myself?'

'Help yourself to whatever you like. You're in luck. It's Friday, so it's fish and chips.'

'Really? Even on an international station?'

'We all take turns helping Rajiv prepare the evening meal,'

Caro explains. 'Fridays are for Britain, Ireland, New Zealand and Australia, and we generally stick to fish. France and Belgium have Sunday; Italy and Spain are Saturday – usually pizza or paella. US and Canada are on Tuesday – that's often burgers, though Sonya makes a mean spicy fried chicken. Russia and the Baltic states on Wednesday, and Thursday used to be South America, but now most of the summer staff have gone, that slot's up for grabs. Oh, and India and Asia on Mondays,' she adds, nodding towards Rajiv, busy behind the hatch. 'His curry's the best meal on the base.'

I collect some food and follow Caro to her table, saying hello to Arkady and a guy I don't recognise. Ark, as he insists I call him, seems pleased to see me, his wide smile revealing a couple of Soviet-era gold teeth that give him the air of a Bond villain. The other man, however, offers only the briefest of nods; it's Alex, I realise – the guy with Drew who met me off the plane.

I can see his face now at least: clean-shaven, unlike Ark and many of the summer staff, whose Antarctica beards make them look like Portland hipsters. Alex is boyishly handsome with his floppy dark hair and fresh-faced skin, lightly tanned from time spent outdoors. Mid-twenties, I'm guessing – I make a mental note to check his medical file tomorrow. I smile at him, but he barely returns the favour before he turns away, something cold in his expression that reminds me of Sandrine.

'Ark made a borscht last week,' Caro says as we sit opposite. 'It was pretty good.'

He gives her a thumbs-up. 'Better than trifle you make,' he quips in his thick Russian accent. 'What kind of shit was that?'

Caro laughs and flips him the finger. 'So shit you had seconds, huh?'

'What can I say? I am fat old pig.' Ark rubs his ample belly and guffaws.

'Obviously the whole meal rota works better in the summer when there's more people,' Caro tells me as I pick at my battered fish. 'But we try to ring the changes – we don't want anyone getting homesick.'

'So what do you do here?' I ask Alex, busy piling into his food with the concentration of a man who's either borderline starving or hoping to avoid conversation.

His expressive brown eyes flick up to mine. 'Field assistant.'

I finally identify his accent. 'You're from Ireland?'

'Yeah. Donegal.'

'Nice. I went camping there once.'

Alex's expression registers brief surprise. 'Get wet, did ya?'

'A bit.'

He allows himself a half-smile, then his gaze skirts to Drew, who's approaching with his plate piled high. He sits next to me, nodding at my own sorry effort. 'You not hungry?'

'Not much of an appetite,' I admit.

Caro gives me a quick once-over. 'You could do with one.' She grins to show she means no offence.

'Probably just tired,' I say, managing a couple of chips before I give up. In truth, any pleasure I once took in food seems to have vanished since the accident.

Though I suspect the pills aren't helping.

'Give to me.' Ark takes my plate and scrapes the food onto his own. 'Would be shame to waste.'

Beside me, Alex gets to his feet, dumps his empty plate and glass by the hatch, then leaves without comment. Caro stares after him, but Drew simply raises an eyebrow, unperturbed, then turns to me.

'So, what do you think of it so far?'

I take a sip of water. 'Great. I mean, it's all rather over-whelming, but I'll get there.'

'Well, we're very pleased to have you.' Caro gives my arm

a friendly squeeze. It's a small gesture, but the kindness moves me. I like her and Drew, I realise, feeling relieved; I'll have two friends here at least.

Would this be the moment to ask more about my predecessor? I wonder. I know almost nothing about Jean-Luc, the French doctor whose death led to me sitting here right now. Only that he died out on the ice, in some kind of abseiling accident.

Somehow, I sense nobody is keen to talk about it. After all, Antarctica is dangerous – that much was clear from UNA's crash course in remote medicine. Any number of things could happen out here, and we're a very long way from help. Easier to get someone back from the International Space Station, one UNA doctor in Geneva pointed out, than from this place in the depths of winter.

Does anyone here feel the same anxiety about that as I do?

I glance around, but the atmosphere amongst the twenty or so people in the dining room seems relaxed and unconcerned – if they're bothered about how isolated we are, they're concealing it well.

Undoubtedly that's the best way to cope, I decide. Simply put it right out of your mind.

3

13 February

Where on earth am I?

I wake, disoriented, in the twilight created by my half-closed blind. For a few seconds I'm back there, in the hospital, coming round after the accident. The same sense of confusion, of time suspended. The gradual intrusion of memory.

Those fox eyes in the headlights, the onward rush of trees.

Never, thankfully, the moment of impact.

Nor the aftermath.

But I'm not there. I'm in Antarctica. I arrived on the plane yesterday. I'm going to spend the next twelve months here on the ice, eight of them with only a dozen other souls for company.

The thought prompts a stomach flip of apprehension, followed by a sudden rush of nausea. I scramble out of bed and run down the corridor, make it to the cramped little bathroom just in time to vomit into the toilet.

Oh God. I lean against the white tiled wall, breathing heavily. I feel dizzy too, with a burgeoning headache. For a second or so the room spins, and I worry I'll faint, but the sensation passes with a few more deep breaths.

Altitude sickness. Everyone gets it after arrival, but I'll need to keep a close eye to make sure it doesn't progress into anything worse. The last thing I need is pneumonia – a rare but dangerous complication of high-altitude exposure.

Getting to my feet, I cup water from the tap and sip it, then splash some on my face, avoiding my reflection. It's a habit I got into during my recovery. I don't want to look at my scar, my ruined features, any more than I have to – bad enough enduring the reactions of other people.

Back in my cabin, I take a couple of hydrocodone from my stash then check the time. Five forty-six a.m. I've slept for seven hours – the longest stretch in many months.

Getting dressed in tracksuit bottoms and a light T-shirt sets off a flurry of sparks and crackling. Another feature of the station I hadn't anticipated – thanks to the dry atmosphere, static shocks are frequent. Yesterday Drew pointed out the strips of aluminium tape on all the desks, leading to radiators or other earthed parts of the building, so you can 'discharge' yourself before touching computers or sensitive equipment. On the way to the canteen I drag an elbow along the wall, just as he showed me, to dissipate the build-up of static – less painful than having it arc from a fingertip.

When I arrive, I'm surprised to find I'm not the first for breakfast. Alex is sitting alone, hunched over a book. I pour myself a coffee, praying I can keep it down. I should stick to water, but I need caffeine to perk me up and wash the awful taste from my mouth.

'Is it good?' I sit opposite Alex and nod at his book.

'Yeah. It's pretty creepy.' He shows me the cover – *Dark Matter* by Michelle Paver – then closes the novel and sits back, not quite meeting my eyes. There's something about him I can't put my finger on. A tension in his stance. A sort of wariness. I notice his right leg jittering up and down as he swallows his last piece of toast.

'So how're you feeling?' he asks eventually, pushing his hair from his forehead in an impatient gesture. It's a polite enough question, but his tone suggests he's just going through the motions.

I grimace. 'Like the walking dead.'

A shadow passes across the field assistant's face. He blinks at me, then looks away.

'A touch of altitude sickness,' I add quickly. 'It should be okay.'

'Well, you're in good hands, aren't you? You being the doc.' He smiles tightly then gets to his feet, as if he can't wait to get away. 'Gotta go. Trouble with the showers. I should help Caro fix them before she gets it in the neck.'

I sip my coffee, deflated, as Alex loads his plate and cutlery into the industrial washer – mornings we deal with our own dishes, Drew explained to me yesterday; other meals we take it in turns to clear up. As he retreats from the canteen, I'm unable to shake off the sense that he resents me being here.

But why? Surely I haven't done anything to offend him?

'You must be Kate.'

I turn to a tall, well-built man. In contrast to Alex, he looks genuinely pleased to see me, a welcoming smile spread across his face. 'I'm Arne. Sorry I didn't get to meet you yesterday. Problem with the cat – it took most of the afternoon and evening to fix it.'

'The cat?' I frown, rising to shake his hand, hoping he can't detect the exhausted tremor in mine. 'I thought animals were banned in Antarctica.'

He laughs. 'It's short for Caterpillar, the tractor we use to collect snow to melt for drinking water.' His English is softly accented with a Scandinavian lilt.

'Ah. Kind of essential then.'

'More essential than an actual cat, that's for sure.'

I study him as he gets his breakfast. Late thirties, I reckon. Short dark hair, graying at the sides, but with a tuft of white at the front. It's the most distinctive thing about him; otherwise he's what my mother, with a hint of disparagement, might describe as 'pleasant'.

'So you work with the vehicles?' I ask as he returns with muesli and a glass of long-life orange juice.

'Station vehicle mechanic. Plus I help out with other stuff. Anything involving an engine basically.' He nods at my lone mug of coffee. 'That all you're having?'

'Touch of nausea from altitude sickness. I'll be fine.'

'It's the worst,' he says, tucking into his breakfast. 'Guy I came out with had to be flown off the ice after a week, he got so sick with it. Cerebral . . .'

'Cerebral oedema?'

'Yeah, that's it. He was pretty bad. Thankfully he recovered, once they got him back to Christchurch.'

'Where are you from?' I try to recall the list of fellow winterers I was given in Geneva. 'Sorry, I should know, but I'm still reeling a bit from arriving.'

'Iceland.'

'Nice,' I reply, mentally kicking myself for my blandness. 'How long have you been here?'

'A few months.' He takes a slug of his juice. 'But I've been on the ice before. McMurdo.'

'Party central, so I hear.' The US ice station, the largest on the continent, is renowned for its drinking culture. With over a thousand staff in summer, it's more a small town, equipped with ATMs and a bowling alley. Even, apparently, a decommissioned nuclear reactor.

Arne smiles, but doesn't comment. I have the feeling he's humouring me, the new girl – not a role I relish.

'So you really know the ropes,' I venture, after half a minute of uncomfortable silence.

'Yes.' He sighs. 'Literally.'

'How do you mean?'

'Have you been outside yet?' His eyes flick towards the bright light streaming in through the windows.

'Only the walk from the plane to the station.'

'Did you notice the ropes around the building?'

I shake my head. I'd been too busy trying to keep up with Drew and not freeze to death.

'Well, they're there to stop you getting lost in bad weather or if you drop your torch when it's dark – you can use them to guide yourself back to the base. That way you won't wander off in the wrong direction.'

'I guess that wouldn't be good.'

'You're the doctor. You tell me how long you'd last in minus sixty Celsius.'

'Not long,' I admit, wondering exactly how much time you would have. Ten minutes? Twenty? It doesn't bear thinking about.

'Anyway, that's not going to happen.' Arne stands up, and I notice again how tall he is. Easily six foot, maybe a little more. But unlike Luuk he wears his height lightly, like someone completely confident in his own skin. 'Just take the normal precautions and you'll be fine.'

'Like Jean-Luc Bernas?' I blurt. 'What exactly happened to him?'

Arne pauses. I wait for him to sit down again and fill me in, but a tension creeps across his face, the look of someone who wants to end the conversation. 'It was simply an unfortunate accident.'

A second later he's gone.

I make my way back to my cabin, pausing to examine some of the photographs lining the walls of the main corridor. There's a framed photo of Shackleton's wooden hut, with its old stove, and shelves lined with ancient tins of supplies. Further along, group shots of people out on the ice, dressed in UNA regulation red.

I linger, studying those taken in the summer, when it's possible to go outside with your face exposed. Spot Drew and Caro. Ark giving a thumbs-up to the camera, ice crystals glistening in his shaggy beard.

Next to this is a picture of two men, both grinning at the photographer, their red jackets casting a healthy glow on their bare faces. One of them is Alex. He looks different. Excited, carefree, and even younger, somehow, as if the intervening months have worn him down. That's what struck me about him this morning, I realise – an indefinable air of . . . unhappiness.

Next to him, arm around his shoulder, is a handsome older man in his forties. Short silvered hair. Tanned face and a broad smile, his eyes crinkling as if in the wake of something amusing.

Underneath, a scribble of letters in blue biro. I peer at them. RIP.

Rest in peace. This must be Jean-Luc Bernas. My predecessor.

A twinge of some emotion I can't name. Sorrow? Pity? I return to the cabin reflecting on how much his death would have impacted the rest of the base. Everyone must have been devastated. And scared – several weeks without a doctor while UNA scrambled to find a temporary replacement would have been an anxious time for all.

No wonder they seem reluctant to talk about it.

I picture the friendly face of the doctor. Alex's happier demeanour. Jean-Luc was clearly well-liked, probably deeply mourned. Hardly surprising Alex is finding my arrival difficult.

I sit on my bunk for a while, trying to pull myself together, but I can't shake a feeling of insecurity, of somehow being an imposter. Rationally, I know that's ridiculous – I won the contract after a gruelling three-day interview and assessment in Geneva, not to mention an intensive medical and psychological examination. I'm as qualified to be here as anyone.

All the same, I feel a poor substitute for the man they'd known – and possibly even loved.

True to his word, Raff has left things in good order. There's a file on my clinic desk filled with detailed notes on where to find everything, how to access and navigate the medical area of the IT system, plus an update on all the experiments. He's even drawn a flat plan of my surgery and its supplies.

How did Raff manage when he arrived? No one then to show him the ropes. I'm touched by how much he's gone out of his way to avoid leaving me in the same boat.

'Please don't hesitate to contact me if I can be of further help,' reads his handwritten note. Underneath, an email address at a hospital in Naples – I resolve to thank him as soon as I get online.

Fighting off another wave of dizziness and nausea, I explore my little domain. Two rooms, linked by a double door. One a surgery with an exam bed and most of the medical gear, the other my office and clinic, housing all the drug supplies. There's a decent range of equipment, including a ventilator, anaesthetic machine, cylinders of oxygen, and various surgical and dentistry tools, as well as facilities for taking X-rays, and simple blood or urine analysis. It's reassuring to find it fully functional, as far as I can tell.

I pick up a pair of dental forceps, praying I'll never have to use them. Despite the crash course in Switzerland, I've limited experience with some of this stuff.

You'll be fine, I reassure myself. After all, there's a 24-hour direct link to the UNA team at the Geneva University Hospital; anything I don't know or am unsure about, they can talk me through. Even teeth.

Using my keys, I unlock each of the cupboards and go through the impressive stockpile of medication, including, I can't help noticing, plenty of benzos and some pretty strong opiate-based painkillers.

I pick up one of the packets and break the seal, studying the sachet of pristine little pills. Pushing down a surge of longing, I put it back inside and lock the cupboard door, remembering my promise to myself: once my own stash runs out, that's it – no dipping into station supplies.

I distract myself by going through all the medical notes – UNA has provided hard copies, as well as those stored on the computer system. I pick out each file one by one, quickly flicking through. Notice a number of the staff – Alex, Alice, Tom – have been prescribed sleeping pills since Jean-Luc died.

Is that because of the constant daylight, which can play hell with the circadian rhythms? Or is it more to do with the doctor's death, hinting at darker feelings running beneath the social front they present to the world?

I guess I'll find out in good time.

With my little orienteering session out of the way, I run a few checks. Attaching the pulse oximeter to my finger, I note my blood oxygen saturation has fallen to 89 per cent, as my haemoglobin levels react to the low pressure from the altitude. Way off the normal 97–98 per cent. And at 109 beats per minute, my pulse rate is too high. I'll need to keep tabs on myself for the next few days.

'How you doing?'

I give a yelp of surprise and spin to see Drew in the doorway. 'Sorry.' He looks embarrassed. 'Didn't mean to startle you.'

I smile. 'My fault. I was miles away.'

'Everything as it should be? What's that phrase? Shipshape and . . .' he pauses.

'Bristol fashion?'

'Yeah, that's it. Though I don't have a clue what it means.'

'Me neither,' I admit. 'And I live there.'

'We'll have to google it later,' he says, 'if we can access the damn internet.'

I grimace, remembering my conversation with Tom after dinner last night. He'd patiently explained how to get online, warning that it was slow, with usage restricted to essential email and communications.

'Consider it a chance to detox from social media,' he'd said in his clipped German accent, so deadpan that I couldn't tell if he was joking. He still had a hard time looking me in the eye, I noticed. Perhaps he really is just painfully shy.

'See Raff left you plenty of homework.' Drew nods at the open folder on my desk. 'Better leave you to it. I was wondering if you fancy a trip outside after lunch? The weather's good.'

'Thank you.' I smile again. 'I'd love that.'

A few hours later I find myself back in the boot room, hauling on cold weather gear. Given the heat indoors, it feels stifling, but the moment we're outside it'll be barely adequate.

I check and double-check my clothing, making sure I have my hat and goggles, nervous about leaving the warm cocoon of the station, then follow Drew out into the blinding sunlight. Freezing air rushes into my lungs and stings the exposed skin on my face. Almost instantly the tiny hairs in my nostrils stiffen and freeze.

You're fine, I tell myself fiercely, trying to inhale and exhale slowly. Nothing bad is going to happen.

'Thought we'd take one of the skidoos,' Drew says as we descend the steps to the ice. 'Save you too much walking till you're up to speed.'

Oh hell, do I look that bad? I still feel a bit nauseous, though my headache abated with a few more painkillers. Clearly my exhaustion is still showing.

Drew leads me around the side of Beta to a large hangar where several black snowmobiles are parked. He mounts the nearest, motioning me to get on behind. I climb on awkwardly, feeling the biting cold of the seat through my padded trousers.

'Hang on tight!'

As he revs the engine and takes off across the ice, I clutch onto his waist. It makes me feel awkward and self-conscious, but we're circling the whole complex at unnerving speed, swerving around the ropes Arne mentioned earlier that arc out from Alpha and Beta towards the surrounding outbuildings.

'That's where we keep the emergency generator,' Drew shouts back, as we pass the largest of the sheds. He points out the massive fuel containers full of diesel as we skid past, cutting a path towards a smaller hut in the distance.

I try to contain my rising unease as we head into the vast white space and Alpha and Beta recede behind us. I'm scared to leave it, our tiny refuge in this frozen oblivion. Afraid that somehow I won't make it back.

Suddenly we hit a rut in the ice and I squeal in alarm, clinging to Drew even tighter.

'You okay?' he yells above the noise of the engine.

'Yes!' It's a lie. I'm utterly terrified. If I fall off, I'm looking at a concussion or a fracture at the very least. I close my eyes, trying not to think of the crash, the sudden sensation of weightlessness as the car left the road and flew through the air.

You're fine, Kate. He's probably driven this thing a thousand times.

A minute later we pull up outside the little building. 'This is the meteorology hut,' Drew says as I clamber off the skidoo, thankful I'm still in one piece. 'It's pretty much Sonya's domain.'

We step inside. After the cold air that whipped around my face on the skidoo, penetrating right through the necker I'd pulled up over my nose, this place feels surprisingly warm. Almost cosy, though there's no heat source I can identify. The paraffin heater in the corner isn't lit.

'Most of this stuff is for snow samples and measuring ozone concentrations,' Drew waves at a bench covered in unidentifiable equipment and containers, 'but Sonya walks out here to release the daily balloon.'

'Balloon?'

'Helium. It carries instruments to measure things like temperature, humidity and so on, and transmits data back to the base for about 150 kilometres.'

'Sonya comes out here to do that *every day*?' I try to imagine braving this harsh white world day in, day out. Being out here, on your own, undaunted by the size and inhospitability of this landscape.

'Pretty much,' Drew says. 'She only missed a couple when the weather was bad. She loves it though, says it's her daily constitutional.'

I remove my goggles and rub my eyes, picturing Sonya bundled up in her outdoor gear, trudging all the way out to this shelter. I'm filled with admiration. I'm not sure I'd have the courage. Or tenacity.

'You okay?' Drew asks, studying me.

'I think so.'

'I was as nervous as fuck. First time out on the ice I had a straight-up panic attack.'

'Seriously?' I return his gaze, wonder if he's exaggerating to be kind.

'Seriously. I nearly threw up I was so scared. It gets you like that sometimes . . . the vastness. How inhospitable it all is,' he says, echoing my own thoughts. 'This place has a way of letting you know who's boss.'

I think again of Jean-Luc, unable to shut down the image

of him dying out here, somewhere in this frozen world, and bite back the urge to ask Drew about the accident.

Not the time or place.

We visit the atmospheric science hut, where Alice spends much of her time on air sampling, then tour the other shelters erected for various experiments. Some have been abandoned with the departure of most of the summer crew, Drew explains; others, including a round cave excavated in the ice on the south side of the station, are used all year long.

We move on to Omega, the aluminium tower I spotted from the plane. 'Tallest in Antarctica,' Drew shouts to me as he weaves through the network of guyropes tethering it to the ground. 'Fifty metres high, and a kilometre from Alpha. Holds much of the meteorological equipment.'

'Does Sonya have to come out here every day as well?' Heaven forbid.

Drew shakes his head. 'Only about once a week. Then she takes a skidoo.'

He slows to a crawl, glancing up at the tower then back at me. 'Fancy checking out the view at the top? I brought some harnesses and climbing gear in case.'

I peer up through the ice-encrusted girders, the sky beyond so blue it's almost black. 'Perhaps another day. Not sure I have the stomach for it yet.'

'Probably wise,' he agrees. 'It's a great outlook, but it can be pretty hairy up there, especially if there's any wind. Not ideal if you're feeling under par.'

Instead we head off in the opposite direction, towards a series of large domed tents on the horizon. I'm really starting to feel the cold now, the freezing air penetrating the thick downy layers of my clothing, making my toes and fingers pulse and ache.

'What's that?' I ask Drew, as we pass a small dome on top of the ice.

'Igloo,' Drew shouts back as we roar past. 'Couple of guys built it a few winters ago.'

'What's it for?'

'Nothing much,' he laughs. 'It's empty. A few of the summer staff slept there once, for a dare.'

I shiver at the thought – even in the summer, temperatures here are well below freezing.

After another minute or two bumping across the ice, Drew slows up alongside the tents, some half a kilometre from the main station. 'Welcome to Gamma,' he announces. 'Aka summer base. It's got its own water supply and internet, even a coffee machine and washing facilities.'

'How many people stay out here?'

'Thirty odd. It can get pretty crowded. It's also our official evacuation point if we have an emergency in Alpha or Beta. Wanna take a look?'

He stops outside the entrance and I follow him inside. There's not much to see now the remaining summer staff have moved back into the main building, just neat rows of bunk beds, crammed surprisingly close. A couple of small bathrooms and a minuscule kitchen. It makes my claustrophobic little cabin look like the last word in luxury.

'Can you give me ten?' Drew asks. 'I have to check one of the supports.'

All at once I'm assaulted by another swell of nausea. I inhale deeply. Oh Jesus, don't let me be sick in here. Not in front of Drew.

'Actually, I might walk back,' I say hurriedly. 'I need to warm up a bit.'

'You sure?' Drew frowns, clearly uncertain whether that's a good idea.

'It's not far. And I could do with stretching my legs.'

'Okay, but take the walkie-talkie,' he insists, handing his set to me. 'Any problems at all, just radio the base. I'll see you back at Alpha.'

I seal the handset into the pocket of my jacket, then leave the tent and set off towards the main building. Within seconds, however, I'm struggling to breathe.

Shit. This is a really bad idea – I'd forgotten how exhausting it is walking any distance at this altitude. I pause, trying to rake more oxygen into my lungs, thankful Drew can't see me.

When I've caught my breath, I set off again, consciously slowing to a fraction of my usual pace, eventually finding a rhythm I can sustain. Weirdly, moving steadily seems to settle my stomach, and the dizziness that accompanies the nausea subsides. Without the wind chill from the skidoo, I can even lower my necker and allow the sun beating down from the cloudless sky to warm my face. In mid-summer, Sonya told me last night, you have to wear a thick layer of sunscreen to combat the lack of ozone, but this close to winter I should be okay – for a few minutes at least.

Halfway back to base, I spot a strong halo in the sky to the left of Alpha, two intense bursts of rainbow either side. I stop to take it in. A sundog. I've read about them but never actually seen one before. The horizon shimmers, fluctuations in the light subtly changing the colour of the ice below.

It's beautiful and mesmerising.

Out of nowhere a breeze appears, picking up little flurries of ice crystals, spinning them into tiny tornadoes that dance along the ridges and pinprick the exposed skin of my face.

What are those ridges called? Ark told me last night, the Russian for these parallel lines in the snow, so reminiscent of waves.

Sastrugi, that's it. I say the word out loud, enjoying the sensation of it in my mouth.

Sastrugi.

All at once any lingering misgivings about coming out here to Antarctica disappear. For all its harshness, its bleakness, there's something magical about this world and its vast, unfathomable emptiness. The air feels impossibly clean and sharp after the pollution of the city. Away from the constant chatter of the station, inside and out, the quiet wraps itself around me like a blanket, soft and soothing.

I breathe in deeply, ignoring the piercing cold in my lungs, the ache of my frozen fingers and toes, as I gaze up into the fathomless blue. No clouds, no contrails from aircraft. We're so remote that even satellites seldom pass over.

Peace, I think, my heart lifting as I embrace the stillness, the silence.

This place is a gift. A privilege.

Nowhere in the world right now I'd rather be.

4

15 February

'How are you doing? You settling in?'

'Great,' I reply, trying to sound more upbeat than I feel. Though my blood sats are better and my pulse rate is down, the headaches and nausea are still plaguing me. And the near constant snow-bright daylight that streams in through every window is playing havoc with my body clock – I barely know whether I should be eating or sleeping.

Alice squints at me, her smooth forehead wrinkled with concern. 'You sure you're okay? You look a bit peaky to be honest.'

'*Peaky*?' Ark frowns. 'What is peaky?'

'She means I don't look very well. Unhealthy,' I add for good measure.

Ark grunts and scratches his beard. 'You be fine. It is,' he searches for the right words, 'height sickness?'

'Altitude sickness. And yes, I'll be over it in a day or two.'

'Hope so,' he says gloomily. 'Don't want to lose you too.'

Sonya frowns at him but Ark ignores her, breaking off a piece of poppadum and dipping it into his curry.

'Once summer crew has gone,' he continues, raising his voice as if challenging everyone to join in. 'Then you stuck with us. And if that don't make you sick, nothing will.' He guffaws at his own joke, gazing around for a reaction.

A few people smile, but it's subdued. My fourth day here and some of the winterers are letting their guard down. The veneer of cheerfulness that greeted my arrival has slipped into something more . . . what? I try to put a finger on it. A wariness, a sense that everyone is treading on eggshells around each other.

There's a lull in the conversation, one of those awkward pauses that arise out of nowhere.

'Well, this is delicious.' Caro raises her glass of wine to Rajiv, whose face still glows from the heat of the kitchen. His turban today is a warm deep orange – apparently he wears a different colour each day of the week, to help him 'keep track of time'.

'You're most welcome.' Rajiv wiggles his moustache and tips a wink back at Caro, making her laugh.

Supper time is fast becoming my favourite part of our daily routine. With station numbers now drastically reduced, Drew and Rob have pushed the tables into a large square so we can all sit together. Every evening, Alice pulls down the blinds in the dining room and lights a trio of candles, shutting out the ever-present glare of the sun and giving the place a more cosy atmosphere.

Caro turns to me. 'What do you think of the food so far?'

'It's fabulous. Much better than I expected.'

'Antarctica has an odd effect on the appetite,' she muses, eyeing my meagre portions. 'Either you're hungry all the time or you barely want to eat at all. Sadly, I'm the former.' Caro pats her stomach and grins – though frankly it's hard to tell what shape she's in under the baggy top and dungarees she usually wears.

'You've done this before then?' I ask.

'Only once. Out on Mawson, the Australian base. I was due to visit Halley too, but it closed.'

I nod. Halley, the flagship UK ice station, had to be evacuated in winter when a huge section of the Brunt ice shelf began to crack away from the Antarctic mainland. 'So you're an old hand then?'

'Guess so. I swore on Mawson it'd be the one and only, but here I am. Go figure.'

'Was it that bad?' I try to keep my tone light-hearted.

Caro tilts her head, considering. 'Let's just say it was interesting, in a tedious sort of way. Winter sorts the men from the boys, if you'll excuse the sexism – though it has to be said, in my experience, women cope better.'

'Why's that?' Luuk leans back in his chair, swigging beer from his bottle. His expression is challenging, almost defiant, as though he's ready for an argument. Despite my best intentions to get along with everyone, there's something I instinctively dislike in him. A kind of insouciance that borders on arrogance.

Caro stares him down, refusing to be intimidated. 'No idea. It's only an observation.'

Luuk eyeballs her for another moment or two, then returns his attention to his food. I gaze around the table. There are still half a dozen summer scientists here, due to leave in a few days – once that plane takes off, just thirteen of us will remain.

Thank heavens I'm not superstitious.

I've got to know most of the winter crew, at least a little. Chatted over meals, and in my clinic, as I ask each to come in for a basic check-up. Raff has done an excellent job, but I want to establish my own baselines.

Only two have yet to show up for their medicals: Alex, who seems to be actively keeping his distance, and Sandrine, who also hasn't improved on closer acquaintance. I study her, sitting at the far end of the table, talking to Tom and Sonya, her expression blank with concentration. Despite the make-up, there's no hiding the dark circles under her eyes, the heavy frown lines in her forehead. Too much work, and not enough sleep.

For a second, our eyes meet, then her gaze flicks away again without acknowledgement. I haven't been able to shake the sense that she doesn't like me, that Sandrine somehow resents me being here. Surely she's relieved to have a permanent doctor back on the base?

'Fucking shame about the naan bread.'

I glance at Rob, who's pulled his hair up into a kind of samurai topknot that looks pretty bad-ass. 'Sorry,' he says, catching my eye.

'What for?'

'My language. Mum's always nagging me about it. Though she knows just about every curse word in English and Taiwanese.'

I laugh. 'Don't worry about it. You should work in a busy A&E – plenty of swearing, I assure you. Anyway, what's the deal with the naan bread?'

'Haven't you heard?' Alice's voice is dramatic. 'We've got weevils!'

'Weevils?'

'In the flour.' Rajiv looks disconsolate. 'Half the consignment is ruined, and there's no room to fly in more. So bread's rationed from now on.'

That'll hit everyone hard, I think. I may have only been here a matter of days but I'm already aware that Rajiv's freshly baked loaves, which he garnishes with all sorts of extras – dried onion, garlic, caraway, different nuts and seeds – are one of the highlights of the station diet.

'What is wrong with weevils?' booms Ark. 'More protein!' He breaks out into another round of laughter as he registers the disgust on the faces around him. 'You babies not last long in gulag!'

'This *is* the fucking gulag, isn't it?' Alex mutters, only half to himself.

Luuk snorts, his expression mocking, but Alex ignores him. I study him, curious. What on earth does he mean? But Alex keeps his focus on his food, avoiding eye contact with anyone.

Probably he's still upset about Jean-Luc's death, I decide, remembering that photo, the easy camaraderie evident between them. Perhaps he's finding it harder to deal with than some of the others.

I try to finish my curry. Caro's right. It's really good, making the most of the few vegetables we have left in store. Once the final boxes arrive on the plane tomorrow, that'll be it – the only fresh food we'll taste for eight months will be Drew's meagre supply of salad.

As people get up to serve themselves dessert, I lean in to Alice. 'Do you mind if I ask you something?' I say, voice lowered.

She fixes her clear blue eyes on mine. 'Sure. Fire away.'

'What exactly happened to Jean-Luc?'

'No one told you?' Her eyebrows lift in surprise.

'Not in any detail. Just that he had an accident out on the ice.'

Alice chews the side of her lip. Takes a long slug of wine, then lowers her voice to match mine. 'He died on a group expedition to the Transantarctic Mountains – about three days from here by skidoo. There are some big crevasses out there, and we were practising ice climbing. Well . . . he was abseiling into one of them, and his equipment failed. He fell right in.'

'Shit.' I let out a long, astonished breath. 'How did you get him out?'

Alice looks uncomfortable. Her eyes flit around the table before she drops her voice to a murmur. 'We didn't.'

Shock hits me like a punch in the lungs. 'You mean . . . he's still out there?' I flash back to those photos on the wall. That kindly, handsome face beaming at the camera.

Oh God. It doesn't bear thinking about.

'There was no way to recover his body,' Alice explains. 'You have to understand, Kate, the ice out here can be up to six kilometres deep. Those crevasses go down very, very far.'

'Jesus.' I try to digest the horror of this. 'So how do you know . . . that he . . .' I can't bring myself to say it.

'That he died in the fall?'

I glance up in surprise as Alex cuts into our exchange. Oh hell, he's heard what I was saying. Heat rushes to my cheeks as I see he's staring at me. No, that isn't the right word. He's *glaring* at me.

The conversation around the table dies away as everyone turns their attention to us. 'The answer, *Doctor North*, is that we've no idea,' Alex says. 'For all we know Jean-Luc could have been hanging there, injured, for hours before he died. *Fucking hours*,' he repeats, his voice rising with emotion.

That strikes me as unlikely, given the temperature, but I'm not about to argue. He looks pissed off. Like someone on the edge.

'Alex,' Sandrine shoots him a warning look, 'this is neither the time nor the place.'

He swings to face her. 'It never fucking *is*, is it, Sandrine?'

She narrows her eyes at him, lips tight with emotion. Whether from anger or some other feeling, I can't tell.

Out of the corner of my eye, I see Tom's pale features freeze in a rictus of tension. He closes his eyes for a couple of seconds, as if keeping something under control.

The sound of a chair scraping against the floor snaps my focus back to Alex. He gets to his feet abruptly and leaves the dining room, everyone gazing after him.

At the far end of the table, I glimpse Sandrine swallow down some emotion, refusing to make eye contact with any of us.

My fingers tremble as I pick up my glass and take a large gulp of wine, overcome with a paroxysm of guilt and embarrassment. I should have kept my mouth shut. Should have been more discreet.

But one thing is clear.

The death of Jean-Luc hangs over this ice station like a curse.

5

16 February

4.02 a.m.

I've been awake for what feels like for ever, lying in this
uncomfortable bunk in this claustrophobic little room, fighting
the lure of the super-strong sleeping pills in my surgery.
Anything to stop my mind churning over last night. Alex's
outburst, Sandrine's tight-lipped rebuke. My own sense of
having blundered into a minefield.

Beneath it all, the image of Jean-Luc, my predecessor, out
there somewhere suspended in that icy tomb.

Frozen, perhaps, for all eternity.

I close my eyes against the light streaming underneath the
crack in the blind, recalling a documentary on ice climbing I
watched with Ben, a few months before the accident. Both of
us transfixed as the climber dropped backwards into a crevasse,
legs swinging precariously over the abyss. Fear in his breathing,
ragged and staccato, as he lowered himself into that fathomless
blue void.

What did he feel, Jean-Luc, in that moment when the tension
of the climbing rope dissolved and he plunged down into those
icy depths?

What terror? What disbelief?

I pray his agony was momentary, that some blow to his head
knocked him unconscious. That he didn't lie there for long

minutes, the cold seeping into his bones, knowing there was absolutely zero chance of rescue.

Pushing the image from my mind I heave myself out of bed, limbs laggy and tired, to rummage in my wardrobe for some pills. Already the bottle feels lighter. I peer morosely inside, remembering my resolution to kick the habit once I arrived on the ice.

Where better than Antarctica? I'd thought. Away from my usual routine, the lure of the prescription pad.

But right now it doesn't feel so easy. After a moment of hesitation and self-loathing, I chew a couple of hydrocodone to get them into my bloodstream as fast as possible, then pull on some clothes and make my way to the canteen.

Only Tom is there, sitting in the corner, staring out of the window. He nods hello, then turns away. I hesitate, studying the back of his head, his short neat haircut and immaculately pressed shirt and black trousers, wondering if I should make the effort to get to know him a bit better.

But something about his hunched shoulders, his studiously averted attention, tells me he'd rather be left undisturbed. I brew some coffee, make a slice of toast, then escape to my clinic instead. Work, I've learned, is the antidote for pretty much everything.

After all, it's helped me survive since losing Ben.

Fortunately, there's plenty of it. I spend several hours reviewing the various medical experiments I've inherited as station doctor. Jean-Luc and Raff have already collected prodigious amounts of information from each of the winterers: regular blood pressure, temperature, oxygen saturation, and respiratory rate readings, plus weekly blood tests to check cholesterol and haemoglobin levels. Not to mention frequent urine and stool samples to keep tabs on how our immune systems are reacting to the closed environment, given no viruses, bacteria or fungi can survive outside our little cocoon.

On top of all that, there's a raft of behavioural data from the wristbands we're all required to wear, designed to monitor activity levels, heart rate and sleep, as well as our location on the base, and even who we're with. Supplemented with questionnaires and video diaries, it's all designed to study how darkness and isolation affect mood and social interaction. Our real mood, that is – not the social façade we try to maintain.

All a bit Big Brother, without a doubt. But that's what we signed up for.

I scan the results, hoping they might shed light on the tensions I've already witnessed in the station. But it proves impossible to discern a pattern and I lack the energy to dig deeper, so I click into a different screen to check the testing schedule.

Oh hell. Bloods were due two days ago – I'm already falling behind. I get up and open the supplies cupboard, looking for fresh needles and syringes. I'm just pulling out a box of antiseptic wipes when I spot an envelope wedged underneath. I pick it up and peer at the writing on the front, the distinctive cursive longhand the French learn at school.

Nicole Bernas, it says, with an address in Lille. Jean-Luc's wife, I assume, or perhaps his mother or sister.

But it's the words in the corner, printed carefully in capitals in English, that stop the breath in my throat: IN THE EVENT OF MY DEATH.

What the . . . ? I stare at it in disbelief, then check the reverse: no writing, but the envelope is firmly sealed.

What is this doing in the supplies cupboard? Did Jean-Luc hide it deliberately?

I stare at the envelope, wondering when he wrote this and wrestling with the temptation to look inside. All the while trying to get my head around the more obvious question – why on earth did the doctor feel compelled to leave a posthumous letter?

He couldn't possibly have anticipated what would happen out there on the ice, could he?

Before I can speculate any further, an unfamiliar buzz catches my awareness. I rush to the window and peer outside. There, on the horizon, a small speck in the otherwise cloudless blue sky.

The final flight. It's here.

I feel an unexpected swoop of anxiety as I watch the little aircraft grow ever larger, carrying with it the last chance to change my mind. It's now or never, I realise. Once that plane takes off again, I'm here to stay. No way to leave the base for another eight months.

I glance at the letter in my hand, seized by a sudden and unsettling sense of foreboding. I've been here less than a week, but there's no denying the air of palpable tension on the station, of barely concealed unease.

What, exactly, have I got myself into?

Another headache begins to pulse behind my temple, as I watch the aircraft bank around to line up with the makeshift runway. I think back on the monotony of my existence in Bristol – long hours at the hospital, solitary evenings at home, ready meals shoved in the microwave, watching Netflix curled up on the sofa.

My life since the accident.

My life alone.

Do I really want to return to that?

The wheels of the plane make contact with the ground, bouncing a few times and sending up a spray of ice crystals that sparkle in the light, sun glinting on the cockpit windows as the Basler drops its speed and turns towards Beta.

I've no choice, I realise. To go home now would mean leaving the base without a doctor all winter – it would be next to impossible for UNA to recruit and train up another at this late stage. Plus the risks of getting someone out here escalate exponentially as winter closes in and flying becomes too dangerous. Hell, they might even be forced to evacuate the whole base.

What would that do to my professional reputation? Let alone my conscience.

A knock on the door behind me. I quickly stuff the envelope into my jeans pocket as Caro appears, dressed in outdoor gear. 'Hey, Kate, you coming to wave them off?'

'Aren't the pilots staying for a while?'

She shakes her head. 'Too cold today. They've got to keep the engines running or they'll freeze up.'

I lock the clinic door and grab some warm clothes from my cabin, down two more pills, then hurry to the boot room, where I find the last of the summer team saying their goodbyes. Sadness and relief on their faces as they hug everyone, me included. I pull on my outdoor gear, then descend the steps, gasping as the cold air hits my lungs, making my eyes water and chest contract with shock.

Impossible ever to get used to it.

Around me a hive of activity, everyone hurrying towards the refuelling rig. As I trudge across the ice, I pass Luuk and Drew already returning on the skidoos, towing sleds loaded with crates of apples and potatoes, avocados and kiwi fruit, hurrying to bring our last precious supply of fresh food inside before it freezes.

Up ahead, a small figure makes her way towards the plane. 'Sandrine!'

The station leader turns at the sound of her name, pausing to let me catch up. I remove my glove and shove my hand into my jeans pocket, pulling out the envelope, already a little crumpled.

Her eyes widen as I hand it to her and she reads the name. 'Where did you get this?' She frowns at me, her expression faintly accusing.

'I found it in the supplies cupboard. I assume Jean-Luc left it there.'

Sandrine stares down at the writing on the front. Her hand is shaking, I notice; whether from cold or this unwelcome reminder of the death of my predecessor, it's impossible to tell.

'You haven't read it?' she asks.

'Of course not!' I say indignantly. 'That's exactly how I found it.'

With a brief glance around her, Sandrine shoves the letter in her pocket and nods towards the plane. 'They're waiting.'

We join the small group huddled around the Basler, jumping around and flapping their arms to stay warm while the summer team boards the plane and settles into their seats.

'You okay?' Arne asks, as I pant from the effort of hurrying across the ice. Most of his face is exposed, seemingly unfazed by the bitter cold. He's studying me with that quiet air of concern I saw on Alice; as if I'm fragile, or that I, too, might suddenly disappear on them.

'Of course,' I reply, but my voice sounds brittle. I'm still smarting from my interaction with Sandrine. How come every encounter with her leaves me feeling wrong-footed?

I feel another surge of panic at the thought of being left here. Despite the thick necker and goggles, I have an uneasy feeling people can read my mood, that they're aware some part of me wants to grab my things and follow the summer scientists onto that plane.

I glance around, but everyone's attention is fixed on the

departing crew. Only Tom, standing slightly apart from the rest, catches my eye, quickly looking away again.

I'm suddenly certain he knows exactly what I'm thinking.

'Hey, don't forget these!' Caro passes over a small bundle of envelopes to one of the pilots. I realise it's our last chance to deliver any post to friends and family for the next eight months. Damn. I should have included birthday cards for my sister, for my nephews.

Too late now.

I glance at Sandrine, waiting for her to produce the letter from Jean-Luc. But the station leader just stands there, unmoving, as the air crew closes up the doors then clambers back into the cockpit.

What the hell? Surely she should send that letter on to UNA, so they can pass it on to his wife?

I stare at her, but Sandrine ignores me, keeping her eyes fixed on the plane as the pilots give us a thumbs-up. Seconds later they're taxiing away, all the summer crew waving goodbye through the little porthole windows.

'Have a good flight!' Alice yells, swinging her arms wildly and jumping up and down on the spot. 'See you on the other side.'

Drew and Luuk arrive on the skidoos as the plane lines itself up on the runway. With an ear-splitting roar, the engines rev and it hurtles forward across the ice, then slowly, inexorably, lifts into the air.

We stand there, watching, as the Basler grows smaller and smaller, shrinking to a little black dot before finally disappearing into the fierce blue sky. For a minute or so we all remain silent, absorbing the fact of its departure. Red jackets on white snow. The only life for hundreds of miles around.

Thirteen of us. All alone.

'Well, that's it,' Ark declares solemnly, swiping the snow crystals from his beard. 'You stuck with me now.'

Sonya sighs. 'That definitely calls for a drink.'

Slowly she leads the trek back to Alpha, and I follow in her wake, fighting down the feeling that I've just made one of the worst mistakes of my life.

6

30 March

Six weeks later

'You sleep all right?' Drew pulls up an empty chair at breakfast.

'Not really. I keep hearing people in the corridor.' I start on my muesli, longing for some fresh fruit and thick Greek yoghurt to go with it.

Arne yawns. 'That'll be Tom, or Rob. They're becoming . . . how do you say . . . diurnal?'

'Nocturnal?' Alice suggests. 'You mean awake all night and sleeping during the day?'

'Yes, that.' Arne nods.

Quite a crowd for breakfast this morning, I notice. Drew, Arne, Alice and Luuk sitting at one end of the dining table, Alex at the other, head buried in a magazine. As the hours of darkness have increased steadily, attendance at mealtimes has become more erratic, as if the dwindling daylight triggers some primitive urge to go into hibernation.

'Anyway,' Drew turns to me. 'How about that trip up the tower? You really should see the view before it's too dark and cold to risk it. Forecast is for a nice day, and I promised Sonya I'd check on some of the weather equipment.'

I hesitate. Do I really want to go? I'm not scared of heights exactly, but that is one tall tower and the climb looks precarious.

Plus I lack the energy. The disorienting effect of the rapid shift in seasons on my already disordered sleep patterns has rendered me permanently groggy. Tiredness drags at me constantly, making my eyes ache and my mind sluggish, and the thought of dragging myself up that tower is less than appealing.

'It's now or never, kiddo,' Drew urges. 'This is pretty much your last chance till spring.'

He's studying me in that searching way that made me feel stupidly self-conscious when I first arrived. But after six weeks I've given up trying to mask my scar, fending off the occasional question with the simplest of answers: car crash.

'Okay,' I agree, reluctantly. 'Before lunch? I have to do the bloods later.'

Out of the corner of my eye, I sense Arne regarding us thoughtfully. 'I'll come too,' he says. 'I could do with the fresh air.'

Drew lifts an eyebrow. 'Thought you were busy with that dodgy skidoo?'

'It will wait.' Arne glances across the table at Alex. He's still studying his magazine, but something in his demeanour suggests he's been listening to every word. 'You coming too?'

Alex glances up. 'I'll pass, thanks. I'm sure you three can take care of yourselves.'

'You'll need the climbing equipment,' Luuk chips in, chewing a slice of toast. 'Best give it a once-over first though.' Though his comment is clearly addressed to Drew, I notice his eyes are fixed firmly on Alex.

Arne flashes Luuk a warning look and I frown, puzzled. It seemed a pretty innocuous thing to say. Sure enough, Alex's features stiffen. He leans back in his seat and regards us steadily. 'You know where it is, Drew. All checked over, ready to go.'

Drew nods, but Luuk's mouth twitches into a smirk. There's a palpable tension in the air and I have the distinct feeling something is being left unsaid. But Alex ignores him, returning his attention to the magazine.

'Take care of Kate,' says Alice, a little too brightly, like someone trying to defuse a tricky situation. 'That thing is damn slippery in the cold.'

Arne glances at his watch. 'See you in the boot room at midday?'

Drew nods again, and stands. 'Wrap up warm,' he tells me, then disappears.

Mindful of the climb, I put on several more layers than usual; I'm sweating profusely by the time I arrive in the boot room, and I haven't even got my snow gear on yet.

'Your face is almost as red as your jacket.' Drew grins.

I grimace. 'I feel like the Michelin man.' Probably look about as attractive too, I think grimly.

'The what?' Arne's expression is confused.

'It means well padded.' As I put out a hand to steady myself on the racking while I pull on my boots, static arcs to my fingers. 'Ouch!' I yelp, making both Drew and Arne laugh.

Wrestling into my jacket, I search for my glove liners in the pocket; as I pull them out, something drops to the floor.

My pills.

I bend to snatch them up, but Drew beats me to it. 'Strong stuff,' he says, glancing at the label on the foil sachet as he hands them to me.

'They're not mine.' I quickly shove them back into my pocket. 'They're for someone else.'

It's a ridiculous lie and we all know it. I feel my face turn red and pull on my balaclava and goggles to hide my embarrassment.

I daren't look at either of them, just follow them into the garage, feeling mortified.

'Okay, we ready?' Drew loads the climbing gear onto Arne's vehicle, then he and I follow on the other skidoo out onto the ice. We ride in convoy, bouncing across the ridges in the snow, the rays of the rising sun bathing it in a warm golden glow.

I'm going to miss this, I think, as we cruise past the outbuildings and head off towards Omega. In just a few more weeks the light will be swallowed up entirely by twenty-four-hour darkness.

Four long months of it.

A flutter of apprehension, deep in my solar plexus. Will I be able to cope? Will any of us? The tension at breakfast this morning doesn't bode well for a whole winter cooped up together.

Arne pulls up his skidoo at the base of the tower, proceeding to unload the climbing gear. We slide to a halt beside him.

'You used one of these before?' he asks, as he helps me into my harness.

Out of nowhere I'm assaulted by a memory. Ben and I, abseiling in Avon Gorge, a few miles outside Bristol. The two-day course, long on my bucket list, had been his birthday present.

All the same, I had an attack of nerves moments before my first descent. 'I don't think I can do this,' I'd whispered out of earshot of our instructor.

'Horseshit,' Ben said, then kissed me lightly on the lips, in that tender way he did back when he still loved me.

Another rush of sadness and longing assaults me, as fresh and sharp as the day he left. I fight the urge to smuggle those pills from my pocket, and swallow a couple. Too risky – especially after what just happened in the boot room.

I take a few deep breaths instead and follow Arne and

Drew to the base of the first ladder, pushing down the reeling sensation of vertigo as I peer up through the aluminium girders of the tower.

Do I really want to do this? It looks impossibly tall.

On the other hand, I can't stand around out here or I'll freeze. I glance back at Alpha, nearly a kilometre away – a long walk and not one I fancy on my own.

'Have you changed your mind?' Arne is gazing at me. 'I can take you back.'

There's enough of his forehead exposed to see it's furrowed with concern, and not for the first time I find myself envying Arne's girlfriend in Iceland. He might not be as handsome as Drew, or as outgoing, but he exudes a calm self-assurance that's good to be around.

Like Ben, I realise, with another twinge of regret. Back before it all went bad.

'She'll be fine.' Drew mock punches my arm. 'Won't you, Kate?'

'Let's do it,' I say, mustering some enthusiasm. What did my mother say after the accident, when first confronted with the wound on my cheek? What doesn't kill you makes you stronger.

And uglier. She didn't say it, but it was there, in her eyes. The way she winced when I removed the dressing.

'Okay, we're ready.' Drew secures the ropes and karabiners. 'Kate, you want to go first?'

'Why don't you?' Arne suggests instead. 'Kate can follow and I'll take the rear.'

Drew nods and sets off. I grit my teeth and start to climb behind him, gripping the rungs of the ladder firmly, my ears ringing with the clang of boots on metal as we ascend each level then traverse the little platform to the next. Slowly, carefully, we zigzag upwards, Drew adjusting the climbing gear as we go.

By the time we're halfway, my fingers are achingly numb, the cold penetrating through my thick down gloves. But that's nothing compared to the uncomfortable knot in my stomach that tightens as we rise ever higher.

You're fine, I tell myself repeatedly, trying not to look down. You can't fall.

But Jean-Luc did, counters a voice in my head. The climbing equipment didn't save him, did it?

The picture of my predecessor plunging into that crevasse fills my mind again. My legs go rigid and I stop on the ladder, breathing ragged, on the verge of panic.

'You okay?' Arne's voice behind me. 'We can go back down if you like.'

'I'm fine,' I insist. 'Just need to catch my breath.'

Inhaling deeply, I set off again, keeping my focus on the horizon, the wider landscape opening up around us. Drew was right. It has turned into a lovely day, with no mist or low cloud to obscure the view for miles around. In the distance, Alpha and Beta look small and remote, reminding me of my first glimpse of the ice station from the little Basler plane.

Just weeks ago, yet it feels like a million years.

A few minutes later we reach the top platform. Drew lets out a long slow whistle as Arne and I join him. 'Amazing, isn't it?'

I take in the three-hundred-and-sixty-degree view, trying to ignore the sway of the tower in the wind. He's right. It is absolutely stunning. Wave upon wave upon wave of snow, an ocean of white rippling out as far as the eye can see. Above, the endless crush of deep blue sky. I'm beginning to understand what draws people back to this place, winter after winter. The emptiness is mesmerising, hypnotic.

Holding the handrail firmly, I let my gaze drop downwards and see, beneath, the shadow of the tower on the snow, the three of us in silhouette. I lift a hand and wave, and my shadow waves back at me.

'What are they up to?'

Arne's voice pulls my attention to the horizon. He's pointing to a space a few hundred metres to the rear of Alpha. Squinting into the sunlight, I spot a tiny skidoo arcing away from the station; behind it a red-clad figure, sliding across the ice at great speed.

For a moment I can't make sense of what I'm seeing, then realise they're being towed on a snowboard.

'Luuk, I reckon.' Drew peers at them. 'Probably Rob driving.'

'They're going way too fast,' Arne says as they swoop towards Gamma, bucking over waves of compacted snow.

Suddenly, as if we've conjured it into existence, the board catches on a ridge and its rider goes flying into the air, landing heavily on the ice.

I wait, heart in mouth, for whoever it is to get up. 'Shit,' I gasp when they don't. I lurch towards the ladder, feet skidding on the icy metal platform.

Drew pulls me back. 'Kate, hold up! Let me go first. Arne, you take the ropes and make sure she gets down safely.'

He shucks off his climbing gear and descends the ladders with unnerving swiftness and roars away on the skidoo. I follow as fast as I dare, trying to suppress a groan of frustration each time Arne pauses to readjust the climbing gear. All the way down I mentally run through the possible scenarios – head injury, leg fracture, dislocated shoulder.

None of them good.

'Hold on tight!' Arne calls once we're back on the ground and aboard the skidoo. He revs the engine and we speed away. After another few torturous minutes we finally reach the small huddle of people on the snow and I'm relieved to see Luuk now sitting up, tentatively flexing his right leg.

'Are you hurt?' I drop down beside him.

To my surprise he pulls off his balaclava and grins. 'Just smashed up my goggles. No need to panic, Doctor North.'

'Are you sure? You took one hell of a fall.'

'Hey, chill out.' He sounds slightly annoyed, as if I'm spoiling his vibe. I frown at him, then notice his dilated pupils.

Jesus. *He's high.*

I glance around at Rob, hovering nearby. His snow goggles obscure his eyes, but something tells me he's in the same condition as Luuk.

I'm wondering how to tackle the situation, when Alex appears, almost sprinting across the snow. Even with his face covered, I can tell he's furious. Sandrine is at his heels, puffing with the effort of keeping up.

'What the hell were you doing?' Alex yells, looking from Rob to Luuk and back again. 'You're not even wearing helmets. Are you both fucking insane?' He glares at Luuk, at the ice crystals already forming on his face, the exposed hair beneath his hat, then takes a step towards him.

'Jean-Luc warned you.' He pokes his finger at Luuk's chest. 'I should fucking report you to UNA.'

'Really,' Luuk sneers. 'That's a bit rich, isn't it, coming from you?'

Alex's gloved hand clutches into a fist. For a second I think it's all going to kick off, but after a moment of hesitation, Alex spins on his heels and heads back to the base.

'Not cool,' Arne turns to Luuk. 'Not cool at all.'

Luuk shrugs. 'He'll get over it.' With a grunt, he heaves himself to his feet, waving away Drew's proffered hand.

'I really should get an X-ray before you walk on that leg,' I say, but Luuk waves me away, hobbling off to collect his snowboard. I feel a mix of irritation and relief. Probably just pulled a muscle or sprained his knee.

I turn to Sandrine, wondering what she'll do; after all, this is a serious breach of safety, even before you factor in that they're obviously off their heads.

But she ignores me, looking instead at Drew. 'Go check he's all right, will you?' She nods at Alex's retreating form. 'You two can walk to the station,' she says to Luuk and Rob, then climbs aboard their skidoo, revs the engine, then roars away.

I stare after her in disbelief. What the hell? Isn't she going to do *anything*?

A light pressure on my arm. 'Forget it.' There's warning in Arne's voice. 'Let's get back.'

'Should we leave them here?' I glance at Luuk and Rob, both debating what to do with the snowboard. 'It's a long way to walk with an injured leg.'

'You heard Sandrine,' Arne mutters as he turns away. 'That's their problem.'

7

1 May

I'm freezing – the kind of deadening, head-numbing chill that makes your teeth hurt and jaw ache. Despite the kerosene heater in the makeshift shelter, my fingers are so cold I can barely hold the sample pots as I work.

'Many more to go?' Drew trains the torch on my hands.

'Just a couple.' I fumble with the lid from the next pot, wishing for the thousandth time that I hadn't volunteered to collect the weekly snow samples. Ten weeks ago, when the last of the summer team left and someone had to take over the task, there'd been near twenty-four-hour daylight; I didn't factor in how difficult this would be in the dark.

And after tonight, there'll be plenty more of that, I think grimly as I stuff snow into the pot.

'I hope those geeks in Geneva find something exciting,' Drew mutters, stamping his feet to stay warm. 'Alien life forms, at the very least.'

I laugh. That's what I like about Drew, he always manages to lift my mood – no mean feat given the increasing air of tension on the station as the daylight hours have shrunk to a vague twilight and the sun sulks ever lower on the horizon. I'd underestimated how much prolonged darkness messes with your circadian rhythms and any sense of routine, draining your energy and fogging your brain, making a challenge of even the simplest chore.

'Shit.' My fingers ache so much I drop the last container, losing it somewhere on the snow. Drew sweeps the torch across the ground while I look for it.

I suppress a groan of frustration. How will I manage this for the next four months of permanent night? I can't face doing it alone, and I'm loath to admit my longstanding fear of the dark to my colleagues. But there's a limit to how many times I can ask Drew to accompany me; not that he ever objects, but I don't want to strain our friendship.

Over the last couple of months Drew's become my closest ally. As winter deepens, and my polite reminders have been met with increasing apathy and evasion, he's chased people up for blood and stool samples, defending me when they bitch about completing their video diaries and questionnaires. He volunteered to train as a surgical assistant, even offered to help with the endless data updates on the medical systems.

And all that on top of his own workload.

'That's it.' I finally locate the missing pot and stuff it with snow. 'Let's get the hell out of here.'

Drew sighs with relief. 'I really need a beer. I could do with a shower too, but I'll settle for the beer.'

I grunt my agreement, but can't help feeling sorry for Caro, who's had flak for days since the plumbing gave out again, for reasons she still hasn't identified. We've all been forced to wash down using water boiled in the kitchen, exacerbating the deteriorating mood on the base.

As Drew extinguishes the heater, I load the samples into my knapsack, pull on my thick outer gloves, and step outside, listening to the faint tinkling sound as the vapour in my breath freezes and falls to the ground like powdered glass. My fingers and toes throb painfully as we trudge back to Alpha, but that's preferable to numbness; it's when you can't feel anything at all that you need to worry.

'Shit.' Unable to see clearly through the ice crystals sticking my eyelashes together, I trip on a ridge in the snow and lurch forwards.

Drew shoots out a hand to grab me. 'Steady there.' He pulls me upright, his hand lingering on my arm momentarily. I turn, puzzled, but he simply nods and releases me.

We reach the steps and climb back up into Alpha. I flop onto one of the seats in the kit room and pull off my outdoor gear, grateful I don't have to do that again for another week.

'I'll stick these into cold storage for you,' says Drew, picking up the knapsack with the snow samples once he's stripped down to his T-shirt and jeans. 'See you at lunchtime. We're gonna give our favourite star a good send-off, so get your glad rags on.'

Who am I kidding?

I examine the black Lycra dress in the little mirror inside my wardrobe door, careful not to lift my eyes to my face. Once tight-fitting, with a deep plunging neckline, the material now gapes around my breastbone and my hips. I pull it off in disgust and slip on a pair of jeans and a fresh T-shirt, then retrieve my pills from the wardrobe. I swallow two, then add a third for good measure.

Seriously, Kate?

My sister's words reverberate in my head and I squeeze my eyes shut to drive them away.

Soon, I promise myself. Soon.

I arrive in the lounge an hour before sunset. In the adjacent games room, Alice and Drew are engrossed in a table football match; from her victorious cheering, it sounds like Alice is winning.

Sonya sits in the corner, headphones on, knitting something I can't identify – a scarf perhaps? With her round figure and curly grey hair, she looks every inch the benign Southern grandma, but that fools no one with even a passing acquaintance. Sonya is far and away the most intelligent person on the base – I've already clocked her impressive IQ scores in her medical file – and as Professor of Meteorology at the University of Toronto, clearly a leading light in her field.

She also has the stoical patience of a clever black woman who's endured a lifetime of being underestimated.

'Hey.' Sonya catches my eye as I help myself to a glass of red wine, then removes her ear buds and pats the seat beside her. 'Come and join me.'

I sit, grateful for her friendly attention. 'What are you listening to?'

'*The Clay Machine-Gun.* Victor Pelevin.'

'I don't know it.'

'You should read it. It's extraordinary. Ark downloaded the audiobook – he's educating me in the masterpieces of Russian literature.'

I raise an eyebrow, and Sonya smiles. 'Don't underestimate him. He probably knows as much about Russian novels as he does generators. Which is to say, a lot.'

'Where is he anyway?' I glance around. 'And the others?'

'Ark and Arne are helping Rajiv in the kitchen. Alex and Caro are getting changed, Sandrine's still letting off steam in Beta.'

This last comment makes me smile. Our station leader, it turns out, is a keen golfer. During the summer, she set up her own course on a smooth area of ice, covering her balls in red marker pen so she could see them against the snow. But since the encroaching darkness drove her indoors, Sandrine has been forced to mock up a putting green in the largest of the Beta storerooms.

'As for Luuk and Rob . . .' Sonya raises a cynical eyebrow. 'Well, your guess is as good as mine.'

I don't need to ask what she's getting at. Luuk and Rob – or Beavis and Butt-Head, as I've heard Caro refer to them – have taken to disappearing for protracted periods, turning up at supper looking wasted. Not to mention the lingering herbal smell in certain areas of Beta.

I've half wondered whether to broach the subject with Sandrine, but there's no way she can't have noticed – especially after the incident with the snowboard. Presumably she's concluded it's relatively harmless. Whatever gets you through the winter, as Ark is fond of saying.

Besides, it's not as if I'm in any position to criticise.

'So, how's it going?' Sonya pulls more yarn from her ball and starts a new row.

'Busy, which is good. I'd probably go a bit crazy without plenty to do.' Though I'd happily give up the snow sampling, I nearly add.

'It must be a tough job, dealing with all of us. Jean-Luc said it was what he liked least, having to constantly nag people.'

I squint at her in surprise. In all the weeks I've been here, this is the first time anyone has mentioned Jean-Luc without prompting. 'What was he like?' I ask, seizing the opportunity. 'Nobody seems keen to talk about him.'

For a moment or two Sonya doesn't respond, and I worry I've put my foot in it again. Then she lays down her knitting, props her elbow on the side of the armchair, and rests her chin in her hand as she gazes at me.

'He was a good man, Kate. Kind, committed to helping others. Very clever too. Always interested in other people's field of work, forever scribbling away in his journal – or his Antarctic adventure log, as he liked to call it. He was planning to write a book about his time here.'

'Really?' I picture again that face from the photos and feel another wave of sadness. I reckon I'd have liked Jean-Luc a lot.

What a terrible waste.

Sonya smiles at some memory. 'I told him if he was gonna put me in his book, he had to make me thin and twenty years younger, or I'd sue.'

I laugh. 'You must miss him,' I say gently.

She considers this. 'I do. Though he could sometimes be rather . . . intense, he generally had a light touch with people, always knew how to defuse a situation with a joke.' Her face betrays a ripple of emotion. 'No offence meant, but this place hasn't been the same since he died.'

'I can't imagine how devastating it must have been.' I picture the expedition party returning without him, having to impart the news to those left in the station that they'd been forced to abandon Jean-Luc there on – *in* – the ice. Even after all these weeks, I'm still haunted by that image of him. The utter bleakness of it. The terrible isolation. Though he's dead, it's as if we've all somehow let him down.

'I guess a lot of people miss him.' I watch Sonya's fingers form the stitches; it's mesmerising, like a kind of visual meditation.

'Some more than others,' she replies cryptically.

I frown. 'How so?'

Sonya pauses, considering. 'Well, let's just say Jean-Luc didn't always see eye to eye with everyone. There were . . .' she hesitates '. . . disagreements.'

'What about?'

But our conversation is interrupted by the arrival of the others. Rajiv, carrying a couple of bottles of wine, is wearing a long black shirt and his best crimson turban, his beard and moustache freshly clipped and oiled, while Sandrine looks particularly chic in a scarlet shift dress and matching lipstick.

I kick myself, feeling dowdy now in my jeans and plain

T-shirt. I'm about to return to my cabin and get changed when Caro appears, sporting her usual dungarees. Luuk, Rob, and Alex trail behind her – Alex looks positively dishevelled, his face bleary with fatigue, Luuk wearing a pair of cargo shorts and his usual sardonic, slightly aloof expression.

'Where's Arne?' Sandrine asks.

'Gone to freshen up,' Rajiv says. 'He'll be here in a minute.'

As if on cue, Arne arrives. Despite the broken showers, he's managed to wash his hair, I notice; it's still glistening with damp. He's looking pretty smart, in grey trousers and a thin weave jumper that shows off the muscle tone he maintains in the gym. Few of us have the discipline to work out every day, and on Arne it really shows. Drew too.

'It's nearly time,' Sandrine announces, checking her watch. Barely 2 p.m., and we're already saying goodbye to the sun.

Ark hurries in, and Drew and Alice abandon their pool game as we turn off the lights and crowd around the wide lounge windows that overlook the ice. We're in luck: the sky is unclouded, and a clear streak of pink surrounds the sliver of sun that has barely dragged itself into view.

I gaze out over the landscape, feeling strangely apprehensive. These last few weeks I've taken to observing every sunset, fascinated by the sight of our life-giving star losing its daily battle with the northern horizon. Each day it struggles to rise above the ice, each day giving up more quickly, turning the clouds orange and the snow purple as it sinks back down, smearing the sky with the colours of blood and bruises.

The minutes tick by as we stand there silently, watching the light slowly fade, dwindling to a point before disappearing entirely.

'That's it, folks,' Drew declares, switching the overhead lights back on. 'Welcome to winter.'

He sounds cheerful, but the atmosphere in the room is uneasy.

Though the days have been short and dim, the fact the sun put in an appearance at all was oddly comforting.

It's as if we've been somehow abandoned.

Rajiv disappears then reappears with a tray full of snacks – red and green olives, stuffed with pickled lemon and fried halloumi, along with an array of nuts and various flavours of crisps. 'Supper will be served early,' he declares, 'but there's more in the kitchen if you can't hold out till then.'

We help ourselves to drinks and nibbles then settle into the chairs and sofas. Though most days we work and do our own thing, Sandrine has decided we should spend the rest of today together. 'Bonding', as she called it, making it sound more like some painfully awkward group training exercise than anything we might actually enjoy.

I turn to speak to Drew, but see he's watching Alex, who's still standing by the window, staring out into the darkness as if searching for something in that impenetrable gloom.

'Hey, kiddo, what's up?' Drew asks. 'Trouble on the ranch?'

Alex inhales, rubs his hair and turns to face us. His features are stiff, and he looks miserable. 'Just heard my sister's getting married,' he mumbles. 'In a few months.'

'Shit.' Arne's voice is full of sympathy. 'I'm guessing this is a surprise?'

Alex sighs. 'You could say that. She recently discovered she's pregnant – if she waits for me to get home, she'll have had the baby.'

'Shotgun wedding?' Rob jokes, and I see Sonya nudge his foot.

'They've been engaged for a couple of years, actually – this has just brought the whole thing forward.' Alex presses his lips together, as if making a supreme effort not to snap. 'It's going to be a big wedding. Relatives coming over from America, the works.'

I feel a swell of sympathy. He looks really gutted. For all his adventuring – Alex trained as an outdoor instructor and spent several years working in New Zealand – he's clearly a family guy.

'That is hard.' Ark walks up and gives him a bear hug. For an awkward moment or two it looks as if Alex might cry.

'Could be worse,' he says ruefully. 'At least no one died.'

There's a tense silence before Alice speaks, her tone deliberately cheerful. 'And think, you'll have a new niece or nephew to greet you when you get home.'

This finally brings a smile to Alex's face. 'Yeah, the first grandchild. My parents are psyched. Mam's already buying baby clothes.'

'Baby clothes!' Sonya beams, delighted. 'Now that's exactly the excuse I need. Good thing I brought plenty of yarn.'

'Bread!' squeals Caro, grabbing a slice and slathering it in butter.

Rajiv has pulled out all the stops for our first winter supper. Along with the warm walnut loaf, he serves up lobster ravioli, and a mushroom risotto made with dried porcini and ceps. There's even a tiny portion of salad, courtesy of Drew's hydroponics. I groan with pleasure at the taste of the little leaves in my mouth; our supply of fresh vegetables has dwindled to a few potatoes and mealy apples, both shrivelled and soft.

'Drink?' Drew passes several bottles of champagne around the table and everyone pours themselves a glass. Everyone except Ark, that is; in defiance of his Russian roots, he's teetotal. His father was an abusive alcoholic, he told me during my first week here: 'Drank himself to death, which mean we not have to endure him any longer.'

'I'd like to propose a toast to our wonderful chef,' Sandrine announces, her face already a little flushed. I flash her a smile,

feeling a stab of annoyance as she pretends not to notice. 'To Rajiv.'

We raise our glasses as he stands and takes a little bow.

'Don't forget Drew.' I hold my glass up to my friend. 'For the delicious salad.'

We take another drink, Drew giving me a wink of solidarity. Out of the corner of my eye I catch Arne regarding me thoughtfully, and feel suddenly self-conscious, for no reason I can put my finger on.

The atmosphere begins to loosen as the alcohol hits our bloodstreams. Alex and Luuk look noticeably tipsy; Rob and Drew are chatting and laughing happily. Even Tom, who seems always to be on the periphery, is engaging Ark in an argument about the best *Star Wars* film, Alice and Caro listening with bemused smiles.

I study Alice's face. She has the kind of features you can barely tear your eyes from. A constant source of torment to several of the men here, especially as she's entirely off limits – Alice lives in Brighton with her Italian girlfriend, and their five-year-old daughter Lydia.

Not for the first time, I wonder how she can spend twelve months away from a child that young. But I already know the answer. Alice is studying the effects of climate change, and the Antarctic is an invaluable source of data on the impact of human activity on the planet.

She's here for the sake of her daughter, not despite her.

'More champagne?' Drew hovers the bottle above my glass.

I place my hand over the top. 'I should pace myself. After all, I'm the only doctor on the base.' What if something happens and I'm not in a fit state to deal with it?

'Relax,' he reassures me. 'We'll be fine. Live a little, Kate – it's a long winter ahead.'

I relent and let him refill my glass, resolving to sip it slowly.

As Rob and Rajiv hand out the desserts – chocolate mousse topped with little slivers of crystallised fruit – Sandrine bangs her spoon on the table and waits for silence.

'To absent family and friends,' she proposes, gazing around at everyone with a strangely pained expression, her smile tense and artificial.

A general murmur as we raise our glasses and return the toast, followed by a silence that lasts a few beats too long. How many are remembering Jean-Luc, I wonder?

In the event of my death.

I think again of that letter, the one I found in my clinic, the one that has played on my mind ever since. The strangeness of it. Antarctica can be hazardous, sure, but rarely lethal. What prompted him to write it? And why hide it away like that?

My eyes drift to Sandrine, now talking to Sonya, and I ask myself for the thousandth time why she didn't send it on to UNA. What possible reason could there be for keeping that letter here? In the couple of months since that plane left, I haven't come up with any explanation.

It hasn't helped warm me to our station leader. Plus there's something aloof in her manner, something rigid and unyielding. The kind of woman who never breaks out of their role, like a bossy headmistress who treats the adults around her like wayward children.

There's no faulting her experience though: a doctorate in environmental science from the Sorbonne, plus two years on the French/Italian base, Concordia. No family, according to Caro, bar a pair of nieces.

I take a sip of wine and find my gaze meeting Arne's. My cheeks flush. Has he read my feelings about Sandrine on my face? I should make more effort, I decide. Try to get to know her. Give her the benefit of the doubt.

'How's the family holding up?' Arne asks, turning to Ark.

Ark nods genially. 'Good. You know, waiting for chance to depose that *pizdah*.'

'*Pizdah*?' I frown.

Caro comes to my rescue. 'That cunt. He means Putin.'

Ark nods. '*Da*. Is crook.'

I raise an eyebrow at Caro. 'I didn't know you spoke Russian?'

'Ark's teaching me.' She grins. 'Starting with all the dirty stuff.'

Ark laughs, but his expression remains wistful. Clearly he's thinking of home. 'You must miss them all,' I say to him.

'Of course. And my country too.' He follows this with a deep sigh. 'Is curse of all Russians – even if you hate the place, the system, it is in your blood, in here.' He thumps his chest with one of his enormous fists. 'I miss it all the time. *Nasha rodina* – my homeland.'

He sniffs, then lets out another of his long guffaws. 'But then you remember the money!'

Everyone laughs, but Sandrine's lips purse with disapproval.

I lean towards her, determined to strike up a conversation, but my words are cut short by a loud thump as a fist hits the table, making the surrounding plates and cutlery jump with a clatter.

'What the fuck?' Alex shouts, glaring at Drew. 'Are you serious?'

'Calm down, man.' Drew raises his hands in the air. 'I didn't mean anything by it.'

Alex eyeballs him for a second, then stands so abruptly he nearly tips his chair. His eyes dart from one of us to the next, his expression full of accusation. We stare back at him in stunned silence.

'You all think it was my fault,' he slurs, swaying slightly. 'Don't you?'

Ark rises to place a cautionary hand on Alex's shoulder, but he shrugs it away.

'You do,' he shouts. 'I know you fucking do. You think it's my fault. You don't say so, but that's what you all believe.'

He spins around and walks off, fists opening and clenching. Suddenly he raises his right arm and punches the wall so hard there's an audible crack. As Alex slams out of the room, a fragment of plaster falls to the floor, revealing a sizeable dent in the plasterwork.

That must have hurt.

A lot.

Caro turns to Drew, her expression perplexed. 'What did you say to him?'

'Nothing,' Drew says, eyes wide. 'The guy's drunk is all, and upset about his sister's wedding.'

'I'll go check he's okay—' I get to my feet.

'No,' Caro interjects. 'Let me. I'll fetch you if his hand needs attention.'

'I'll come with you.' Sandrine folds up her napkin and follows Caro out of the door.

For a minute, nobody speaks. Suddenly Alice bursts into tears. Long gulping sobs. Sonya puts an arm around her, hugging her until her emotion subsides.

'Sorry,' she says, sweeping a napkin across her face. 'It's just getting to me, that's all.'

Drew seems nonplussed, but I watch him take a particularly long slug of his beer.

What on earth did he say to Alex?

I want to know, but have the sense not to ask. We've had more than enough drama for one evening.

8

1 May

'Alcohol. Argument. Is like being back home.'

Ark raises a few weak smiles as we sit in the lounge, feeling awkward, listening to the Abba track playing in the background.

After a few minutes Tom shakes his head and gets to his feet, body rigid with tension, his expression an odd mix of confusion and dismay. 'I've had enough,' he says in his soft German accent. 'I am going to do some work.'

I nurse the dregs of my wine, wondering what to do. Should I go see Alex? Or wait for Caro to come and get me?

You all think it's my fault, don't you?

What did he mean? I recall Luuk's taunt after the snowboarding accident out on the ice: *That's a bit rich coming from you.*

I try to quell a growing sense of disquiet. Something isn't right. Something I can't put my finger on.

What is going on here?

I consider asking Alice, but I'm wary of setting her off again. Whether it's grief for her dead colleague or distress at Alex's outburst, the last thing I want is to unsettle her further.

Sonya's eyes linger on the doorway, her face clouded with concern – clearly she's as troubled by this as I am. I glance at Arne, but he's sitting back in his armchair, staring up at the ceiling, lost in thought.

I take the opportunity to study him more closely. He has the kind of looks that grow on you, I've noticed. The sort that become more attractive on closer acquaintance. I've come to admire Arne's steadiness, his air of self-sufficiency, of keeping slightly aloof from the rest of the group.

Ben was like that too. The kind of guy it was easy to overlook until you knew him better.

But you didn't really know him, did you? I remind myself, feeling the twitchiness that precedes the urge for another dose of medication. I think longingly of the pills in my wardrobe, wishing I'd brought some with me – but after dropping them that time in the boot room, I didn't want to take the risk.

'I really should check on Alex,' I say, seizing the excuse, but Drew puts out a hand to stop me.

'Let him sleep it off.' He gets to his feet and fetches a bottle of wine. 'Here. Have another drink instead.'

Instead? I wonder for a moment if my friend has me sussed. If he put two and two together back in the boot room that day. But he's right, I decide, as he pours me another glass of red. It would be better to check on Alex in the morning, when he's calmed down. And sobered up.

Sadly his outburst has taken the shine off the evening. One by one the others disappear, until only Drew, Alice, Luuk, and Rob remain.

'Well, that was heavy,' Drew says, after Arne bids us goodnight. 'Not quite the evening I was expecting.'

Rob sighs. 'It's the alcohol. The altitude makes it worse – one minute you're slightly buzzed, the next you can barely stand up.'

'And the rest,' snorts Luuk. 'It's not just the booze making him paranoid.'

I frown. Has Alex been smoking? But he didn't seem stoned,

more upset. I make a mental note to ask Caro – of all the people in the station, she seems closest to him.

I attempt to engage Rob in conversation – he's been friendly enough since my arrival on the ice, but in a bland, distant kind of way that leaves me knowing little about him. He has a chameleon-like quality, clearly happy in his role as Luuk's sidekick.

But before I get anywhere, Alice proposes another pool tournament, and Rob and Luuk leap to the challenge, leaving Drew and me alone.

'Penny for them?' Drew breaks my reverie, as I listen to the others baiting and teasing each other in the games room.

I sigh. 'Nothing much. Thinking over what I need to do tomorrow.'

'Shelve it. It's Sunday – you don't need to do anything at all.'

He's right, though we rarely bother with weekends as such, given most of our work isn't tied to standard hours. But we do aim to have one day a week – usually a Sunday – when we try to do other things. In my case, that's not much. A video chat with my mother or sister. Perhaps summon up enough concentration to read a book.

'You sure you're all right?'

Drew's studying my face – though not in the usual way people do, eyes drawn inexorably to my scar. This is more penetrating, as if he's trying to figure out something about me.

'I'm fine. Just tired.' I check my watch – not quite time for bed.

'You work too hard.'

There's no response I can make to that beyond a wry smile. It's true, I do work too hard. It's been my refuge ever since the accident, and I returned to my job in the hospital as soon as possible – when you focus on the bad stuff that happens to other people, it leaves less room to dwell on the bad stuff that's happened to you.

'There you go again.' Drew laughs. 'Off with the fairies.'

'Sorry.' I take a slug of wine. It's a decent Italian red – Rajiv clearly knows his vintages, and UNA has the good sense not to fob us off with rubbish.

'Well, so much for pool,' says Alice, as she and the other two emerge from the games room. 'Having had my arse whipped, I'm off for an early night.' She gives us each a hug and kiss on the cheek. 'Thanks for a lovely evening.'

We murmur our goodnights, and Alice leaves, Rob and Luuk's gaze following her out of the room.

'Forgeddaboutit,' Drew quips in a NY accent, which makes them both laugh.

The four of us fall into a long and rambling conversation. Luuk, I discover to my surprise, studied fine art in Utrecht before deciding to retrain as an electrician. I ponder this as the banter flies back and forth. Is that why he's so . . . antagonistic? Some by-product of thwarted artistic ambition?

I'm not about to ask, but I learn more about Rob, who describes growing up in Australia as the child of Asian immi-grants – his imitation of his mother's hybrid Aussie-Taiwanese accent makes Luuk and Drew laugh so hard they have tears in their eyes.

Gradually I find myself relaxing, though part of my mind still niggles at what happened with Alex earlier. What did he mean? What does everyone think is his fault?

Should I ask Drew?

No, I decide. The person to ask is Alex himself. I'll deal with that tomorrow. And check in on Tom, too, while I'm at it.

'Well, I'm gonna hit the sack,' Rob says eventually. Luuk drains the rest of his beer and joins him. 'Don't stay up too late,' he calls back to the two of us, with only the hint of a smirk.

I watch them leave, wondering if they're going off for another smoke. Seems more likely.

'I should go to bed too,' I sigh. 'I really do have lots of work to do tomorrow. Sunday or not.'

'Hey, the night is young,' quips Drew. 'We've got four months of it yet. You can't spend all of it hiding away in that clinic.'

I hesitate.

'Stay and keep me company,' he insists. 'My body clock's screwed and I can't sleep anyway, so what's the point of trying?'

He's right. I doubt I'll sleep much either, especially given what's happened tonight. So I allow him to top up my glass again, knowing full well I'll regret it in the morning. But I'm past caring. The events of the evening have me rattled and I'm grateful for the opportunity to blot it from my mind.

'You didn't say much,' Drew prompts. 'About yourself, earlier. In fact you never do. I hardly know anything about you.'

I nod, surprised he's picked up on my reticence. Whereas once I'd have been happy to talk openly about my life, these days I avoid it as much as possible. All roads seem to lead to Ben, to that night.

'I guess I don't find myself a very interesting topic of conversation,' I hedge.

'Big on self-censorship, aren't you?' Drew grabs a handful of peanuts and chews them slowly, pinning me with his gaze. He really is insanely handsome, I think, feeling slightly drunk. His clear brown eyes and light tan. The perfect hint of stubble.

Entirely out of my league. The thought is vaguely comforting, as if I no longer have to bother trying.

'How about you pick one thing,' he persists. 'Tell me the last time you were happy.'

The last time I was happy? To my dismay, I find I can't remember. Happiness seems an impossibility now, about as attainable as becoming a concert pianist or flying to the moon. Happiness is for other people. All I aspire to is numbness, an absence of pain.

Then an answer occurs to me, but not one I can tell Drew. I recall those first days after the accident, when I was moved from morphine to prescription painkillers – the good stuff, not the pale imitations you can buy over the counter at Boots. I remember perfectly the rush of well-being they gave me – relief not simply from the physical pain of my smashed knee and whiplash, but from all the grief and guilt and trauma.

Of course, it's not real, that blissful detachment – merely the chemical effects of opioids attaching to receptors in the body and brain. But that didn't stop me craving it, always chasing that soft, soothing blankness.

Though now it mostly eludes me.

I look up to see Drew frowning at me. 'Okay then, how about the last time you got drunk. I mean really drunk, not just a bit "squiffy".' He says this last word in a mock English accent that makes me laugh.

I sigh, trying to recall. It must have been that night, six years ago, when Ben and I went for a summer barbecue in Clifton with a crowd of our medical friends. I got through nearly a whole bottle of designer gin, then dragged everyone to a club in town to dance our arses off.

I tell Drew about it, all the while marvelling at that light-hearted version of myself. Did I actually do things like that? Impossible, now, to imagine I was ever that person, that I was once that relaxed, that carefree.

And not a painkiller in sight.

Somehow Drew coaxes more from me and I end up telling him about my family. How both my parents were doctors, but my elder sister Clare managed to break the mould by studying law at Cambridge instead of medicine. My brother Richard, however, dutifully followed into the family business, eventually becoming head of surgery at a leading hospital in Australia.

'You sound a clever bunch,' Drew comments.

I pull a face. 'We're a family of over-achievers. The kind that looks great on paper but feels hollow on the inside. Nothing is ever good enough when the minimum standard is perfection.'

'So you're not close to them then?'

I shake my head. 'Dad died five years ago, and Mum lives in India now – she took a job in Delhi as a consultant psychiatrist. My brother works in Melbourne, and we've pretty much lost touch.'

'Don't you miss her? Your mum.'

'Sometimes.' I keep my voice noncommittal. 'She was never exactly the stay-at-home, nurturing type. I'm closer to my sister, Clare.'

Drew looks thoughtful. The expression on his face is uncomfortably close to sympathy. 'Sounds a bit lonely, your childhood.'

I squint at him in surprise. Is it that obvious? Or maybe I've underestimated him. Just because he's ripped and fit, it doesn't mean Drew's some kind of emotional caveman.

'Yeah, I guess it was. But hey, it's my life now.'

'And is there anyone in particular you share it with?' He asks this casually, as if it isn't a loaded question, one I've dodged a number of times since coming here. This time, I suspect, I'm not going to sidestep it so easily.

'Not any more.'

Drew studies me with an inscrutable expression. 'So you're single?'

'I've been talking too much,' I say quickly, anxious to change the subject. 'What about you? Tell me more about your life – you don't really mention it either.'

Drew shrugs. 'Not a lot to say. Born and raised in the Midwest. Parents were arable farmers. My brother went to college, got the hell out of Dodge.'

'Got the hell out of Dodge? You mean your home? Wasn't it happy?'

He sighs. For a moment I worry I've hit a nerve. 'He left Nebraska. Took me a few years longer. When my parents sold the farm, retired to Florida, I rented a place in town and worked at the local Target for a while, before I realised that if I didn't get my shit together, that would end up being my whole life. So I joined the army and trained as a combat engineer.'

'How long did you do that for?' I feel bad I don't already know, but there's an unwritten rule on the base that no one pries, or asks too many questions. Out here, it seems, we can be whoever we choose; fresh versions of ourselves – at least for the duration of our stay.

'I was in the army four years, maybe five,' Drew replies. 'A couple of tours in Afghanistan was enough for me.'

He chews the side of his lip and I sense we've strayed into territory he too would rather forget, so I grasp for a change of subject. 'So you've no one special waiting for you either?'

Fuck's sake, Kate. I kick myself the second the words leave my mouth. Why on earth would you ask him that?

Because I'm drunk, I realise, blurrily.

Drew turns to me – to my relief I see he's grinning. 'Why are you asking me that, Kate? You interested?'

'Of course not,' I say quickly, heat rushing to my cheeks. 'I'm sorry . . . I mean, you're a good-looking guy, I was simply wondering why you'd be single.'

Jesus, Kate, you're actually making this worse.

Drew's smile is playfully mocking. 'FYI, Doctor North – not

that you're interested – I had a girlfriend back in the US for five years. We broke up last year.'

'Oh.' I can't think of anything to say to that.

'She didn't like me disappearing off to the ice. Plus she wanted children, and I wasn't that keen.' He downs the rest of his beer. 'Do you?'

'Do I what?'

'Want children.'

I shrug. 'No . . . not really.'

To be honest, it's no longer a question I give much thought to. Ben and I had assumed it was on the cards, one day, when our careers were more settled; but now he's gone, it seems irrelevant.

Besides, who'd want me now? I'm making a fool of myself even having this conversation, I realise, remembering my scar. I get to my feet, the room spinning. 'I'm going to bed,' I say, trying not to think about the hangover waiting for me tomorrow.

'Wait up.' Drew drains his beer and turns off all the lights in the lounge. We walk quietly through the corridors, wary of disturbing anyone.

'Hey, you like whisky?' Drew asks, as we approach his door. 'I've got a bottle stashed under my bed.'

'Under your bed?'

'Can't be too careful.' He gazes at me. 'Well? Fancy a nightcap?'

Despite everything, I'm tempted. The alcohol has dissolved my usual inhibitions, all those protective layers I've carefully assembled around myself. And there's something else, a sensation as unfamiliar now as happiness: an undertow of desire.

Don't be stupid, I tell myself fiercely. There's no chance someone like Drew would be interested in you. Even here, where there isn't much in the way of choice.

'It's a single malt,' he leans in, whispering. 'If that doesn't tempt you, I can't imagine what will.'

He lifts a hand and pushes my hair from my face. With his index finger he traces the line of my scar from the top of my cheek almost to my jawbone. Despite myself, my skin tingles beneath his touch.

I wait for him to ask exactly how I got it. That inevitable question. I'm amazed he's managed to hold it in so long.

'Kate,' Drew murmurs, lifting my chin so I'm forced to look at him. 'It doesn't make any difference, you know. It's not as bad as you think.'

I stare at him, speechless. Then let him pull me into his cabin and shut the door behind us. As soon as we're inside he draws me into a kiss. Soft, at first, tentative, then quickly fierce and hungry and urgent. It's been so long since I've kissed anyone, and desire rushes up with shocking force.

I thought all this was behind me.

'You okay with this?' Drew draws back to look in my eyes. 'Just want to make sure I'm not taking advantage of a lady while she's drunk.'

'Shut up,' I say, kissing him again. Seconds later, we're removing each other's clothes. I try not to stare at Drew as he pulls off his top – his body is strong and toned and there's still a faint tan line at the base of his abdomen. I'm guessing he spends quite a bit of time at home with his shirt off.

'Come here,' he says, pulling me down onto the lower bunk.

These beds are definitely not built for fucking, we discover. There's not enough headroom for anything but missionary – not that I care; it's been so long that even vanilla sex feels exotic.

I'd forgotten, I realise, as Drew pushes into me. I'd forgotten how good this is, the sensation of being touched, of skin on skin, the ebb and flow of pleasure.

But suddenly, stupidly, silently, I find I'm crying. I turn my head to the wall, stifling a sob, praying Drew won't notice. All at once I want this to be over . . . it feels wrong.

Too much, and too soon.

Ben's face hovers in my mind. That look in his eyes, gazing at me but not seeing.

Gone already.

'Stop!' I push Drew away.

He stares at me, confused. 'What is it?'

I shake my head.

'Kate, I thought you were into it. I didn't mean to—'

I cover his mouth with my hand. 'It's not your fault. It's me . . . I'm sorry. I just can't . . . and I can't explain it either.'

I pull the covers up around me and we lie there silently for a minute or two as it gradually dawns on me what a mess I've got myself into.

'I feel bad about Alex,' Drew says out of the blue.

I turn to him, surprised. 'Why?'

'I didn't mean to upset him. I want you to know that.'

'What did you say to him anyway?' The question pops out before I can stop it, the wine loosening my tongue.

Drew inhales. Props his head on his elbow and peers at me. 'It was nothing. I simply asked about the field safety audits and risk assessments. He's in charge of them.'

I frown. 'Why would you mention those?'

Everyone blames me.

'Because they haven't been done, Kate. After Jean-Luc died, Alex was supposed to write a report, review all the safety procedures, but he hasn't.' Drew rolls onto his back. 'Look . . . I don't want to stir things up.' He pauses, as if wrestling with himself.

I wait for him to go on.

'Okay, listen. It's not the first,' he says reluctantly.

'What do you mean?'

'It's not the first time Alex, you know . . . has been involved in an incident.'

'An incident? I don't understand.'

Drew frowns at me. 'Hasn't anybody told you exactly what happened?'

I shrug. 'Not really. No one seems keen to talk about it.'

'One of the karabiners sheared off while Jean-Luc was abseiling into the ice. He fell over fifty metres into the crevasse, nearly pulled me in too.'

'Jesus. Is that true? But what's that got to do with Alex?'

'Think about it. Alex is in charge of all the field equipment. It's his job to make sure it was all good before we went out.'

Drew's right. But it never crossed my mind that Alex was in any way responsible for what happened. Surely, if that were the case, he wouldn't be here now? At the very least he'd have been sent home.

I say as much.

'Some of us wanted that to happen, but Sandrine flat refused. She believed there wasn't sufficient proof that Alex had been negligent.'

'So it was an accident then?'

Drew leans over slightly, so we can see each other properly. 'Thing is, Kate, like I said, it's not the first time. Someone died when Alex was working in Queenstown. A bungee jumping incident, on his watch. Another equipment failure, apparently.'

I pull away a little so I can focus better on Drew's face. 'Really?'

He shrugs. 'Nothing was ever proven, but a girl died. It was in the papers.'

'Are you saying he did this *deliberately*?'

'No, not at all. I mean . . . he's sloppy. Doesn't check things thoroughly. Then tries to blame other people.'

I consider this. If that were the case, why would UNA have taken Alex on in the first place? At the very least, they'd have overruled Sandrine and sent him home after Jean-Luc died.

'How do you know all this?' I ask Drew.

'Luuk told me. Anyway, it's common knowledge.'

You all think I did it.

Christ, no wonder Alex is so paranoid. I feel uneasy even discussing this behind his back.

'Who was on this trip?' I ask.

'Pretty much all of us – it was supposed to be this team bonding thing for those overwintering. Sonya didn't go – she didn't want to trust the weather balloon to one of the summer staff, plus Rajiv and Caro volunteered to stay and run the station.'

I pause, then ask a question I probably shouldn't. 'What Luuk said earlier, about Alex, did he mean he smokes a lot of weed?'

Drew shrugs. 'It goes on.'

'And you?'

'Not my thing. Seen too many people messed up by drugs to ever want to go there.'

He gives me a long look and I feel my face flush, remembering again the pills that fell out of my pocket. Does he think I have a serious problem?

Do I?

Gingerly, I slip off the bunk and reach for my clothes in the semi-darkness. 'I should get some sleep. No chance with two of us in that bed.'

'Yeah, you have to figure these bunks are a deterrent.'

I turn to look at him. 'Listen, Drew,' I say, then pause, trying to sort through the confusion of my thoughts, my feelings.

His smile melts away. 'That sounds ominous.'

I hesitate, choosing my words carefully. 'Don't get me wrong, I like you, really, and I'm flattered. But we shouldn't have let it happen. I'm the station doctor, which means remaining completely impartial and available to everyone, and I don't want anything getting in the way of that.'

The silence lingers a second or two. 'That didn't seem to bother you just now,' he says, eyes no longer meeting mine. 'You seemed kinda into it – at first, anyway.'

'I . . . I shouldn't have drunk so much. I wasn't thinking straight.'

'You were drunk. Well, thanks for the compliment.' He blinks at me, his expression hurt.

Oh God, I'm not handling this well. 'Drew, that's not what I mean. You know that.'

He studies my face for a moment. 'No problem, Kate. Let's simply park this in the friend zone.'

'You're okay with that?' I stand there feeling, despite his words, that this hasn't gone well. But then what did I expect?

I expected him not to be bothered, I realise. It never occurred to me that this was anything but a momentary diversion from the monotony of life on the base.

But he seems . . . crushed. I kick myself for my carelessness. My silly assumptions. Just because Drew's good-looking, it doesn't mean he hasn't got feelings, I remind myself again. It was stupid, letting our friendship slide into casual sex; the last thing I wanted to do was make things difficult between us.

'I'm sorry,' I say, meaning it.

Drew gives me a rueful smile. 'Me too. But it's fine. We won't let it spoil things, okay?'

'Okay.' I give him a quick hug before I leave. It's only as I'm creeping back through the corridors, hoping I don't bump into anybody, that it occurs to me to wonder if Drew has done this before.

Am I the latest in a line of conquests? There were plenty more women here, after all, over the summer.

It hardly matters, I decide, as I let myself into my cabin, down a couple of sleeping pills and fall into bed, the first throb of a headache beginning to pulse in my temple.

Either way, it's a mistake I'd be foolish to repeat.

9

2 May

I sense the weight of it first, sitting on my chest. Two brown eyes staring into mine, dark slits at their centre.

That narrow vulpine face.

I open my mouth to scream, but nothing emerges.

The fox vanishes. I'm awake, heart pounding. I sit bolt upright, still in the panic of the dream. Feel, initially, the pain in my head. The creeping dread that heralds a really bad hangover.

Then I remember last night.

I groan out loud. Why the hell did I do that? Rule number one of surviving in a small group in the middle of icy nowhere – don't screw anyone, Kate. Don't risk a friendship turning sour, don't become the source of unnecessary gossip. Anybody passing in the corridor might have heard us, after all.

How could I have been so colossally, monumentally, spectacularly stupid?

For a minute or two I contemplate staying in bed. Heaven knows, I feel dreadful and deserve a day off. But that would be cowardly – and simply postponing the inevitable. Plus I need to check on Alex, and talk to Caro.

Nothing for it but to pray no one picked up on what happened.

I swallow a couple of hydrocodone, then open the blackout blind and stare out into the darkness. No sunrise to look forward to, only a twilight glow for a few hours around midday. From now on I'm stuck with the harsh white glare of the LED bulbs that light the station.

To my surprise – and relief – I find only Arne in the canteen, watching something on his iPad while eating a bowl of muesli.

'Don't let me interrupt,' I say, as he glances up.

'No worries.' He turns it off. 'I've watched it three times already.'

'What is it?'

'A film called *Solaris*.'

'Andrei Tarkovsky,' I smile. 'One of his best.'

A look of delight passes across Arne's face. 'You like his films?'

'Very much.' I picked up my love of Tarkovsky from Ben, who took me to see a retrospective of his work at an indie cinema in Bristol, not long after we got engaged. I quickly fell under the spell of those haunting images, the long lingering camera shots, the persistent sense of the ineffable.

I remember *Solaris* well. The melancholy tale of a psychologist sent up to a remote space station occupied by three scientists who've all fallen into deep emotional crises. He quickly discovers the base is inhabited by monsters, elements of their subconscious given bodily form by the sentient planet they're orbiting.

The parallels with this place don't bear thinking about.

'How are you feeling?' Arne scrutinises me carefully. But there isn't anything in it beyond concern, I decide. He's simply one of those guys who likes to observe people.

'A bit hungover,' I admit. 'Hit the wine too hard yesterday.'

'Well, it was a difficult occasion.' He presses his lips together, his expression thoughtful. 'Alex is in a bad place. I worry about him.'

I take a gulp of my coffee. 'Do you talk to him much?' Aside from Caro, Arne seems to be the only person I've seen Alex hang out with.

'A little. But he's . . . well, a typical block.'

'Block?' I frown, confused.

'You know, a man?'

'Oh,' I give a little laugh. '*Bloke*. He doesn't open up much, you mean?'

'Exactly.'

I blink at him in surprise. To be honest, that's exactly how I'd describe Arne himself.

'So Alex hasn't told you what's bothering him?'

Arne regards me carefully. 'I didn't say that.'

I'm about to ask what he means when Alice appears with Rob in tow. 'Morning,' she says cheerfully, boiling the kettle for tea. Rob gives me a nod, then gets his breakfast.

No sign that anyone suspects anything, I note with relief. I clear my things and wash them up in the kitchen, planning my schedule. First up, I need to catch up with Alex. Tom too – the way he rushed off last night is another thing on my mind.

But given it's Sunday, it isn't obvious where to find either of them. Sonya likes to knit in the lounge on her days off, basking under one of the UV lamps UNA provides to offset the worst effects of no sunlight. Sandrine will invariably be found on her makeshift putting green in Beta. But Alex? Or Tom? I'm not sure what they like to do in their free time – mooch around in their cabins, I suspect.

That's exactly where I find Alex, reclining on his bed. He doesn't bother to sit up when I knock and stick my head around his door.

'Can I come in?'

He nods at the desk chair, so I shut the door behind me and sit. 'You okay?'

Alex doesn't answer, just regards me for a moment then

shifts his gaze to the window. Unlike me, he doesn't keep the blind down all the time to ward off the darkness lurking outside.

I glance into that impenetrable night, then look away, skin crawling. The sensation is similar to being on a boat, peering down into the fathomless depths of the ocean. The horror of the unseen. Anything could be out there, says a primitive part of my brain, though the rational part knows there's nothing but air and ice.

'How can I help you, Kate?'

Alex's voice reclaims my attention. I glance down at his right hand. The skin is mottled with bruising, blood crusted around the split in his knuckles.

'We should clean that up and examine it properly,' I tell him. 'Want to come to the surgery?'

I'm fully expecting him to refuse, but to my surprise he gets up and trails after me. I flick on the clinic lights and sit him in the chair by my desk. Fetching an antiseptic wipe, I crouch opposite and gently clear away the dried blood.

'Can you flex your fingers for me?'

Alex does as instructed.

'Make a fist.'

He clenches his hand, wincing. But the swelling is minimal and I'm pretty sure nothing is broken. I fish a dressing from the cupboard, douse the wound in more antiseptic, then dab it dry.

Applying the tape, I feel his fingers trembling. From pain, I wonder, or something else? 'Do you need some painkillers?' I ask.

Alex shakes his head. 'I don't want anything.'

I glance up at his face. He really does look awful. Not just hungover, but as if he's been putting on an act ever since I arrived, and now it has completely fallen apart. He looks crushed . . . defeated.

What on earth is going on?

I recall again those stories about people cracking under the strain. Guys who decide to leave the pole in the middle of winter, setting off on skis or snowmobiles. People bursting into tears over breakfast, or locking themselves in their room, refusing to come out. The blank Antarctic stare known as 'toast', the mind lost in a world of its own. Not to mention numerous fights and arguments, bruised fists and broken jaws.

Not every psyche is robust enough to deal with the extreme isolation, the sense of being imprisoned with a small cohort of people. Minor issues can easily escalate into major feuds. Hostilities break out over a simple misunderstanding.

'You going to tell me what that was all about yesterday?' I ask gently.

He doesn't answer.

I try again. 'Alex, please talk to me. Tell me what's wrong.'

Finally he looks up. I have the sense he's assessing me, coming to some kind of conclusion.

'They think it's my fault,' he mumbles, 'what happened to Jean-Luc.'

I stay silent, waiting for him to continue.

He rubs his forehead with his uninjured hand, closes his eyes for a moment. 'Did you know we spent four hours trying to reach him? But he was wedged head down, out of sight. He . . .' Alex swallows, inhales. 'We couldn't get him out. We tried, but we couldn't get him out.'

'Alex, I'm so sorry.' I take his good hand in mine.

'Huh . . . well, you're pretty much the only one. You and Caro. Everyone else blames me.'

'Alex,' I choose my words carefully. 'I don't think—'

'It's my job, you see, to make sure everything is safe and secure before any trip out on the ice. And I did, Kate. I always go over all the equipment meticulously. There was absolutely no sign of anything wrong. But a failure like that . . .'

94

He falls silent again.

'A failure like what?' I prompt.

'Those karabiners are designed to take huge weights. Much heavier than Jean-Luc. No way one of them would spontaneously shear off. It would have to be visibly defective for that to happen, and I'd have noticed.'

'Did you examine it? Afterwards, I mean.'

'There was nothing to examine. Everything fell into the crevasse with him.'

I frown. 'So what are you saying?'

Alex shakes his head. I sense he's holding back, that he doesn't trust me enough to go further.

'Listen,' I urge. 'I'm a doctor, so I am duty bound to keep anything said in this room confidential, okay?'

Alex grunts in response.

I sigh. 'Alex, please don't take this the wrong way. But I'm wondering if you . . . well, if you . . .' I pause. 'I'm aware some people on the station smoke marijuana. I wondered if that applies to you.'

Alex's eyes widen. 'What are you implying, Kate? That I'm fucking paranoid? Or that I got high and didn't check the equipment properly?' His voice is rising and he looks furious.

I hold my hands up in an attempt to pacify him. 'No, I only meant perhaps it wasn't helping—'

'Fuck you!' He glares at me, cheeks reddening as if I've reached out and slapped him. 'You're as bad as the rest of them.'

'Alex, wait—'

But my words are cut short by the sound of the clinic door slamming behind him.

IO

2 May

Locking the clinic door, I hurry back to my room and stand by the window, lifting the blind and forcing myself to gaze outside. But a thick blanket of cloud obscures the myriad stars that are the single upside of constant darkness and zero pollution, leaving nothing to see beyond my own reflection in the glass.

I picture Jean-Luc again in that cold, cold ice. There's no room for error in this unforgiving place, I think – a single mistake can have fatal consequences.

And I've just made a grave one with Alex. Why on earth did I mention the marijuana? I should have waited for a better time.

Stupid move, Kate.

In the corridor, voices echo, coming closer then fading. Somewhere, more distant, the faint hum of the diesel generator keeping us alive in this ice-bound oasis. I listen for a while before retrieving the vitamin bottle from the back of my wardrobe. My hangover is rapidly blooming into a killer headache, and the pills I took earlier are barely touching it.

As I open the lid and peer inside, a wave of nausea rushes up and threatens to engulf me.

It's empty.

Every single one of my remaining pills has gone.

With a rising feeling of panic, I rummage around in the wardrobe, assuming the bottle had somehow spilled its contents.

But there's no sign of any of my medication. Not even one tablet.

What the hell?

I search my rucksack, find a couple of hydrocodone wrapped in a tissue in one of the side pockets. I crunch them between my teeth then swallow them down, desperate to take the edge off the pain in my head so I can think more clearly.

Is it possible I put my pills elsewhere and somehow forgot? Could I have had some kind of lapse, a side effect of the medication?

I'm not one of those people who thrives on denial. I'm well aware I've been taking too many prescription drugs, and for too long. Though my dependence started legitimately enough – the accident left me with chronic pain from whiplash and a broken knee – I can't deny it's morphed into something else entirely. Thanks in no small part to my sister, who six weeks after the crash confronted me with a pile of empty pill packets retrieved from my recycling bin.

'*Seriously*, Kate?'

Clare hadn't had to say any more. It was as pointless trying to bullshit my sister as myself.

All the same, I've managed to function well enough until now. No obvious gaps or lapses in attention. I wind back to this morning, trying to remember exactly what I did. I can visualise it clearly, taking the hydrocodone out of the bottle then replacing it at the back of my wardrobe, underneath my outdoor clothes.

No way I imagined that. I may have a problem, but I'm not crazy.

Though the alternative is worse. If I didn't lose or misplace them, then this is . . . down to someone else.

Somebody has been in my room and taken my pills.

But why? I sit on the bed and try to think through the fog

of my hangover. I'm happy to prescribe whatever anyone needs. UNA recognises that getting through an Antarctic winter can be physically and mentally gruelling, and has no qualms about giving people any pharmacological support they need.

So if not for their own use, why else might someone steal my pills? To report me to Sandrine?

The thought sends a chill right through my limbs. While I haven't broken any rules – UNA doesn't forbid people bringing their own medication onto the ice – I suspect the station leader might take a dim view of my stash.

It doesn't make sense though. Surely, if their purpose was to expose me, they'd have taken the vitamin bottle too? After all, it's pretty much proof I'm trying to conceal my habit.

A surge of anxiety makes my head throb even more. I lie back and close my eyes for a minute or two, trying to calm down. When I open them again I notice something strange – the notebook I keep on the left side of my desk has shifted to the right. I get up and check, certain I didn't move it – I use it to hide a large mug stain left by a previous resident.

Slowly, carefully, I go through the rest of my room, starting with the drawer where I keep my toiletries. Everything looks normal, but slightly off, as if someone searched through my belongings, covering their tracks in a hurry. It's the same story with my bedside table, and all the stuff stashed on the top bunk. Nothing I can put my finger on, just a creeping sense that things have shifted since I left them this morning.

Returning to the wardrobe, I inspect my clothes. Notice my long-sleeved T-shirts have been folded differently, their arms no longer tucked inside. My underwear, too, has been rearranged, all my socks now at the back of the shelf instead of the front.

The conclusion is inescapable. Someone has been in my room and gone through all my possessions.

But the question is why?

And what am I going to do about it?

Nothing, I realise, with a sinking feeling. There's absolutely nothing I can do. I can't report the missing pills, for obvious reasons. And I don't think anything else has been taken.

Is there another way I could find out who did it? From the tracking data on our activity bands perhaps?

But I'd need help – I've glanced at the data before and couldn't make head nor tail of it. Anyway, whoever came in here probably had the sense to remove their activity band beforehand.

Oh God. I lie back down, fighting another swell of panic that makes my pulse race. Someone knows. Someone knows my dirty little secret.

I grit my teeth, trying to steady myself. I can't think about that now, I decide – all I can do is keep my head down and carry on as normal, hope whoever did this keeps it to themselves. And if they choose to expose me, well, I'll just have to fess up and throw myself on Sandrine's mercy.

Christ, it's not as if she can sack me, is it? I'm the only doctor they've got until that plane arrives next spring.

Perhaps my intruder has done me a favour, I think, as my headache finally eases enough to go and see Caro. After all, knowing you have a problem isn't the same as dealing with it – that's a battle I've always been happy to fight tomorrow.

Maybe, ironically, this is exactly the push I need.

I find Caro alone in the library, writing a letter. Odd, given there's no way to get it to its recipient for another six months.

'I write to my parents every few weeks,' she says, catching my puzzled expression. 'An account of what I'm doing, updates on the station and so on. They love receiving them, even if they arrive in one big pile.'

They're cattle farmers, I remember, farming in the hills near Dunedin. After a life as an only child – and by her own admission always something of a tomboy – Caro trained as a plumber.

In truth, she still has plenty of the tomboy about her, eschewing make-up, invariably dressed in that old sweatshirt and baggy dungarees. But I'm pretty certain she's straight; Alice, on the other hand, who's as ethereally feminine as you can get, is very much not.

I bite my lip, hesitating. Wondering whether to go ahead. 'Caro, may I ask you something?' I glance around to check we're not being overheard.

'Sure.' She puts down her pen and gives me her full attention.

'Can you shed any light on what went on yesterday? Has Alex talked to you about it at all?'

Caro chews her lip. 'A little. He thinks people blame him for what happened to Jean-Luc. But it wasn't his fault, Kate.' She looks at me earnestly. 'Alex is super careful. I mean meticulous.'

Despite what Drew told me last night, Caro's words ring true. After all, if you've been involved – or at least present – when someone died like that girl in New Zealand, the experience would surely change you. And contrary to what Drew suggested, wouldn't it make you more anxious to ensure it never happened again? More careful?

On the other hand, does lightning ever strike twice? Could it be coincidence that two people died on Alex's watch?

I'm tempted to ask Caro if she knows more about that bungee incident, but decide to track down the newspaper reports first. Besides, the person I really should talk to about it is Alex himself.

If he'll give me another chance.

'I think I've upset him,' I confess. 'I asked him about smoking marijuana. He took it as some sort of criticism.'

Caro frowns. 'He doesn't smoke,' she says. 'Not any more. Not since Jean-Luc died, and not much before then.'

'Okay.'

'He's a good guy,' she adds almost fiercely, as if I've implied otherwise. 'I mean it, Kate. He's one of the kindest, most gentle people I've ever met. He's absolutely devastated about Jean-Luc. They were friends, you know. Alex was kind of lost when he first came out here, and Jean-Luc took him under his wing. They spent loads of time together, trekking out on the ice in summer, playing poker, hanging out when they weren't working.'

To my surprise, her eyes well up. Caro really cares about Alex, I realise, and it makes me glad. I sense he needs all the friends he can get in this place.

'I'm scared,' she whispers, voice husky with emotion. 'I don't think he's coping very well.'

'I'll keep a close eye on him and give as much support as I can, all right?' I squeeze her hand. 'I'm sure he'll be fine.'

Caro smiles at me gratefully. 'Thanks.' She glances down at my fingers then up at my face. 'You okay, Kate? You look kind of pale, if you don't mind me saying. And you're trembling. Is everything all right?'

I remove my hand from hers, suppressing the urge to tell her what just happened. The shock of my discovery.

'Just hungover,' I say, trying to sound brighter. 'Hit the wine a bit too hard last night. Always leaves me jittery.'

'Me too.' Caro's expression is sympathetic. 'Go grab yourself something from the kitchen. Nothing like a hefty dose of fat and carbs to chase away a hangover.'

I get up. 'Good plan. I just want to check in on Tom first, then I'll follow your prescription.'

I find Tom alone in the comms room, sitting at his desk, laptop open. He seems startled when I knock then poke my head around the door.

'You okay?' I ask. 'You seemed a bit out of sorts yesterday.'

'Out of sorts?' Tom stares at me blankly, then looks away again, as if holding my gaze is painful.

'Upset,' I explain. 'Sorry.' Despite the high level of English spoken amongst the winterers, it's impossible not to trip up over the occasional idiom.

'There is nothing wrong with me,' he says bluntly.

'I wasn't suggesting there was, Tom. I simply wanted to check everything was all right, that's all. I'm responsible for everyone's welfare on the base.'

'I'm fine, Kate.' He keeps his eyes fixed on his screen. 'Thank you for asking.'

'If you're sure,' I add. 'But remember, you can talk to me any time, in total confidence. And please, could you come in for a blood test and complete your video log? I see you've missed the last couple of weeks.' I refrain from explaining, yet again, why they are necessary – as data manager, I'm sure Tom understands their importance.

'I will,' he says, flicking his gaze briefly to mine and away again in an obvious gesture of dismissal.

Was it him? I wonder, as I take the hint and head for the kitchen. Could it be Tom who searched my room?

Stop it, Kate. Just don't go there. It could have been anyone.

I take Caro's advice. Make myself a large cheese and pickle sandwich, and boil the kettle for a cup of tea, trying to push everything out of my mind while I go to the storeroom to find a new box of teabags. As I'm heading back, my elbow catches a tray on the stainless-steel counter.

There's a loud crash as it hits the kitchen floor.

Oh shit. I stare in horror at the mess, glistening pieces of fish scattered everywhere. They must have been defrosting for tonight's supper. I pick up the tray and retrieve each fillet, start rinsing them under the tap, hoping no one will notice;

after all, this place is spotless and I can't imagine we'll come to any harm.

'What are you doing?'

I turn to see Rajiv watching me. 'I'm so sorry,' I say, mortified. 'I was getting some teabags and accidentally knocked them over.'

He doesn't speak. Just looks at the wreckage of fish on the tray. 'Leave it,' he says sharply.

'Rajiv, I—'

'It isn't necessary to apologise.' He picks up the tray and dumps it all in the bin. 'I will find something else for Tom.'

Oh hell. I completely forgot it's Tom's birthday today. Didn't even think to mention it when I spoke to him just now. Rajiv was evidently planning a special meal, and now I've ruined it.

'I'll help you.' I glance around the kitchen, looking for inspiration.

'No,' Rajiv says, his voice stiff. I can tell he's working hard to contain his anger.

Tears prick my eyes. 'Just let me—'

'Drop it, Kate. Please.'

I can see he means it. Abandoning my tea and sandwich, I hurry back to the clinic, locking the door behind me. Sinking into my chair, I drop my head into my hands, fighting the urge to cry.

Pull yourself together, I tell myself fiercely, breathing deeply to get my emotions under control. But it doesn't work. I sense my mood, already on a downhill trajectory, plummeting further. The hangover, my bungled conversation with Alex, the discovery of my missing pills, and the incident in the kitchen, all tipping me towards some kind of edge.

Before I can stop it my mind spins back to that argument with Ben, the one that blew up out of nowhere, the Sunday before the accident.

He'd been aloof and cold, mooching around the house, barely saying a word. I recall my increasing bewilderment, and my growing resentment; I'd been working seventy hours a week at the hospital, as well as renovating our kitchen and planning our forthcoming wedding. Though Ben worked long hours himself, he never offered to help.

Impossible to forget the anger on his face that afternoon when I challenged him, pouring out my frustration.

'Yes, I know, you're a bloody saint,' he snapped back. 'The Norths are all perfect, no one else can measure up. That's a given.'

I stared at him in astonishment. Where on earth had that come from? Ben had never before said a bad word about my family. Seemed, on the contrary, to get on well with them – on the rare occasions we met up.

'What the fuck, Ben? I'm trying to do all of this, keep all these plates spinning, and *that's* your response?'

He sighed and turned away.

'So, what, you're just going to ignore me?'

Ben swung back on his heels. 'I can't compete, Kate. Whatever I do, whatever anyone does, it's not enough. It's never good enough. You're so . . .' He stopped. Closed his eyes briefly, then walked out of the house, got in his car and drove off; when he returned later that evening, it seemed easier to pretend the whole thing hadn't happened.

You're so . . . The words reverberate in my head. I never did find out what he was going to say.

A sudden sharp pain in my heart, raw as a wound. I feel like wailing, with grief and fury.

Fuck you, Ben. *Fuck you.*

Taking the keys from my drawer, I get to my feet and unlock the cabinet containing the benzodiazepines. I examine the neat boxes lined up on the shelf, the allure of their pristine packaging.

I pick up the nearest packet of Valium, pull out the sachet and run my fingers over the little foil capsules with an intense rush of longing.

Seriously, Kate?

Pushing my sister's voice aside, I pop out two of the pills and swallow them down. Hesitate for a second or so, then take another couple for good measure, stuffing the rest of the packet in my pocket. Then I shut the cabinet and rest my head on my desk, inhaling slowly until everything fades and recedes back into the shadows.

11

27 May

'I've already told you, it has nothing to do with the plumbing! I sorted that out ages ago.'

Caro's voice, sounding exasperated. I detour from my trip to the Skype room to the laundry, pausing to listen outside the door.

'I reckon the drain hose is clogged,' she says.

'Always some excuse.' Luuk's tone is aggressive. 'Nothing ever works in this place – the showers, the washing machines. I mean, look!'

'Yeah, I see it. Water on the floor, Luuk. You know where the mop is.'

'I just want to wash my fucking clothes. It's not a big—'

I don't catch the rest. Alex almost shoulders me out of the way as he barges past, his face thunderous. Clearly I wasn't the only one within earshot. I follow him inside, sensing things are about to get nasty.

Damp seeping into the knees of her dungarees, Caro kneels on the tiled floor of the laundry room, surrounded by a pool of greyish water. She's examining the coils of piping at the rear of one of the washing machines.

'What's going on?' Alex demands, gazing from Caro to Luuk.

'Drain hose is completely blocked,' Caro replies, relief on her face as she clocks the pair of us. 'Could either of you hand me a bucket?'

I fetch one from the cupboard and Caro angles it beneath the outflow as she unscrews the hose. It's not entirely successful. A gush of water expands the puddle on the floor.

'*Kut!*' Luuk jumps out of the way as it splashes onto his Vans. 'Look at this fucking mess.'

'*Your* fucking mess,' Caro corrects, peering into the hose. Tipping it downwards, she shakes it hard and something drops on the floor.

Alex scoops up the disposable cigarette lighter, decorated with little green marijuana leaves, and hands it to Luuk. 'I believe this is yours.'

Luuk takes the lighter without a word. Doesn't apologise to Caro, or even appear particularly abashed.

'How many times have I asked people to empty their pockets before putting their clothes in the machine?' Caro complains, her eyes welling. 'And not to overfill these top loaders. You can't simply not bother for weeks then shove all your stuff in there in one go.'

Luuk mutters something I don't catch. Suddenly Alex springs forward and grabs his T-shirt, aiming a punch at the side of his head. Caro squeals as Luuk spins around and hits back, his fist grazing Alex's chin. Alex stumbles, and Luuk manages to get him into a stranglehold.

'Leave him alone!' Caro shouts. In a flash she grabs the bucket of dirty water from the washing machine and flings it in Luuk's face. He stares at her, astonished, hair and beard dripping.

'You stupid bitch!'

Alex gets free of Luuk's grasp, then kicks his legs from under him.

'Stop it!' I yell, as Luuk goes down hard onto the wet floor. Shit, what do I do?

A few seconds later, Arne and Drew run in, alerted to the

rumpus. Arne grabs Alex, who's aiming a kick to Luuk's belly, and pins him against the wall.

'It's not his fault!' screams Caro, crying now. 'Alex was defending me.'

Drew glowers down at Luuk as he tries to scrabble to his feet.

'What the hell is going on?'

We all turn to the sound of Sandrine's voice from the doorway. Jesus, I think. Bad news travels fast in this place – any hint of trouble and half the station soon turns up.

It's not the first fracas I've witnessed in the last few weeks. As the Antarctic winter deepens, so have tensions on the base. Our days are increasingly punctuated by low-grade sniping and backbiting, occasionally erupting into a full-blown argument – a fortnight ago Drew and Rob went head-to-head over whose turn it was to empty the food waste bins, with Ark and Arne having to physically restrain them before they came to blows. Several days later Sonya lost her temper with Luuk for playing thrash metal at full volume in the lounge.

'He was threatening Caro.' Alex glares furiously at him as Luuk pulls himself to his feet. There's blood on his beard, I notice, though not much.

'Like hell I was,' growls Luuk, running a hand through his wet hair. 'Look what she did to me!'

Sandrine turns to Caro. 'Did you?'

'None of this is her fault!' Alex protests. He's shaking with anger now, jaw clenched with emotion. 'You!' He takes a step closer to Luuk. 'It was you, wasn't it?'

Out of the corner of my eye, I see Caro shake her head at him. Don't do this, her wide-eyed expression says. At the same time I catch a whiff of something like whisky from Alex's direction, and realise he's been drinking.

Hell. It's not even midday.

'Let's leave this here.' Arne raises a hand in warning, but Luuk ignores him.

'What was me?' he glares back at Alex. 'I've no idea what you're talking about.'

Alex jabs his finger towards his face. 'You were on that climbing trip. You never liked Jean-Luc, did you?'

Luuk sneers. 'What the fuck are you on about, man?'

'You know exactly what I'm talking about.' I get another whiff of alcohol as Alex spits the words at Luuk.

'Hey,' Drew moves in closer, 'you need to calm down—'

'No, let him get this off his chest,' Luuk says. 'Let's all hear Alex's pathetic attempt to deflect blame from himself. He can't accept that Jean-Luc's death was his fault, so he's trying to find a scapegoat.'

Sandrine frowns. 'What exactly are you insinuating, Alex? Are you suggesting someone *tampered* with Jean-Luc's equipment?' The lines on her forehead, around her mouth, seem more pronounced than even a week ago, as if she's ageing right before our eyes, worn down by some emotion I can't fathom. 'That cannot be a serious accusation. How on earth would anyone do that?'

'I'm not sure.' Alex shakes his head. 'Messed with the karabiner, most likely. But we'll never know, will we, Sandrine? It's all down there with him, half a mile deep in that crevasse.'

Anguish flashes across the station leader's face as she's assaulted by the same image that's haunted me these last three months.

'It was sabotaged,' Alex insists. 'It's the only explanation. I've gone over and over it. That equipment was fine when I checked it before we left, but I didn't have eyes on it the whole time. I might not have seen if someone—'

'But why?' Arne cuts in, his expression confused. I feel

inexplicably drawn to him, wanting to move physically closer, as if he's a safe haven in this storm. 'Why would anybody do that?'

'Yes, why?' demands Sandrine. 'Why would anyone hurt Jean-Luc?'

Alex shakes his head slowly, as if in disbelief. How much has he had to drink, I wonder? And has this become a regular habit?

Keeping an eye on him, as I promised Caro three weeks ago, has proved easier said than done; Alex has become increasingly withdrawn, avoiding everyone bar her and Arne. He's completely abandoned the medical tests and video diaries, forcing me to keep tabs on him the only way I can – checking his activity monitor. Even if I can't fathom the data, the heart monitor at least reassures me he's still alive.

'Why don't you ask Luuk that question?' Alex addresses Sandrine. 'You know damn well they had several run-ins over his little stash.'

Luuk grits his teeth, looking furious. For a second or two he seems on the brink of launching himself at Alex again. 'You can't be serious,' he splutters. 'You honestly think I'd kill someone? Over a thing like that?'

'Jean-Luc threatened to report you, didn't he?' Alex persists.

'Alex, please.' Caro's voice is heavy with warning.

'Well?' Alex appeals to Arne. 'You believe me, don't you?'

Arne doesn't respond, and Luuk looks around wildly. 'What is this? Some kind of fucking *trial*?' He turns to Sandrine. 'You going to do anything? Or would you rather just stay out of the spotlight?'

The station leader stiffens, her face rigid with tension. She seems almost paralysed.

'And what about him?' Luuk nods at Arne. 'I seem to remember he and the doc had their disagreements. Why isn't he in the picture for this so-called murder?'

'This is not helping,' Arne says coldly, directing his comment at both Luuk and Alex. 'We all have to live with each other for the next six months.'

'For heaven's sake, there's been no murder,' Sandrine snaps, seeming to come to and remember she's supposed to be in charge. 'Jean-Luc's death was an accident, pure and simple. This has to stop.'

'Alex, why don't you come with me to my clinic,' I say, desperate to talk to him, to calm him down.

'Thank you, Kate,' Sandrine's voice is clipped. 'I'll handle this. I don't need you interfering.'

Heat rushes to my cheeks. I stare at her, stung and bewildered. Can't she see I'm concerned about Alex's psychological welfare? The man's clearly a wreck, and suspicious of everyone.

Unusually so, I wonder? The ice station in winter has become a curious mix of claustrophobia and loneliness. It's difficult to get any real privacy, to escape the sense that you're living in a goldfish bowl, under constant scrutiny, and everything you say or do is being observed and evaluated.

It's enough to make anyone paranoid.

'Luuk, I'd like to speak to you in my office,' Sandrine says, ignoring me. 'Alex, go back to your room and sober up.' With that she disappears. It's then I notice Tom hovering in the doorway, observing us all. I try to catch his eye, but he turns and vanishes in Sandrine's wake.

A hand squeezes my shoulder. Drew. 'Don't take it to heart,' he says as he gets the mop out of the cupboard to help Caro clean up. 'She's under a lot of strain.'

I flash him a grateful smile, but I'm angry and humiliated. Can't Sandrine see I'm trying to do my best? What the hell is her problem with me anyway?

However hard I try, I can't get past the feeling the station leader resents me for even being here. Though, thankfully, there's been no mention of my missing pills – it seems whoever took them wanted them for themselves.

I glance over at Arne, who's standing in the corner, his expression deeply troubled. Without a word, he turns and leaves. I hear him heading up the corridor towards the skype room, probably to call his girlfriend.

The thought is oddly painful. For the first time since losing Ben, I find myself wishing I had someone else. Someone I could confide in. Someone who could soothe and reassure me, even from a distance.

In all my life, I realise, I've never felt more alone than now.

12

12 June

'You seem low.'

The screen flickers, and my sister's face blinks out for a moment. I pray we're not about to lose the connection again. Skype calls, given our limited bandwidth, are hazardous at the best of times, and we're restricted to one ten-minute slot a week.

Not that I often use mine.

'I'm fine,' I lie, knowing she won't be fooled. Even ten thousand miles away with a dodgy internet connection, Clare's emotional radar is infallible.

'You don't look it.' She studies my grainy image in her monitor. 'You look pretty terrible, actually.'

'Thanks,' I mutter, although my sister's right. With no sunlight, my skin is pale and pasty – a fate only Rajiv and Sonya have escaped – and the pink line of my scar looks worse than ever. Plus I've lost weight since my body clock went haywire – it's hard to eat when your brain insists you should be in bed.

'You sleeping okay?' Clare wears the expression I've come to know well since the accident – a mix of concern and barely suppressed exasperation.

'Only a few hours at a stretch,' I admit, shifting on the plastic seat in the tiny box room reserved for these calls. 'It's the lack of light.' Despite the disorienting effect of twenty-four-hour

days when I arrived, waking to darkness is worse, both demor-
alising and physically draining. I feel as if my body is falling
apart, little by little, the longer I'm here.

'So are you taking anything for it?' My sister's tone is loaded.

'Pills, you mean?'

She gives a curt nod.

I inhale, wondering how to reply. Clare's already read me
the riot act and threatened to report me, back when she rumbled
the contents of my bin. But it's not illegal for doctors to
self-prescribe in the UK, just severely frowned upon, and I
knew Clare wouldn't risk losing me my job. It was the one
thing I had left, after all. I had to sell the house after Ben had
gone, unable to pay the mortgage on my salary alone, and was
forced to rent somewhere smaller.

'No, I'm not,' I lie again, keeping my expression deadpan
as shame washes through me. If Clare knew the truth, that I
was helping myself to precious station supplies, she'd probably
disown me.

I wait for her to call my bluff, but she evidently decides it
will get her nowhere. 'Are you eating?' she asks instead.

I imagine my sister working through a mental checklist.
Sleep – tick. Addiction – tick. Eating habits – tick. Next she'll
be asking if I'm getting enough fresh air – to which the answer
is obviously no; I go out into that impenetrable darkness as
little as possible.

'Yes, I'm eating.' I try not to sound annoyed. I owe Clare
patience and politeness at the very least. With our father dead
and our mother so far away, it fell to my sister to keep vigil
by my hospital bed in those first days following the crash. To
warn me about the extent of my injuries before handing me
the mirror I was demanding. To take me into her busy family
home during those weeks of recuperation before I could find
a new flat and return to work.

'You sure?' Clare looks unconvinced.

I ignore the question. 'So how are things your end?' I ask instead, hoping to divert her from 'project Kate'.

'Same old,' she sighs. 'Eleanor hates her new school, and Toby . . . well, you know Toby. I've had to hide his Xbox. He's currently mounting a one-boy war of psychological attrition.'

This makes me smile. My nephew has inherited his mother's obstinacy and doggedness, which naturally leads to frequent clashes.

'And John?'

Clare grimaces. 'In Bahrain.'

I pull a sympathetic face. My high-flying brother-in-law, with his position in the Foreign Office, is more frequently out of the country than in it, leaving my sister to manage the bulk of the childcare and domestic responsibilities on top of a demanding job as a human rights lawyer.

I often wonder how she puts up with it. Then again, I'm hardly the oracle on relationships.

'Plus it's insanely hot here,' she complains. 'Another bloody heatwave. As soon as John comes home he's promised we can go away for a week. Take the kids to the beach.'

I try to imagine a world that isn't endless ice, where water is liquid without being heated, and you can sit outside in a T-shirt and shorts. It seems impossible. My sister lives on another planet. In another galaxy.

A couple of seconds of blankness as the call stalls again. When it resumes, I only catch the tail end of Clare's question: '. . . you'd tell me if there was something wrong, wouldn't you?'

'Of course,' I lie a third time, but I'm betrayed by the tears that suddenly prick my eyes. How does my sister do that? Manage to home in on the core of my unhappiness? Perhaps it's her job – I guess you develop an instinct for other people's anguish.

Clare chews the side of her lip and sighs again, and I wish I could confide in her. Could tell her about someone stealing my pills and going through all my things, and how it has played on my mind ever since. How, despite my best efforts, it has made me suspicious of almost everyone.

But it's out of the question. I consider telling her instead about the atmosphere on the base. Though there's been no more actual fights since the incident in the laundry room two weeks ago, the general mood hasn't improved. Everyone is on tenterhooks, either avoiding company or sticking to safe little cliques. Luuk and Rob are rarely seen apart, while Caro hangs out with Alice and Alex, who's still shunning me. I spend most of my free time with Drew, who thankfully seems happy with life in the friend zone. Arne too, although mostly he keeps himself to himself.

But why burden my sister with all this? The last thing I want is her worrying about me even more.

'Lisa messaged me the other day,' she says out of nowhere. 'She was asking how you are. Said you hadn't replied to her recent email.'

I feel my cheeks flush. 'I've been busy.'

My sister narrows her eyes at me. 'She's your best friend, Kate. She worries about you. For Christ's sake email her. Mum too. She says she's written to you twice and not heard anything.'

A commotion breaks out in the background. Toby's voice, indignant, yelling something at his sister.

Clare rolls her eyes. 'I'd better go. It'll be open warfare if I don't intervene.'

'Give them my love,' I say quickly. 'Tell Toby to cut you some slack, or I won't bring him back a penguin egg.'

'There's no penguins where you are,' my literal-minded sister points out. 'Nor would you be allowed to take one home.'

'Nope. But he won't know that.'

She grins, gives me a little wave. 'Call Mum,' she says again, then logs off.

I sit in the Skype room for another ten minutes, trying to pull myself together, swiping my eyes with the heel of my hand. Speaking to my sister makes me feel lonelier than ever – as if she were my sole connection to the outside world.

Hell. She pretty much *is* my sole connection – though that's largely my own fault. Most of my friends – bar Lisa, who I've known since med school – have melted away. Or rather been pushed; after my first meet-up post-accident resulted in actual tears from a work colleague, overwhelmed by the sight of my injured face, it felt easier to keep my distance.

I didn't deserve all that sympathy, that concern. Nor could I endure everyone carefully avoiding the topic of Ben.

My mother, on the other hand, can never leave it alone, on those rare occasions we talk. Always asking probing questions about him, as if I'm a patient rather than her daughter. Trying to get into my head in a way I can't handle.

I'll email her tomorrow, I resolve, glancing at my watch.

Nearly supper time.

'Reckon it might be quite a show tonight,' Sonya announces over a delicious lasagna, made to a recipe Raff taught to Rajiv.

'You think?' Alice looks hopeful.

'Weather conditions are perfect. No cloud cover or bright moonlight. Fair chance of a good display – if not, it'll be great for stargazing. We're bound to spot a few meteors.'

'Yes, let's go outside when we finish up here.' Sandrine sounds excited. With the upcoming midwinter festivities – the highlight of the Antarctic social calendar – still a couple of weeks away, she seizes any opportunity to raise morale with some group bonding.

Everyone murmurs agreement – all except Alex, I notice.

Sure enough, when we're kitting up in the boot room, there's no sign of him.

'Anyone know if Alex is coming?' I ask. I've been trying to keep tabs on him since the fight in the laundry room, given his wild accusations about what happened to Jean-Luc. But he's become increasingly elusive outside meal times, hiding away in various corners of Beta and avoiding almost everyone.

Caro shakes her head. 'I don't think so.'

'I'll go check.'

I make my way to the cabins. Knock on his door. No answer. I check the common areas, then give up, returning to the boot room to put on my outdoor gear as quickly as possible. The trick is to get kitted up and out of the building before you start to sweat – there's nothing worse than damp clothes next to your skin in temperatures well below freezing.

Grabbing a torch and ignoring the pain in my lungs from breathing so hard, I hurry to catch up with the others – the thought of being alone out in the darkness fills me with dread.

I find Sonya leading everyone a good distance from the station, so any internal lights won't detract from the show. Standing in a rough line, we switch off our torches and wait. Above us, countless stars crowd the sky, the pale band of the Milky Way more pronounced than I've ever seen it. A small crescent moon, low on the horizon.

Sonya was right: this is the perfect time and place for star-gazing. I should do it more often. Get someone to come with me who knows their constellations.

After ten minutes or so, my fingers start to go numb, so I put my torch down by my feet and shove my gloved hands deep into the pockets of my thick down jacket. Somewhere to the left of me drifts a faint smell of marijuana.

Has Sandrine noticed? If so, she's studiously ignoring it. Picking her battles, I suppose.

Another five minutes and I'm concluding we're out of luck, when Alice gasps. 'Look!' she exclaims, pointing over my left shoulder.

I turn to see. At first I can't discern anything more than a faint glow on the horizon, but gradually it grows, spreading across the sky in a fire of purple and green, twisting and undulating, sometimes brighter, other times fading almost to blackness.

Aurora australis. The Southern Lights.

'Wow!' I gasp, and Luuk lets out a long low whistle of approval as the aurora expands, building into huge columns of violet and green that soar ever upwards, running from south-east right around to the north-west. The sky has transformed into something solid, a bright fabric that billows and bends in a magnetic wind.

I grab my phone from my jacket. Shielding it from the cold inside my sleeve, I take a few quick snaps and stuff it back in my pocket. Then stand and admire the show. It's truly mesmerising. Ethereal, too, though I understand the physics – charged particles from the sun striking atoms in the Earth's atmosphere, causing them to release photons of light.

Knowing this, however, doesn't make it any less awe-inspiring.

I watch, entranced, the vicious cold forgotten, losing all sense of time, unable to look away for even a second, spinning on the spot to follow each dancing column of light as it moves across the sky.

I feel suddenly, gloriously, elated. As if everything in my life has conspired to bring me to this moment.

Around me, various people call it a night, but I can't yet tear myself away. It's like a magic show, and I'm filled with the same wonder as when my father set up a firework display in the garden for my fifth birthday. I thought they were the most amazing thing I'd ever seen.

He'd have loved this, I think, with a pang of old grief as I remember his passion for astronomy, how he used to coax me outside on cloudless nights to show me the stars. Always keeping a few lights on in the house behind us so I wouldn't be afraid.

'Coming in?' Alice asks.

'I'll stay a bit longer.' Drew's voice.

'Me too.' Luuk.

A moment later another beautiful plume of jewel colours ripples across the sky, even brighter than before. I watch it, fascinated, unaware of the minutes ticking by. It's only as the aurora finally starts to fade and my feet and fingers throb with cold that I realise I'm alone.

'Drew?' I call into the darkness. 'You there?'

No reply.

Where have they gone? Surely they wouldn't have left without me?

I bend to retrieve the torch, but my fingers close on empty space. I drop to my knees, peering in the dwindling light of the aurora.

Shit. Where is it?

I feel around me, gripped by a surge of anxiety. *Where is my torch?* It was here. I'm sure it was. I've barely moved from this spot the whole time.

How could it have disappeared?

My phone. I get back onto my feet, retrieve it from my pocket and turn on the flashlight, holding it tight in my glove to protect it from the cold. It's pitifully weak, but casts enough light for me to check the surrounding area. Advancing cautiously, keeping to the footprints in the snow made by the other winterers, I swing my phone to either side of me to look for my torch.

Nothing.

I retrace my steps, anxiety building towards panic.

Where the hell is it?

A second later my phone dies – whether from the cold or a flat battery, there's no way to tell. I stand there, heart thudding in my chest, deciding what to do. I peer back to where I reckon the base should be, but there are no lights visible from this side. Turning slowly, I try to find Alpha's silhouette against the dark sky, but can't see anything at all.

Fuck.

With a rush of dread, I realise I've lost all sense of direction. I gaze up into the cloudless heavens, into the crush of those billions and billions of tiny stars, but now it all seems so vast and inhospitable it makes me dizzy. I have a sudden sharp sensation of vertigo, an urge to lie on the ground and cling to the ice, as if I were hanging upside down and might fall upwards.

Shit, Kate. *Pull yourself together.*

Trying to steady my breathing, I turn on the spot again, but the blackness around me is absolute, and I've no idea which way to go. My pulse quickens as I try to work out what to do. I'm getting seriously cold; I need to move, and fast.

But what if I start walking in the wrong direction? What if I head *away* from the station? I could end up truly lost, and freeze to death in a matter of minutes.

The only sensible option is to stay still and wait for someone to realise I haven't returned. But how long might that take? What if no one notices, or simply assumes I've gone to bed?

Stupid, I think, with a moan of fear and frustration. Why was I so careless? I should have returned with the others. None of us is supposed to be outside alone in the dark, but as with many station rules, observance has slackened as the winter progresses.

'Help!' I yell into the endless night, stamping my feet on the ground – my toes now so numb I can barely feel them and I'm shivering so violently I can hardly stand.

I'm going to die out here, I decide, in another wave of pure, blind panic. I'm going to freeze to death in this fucking hell-hole.

'Help!' I shout again, listening for a reply. But it's pointless. I'm too far from the base for my voice to carry; besides, the buildings are so well insulated that barely any outside sound penetrates.

Desperate, I plunge forwards into the darkness in what I hope is the direction of the building; if I stay here any longer, I'll die anyway. But almost immediately I stumble over a ridge in the ice. A searing pain rips through my bad knee, making me gasp and pitch forwards. An audible crack from my goggles as my head hits the ground.

'Shit.' I start crying in earnest, but that only serves to near blind me as the tears instantly freeze, clinging to my lashes.

I squeeze my eyes tightly shut, forcing myself to stop, and for a second or two I'm back in that car, pinned at an impossible angle. Time suspended. The ticking of the engine as it cools. A sensation strangely like peace.

Everything resolved at last.

Everything forgiven.

Isn't freezing to death supposed to be like falling asleep? How easy it would be, simply to give up and let go, succumb to the inevitable.

Then I hear it. A noise, somewhere out on the ice.

A voice, calling my name.

I scramble to my feet, peering into the night. 'Here!' I yell, waiting for a response, but nothing comes. I spin around, unsure if it was simply my imagination. Perhaps this is what dying of cold is really like, a slow fading into dreams.

'Kate?' The voice again.

Not a dream. 'I'm here!' I shout again, as loud as I can, waving my arms idiotically, although no one can see me. There, finally, I catch a faint beam of torchlight in the distance and start limping towards it.

'What the fuck, Kate?' Arne says as he reaches me, Drew close behind him. 'What are you doing out here? We only just realised you were missing.'

'I couldn't find my torch.' My words come out as a gulping sob. 'Someone took it.'

'You sure?' Drew scours the ice with his own flashlight, but we're too far now from where I was standing.

'I had it with me,' I insist, teeth chattering uncontrollably. 'And then it was gone.'

'Never mind.' Arne turns his attention to my leg. 'You're limping.'

'I fell over. Wrenched my knee.'

'We'll give you a hand.' Drew hooks his arm under my shoulder and gestures Arne to do the same. 'Let's get you inside before you die of hypothermia.'

13

12 June

By the time we reach Alpha and climb the stairs to the boot room, I'm shaking so hard I can barely stand. My face tingles with a thousand tiny needles from the ice crystals that have formed in my skin – I know if I looked in the mirror I'd see the red flush of frostnip, the precursor to frostbite.

'Thanks,' I stammer to Drew and Arne as they release me and I sink onto a bench.

'You okay?' Drew's eyes lock with mine for a beat or two.

'I think so.'

'Anything you need? Hot drink, something stronger?'

'No, really, I'm fine. Honestly. Thanks, Drew.'

He nods. 'I'd better find Sandrine and let her know you're safe. Have a hot shower – that'll warm you up fast.'

I think longingly of the bathtub back in my flat in Bristol. What wouldn't I give right now for a long hot soak. I try to remove my outdoor gear, but my fingers are too numb. I fiddle with the zip of my jacket until Arne comes to my rescue.

'Here, let me do it.'

Feebly, I let him peel it off me, then pull off my boots. My feet are so cold it's almost painful. 'Keep your salopettes on,' he advises. 'Wait till you warm up a bit.'

I nod, following him to my room, my injured knee throbbing painfully. Arne pulls back the duvet and I flop onto the bed, still fully clothed. 'Forget that shower, I'll fetch you a hot drink instead. I insist.'

I do as he says. Pull the duvet over me, and lie there shivering. Tentatively, I lift my left leg and try to bend my knee; a dart of pain, but I reckon the ligaments are okay. It's never been quite right since the accident, and clearly falling on the ice hasn't helped.

I reach underneath the mattress for some of the painkillers I've hidden and quickly swallow them down. Then lie back again, ignoring the discomfort in my leg and focusing on a lingering sense of unease.

What happened to my torch? How did I manage to lose it?

My chest still feels tight with the terror of being out there, lost, alone, growing ever colder and more convinced I was going to die on that unforgiving ice. 'I told everyone you were okay.' Arne returns, a mug in each hand, a bottle of bourbon tucked under his arm. He sets the mugs on my desk and tops them up with generous measures of alcohol. 'Here.'

I try to take it from him, but I'm shivering too hard.

'One sec.' He disappears again and returns this time with a metal straw and a large blanket. Dropping the straw into the mug, he places it on my bedside table, then drapes the blanket over my duvet.

I lean over and take a sip. It's delicious – sweet hot chocolate, with a distinctive nip. Within moments a welcome warmth spreads into my core.

Arne pulls up the desk chair and sits. He studies me, looking concerned. 'You all right?'

'I will be. Thank you for coming to my rescue.'

He nods, and carries on scrutinising my face. Despite his height, his formidable physical presence, Arne doesn't seem to take up much space in the room. Something to do with the quiet confident way he holds himself, perhaps, a kind of internal poise.

'Somebody took my torch,' I say. 'I put it on the ground by my feet, and I didn't move the whole time.'

Arne frowns, and I realise how paranoid I sound. 'Kate,' he says gently, 'it's very easy to get disoriented out there, to lose track of things. We shouldn't have left you, even for a few minutes. We assumed you were following on behind.'

I have another sip of my drink, then rest my head on the pillow and close my eyes. Maybe he's right. I must have lost track of what I was doing – easily done, after all, when your attention is fixed elsewhere.

Then I remember my missing pills. No easy way to explain those.

'If you like, I'll take the skidoo out tomorrow,' Arne offers. 'I'll go and find your torch.'

'Would you?' I give him a grateful smile. I can't face going back out there myself. I flash back again to that enveloping darkness, the horror of being alone in its deadly embrace.

Stop it, Kate. I force my attention to the here and now. I'm warm, and safe. A soft glow inside from the hot chocolate and the numbing effect of the painkillers. I run my fingers over Arne's blanket. It's hand-knitted, a mix of complicated geometric shapes in natural tones of grey and brown, giving off a faint aroma of sheep.

'Has Sonya seen this?' I ask. 'It's lovely. And very cosy.'

Arne grins. 'It's made with yarn from Icelandic sheep. Their wool is well known for its thermal properties.'

'Where did you get it?'

'My girlfriend knitted it, actually. Took her months. She was cursing me by the end.'

'I bet. What a lovely gift.'

I watch stealthily as he leans back in the chair, inspecting my room. Again, I'm struck by his appearance. Not in-your-face handsome like Drew, but quieter, more affecting.

His girlfriend must really miss him.

'You feeling any better?' he asks, stretching out his legs until they almost touch the base of the bed.

I nod. I've finally stopped shivering, and the warmth is now flowing out from my core to my extremities. 'Have you seen Alex, by the way?'

Arne shakes his head. 'No sign of him all evening.'

I finish the rest of my drink and replace the mug on my bedside table. 'Can I ask you something?'

'Fire away.'

'Have you seen Alex smoking at all? Marijuana, I mean.'

Arne gives me an assessing look, evidently weighing his answer. 'I haven't. Why do you ask?'

'It could explain a few things.' Despite both Alex and Caro denying he smokes, it made sense. 'I thought it could account for his behaviour, his conviction that someone tampered with Jean-Luc's equipment.' It would explain, too, how he might have missed stuff, how accidents might happen, but I don't say that to Arne.

'It could,' Arne agrees. 'Have you talked to him about it?'

I wince, remembering Alex's outrage when I brought it up six weeks ago. I've tried several times to speak to him since, but he shut me down immediately. There seems little point in persisting.

'Where do they get the stuff anyway?' I sidestep Arne's question with one of my own.

He shrugs. 'Possibly Luuk brought it over, or somebody sent it to him. There's a rumour that it's grown somewhere on the station, using hydroponics, but that's just another Antarctic urban legend. You get those kinds of stories on every base.'

I think of Drew, his hydroponic system for the salad. The neighbours down the road from me who were arrested for growing weed in their roof space. 'Doesn't sound that implausible,' I say.

'You can't keep anything hidden here for that long. Sandrine turns a blind eye to people smoking, but there's no way she'd tolerate them cultivating their own supply.'

I consider this. He's probably right.

'So you're cool with it?' he asks, studying me. 'People smoking out here?'

I shrug. 'It's probably better than getting drunk.'

'Jean-Luc hated it. Said it screwed up his experiments and that it was too risky out here. Some people react really badly to the stronger strains, especially skunk.'

My predecessor had a point. I've seen quite a few cases of psychosis in my time on the ER, some caused by the super-strength cannabis sold on the streets.

'For what it's worth, I agree with you,' Arne continues. 'But Jean-Luc believed Luuk and anyone else caught using drugs should be thrown off the station.'

'Was that why you didn't get on with him? Luuk implied the two of you didn't see eye to eye.'

Arne lets out a long breath that turns into a sigh. Sits up and rubs his cheek, as if checking whether he needs a shave. 'He could be very . . . what is the word. Dog . . .'

'Dogmatic?'

'Yes. Inflexible.'

We sit in silence for a minute, both thinking. I grapple around for more conversation, finding I very much don't want him to leave. 'Do you have any idea why Alex said that stuff in the laundry room? About Jean-Luc being murdered.'

Arne adds more bourbon to the remains of his hot chocolate and takes a swig. 'They were very close. Jean-Luc was a sort of father figure to him. His death hit Alex hard.'

'Yes, it seems to have really knocked him for six.'

'For six?' Arne frowns.

'Sorry, it's a colloquialism, from cricket. It means you're out of the game, devastated.'

'I see. Yes, knocked him for six.'

'Can you think of any reason why someone might want Jean-Luc dead?'

Arne's mouth turns down in a kind of shrug. 'No, I can't.' He sighs again, then fixes his gaze on mine. I get the sense he's making his mind up about something. 'Did Alex mention Jean-Luc's things? His journal?'

'No.'

'When they got back – it took several days to return from the crevasse – Alex claimed somebody had stolen Jean-Luc's laptop and journal from his room.'

'Surely nobody would actually steal a dead man's belongings?' I raise my eyebrows, aghast. 'Anyway, how did Alex know they were missing?'

'I assume he checked Jean-Luc's room before they cleared it out. It's possible someone decided that since he was dead, they might as well help themselves.'

My frown deepens. The laptop perhaps, but the doctor's journal? Why on earth would anybody want that?

'Anyhow, Alex was pretty upset about it. He insisted Sandrine investigate.'

'And did she?'

'Briefly. She had enough on her hands trying to find a replacement doctor, and dealing with the aftermath of the accident. From what I heard she concluded one of the summer crew took them.'

Maybe not, I think, wondering if I should mention the theft from my own room. Impossible though. I can't tell Arne without admitting what was stolen.

'Alex was pretty upset about it,' he adds. 'He demanded Sandrine report it to UNA, but she refused.'

I reflect on Sandrine's clipped manner. Her coldness. There's a weariness behind it, I suspect, a barely contained anxiety.

After all, she's responsible for this whole station and the safety of everyone in it – not an easy burden at the best of times.

'What happened to the rest of Jean-Luc's stuff?' I ask. 'Was it flown home?'

'It's locked in a cupboard in Beta. I guess it'll get shipped out in the spring.'

I frown. 'How come? Don't his family want his things back sooner?'

'I don't know. You'd have to ask Sandrine about that – it was her decision.' But I detect evasion in Arne's expression, the way his eyes won't quite meet mine. There's something he's not telling me, I sense, but decide not to press him further.

'What was Alex like,' I ask, changing the subject, 'before all this happened?'

He chews his lip, mulling this over. 'That's the thing – he was a pretty chilled, relaxed kind of guy. Happy. Completely different to how he is now.'

I picture Alex in that photo, standing next to Jean-Luc, arm draped over his shoulder. I can imagine that.

'Why didn't he go home afterwards? If it was so difficult for him to be here.'

'I believe he felt . . . feels . . . that people would see it as an admission that it was his fault. He thought he had to stay . . . He—' Arne stops, seems to change his mind about whatever he was about to say.

'He thought what?'

Arne sighs again. 'Alex said he wanted to get to the bottom of it, what happened to Jean-Luc.'

I think this over, then throw caution to the wind. 'I heard there'd been an incident out in New Zealand.' I'd tried, a while back, to unearth more detail on the internet, but found nothing except a brief report in a local paper. A couple of paragraphs that hadn't added much to what Drew had already told me, beyond the girl's name.

'Yeah. Poor kid.'

'The girl, or Alex?'

'Both. It's a tragedy either way you look at it.'

'You don't think it was Alex's fault then? What happened out on the ice, with Jean-Luc.'

Arne shakes his head again. 'I've worked with Alex, he checks everything three times. If he's paranoid about anything, it's about something failing.'

I study him, confused. 'So you, what, agree it was sabotage? That somebody deliberately tampered with the equipment?'

'No, Kate.' Arne pauses, picking his words carefully. 'This is Antarctica. Shit happens. Things don't perform the way they do at home. It's a high-risk environment, we're working at extremes. I think it was a very unfortunate accident.'

'And that girl in New Zealand?'

Arne shifts on the desk chair, clearly uncomfortable. 'Just because it's rare for something to go wrong, it doesn't mean it can't happen twice. Bungee jumping is also high risk, after all.'

He's right, I decide, with a pang of pity for Alex. What a shitty hand he's been dealt. I just hope he can find a way back from it all.

I make a fresh resolution to try to pin him down tomorrow, perhaps talk about medication; after all, I have a whole cupboard full of antidepressants.

'Alex will be okay,' Arne says, as if reading my mind. 'He just needs to get off the ice and away from all this.' He stretches his legs and stands. 'And you look as if you could do with some sleep.'

'Don't forget this.' I hold out the blanket.

'Keep it as long as you need.' He picks up the mugs, then

lingers at the door. 'And be careful in future, eh? Losing one doctor might be regarded as misfortune; to lose both looks like carelessness.'

With that he exits, leaving me gazing after him in surprise. A vehicle mechanic who watches Tarkovsky and paraphrases Oscar Wilde.

That's not someone you meet every day.

14

15 June

A knock on the clinic door one afternoon as I'm updating the blood results. Nothing unusual, though most of us are showing low levels of vitamin D – I need to make sure people are taking their supplements.

I'm pleased to see Caro's face appear, but my smile fades as I spot a telltale redness around her eyes and nose.

'You busy?' she asks.

'Not at all. Have a seat.'

She sits opposite, grasping a crumpled tissue. I feel a twinge of alarm. What's this about? Has she had another run-in with Luuk?

'Has something happened?' I put a reassuring hand on her arm.

Caro fidgets with the tissue, visibly swallowing. Suddenly she bursts into tears. Great convulsive sobs shake her whole body, her breath emerging in ragged gasps. But she still doesn't speak.

'Caro,' I prompt, increasingly anxious to see this level-headed girl in such a state. 'What on earth's the matter?'

She swipes her eyes with the tissue, then inhales. 'I'm pregnant.'

I stare at her, open-mouthed, trying to process this. 'Pregnant?' I repeat dumbly. 'Are you sure?'

She nods. 'I haven't had a period in a while.' She swallows, looks away. 'A long while, actually.'

Oh God. I sit there, winded, unable to disguise my shock. Pregnant.

Holy fuck.

Of all the medical emergencies I've trained for out here – or conjured up in my head in the dead of night – this is not one of them. UNA makes it clear to all female staff that they must maintain reliable contraception – a pregnancy out here in the middle of winter could be disastrous.

'Oh shit.'

Caro flushes, and I realise I've said it out loud.

'I'm sorry,' she whispers. 'I've been completely fucking stupid. I should have told you earlier.'

'It's a surprise, that's all.' I pull myself together. 'It's not your fault.'

'That's not exactly true, is it?' Caro grimaces.

'It takes two,' I retort, wondering about the father. Is it someone currently on the base, or one of the summer team? I contemplate asking, but decide it's none of my business. 'Do you remember the date of your last period?'

Caro looks uneasy. 'I'm not certain, to be honest. I was using a contraceptive patch for a while, and there was never much . . . only spotting. That's . . .' More tears roll down her cheeks. 'That's how I didn't realise . . . for so long, I mean.'

I glance at her belly, but it's impossible to discern anything under those baggy dungarees.

Fuck. *What the hell am I going to do?*

'Right.' I take a breath, collecting myself. 'First things first. Let's do a test to confirm, okay?'

I get up, knee twinging despite the support bandage I've worn since wrenching it on the ice three nights ago, and root around in the supplies cupboard. Do we even have pregnancy tests? I can't remember seeing any.

There *must* be one somewhere. UNA seems to have thought of pretty much everything.

I try to calm myself down, checking through the supplies again as Caro sits silently in the background. I consider what it would have taken for her to come here today, her natural dread at my reaction. She's not stupid – she must know what a terrible position she's put both of us in.

'Here we are.' With a rush of relief, I find a small pack of pregnancy tests hidden behind the more copious quantities of condoms and sanitary products. I remove the instruction leaflet and read it carefully, then hand her the little wand. 'Just pee on the stick. Result in two minutes.'

As Caro disappears to the loo down the corridor, I stand there, taking the weight off my bad knee, mind reeling with a thousand questions. How far along is she? The test will only confirm she's pregnant – without a clear date for her last period, it'll be difficult to assess the due date with any accuracy. Oh Jesus, what do I do about antenatal care? It's been years since my student rotation in the maternity unit.

More to the point, when is the earliest we can get her off the ice? And will we be in time?

I squeeze my eyes shut and send a silent prayer to a God I don't believe in. Please let her be mistaken. Please let this be due to something else – the diet, maybe. Some hormonal disruption.

But the instant Caro walks back into the clinic, her grim expression confirms my worst fears. She hands me the plastic wand without a word, and I glance at the little blue tick in the window marked positive.

I exhale slowly. Try to hide my growing panic.

'Right,' I say briskly, grabbing the paper calendar from my desk. 'Have you any idea when you might have conceived?'

Caro's face reddens. 'Um . . . well, no. I'm not sure.' She hesitates. 'It wasn't only the once, you see.'

'You say you wore a contraceptive patch. You think that failed?'

'I got one before I came out here, but it made me feel sick. So I swapped to progesterone pills instead.'

'Did you remember to take them every day?' I try not to make the question sound accusatory, but her blush deepens.

'Most days.'

I nod. No point pursuing this. The deed's done, and there's nothing to be gained by implying Caro has been careless. Or her partner – whoever that might be.

I take another deep breath, refocus. 'Do you mind me asking something personal, Caro?'

'Sure.'

'Does the father know?'

She shakes her head vigorously, then looks away, her shoulders heaving with more tears. 'To be honest, I'm not certain . . .' She stops herself, pressing her fingers to her mouth as if to hold in her distress. 'Oh shit, what a mess.'

I gaze at her, at a loss what to say. Being pregnant under these conditions is nothing short of calamitous. I run through the possible complications, struggling to recall my obstetrics training. Hopefully we're well past the window for ectopic pregnancy. Though that still leaves things like . . . what? Late miscarriage, hypertension and pre-eclampsia, severe haemorrhage. A congenital deformity with the baby.

'Let's get you on the exam bed,' I say gently, trying to sound calmer than I feel. 'See if we can establish how far along you are. Could you slip off your dungarees?'

She releases the straps and lets them fall to the floor, then climbs on, pulling up her T-shirt. Without the clothes, I can see a pronounced little bump. Surely that means the father has either gone home with the summer team, or that they're no longer sleeping together? Hard to believe anyone seeing her naked now wouldn't notice.

Focus, I tell myself, as I gently palpate her stomach, fingers feeling for the hard roundness at the top of her uterus. Grabbing my tape, I measure down to her pubic bone.

Nearly twenty-six centimetres. I put on my stethoscope, place the cup on her stomach, moving it around and listening carefully.

There. Faint and fast, the little gallop of the foetal heartbeat.

'What is it?' Caro asks anxiously, studying my expression. 'Is everything all right?'

'You seem fine. Get dressed. I just need to check something.' While she's fiddling with the straps of her dungarees, I fire up the computer and navigate to the 'cheat sheets' – a summary of virtually every medical condition us station doctors are ever likely to encounter. I find the antenatal section and check the chart for fundal height. Grabbing my calendar, I calculate her due date. Not easy, given fundal height is just an estimate and I could easily be two or three weeks out.

My heart sinks. There's little chance they'll get a plane out before mid-October – at the very earliest, and only then if the weather is unusually mild.

'Are you going to tell me?'

I straighten up and face Caro. 'Okay. I estimate you're somewhere between twenty-four and twenty-eight weeks pregnant. But without the exact last date of your period or an ultrasound scan, I can't be more accurate.'

She chews the inside of her lip. 'So I'm due when? Roughly.'

'Given the average pregnancy lasts approximately forty weeks, that puts you at . . .' I check the calendar again to be certain. 'Some where between mid September and mid October. But bear in mind pregnancy length can vary by several weeks either side of that.'

Caro's face tightens. 'Oh fuck.'

I don't respond for a moment or two, letting the news sink in. For both of us.

'We'll work something out,' I say, trying to sound more confident than I feel. 'I'm sure UNA will make every effort to get you off the base as soon as it's safe. It could be I'm wrong, that you're not as far gone as I think. Like I said, it's only a rough estimate.'

Caro nods, but she looks devastated. 'I didn't think it would be so soon. I mean, I'm not that big, am I?'

I shake my head. It's true. She's not showing that much, but then that's not unusual for a first baby.

Caro clears her throat. Drops her gaze to the floor. 'I guess it's too late to do anything about it,' she murmurs.

'You mean a termination?'

She nods again.

'There's absolutely no chance of that, Caro. Especially here, and at this stage of pregnancy.' I pause. 'Are you saying you don't want to keep the baby?'

Caro bites her lip, her mouth quivering. 'No. I mean, I do. I do want to keep it.' Another tear rolls down her cheek. 'It's just that I feel so . . . silly. I should have come to you sooner, but I didn't realise for ages – it simply never occurred to me that was what was going on. I thought I was putting on a bit of weight, but that's not surprising . . . I mean, I know you've the appetite of a bird,' she sniffs and gives me a tearful smile, 'but Rajiv's a great cook, and there's plenty of it. And then, when I started to suspect, I guess I went into denial. Kept telling myself it couldn't be true – until I felt these weird sensations in my stomach and realised it was the baby kicking.'

'You didn't experience other symptoms? Nausea? Tiredness? Breast tenderness?'

'I felt a bit sick, yeah, but I put that down to the progesterone pills. I've been tired, but then who isn't out here? I just assumed my biorhythms or whatever were out of sync.'

I give her a sympathetic look. I can't blame her. Would I have caught the signs myself? Not anything I need to worry about, thank God. I had a coil fitted back before the accident, plus I made sure Drew used a condom.

Belt and braces.

'So, are you still taking the progesterone?' I ask.

'I stopped them a few weeks ago, when I finally realised what was going on.' An anxious look crosses her face. 'Could they have harmed the baby?'

I shake my head. 'I'll check with the UNA medical team, but I'm not aware of any evidence that they do.'

'Okay.'

'But in the meantime, no alcohol.'

'Okay,' she repeats.

I pause, trying to think what to do now. 'Listen. You need to consider if – or rather when – you're going to tell everyone else on the station, but in the meantime I have to discuss this with Sandrine. Is that all right?'

She hesitates.

'It's absolutely in your best interests,' I add. 'Yours and the baby's. Sandrine will need to make certain everything is in place to get you out of here at the earliest possible date. And I need to liaise with UNA so I can offer you the best antenatal care. Do you understand?'

Caro doesn't speak for a while, just stares at the blind covering the clinic window, blocking out the darkness. She looks so young, I can't help thinking. So vulnerable.

'Please don't tell her yet,' she whispers. 'That it's me, I mean. I know you'll have to warn her about the situation, but I need more time to get my head around it without Sandrine on my back.'

I consider this. 'All right. I won't mention it for a couple of days. But Caro, there are only five of us on the base – women, that is. One of them is gay, and Sonya, well, she's not in the right age bracket. So it won't be hard for Sandrine to work out.'

She nods, chewing her lip again, then glances down at her clothes. 'It's not that obvious, though, is it yet? To the others?' She works up a tentative smile. 'Good thing I'm a plumber, eh? I can hide under these baggy overalls.'

'That's not going to work for much longer,' I point out gently. 'You should think about telling people before they put two and two together. You know what gossip is like in this place.'

Caro pulls a face. 'Tell me about it. It's like bloody Chinese whispers. Have you heard the rumour that I deliberately sabotaged that washing machine to piss off Luuk?' She frowns with disgust. 'As if I ever would. Not to mention it was his sodding lighter in there.'

'That's exactly why we need to tell them soon. But you should speak to the father first, Caro. He should know.'

'Yeah.' Her gaze drifts back to the window, then, with a sigh, she gets to her feet. 'Anyhow, I should get on with some work. The showers are playing up again.'

'Are you winning?'

'I've isolated the problem down to the boiler feed. But we'll see.'

She looks so tired and forlorn that I cast professional boundaries aside and get up to hug her. 'It's going to be okay,' I insist. 'Whatever happens, you're going to be fine. And the baby. Come back in a few days, and we'll discuss your antenatal care in more detail.'

She nods, but her expression remains rueful. I wait until she reaches the door before I say it. 'By the way, Caro?'

She pauses, looks back.

'Congratulations. I happen to think you'll be a fantastic mum.'

'Thanks.' Caro manages a weak smile, then closes the door behind her.

Once I'm sure she's gone, I let my head sink into my hands. Oh fuck. What am I going to do?

15

'Is this a joke?' Sandrine's expression is pure disbelief. 'If so, Kate, it really isn't very funny.'

I shake my head. 'I'm afraid not. We did a pregnancy test. I can show you the result if you don't believe me.'

She gets up from behind her desk, actually starts pacing the room. Then pauses. 'Are you absolutely sure? Could it be wrong?'

'They're 99 per cent accurate. Besides, I palpated her uterus. It's definitely enlarged, plus I heard the heartbeat with a stethoscope. That's pretty conclusive.'

Sandrine sinks back onto her chair. '*Merde*,' she mutters. 'Where will this all end?'

'With a healthy mother and baby, I hope.'

The station leader ignores my flippant response. Just fixes me with a cold stare. 'So who is it?'

'As I explained, I'm bound by patient confidentiality. She doesn't want me to reveal her identity.'

Sandrine purses her lips in something close to contempt. We both know it's bullshit, and I'm merely playing for time.

'Is it you?' She looks at me accusingly.

My first instinct is to laugh, but then I stop myself, for Caro's sake. No harm letting Sandrine wonder for a few days. She may guess it's Caro anyway, but she won't be sure.

'Kate?' She eyeballs me a moment or two longer, then snorts at my silence. 'Well, it's not *me*,' she says in a tone of disgust.

I sit opposite, wondering how to divert her attention to what we need to do now, rather than who put us in this position. But Sandrine glances at my stomach, drawing her own conclusions. With the weight I've lost since arriving on the ice, my belly is conspicuously flat. I watch her do the maths – a simple enough sum. Sonya, at fifty-four, is unlikely to be in the running; so that leaves Alice and Caro.

She inhales as she comes to the obvious conclusion. I feel bad for Caro, but what can I do? I did warn her.

'That idiot girl!' Sandrine snaps. 'Why didn't she take precautions?'

'She did,' I say, jumping to Caro's defence. 'But no method of contraception is one hundred per cent reliable.'

The station leader makes an exasperated noise, clearly unconvinced. Then all at once her anger deflates. The woman in front of me looks exhausted – and more than a little desperate. From the circles under her eyes, the hollows in her cheeks, it's obvious how much of a toll this winter is taking on her.

Sandrine's clipped efficiency often comes across as disdain, unrelieved by any discernible sense of humour, but right now she looks so beleaguered I'm tempted to extend a comforting hand.

I resist the impulse, knowing instinctively she won't appreciate the gesture. Her opinion of me doesn't seem to have improved; I'm still left with the feeling that I make a poor substitute for Jean-Luc – in her eyes anyway.

'Can't you be more precise?' Sandrine asks, 'About the dates?'

I shake my head. 'Not without an ultrasound. And even then, it wouldn't tell us definitively when she might go into labour.'

Sandrine shuts her eyes briefly, wrestling with some internal demon. 'I'll talk to UNA. See if there is some way they can evacuate her to New Zealand for the delivery.'

Sandrine doesn't reply. Simply gazes despondently at the stack of papers on her desk. 'I don't suppose she's mentioned who the father is?'

I shake my head again.

She runs her tongue over her teeth as she considers the possibilities.

'Do you have any idea?' I ask.

'I have my suspicions.'

'Would you care to share them? Do you think it's someone here now, or one of the summer staff?'

Her smile contains a touch of the sarcastic. 'Like you opened up to me, Kate?'

'I had no choice!' I retort, unable to contain my irritation any longer. 'She specifically asked me not to. I can't break the Hippocratic oath simply because it's convenient, Sandrine.'

The station leader remains mute.

'Fine. Suit yourself.' I get up and walk out of her office without another word.

It's an easier conversation with the consultant obstetrician on the UNA medical team in Geneva, despite the fact the video chat keeps freezing, forcing us to repeat almost everything we say. This, and the lateness of the hour, only adds to my growing exhaustion.

I take the same line with Annette Muller as I did with Sandrine, refusing to name Caro as the patient, though it's probably equally obvious who I'm referring to. Unlike Sandrine, however, Annette neither presses the point, nor gets annoyed.

'Well, we'll just have to manage this as best we can.' Her upbeat smile succeeds in taking some of the edge off my anxiety. 'You say she's around twenty-six weeks? Usually we'd have done an ultrasound scan by now to assess foetal and placental development, but obviously that's not an option. So carry on measuring the uterus – that will be a good indication whether the baby is growing normally – and keep an eye on her blood pressure and check for protein in her urine. Oh, and I'd give her an additional vitamin supplement, just to make sure.'

'Okay.'

'Meanwhile we'll do everything we can here to get her off the station in time to have the baby.' Annette's tone is matter-of-fact, as if this whole situation were entirely run of the mill. 'I've already spoken to the logistics team and they're looking into it.'

I nod, feeling increasingly numb with stress and exhaustion.

'At least she's not R-neg,' she adds, 'so we don't need to worry about rhesus sensitisation should she go into labour before we can evacuate. That would be a real problem with no Anti-D on the base.'

'Small mercies, eh?'

Annette sighs, her expression sympathetic. 'Don't look so worried, Kate. She's not ill, just pregnant. Plenty of women around the world get through this without any medical care at all. Let's not dwell on what might go wrong, and instead focus on the likelihood that all will go well.'

I nod again, taking a little comfort in her calm acceptance of the news. She's right. I need to get my act together before I next see Caro – the last thing we want is to make her any more anxious than she is already. But I am rattled by my discussion with Sandrine. I didn't handle it well, but I'm still too angry to try to build bridges.

I cut off the call and sit at my desk, thinking. Not only about Caro, but Alex too. These last few days he's stopped bothering to turn up even to evening meals. I'm increasingly worried about him, and his state of mind.

It occurs to me to check the video log directory – maybe he's made another entry. With UNA providing dedicated equipment, crew members can make videos in the privacy of their cabin and upload them straight into the system. Though I'm sent a notification every time that happens, it's possible I haven't noticed.

I scan the entries under Alex's name – nothing for the past six weeks. I gaze at the list of those he made earlier. I'm fully aware these video logs are supposed to be completely confidential, but for once I am tempted to break the rules; if I can't talk to the man himself, perhaps I can glean more insight into his mood by watching them.

My cursor hovers over the most recent. Surely it wouldn't do any harm? After all, nobody need ever know.

No.

I return to the main screen, studying the names on the list. Only Arne, Sandrine, Rajiv, Alice, and Sonya are up-to-date with their entries. I need to do some more chasing up. Explain – yet again – why it matters. What we owe to the people who laboriously set up the experiment, how much we could learn, the ways in which it might be used to help others.

But it's a slog, as I know myself. Every week, I struggle to talk to the camera. Impossible, somehow, to be honest about how I feel, what I've been witnessing on the station over the last month or so, the deterioration in everyone's mood as the lack of light takes its toll. So I stick to facts, avoid mentioning anybody by name, simply describe what I've done, what I'm planning to do. Updates on the experiments, that sort of thing.

Of course, there's one person who won't be making any more videos, I think, gazing at Jean-Luc's name, wondering why nobody thought to remove him from the system. I click into his file and examine all the entries. Twenty-six in total, the oldest at the top, recorded back in October in what would have been late spring here in Antarctica. On impulse, I open it up.

Confidentiality doesn't apply to dead people, surely?

I'm harming no one by watching this, I tell myself, though my motives for wanting to at all are less clear.

Why am I so curious?

Morbid fascination? Or am I simply in need of distraction?

A moment later I'm staring at that handsome face. Silver stubble, grey around his temples. A deep tan that suggests he spent a lot of time in the sun.

The second he starts speaking, I realise it's in French. Of course. In the privacy of a conversation to camera, people will naturally use their native language. I feel a flicker of disappointment; though I studied French to A level, I'm far from fluent.

Still, I let the video run, mesmerised by the sight of this man in the flesh, the sound of his voice. Everything about him, his demeanour, his mannerisms, the way he smiles at the camera, speaks of someone relaxed and happy in his own skin. He exudes an air of friendliness and authority – no wonder people warmed to him.

Most of them, at least.

I find I can understand more than I anticipated. His French is clear, with no strong accent or slang, and he talks with thoughtful slowness, describing his arrival on the ice, how happy he is to be here. How much he is looking forward to his year in Antarctica, and how much he misses his family.

'This place, this empire of white,' he says in French. 'It is the most beautiful in the world. So vast and still. So magnificent. It is untamed and wild and it lives on in my heart and my head, even when I'm not here. It teaches you that we are small and we are fragile, but somehow that need not diminish us in a place like this. Being here at all is a miracle.'

I swallow, experiencing a mix of emotions. I'm well aware I shouldn't be doing this, but I can't stop. I click through some of the later entries, playing excerpts. A lot of the time Jean-Luc talks about the experiments. I notice how careful he is never to refer to anyone on the base by name – a consummate professional, I think, feeling increasingly guilty about prying.

Why, exactly, am I doing this?

I return to the main list. With a frisson of unease, I note the date of the final entry: four days before his death. He must have recorded it right before leaving on that fateful expedition. I open up the link and blink at the screen in shock. This Jean-Luc is a different man to the one in the earlier videos. He looks depressed and tired, his tone dejected. His entire demeanour has changed, as if in the intervening months he's gained a whole world of problems.

What the hell happened? This was late summer, and though too much light can certainly mess with your sleeping schedule and other biorhythms, it's rarely as disruptive as the perpetual darkness of winter. But the doctor looks terrible – as if he hasn't slept properly in days.

'*Je ne sais pas quoi faire,*' he says, after a long silence in which he fiddles with something off-screen. Where before he made constant eye contact with the camera, now he seems unable to hold its gaze for more than a few seconds. '*Peut-être rien en ce moment.*'

I don't know what to do. Perhaps nothing at this moment.

His eyes flick away again as he mutters something I can't quite catch. I wind back, replay it. '*Cette pauvre fille. Je dois être certain que nous ne sommes pas vraiment en danger, que celui-ci c'est la même personne. Je dois convaincre Sandy de parler à UNA sans délai. Il faut vérifier les échantillons d'ADN.*'

Then, suddenly, the doctor leans forward and switches off the camera.

I translate his words in my head, and play the clip again, to make certain I understood. *That poor girl. I have to be certain that we're not truly in danger, that this is the same person. I must convince Sandy to talk to UNA urgently. We have to check those . . . what?* I look up the word *échantillon* on the internet.

'Sample,' says the online dictionary. As in DNA sample, I guess.

I frown, studying the now blank screen. What did Jean-Luc mean? Why did he need to insist Sandrine talk to UNA? What DNA samples?

Truly in danger . . .

My head buzzes with a feeling of foreboding. I sit there, trying to make sense of what I just heard. Jean-Luc was clearly troubled by something, that much is clear – he appeared as anxious as I've ever seen anybody, the contrast with his earlier self deeply unsettling.

But what on earth was going on?

There's only one person I can think to ask.

16

18 June

There's no answer when I knock on the door of Alex's cabin, so I tour the station, first checking all the workshops in Beta. I end up finding him where I least expect, tucked in the corner of the empty dining room, hunched over his laptop, a half-eaten sandwich on a plate next to him.

'Hi,' I say, as brightly as I can manage given I've had an exhausting day and it's nearly one in the morning.

Alex acknowledges me with a brief nod.

'How's it going?' I sit in the chair opposite, making it clear I'm here for the long haul.

'Okay.' He switches off his laptop and closes the lid.

I study his face. Alex looks tired and gaunt – par for the course here these days. Refreshing sleep is now as rare a commodity as fresh veg. But there's more, a haunted resignation, as if this place is something he's being forced to endure.

'You sure you're all right?' I ask, but get a blank stare for an answer. 'You don't look it,' I persist.

He sits back with a sigh, pushing back his hair. It's longer, I notice. Ever since the onset of the recurrent shower issues, most of the guys have got into the habit of shaving off their beards and getting their hair regularly chopped, courtesy of Ark and his electric clippers. Either Alex doesn't care for a buzz cut or he's reluctant to ask.

'What do you want, Kate?'

I sit there for a moment or two, deciding how to broach what Jean-Luc said in that video log. I'm wary of admitting to Alex that I watched it; even if I'm within my rights, I don't need him wondering if I've done the same with his.

'Can I ask you something?'

He gives a barely perceptible nod.

'You were friends with Jean-Luc, right?'

Alex stiffens slightly at the name, but nods again.

'Did he ever say anything to you . . .' I stop. Regroup. 'Did he mention having any reason to believe somebody here might be a threat to our safety?'

I sense Alex's attention sharpen. 'Why would you ask me that?'

'Just a note left in his file,' I lie. 'It said he needed to find out more, but that he thought we might be in danger. No indication what it was about.'

'In his medical file?'

I nod. It's sort of true, after all.

'No name?'

'Name?'

'He didn't say who it was?'

'Who what was exactly? I'm not sure what you mean.'

'Isn't it obvious?' Alex sounds irritated. 'I mean whoever killed him. The person Jean-Luc was investigating, the person who stole his laptop and notebook.'

I gaze back at him. 'Do you really believe Jean-Luc was murdered?'

'Yes,' he hisses, with a glance around to make sure we're still alone. 'Jean-Luc told me a couple of weeks before he died that he suspected someone on this station of having committed a serious crime. He—'

I hold my hand up to stop him. 'Wait. What kind of crime?'

'He didn't say. Just that it was very serious. That he'd discovered something suspicious and he needed proof.'

'So he didn't suggest who . . . or what?'

'No.'

I look away, trying to gather my thoughts. Tread carefully, Kate. You're supposed to be helping Alex, not feeding his paranoia. 'Did Jean-Luc say how he intended to prove it?'

'Not exactly. Just that he wanted UNA to run some checks. That the results would confirm whether or not he was right.'

The DNA samples Jean-Luc mentioned, the ones he discussed with Sandrine.

'And did they do it?'

Alex shrugs. 'I've no idea. That's why I went to get his journal and laptop. I knew what happened to him wasn't an accident, so I wanted to know what he'd discovered.'

'But you couldn't find them.'

'No. I went straight to his room after a debrief with Sandrine so she could send a report to UNA, but by that time they'd gone.'

I inhale, taking all this in. 'So . . . this person . . . you've absolutely no idea who it is, or why Jean-Luc was so concerned?'

'Not yet.'

'What do you mean?'

'I mean I intend to find out.'

'How?'

Alex shakes his head fiercely. 'I don't know, but I'm piecing it together. Jean-Luc said other stuff, odd things here and there, when we were alone. He was really cut up about an incident last time he was in Antarctica – some girl who died out on the ice.'

'Who?'

Alex shrugs again. 'He wouldn't say.'

'And you believe Jean-Luc's death was connected to that?' I look at him incredulously. Somehow, somewhere, this conversation has gone right off the rails, and I no longer know what to think. Except that it's not doing Alex any good at all.

Silly move, Kate.

'I reckon so.'

'Alex, listen to me. I'm not sure that . . . everything you're saying makes sense. I know you're upset and possibly a bit depressed. I'd really like you to come and see me tomorrow, so we can discuss this when we're both less tired. Maybe talk over your options for medication.'

The second the words are out of my mouth, I see by Alex's expression that I've said exactly the wrong thing. Again, I realise, remembering his indignation when I asked him about the marijuana. Why do I keep screwing this up?

'Alex, please, I'm only trying to—'

'What the fuck, Kate?' He leaps to his feet, glaring at me. 'You come in here, you start this whole conversation, *and now you don't believe me?*' His face is red with fury, his voice loud enough to wake half the base.

'No,' I stammer, glancing anxiously towards the door. 'Alex, I'm sorry, I didn't mean that. I meant this is clearly getting you down and—'

'Of course it's getting me down!' he yells, so angry I'm almost afraid. 'One of the best men I've ever known has been murdered – yes, *murdered* – and I'm getting the fucking blame, and instead of helping me find out who the hell did this, you want to stick me on antidepressants!'

'No, that's not what—'

'I DON'T NEED FUCKING ANTIDEPRESSANTS! I need to put a stop to this. I'm going to find the bastard who did this to Jean—'

'*Alex, enough!*'

Her voice is loud and commanding. We both turn to see Sandrine standing in the doorway. Behind her hovers Caro, in pyjamas and a loose dressing gown, along with Drew, Arne, and Luuk.

Hell. We really have woken up half the station.

'What bastard?' Luuk glares at Alex. 'What the fuck are you on about?'

But Alex doesn't respond. Instead he makes a sudden rush for the door, forcing everyone to jump aside to let him through.

Sandrine's gaze follows him down the corridor, then swings back to me. 'What was that all about?'

I shake my head, heat rushing to my cheeks. 'I . . . I'm not sure. I was simply trying to talk to him.'

'Like you did before?' The station leader fixes me with a piercing stare. 'I'd say you've done enough damage for one night, haven't you? I suggest you go to bed, but I would like to see you in my office tomorrow.'

With that, she turns and leaves the room.

I stand there, blinking, trying not to cry. Caro comes over and puts an arm around my shoulder while the others regard me awkwardly. 'Ignore her, Kate. She's under a lot of strain.'

I swallow. Nod. But Sandrine's right – I really *have* made this worse.

17

18 June

3 a.m.

Ben's voice in my head. 'I'm tired, Kate, tired of trying to get everything right. Always working so hard to please everyone, to be fucking perfect. When do we get to stop?'

Only by 'we', he meant me, of course.

After all, he chose a different life. He chose someone else, someone more exciting, more spontaneous.

What would Ben think now? I wonder, as I replay last night's disastrous conversation with Alex, Sandrine's stinging rebuke. Me out here in the middle of nowhere, at the ends of the earth, screwing everything up.

Not so fucking perfect after all.

I heave myself out of bed, feeling almost delirious with exhaustion. I picture the high-strength sleeping pills locked away in the clinic, those little white domes nestling in their pristine foil packet. A couple, perhaps, to snatch a few more hours sleep. To get a better grip on things.

Sandrine was right – my judgement is impaired and the insomnia isn't helping.

Pulling on my dressing gown, I pad along the empty corridors to the clinic, praying I won't bump into anyone. I slip my key into the lock, but when I turn it, nothing happens. I frown, peering at the door in the dim lights that illuminate the corridor at night, then pull on the handle.

To my surprise, the door swings open.

I stand there, puzzled. I'm certain I locked it last night – I always do. There are too many valuable and even dangerous medications, too many pieces of sensitive equipment inside this room to ever risk leaving it open.

Shit, I think, remembering the pills stolen from my room. I go in, shutting the door behind me. To my relief, the medicine cabinets are still secured. I take a look inside. Everything seems in order. I double-check the items somebody might be tempted by, but they're all there, neat packets of barbiturates and opiate painkillers, nothing obviously missing.

I sink onto my chair. What's going on? I could swear I locked the clinic before setting off to find Alex. I can actually picture myself doing it, tucking the keys into the pocket of my jeans as I headed towards his cabin.

Then I remember my torch, lost on the ice. My conviction that someone had taken it. Arne told me the next morning that Drew had already found it, right where we'd all been standing. Somehow, even searching with the light of my phone, I'd managed to miss it.

Am I going crazy? I ask myself seriously. Is it possible that I'm imagining things? *Even my missing pills?* Could I have used them all up and somehow blanked it from my mind?

Perhaps denial has me in its grip after all.

It's simply exhaustion, counters another voice. You probably forgot to lock the clinic door. I recall all the times I've worked back-to-back shifts in A&E, driving home with no memory of the journey, as if half my brain had been asleep behind the wheel.

I rest my head on the desk and shut my eyes, trying to think. Without warning, the fox appears, frozen in the headlights, staring in through the windscreen. Our gaze meets, a split second before I yank on the steering wheel and the world becomes a tumbling confusion of trees and rocks and starry sky.

Velocity and kinetic motion. The physics of collision.

Of oblivion.

I open my eyes, shaken by the force of the hallucination. Jesus, I really have to get more sleep. Rising to my feet, I reopen the cabinet containing the strongest sleeping pills. Take two from the nearest packet and go back to bed.

By the time I get to breakfast, the canteen is almost empty. Just Rob and Luuk, hunched head-to-head, talking. They fall quiet as they see me come in.

I pretend not to notice. It's easy to guess what they're discussing – the fiasco with Alex last night.

I take a coffee and a couple of pieces of toast back to my cabin, focusing on the day ahead. I should go to Sandrine first, attempt to build bridges. Perhaps we could come up with a plan for how to help Alex, maybe even tackle him together. See if we can make sense of this whole situation.

I have to be certain we're not in danger.

Why would Jean-Luc say that? Is it possible he meant something else entirely? That I misunderstood, or his meaning got lost in translation? I'll check the video again, I decide – in the cold light of day, it seems likely I made a mistake.

I sit on my bed with my tiny mirror to apply a little make-up. I want to put my best foot forward this morning, and frankly I need all the help I can get – my skin looks pale and ghoulish, and my hair badly needs a cut.

The trick, I've found, is to use a mirror so small you can only see a portion of your face at one time. I rub in some tinted moisturiser, the tips of my fingers tracing the line in my cheek, drawn to it like a tongue to a broken tooth. It fascinates as much as it appalls.

My mark.

Another reminder that, contrary to Ben's accusation, I'm very far from perfect.

'Is now a good time?'

I poke my head around Sandrine's door, mustering my friendliest demeanour. Receive a curt nod for my efforts.

'Shut it behind you, please.'

I steel myself. So this is going to be a proper dressing down. Station protocol is that people rarely shut their doors when outside their cabins. A signal, I suppose, that they're open to interruptions, that nothing is being concealed.

Sandrine indicates the chair opposite her desk, but doesn't speak for several minutes. I can't tell if this is because she's trying to work out what to say or if it's a deliberate move to unnerve me. I don't attempt to fill the silence. Whatever her game, I'll let it play out without reacting.

'Kate, we both know it was a mistake you coming out here.'

I gape at her, open-mouthed. Did she really just say that? Despite my resolve to stay calm, my chest tightens with shock and anger. I steady my breathing, keep my voice cool and measured. 'I'm not sure how to respond to that, Sandrine. Would you care to elaborate?'

A flicker of surprise crosses the station leader's face. Evidently this isn't what she expected. 'You're not sure how to respond . . . well, perhaps you should start by telling me what on earth you were doing last night.'

'Wasn't it obvious? I was talking to Alex. I'm worried about him.'

But that's not entirely true, is it? I am forced to admit, at least to myself. I didn't go to him purely with his welfare in mind; I sought him out because I wanted answers to questions of my own.

In that sense, I failed him.

'You appeared to have made him extremely upset,' Sandrine confirms. 'And not for the first time, by all accounts.'

'That wasn't my intention,' I say, carefully.

'What exactly were you talking to him about?'

I consider my response. Should I come clean? Tell her I watched Jean-Luc's video and explain what he said? Though obviously she knows something about it, I sense the station leader will take a dim view of my breaking protocol and prying into Jean-Luc's private life.

A very dim view indeed.

'I . . . he,' I pause, decide to bite a different bullet. 'I've been concerned about what Alex said that time in the laundry room – he seems convinced the previous doctor's death wasn't an accident.' I keep my eyes trained on Sandrine's face, alert for a reaction. But she doesn't so much as flinch, simply waits for me to continue. 'Do you agree?'

Her eyes narrow. 'Do I agree with what, Kate? That Jean-Luc's equipment was sabotaged? Do you really want me to dignify that with an answer?'

'Yes.'

Another flash of surprise. I watch the station leader re-appraising me. Clearly I'm not quite the pushover she antici-pated.

'Let me put it this way, Sandrine. Do you blame Alex for what happened? And if so, why is he still here?'

She contemplates my questions. The woman rarely blinks, I notice, seems able to maintain the naked stare of a cat. 'No, I do not blame Alex,' she says eventually. 'It was an accident. Nothing more, nothing less.'

Almost exactly what Arne said, I recall, wondering why on earth I'm pursuing this. Has Alex actually managed to persuade me otherwise?

Ask her about those DNA samples, urges an inner voice. Ask her about what Jean-Luc said in his video log. And while you're at it, ask her what she did with his letter.

But I hold back. It won't help to add more fuel to this fire.

'It seems to me you made a very questionable decision.' Sandrine's tone is icy and deliberate. 'I'll be honest with you, Kate, we've already lost an excellent doctor, and been forced to accept a dubious replacement. We now have a pregnancy, and possibly a labour, to deal with, along with somebody who is clearly deteriorating mentally, and you are not helping by stirring things up like this.'

I recoil at her words, stunned once again into silence. *A dubious replacement?* But there's also truth in what she's saying, I remind myself. I *have* been stirring things up.

Heat rises to my cheeks, betraying my confusion. 'I'm a good doctor,' I say fiercely, insisting as much to myself as Sandrine.

'So you say.' She raises an eyebrow. 'But my enquiries suggest otherwise.'

'What enquiries, Sandrine?' I snap, anger getting the better of me. 'What the hell are you talking about?'

The station leader regards me calmly, knowing she has me wrong-footed at last. 'I believe you were accused of malpractice, were you not? Against an elderly woman.'

My jaw drops. How on earth does she know about that?

'For your information,' I clench my hands to stop them trembling, 'I was completely cleared in that complaint. I didn't do anything wrong. On the contrary, I followed protocol to the letter.'

It's your fault!

The daughter's words rise up with all the force they had back then, as she stood in the middle of A&E, accusing me of killing her mother. Perforated appendix leading to peritonitis in a seventy-year-old woman; when she'd arrived in the hospital complaining of stomach pain and vomiting, I misdiagnosed it as gastroenteritis and sent her home.

But I'd done everything I reasonably could – at the time I examined her, her blood pressure and heart rate were normal, and she had only a slight fever. There'd been no red flags for appendicitis.

All the same, the whole experience, coming so soon after my return to work, left me shaken and humiliated. It was one thing to be exonerated by my superiors, quite another to forgive myself. Always at the back of my mind the question of whether my little self-medication habit had tainted my judgement. I didn't think so – but then, who was I to say?

Angry tears prick my eyes. I lean across Sandrine's desk, voice shaking. 'UNA chose me, and has full access to my records. I don't know who you've spoken to, but I want to make one thing absolutely clear – we are stuck with each other for the next eight months, and we both have a job to do. So I'm warning you, stay out of my affairs, and I will stay out of yours.'

The station leader's eyes widen, and her expression hardens. 'What exactly do you mean by—?'

'Oh, go to hell, Sandrine.' I slam out of her office and head for my clinic, passing Alice in the corridor. 'Kate, are you—?'

I wave her away, too choked up to speak. Let myself into my clinic and lock the door behind me, trembling with emotion.

What the hell just happened?

I cross to the medicine cabinet. Without thinking, without leaving any space to talk myself out of it, I remove another packet of Valium, clip off two capsules and swallow the pills with a glass of water. I lean against my desk, filled with shame and indignation and fury.

How dare she?

How dare Sandrine accuse me like that?

I wait for the drug to kick in, for the onset of chemical detachment. The last time, I tell myself, almost believing it. This is the last time.

Extraordinary circumstances.

I turn my mind to Jean-Luc, that vibrant, intelligent human being. Seeing him alive, hearing his voice in those videos, has made that mental image of him out there, suspended in the ice, all the more dreadful.

I have to be certain we're not in danger.

Firing up my laptop, I log into the system, formulating a plan. I'll write down every word of what Jean-Luc said and confront Sandrine with it. To hell with her reaction. Because I know, with a sudden and inexplicable sense of certainty, that something is wrong here.

I navigate to the video logs, click on Jean-Luc's name. Then stare at the screen, heart racing despite the Valium.

His video diaries. All twenty-six of them.

They've vanished.

I click back frantically, and try again. No sign of them. I check other people's files, see all the entries listed as usual.

I sit there, head reeling, but my brain feels sluggish and lazy. *Think*, Kate, I urge myself. Is it possible you accidentally deleted them?

I force my mind back. Exactly what did I do? Closed the last video, clicked out of the file, logged out of the system. I'm positive.

An accident, then? Somehow they've been wiped?

Only one way to find out. I log off, then go and find Rob in the comms room. He's alone, thankfully – no sign of Tom.

Rob gives me a wary look, clearly apprehensive – God only knows what he's heard about last night.

'Can I ask you something?' I point to his screen to indicate it's work-related, noting his expression of relief. 'Some of the video logs appear to be missing, and I'm trying to find out what might have happened to them. Could you check?'

'In the medical system, right?'

I nod. 'Jean-Luc's. I can't see them any more.'

Rob types on his keyboard and calls up a screen. 'Yup. Deleted.'

'Deleted? I stare at him aghast. 'How . . . ? When?' Surely Sandrine didn't have time to do it after I stormed out of her office?

He taps a few more keys. 'Operation performed at 2.18 a.m. this morning.'

'Who deleted them?'

He peers at his screen. 'You did.'

'No.' I shake my head. 'That's not possible. I was asleep.'

Rob shrugs. 'It was done from your terminal, Kate.'

I gaze at him, trying to think, but the Valium isn't helping. 'Are you absolutely sure? It can't be an error?'

'No one else has the permissions. Except Sandrine.'

'And presumably you?'

I see something harden in Rob's expression. 'Yes, and me. But I didn't delete these files, Kate, and I doubt Sandrine did either.'

Then I remember the open door to my clinic. So I hadn't forgotten to lock it after all, I realise with dismay. Someone broke into my office and used my terminal to erase Jean-Luc's video files.

But why?

I can't begin to answer that question, especially not here, in front of Rob. So I pose one instead. 'Are there any backups, do you know? Are they uploaded to UNA in Geneva?'

Rob shakes his head. 'Files are too large. They take up too much bandwidth.'

'So they're gone?'

'I'm afraid so.' He sighs, averting his gaze from mine. Clearly he believes I did this – presumably by accident – and am now trying to cover my tracks.

'Rob, listen,' I lower my voice. 'Please will you do me a favour? Can you not mention this to Sandrine?'

He considers my request. 'Okay.'

'Thanks. I appreciate it.' I turn to go.

'You haven't forgotten about Monday, have you?' he calls after me. 'The decorations, remember, for the party?'

No doubt it's obvious from my blank expression that, yes, I have indeed completely forgotten that this weekend marks the start of the midwinter festivities, and that Rob, Alice and I are supposed to be decorating the common areas – no mean task given the limited supplies to hand.

Hawaiian theme, of all things – the joke being that this place is about as far from a tropical paradise as you can possibly get. My job is to make all the garlands, using paper and string from the recycling bins in Beta.

'Yes, of course. I'm on it.'

'Right.' Rob regards me with an inscrutable expression. 'Just thought I'd check.'

18

20 June

'Kate?'

I spin around, eyes widening with surprise as I clock Tom hovering in the doorway.

'Sorry,' I stammer, trying to swallow the pills I've just removed from the medicine cabinet. Oh hell, did he see me take them?

'Is this a bad time?' Tom's eyes flick to mine, then shift to the mess of paper and string on my desk.

I can't reply. The pills are stuck in my throat. I grab a glass of water from the sink and wash them down, hands trembling from the shock of being caught red-handed. 'Been doing some prep for midwinter,' I croak. 'Have a seat.'

'What are you making?' Tom asks in his flat, slightly formal German accent, as he sits down by my desk.

'Garlands. For the lounge.' I summon up my clinician smile and take the chair opposite. 'So, how can I help?'

Tom sits, dragging his gaze from my inept attempt at crafting to a point somewhere between the floor and my knees, his left leg jiggling nervously.

'I can't sleep,' he says, so quietly I struggle to hear him. 'And I have headaches.'

'Headaches? How often?'

Tom shrugs. 'Most days.'

'Are you taking anything for them? Did you bring any pain-killers out here with you?'

'Only paracetamol. They don't help much.'

'Any other symptoms?' I inquire. 'Visual aura, feelings of nausea, confusion, anything like that?'

'Just the pain. Usually around here.' Tom points to a spot near his temple.

I reach out to touch his head, but he veers away. 'Hey, it's all right,' I say reassuringly. 'I just need to take a look.'

He hesitates, then takes off his glasses and lets me examine his head.

'You've not hit yourself there, had any kind of fall or injury?'

'No.'

'How long have these headaches been going on?'

His eyes rise to the ceiling as he works it out. 'Three weeks or so.'

'And how bad would you describe the pain, on a scale of one to ten?'

Tom presses his lips together as he thinks. 'Five. Maybe four. It's not terrible, more . . . distracting.'

I make a note on my pad before turning back to him. 'Would you mind if we do a quick physical exam? If you lie on the bed, I can check you over.'

'Is there something wrong with me?' he asks, looking worried.

'It's unlikely to be anything serious.' I log into the computer and glance through his notes, checking his recent blood tests – the last one nearly a week ago. 'Everything looks normal, but I'd like to give you a physical exam.'

He climbs onto the bed with a stiff caution. I feel around his neck and torso for any abnormalities. Nothing. I check his blood pressure and pulse rate – both fine. I go through all the motions, more for reassurance than diagnosis – without proper imaging and screening equipment it's impossible to tell if there's some underlying pathology.

Not that I'm particularly worried; like all of us, Tom had extensive medical tests before coming out to the ice – the likelihood of anything serious having developed in the intervening months is low.

'Probably migraines,' I say, once we're seated again. 'Perhaps related to the diet or the altitude. I doubt it's anything to be concerned about. I can give you some stronger painkillers, but be careful not to take more than the prescribed dose.'

Seriously, Kate?

'So you don't think it's a brain tumour then?' Tom's voice is tremulous.

I offer him a reassuring smile. 'Honestly, I seriously doubt it. The chances of that are extremely low indeed. Plus, if that were the cause of your pain, most likely there'd be other signs.'

'Such as?' His tone is wary.

'Sickness, vomiting. Possibly seizures, muscle weakness, other sensory symptoms.'

'Like hearing or seeing things that aren't there?'

I narrow my eyes. 'Is that happening to you?'

Tom's gaze darts briefly to mine as he wipes sweat from his hands on his trousers. 'Sometimes . . .' He falters.

'Sometimes what?'

'Sometimes when I'm outside, on the ice, or when I'm in my room at night, I hear things. See things. Impossible things.'

My attention deepens. With it, a twinge of foreboding. 'Such as?'

Tom swallows again, fixing his gaze now on the scissors on my desk, as if they might leap up and stab him. 'People talking, just out of earshot. Occasionally a dog howling, like it's in pain.'

'You said you see things too?'

He closes his eyes and presses his lips together tightly. For a moment he seems about to cry. 'When I was a child, I had an Alsatian called Lena. Sometimes I see her at the edge of my vision. Or sense her nearby, in the darkness.'

Like my fox, I think, with a small contraction in my heart.

'What happened?' I ask softly, sensing this is not a story with a happy ending.

Tom swipes away a single tear from under his glasses. 'She was run over. My father was speeding down the lane that leads to our house, and . . .' His voice chokes and he looks away. I feel a wave of sympathy. I've heard about his father, a Lutheran mayor in a small town in the Ruhr; apparently he disowned Tom when he came out as gay.

I reach for a tissue and hand it to him. For the first time Tom looks me full in the face, his expression fearful. 'Seeing things, hearing things . . . I thought perhaps it was down to a brain tumour.'

'It must be very distressing,' I say, buying myself a little thinking time. 'And frightening.'

Tom nods, and I consider how withdrawn he's become these last few months. His evident low mood. I'd assumed it was a side effect of winter, the lack of light, the sleep disturbance, but now an altogether more disturbing possibility occurs to me.

Almost as bad as a brain tumour, given my limited ability to treat it here.

'Do you mind me asking if you've been smoking, Tom? Marijuana, I mean?'

He shakes his head emphatically. 'Never.'

I pause, choosing my words carefully. 'Is there any history of mental illness in your family?'

Tom's features stiffen. 'What are you saying? That I'm insane?'

'Not at all. I simply wondered if there was any family history of, say, depression.'

He turns and stares at the black-out blind on the window, as if he can see right through it to the darkness lurking beyond. 'My sister,' Tom says eventually. 'My twin sister was ill.'

'Do you know her diagnosis?'

He inhales, releases his breath slowly. 'Schizophrenia.'

I take this in.

'You think I have it too?'

'I can't say, Tom, but it's a possibility. It would fit the symptoms you've described, and if there's a strong family history, it's something to bear in mind.'

He closes his eyes again, as if to block out both me and the rest of the world.

'But you'll know from your sister's case that there's very good medication now. With treatment, it's a manageable disease.'

We listen to the faint tick of the analogue clock on the wall before Tom finally speaks. 'My sister killed herself,' he says flatly. 'Hung herself by the neck three years ago. It wasn't a manageable disease for her.'

I gaze back at him in shock.

Fuck. I never knew that. Never heard a hint of it around the base – I'm guessing Tom hasn't told anyone. Probably not even the UNA doctors.

My mind reels. How to rescue this situation? I can't help feeling I've blundered again, that I'm not managing this well. I instinctively reach out a hand in sympathy, but his body tenses.

'Listen, Tom.' I withdraw my hand. 'I'll monitor your headaches, and your other symptoms. And in the meantime, if you agree, perhaps we could arrange for you to talk to the psychiatric team at UNA – they can do a more thorough evaluation. More than likely it's simply the effect of being so isolated, of your body clock thrown out of sync by the lack of daylight.'

'But they hate me,' he says abruptly.

'Who?' I ask, taken aback.

'Everyone here. They all hate me.'

'No,' I say quickly. 'That's not true.'

I mean it. Tom's quiet and serious and conscientious, and well liked on the station. He plainly has a huge crush on Drew, who pretends he hasn't noticed and treats Tom with a steady friendliness.

'We all feel like that sometimes,' I continue. 'Everyone cooped up together, little things get blown out of all proportion, people become snappy and irritable. It's easy to feel that everybody's against you, but they're just wrapped up in their own worlds, dealing with their own stuff.'

He blinks back more tears and, without thinking, I kneel down beside his chair and pull him into an unwanted hug. 'I'm so sorry about your sister.' My own voice cracks with emotion. 'But I promise, Tom, that isn't going to happen to you.'

Tom endures the hug for another moment or two before pulling away

'Thank you,' he says as we both get to our feet, then he darts out of the door before I can even say goodbye.

19

21 June

Hell. I examine the sorry little bundle on my cabin desk. The home-made whisky truffles I've made for Rob – the name I'd picked out the hat for the 'secret Santa'– look distinctly underwhelming in the container I've hastily fashioned out of printer paper. Everything about my gift shouts last-minute; despite having a month to prepare, I threw them together this afternoon, unearthing an online recipe and blagging the ingredients from Rajiv.

They'll have to do. No time now to come up with anything else.

I wriggle into my black dress, quickly apply some make-up, adding a touch of concealer to my scar and the dark shadows under my eyes, dusting my cheeks with a liberal application of blusher that only emphasises my pallor.

I check out the effect in the mirror. Definitely a bit Morticia Adams – we should have gone with a Halloween theme; most of us could easily pass as goths or vampires.

Calling into my clinic, I remove a sachet of tramadol from the medicine cabinet, swallow a couple and tuck the rest into my bra. Just to see me through tonight, I promise myself. This much-anticipated dinner marks the winter solstice – as of tomorrow, having endured half our period of total darkness, we'll be officially moving back towards the light.

As good a time as any to turn over a new leaf and kick this habit once and for all.

By the time I arrive in the lounge for pre-dinner drinks, nearly everyone is there. Everyone except Alex, I note – and Tom. I push down my concerns about both and gaze around, impressed with the transformation. Alice has twisted my garlands along strings of tiny coloured fairy lights and hung them across the walls, and dimmed the stark ceiling bulbs with makeshift fabric shades. Large pillar candles complete the effect, softening the harsh contours of the room into something cosier and more intimate. Hawaiian steel guitar music plays softly in the background.

'There you are!' Alice bounds over as I add my gift to the pile on the coffee table. She drapes a lei around my neck and gives me a hug. I'm relieved to see Alex arrive, dressed, like all the men, in a bright Hawaiian shirt and baggy cargo shorts.

Where on earth did they get those? Have they been planning this all along?

'You look nice,' says Alice, approvingly, but I know she's being kind. I admire her bright turquoise blouse and cute yellow shorts, cut high to expose her slender legs and likely driving all the men to distraction – Tom excepted. Sonya, too, has gone with the evening's theme, with a long flowing skirt and a bright lacy crocheted vest. Even Caro has dug out a pair of rainbow-patterned leggings and topped it with another Hawaiian shirt she must have borrowed from one of the boys – it completely hides her swelling stomach. She looks relaxed and cheerful. If she's worried about her pregnancy situation, she's doing a good job of hiding it.

Only Sandrine, like myself, has passed up on the theme of the evening – wearing smart black trousers with a red chiffon blouse and matching lipstick. She catches my eye, her expression blank, then turns away.

I stare at her back, wondering. *Could she be the one who deleted Jean-Luc's videos?*

But why would she? And why do it from my terminal? It doesn't make sense.

Forget it, I tell myself sternly. Enjoy tonight.

Noticing the far wall has been covered in cards and messages, I wander over for a closer look. They're all from the other Antarctic stations – some fifty in total – wishing us a happy midwinter. Most are group photos of the other teams, clustered together on the ice, some waving, all grinning – Rob must have printed them off from various emails. The text underneath is written in half a dozen languages: English, Russian, Spanish, French, German, Japanese, even Chinese.

'Cocktail?'

I turn to find Arne standing behind me, holding out a glass of amber liquid, the rim frosted in sugar, a miniature turquoise parasol leaning on the side.

'Thank you.' I take a sip. It's sweet and fruity with a warm alcoholic kick. 'Mmm . . . what is it?'

'A riki tiki – pineapple and mango juice, with coconut and spiced rum.'

'Wow . . . very tropical.'

'We do our best.'

I nod at the photos on the wall. 'Amazing how many of us there are out here.'

'About a thousand in total,' says Arne. 'Though nearly five times that in summer.'

I imagine them all, like us, celebrating the shift from one season to the next, welcoming our slow but inexorable release from the darkness.

'Did you know midwinter has been celebrated in Antarctica for over a century?' Arne takes a sip from his own glass. 'It's a big deal. When I was at McMurdo it was pretty much a full-on party for a week.'

'Really?'

'Yeah.' He grins. 'We did everything. Costume parties, murder mysteries, games tournaments, drinking competitions, the lot.'

'Sounds like fun.'

'Apart from the hangover. I was in bed for two days afterwards.'

Out of the corner of my eye, I catch Drew watching me. He tips me a wink and I smile back, taking another sip of my cocktail. It really is delicious, and for the first time in days I relax a little. I'm pleased to see Tom, wearing a smart black suit, talking to Sonya. I suppress the urge to go over and give him a hug.

'You look great, by the way,' Arne adds.

I respond with an appreciative smile. I sense people are making an effort to be nice after my showdown with Sandrine three days ago, and I wonder how much they know. Were we overheard? Or have they just picked up on the atmosphere between us?

'You look good too,' I add. 'Where'd you all get those shirts?'

'Kristin sent this one over for me.'

'Your girlfriend?' I'm not sure Arne has ever mentioned her by name – at least not to me.

'Not any more.' He wrinkles his nose and seems a bit embarrassed. 'We split up a few weeks ago.'

I stare at him, surprised. 'Oh shit. I'm sorry.'

'It happens.' He sighs. 'Especially out here. What is it you call them, long-haul relationships . . . ?' Arne looks at me enquiringly.

'Long distance relationships? Though you'd be right about long haul too.'

'Yes, long distance. Well, anyway, they are hard, especially in the Antarctic.' He shrugs. 'It's not as if you can pop home for a visit.'

'All the same, I'm really sorry to hear that. Was it mutual?'

'Mutual?'

'Did you both agree it was the best thing? To split up, I mean.'

'Pretty much. It's normal in Iceland.'

I frown. 'Normal?'

'Women over there aren't so serious, they're more . . .' he searches for the word, 'casual about things. They don't stick around in bad relationships.'

'Was yours a bad relationship then?' I take another sip of my drink – I can already feel the alcohol going to my head, loosening my tongue. 'Sorry, you don't have to answer that. I think I'm a little tipsy.'

Arne smiles at my obvious discomfort. 'Not bad exactly, no. But we'd fallen into a bit of . . .' he sighs, scratching his nose as he searches again for the right phrase ' . . . a bit of a hole. I could have made more effort, I can see that now.'

'Okay.'

'We still like each other, we just don't want to make the kind of commitment you need to take things on to the next level.'

'Kids, you mean?' Christ, Kate, shut the fuck up.

Arne gives me a quizzical smile. 'I guess, though Kristin already has a child. That's one reason we want to stay friends. Margret, her little girl, likes having me around – when I am around, of course. That was a big problem, actually. Kristin felt it's too confusing for her daughter, me disappearing for such long periods. She wants more . . .' He grasps for a word again.

'Stability?' I offer.

'Yes. Exactly that.' He drains the rest of his glass. 'Anyway, how about you? You never talk about your own situation. Do you have someone at home, Kate?'

I shake my head. 'Not any more.'

Arne waits for me to elaborate, and something in his expression tells me he's genuinely interested in my answer. That this isn't just small talk. I have a strange sense that I'm at some kind of crossroads, a chink of light breaking through the gloom that has engulfed my life for the last eighteen months.

A thaw, perhaps, in my icy heart.

I'm about to answer when Rajiv appears, banging a small brass gong. Where on earth did he get that?

'Food is served!' he booms.

The moment is lost, and I've no choice but to trail Arne and the others into the canteen. Drew and Sonya, whose job it was to deck it out, have worked a kind of magic. Fairy lights strung across the walls, pristine white cloths on the tables, and napkins fanned into wine glasses. Candles interspersed with posies of what appear to be fresh flowers.

I peer at them, assuming they're plastic, but find they're actually crocheted with embroidery thread, stalks supported by wire stems.

'Did you make these?' I turn to Sonya, amazed.

She nods.

'Wow, they're incredible.'

'They're not so hard,' she says, nevertheless glowing with pleasure. 'There are lots of patterns on the internet.'

Caro snorts. 'Yeah, I tried a couple. Only mine looked like something a cat might throw up after a banquet of multi-coloured mice. Believe me,' she nods at the posies, 'those take some serious skills.'

Once we're all seated and served with food, Sandrine raises her glass of champagne in a toast. 'Here's to midwinter!' She smiles around at all of us, her gaze sliding quickly over mine.

I ignore the slight, raising my own glass to join the others – all except Caro, who's using migraines as a handy excuse to stay off the alcohol.

'And here's to sun!' says Ark. 'Only fifty more days until we see it again.'

'I'll drink to that,' Sonya adds, and we all take another slug.

That done, we tuck into our food. Rajiv, Ark and Luuk have excelled themselves. Beef wellington for most of us, nut roast for Tom and Alice, the station's two vegetarians. Freshly baked bread with thyme and walnut. And best of all, some of Drew's divine salad with a delicious raspberry balsamic dressing. I eat it in a couple of blissful mouthfuls.

'Wonderful.' I beam at him across the table. 'Great work.'

'Thanks.' He returns my smile, but there's a tightness in it. A little ice of his own. Did he notice me talking to Arne earlier?

Does he think something is going on?

I flash back to that night after the final sunset, our fumbled encounter in that narrow bunk. Feel a renewed sense of shame and guilt.

I shouldn't have done that, and I can't risk making that mistake, I decide, with a surreptitious glance at Arne, who's chatting to Caro and Alice across the table.

However much I might like it to happen.

After the meal, we return to the lounge, stomachs full of fruit tart and Tom's home-made after-dinner mints. 'Gift time,' Caro declares, handing us each our present as we settle in our seats. I examine the pastel stars and flowers stamped in poster paint across the brown craft wrapping paper – whoever made mine has really gone the extra mile.

I watch Rob open his gift first – he seems pleased enough with the whisky truffles, generously offering them around. Then I unfold the pretty paper from my own present. The second I glimpse what's inside I know exactly who they're from. I lift out a pair of exquisite hand-knitted socks decorated with little white snowflakes against a gorgeous sky-blue background. I gaze at them in wonder, then turn to thank Sonya.

'These are just beautiful,' I gasp.

'Try them on.' She nods at my feet.

I slip off my shoes and pull on the lovely socks. They fit perfectly.

'Phew.' Sonya looks relieved. 'I had to guess your size from your boots.'

'Wow, those are gorgeous!' Alice turns to Sonya. 'Would you make me some?'

'My pleasure.' Sonya smiles obligingly, though it strikes me as a big ask; with their tiny, delicate stitches, these must have taken hours and hours.

'Thank you!' I get up to give Sonya a hug. 'I'll treasure these.'

'No more than you deserve,' she replies, patting my hand in a gesture that brings tears to my eyes.

'Okay,' Rob announces, after all the gifts have been opened. 'It's show time!' He disappears for a moment, then wheels in a big flat-screen TV, inserting a DVD into the player beneath. A few people groan – watching John Carpenter's *The Thing* might be an Antarctic midwinter tradition, but some have clearly seen it a few times too many.

'Everyone got a drink?' Drew asks, handing out wine and beer to those who raise their hand. Then Rob dims the lights and settles back in his seat, while Tom distributes the little baskets of toffee popcorn he's made for the occasion.

He carefully avoids eye contact as he hands me mine, I notice – something he's done all evening. Is Tom regretting his visit to the clinic yesterday? Does he blame me for adding to his worries? Maybe I should find an opportunity to take him aside, make sure he's okay.

Not tonight, I decide, chewing my popcorn. I'll catch up with him tomorrow.

Watching the film, I allow myself a rare feeling of content-ment, filled with a good dinner and a sense of . . . what? Family? All the tensions, the rifts, the dilemmas and questions have melted away – for the time being at least. We have endured half the winter, and need only get through another couple of months of darkness before we welcome back the sun.

It is, after all, a significant achievement to have made it this far.

'Refills?' Drew offers, as we take a break halfway through. As I get up to have a pee, I notice Alex slumped asleep on one of the sofas, Caro sitting beside him with her legs tucked up under her and a glass of orange juice in her hand.

'He okay?' I ask her quietly, nodding at Alex.

He opens his eyes at the sound of my voice, then blinks, glancing about as if confused.

'Wakey wakey.' Caro nudges him with her elbow.

He returns her gaze, but there's something unsteady in it. 'I'm going to bed,' he mumbles. 'I feel shit.' He heaves himself to his feet, stands there swaying slightly.

'You want a hand?' Drew gets up to steady him, but Alex waves him away. 'See you in the morning,' he says, staggering off to a chorus of goodnights.

To my relief, Alex's early departure doesn't put a dent in the evening. We watch the second half of the film, then spend several hours telling each other ghost stories. Even Sandrine seems to loosen up as the night wears on, relating a tale of her grandmother, whose house in the Ardennes was supposedly haunted by the ghost of a small girl.

'Every mealtime my grandmother would lay a place for her at the table,' our station leader says, after regaling us with a list of spooky goings-on. 'That way she didn't cause any trouble.'

'Did you ever actually see her?' Alice asks, eyes wide, all her scientific rationalism set aside.

'Only once. I woke up early one morning and caught sight of her out in the garden, sitting on the swing. I knew it was her because she was wearing a white dress.'

'A white dress?' Tom frowns, confused.

'According to village legend she died on the day of her first communion,' Sandrine says solemnly. 'Kicked in the head by a horse.'

We all gaze at our station leader, wondering if any of this was remotely true. Impossible to tell, her face the usual inscrutable mask, giving nothing away.

'I'm too scared to go to bed now,' whispers Caro, with a shiver.

Ark snorts. 'There are monsters, for sure. But not out there, in the dark.'

'What do you mean?' Luuk asks.

'The ones in here.' Ark taps the side of his head. 'Those are monsters you should worry about.'

Sandrine sends him a sharp look, but the others just laugh.

'"Whoever fights monsters should see to it that in the process he does not become one",' says Arne. 'Nietzsche, wasn't it?'

Sonya nods. '"And if you gaze long enough into an abyss, the abyss will gaze back at you." That's the rest of the quote.'

No one laughs at that. A silence descends, and it's obvious why. Everyone is picturing Jean-Luc, their missing colleague, out there in a frozen abyss of his own.

Caro is the first to speak. 'I need to tell you all something.'

Eleven heads swivel in her direction. I glance at Sandrine, who stares at me blankly for a second or two. Of course, we both know what's coming.

Caro's face flushes pink, and I watch her working up the

courage to say the words out loud. Before she can speak, Alice leans over and squeezes her shoulder. 'I know,' she says quietly.

'You do?' Caro's eyes widen.

'You're pregnant.'

Sandrine frowns at Alice. 'How did you know?'

'I've been there.' Alice shrugs. 'I recognise the signs.'

'You're *pregnant?*' Drew stares at Caro, aghast. 'What? When the hell were you going to tell—?'

'She just did,' Arne cuts in.

'It will be fine,' says Sandrine firmly. 'Kate and I are handling the situation.'

'When are you due?' Sonya asks, her forehead furrowed with concern.

'Not for ages,' Caro says evasively, shooting a quick glance at me. 'I'll be long gone, don't worry.'

I glance around at the others. Most are obviously struggling to absorb this news. Only Arne seems to be taking it in his stride.

Did he already know? I wonder. Perhaps Caro is the real reason he split with his girlfriend.

The possibility makes my stomach tighten, and I push the thought away. It's none of my business, I remind myself; my job is simply to keep Caro and her baby safe and healthy.

Drew gets up and helps himself to another beer, then clears his throat. 'Well, here's to his or her good health.' He raises his bottle in a toast to Caro. 'I think you'll make a wonderful mother.'

With a murmur, everyone follows suit, and Caro smiles nervously in return. But it's obvious the news has killed the evening dead. Hardly surprising, I guess, given the circumstances.

'Thanks, guys,' Caro clambers to her feet. 'I should get some rest, but thank you for not freaking out.'

'I'll come with you.' I say my own goodnights, then follow Caro to her cabin.

'Well done,' I say, as she pauses by her door. 'That can't have been easy.'

She shrugs, then lifts her eyes to my face, her expression searching. 'Kate, is this really going to be all right? With the baby, I mean.'

'Of course.' I give her a hug, pushing down my own misgivings. 'You'll be fine, I promise. Now go to bed and get some sleep.'

20

22 June

A noise. Loud and close.

I listen in the twilight of my night light, still half asleep, unsure what it was.

'Kate!' calls an urgent voice, followed by another sharp rap on my door. 'Wake up!'

I glance at the time: 6.02 a.m. What the hell's going on?

'One moment.' I get up and pull on my dressing gown, open the door to Arne, dressed in full outdoor gear, his red down jacket and trousers. Even more incongruous is the look on his face – ashen, stunned.

'What's the matter?' A spike of anxiety focuses my attention. Is there a fire? Has someone been hurt? Oh shit . . . Caro. Has something happened to her and the baby?

'You need to get dressed,' Arne sidesteps my question. 'Quickly.'

I don't move. 'Why?' I insist. 'Tell me!'

Arne leans his forehead against the door jamb in a gesture of pure desperation. 'There's a body outside on the ice.' His voice is stiff and flat, as if he can't quite believe what he's saying. 'Near the tower.'

'A body?' I stare at him, trying to process his words. 'What do you mean . . . who . . . ?'

But the instant I ask, I know the answer. And that I've been waiting for this moment for weeks.

'It's Alex,' Arne confirms. He looks away, blinking, taking a deep breath.

'Oh God.' I stumble backwards into my room, half-winded with shock. 'Are you sure he's dead?'

'We think so.'

I grab my jeans from the back of the chair and put them on under my dressing gown. 'Who found him?'

'Alice.' Arne averts his gaze as I pull on the rest of my clothes. 'She couldn't sleep so decided to go out and release the weather balloon, give Sonya a lie-in. She spotted him on the snow by the tower, and couldn't rouse him.'

I gape at Arne, still struggling to take this in.

'They're carrying him in right now,' he adds. 'You should be ready.'

I nod, following him up the corridor. 'Bring him into the surgery.'

Maybe it isn't too late, I tell myself, as I unlock the clinic door. If he hasn't been out there long, it's possible Alex might still be alive. Seconds later Luuk and Drew loom into view, each holding the end of a stretcher, Sandrine trailing behind. There's an awkward moment as they try to manoeuvre the stretcher through the clinic doorway – no easy feat given the narrow corridor.

No doubt in my mind now. I can tell immediately by his open eyes and the blue tone of his skin that Alex is very, very much dead.

'Put him in the surgery.'

Sandrine waits by my side as they shift his body from the stretcher to the exam bed. In the doorway stands Alice, her arm around a hysterical Caro.

'Let me see him!' she wails between sobs.

'No,' I insist, a little too sharply. 'Caro, you have to let me do what I can.' I turn to Alice. 'Take her into the canteen and make her a cup of tea.'

Alice nods, steering her away by the shoulders. I take a deep breath, then enter the surgery. I gaze at Alex's body, mind numb with horror and grief and regret. My eyes flick to the medicine cabinet, wondering if I could invent some excuse for a minute alone.

'Aren't you going to do anything?' Sandrine snaps, clearly wondering why I'm wasting precious time.

But it's way too late for resuscitation. The angles of the limbs indicate Alex has been dead for a while – rigor mortis, coupled with sub-zero temperatures, has set them rigid.

His face is frozen in an expression of . . . I struggle to name it. Bewilderment. His lips are curled back in a grimace, and his eyes stare straight ahead, as if fixated on some object just out of reach. His hair stands right up from his head, compounding the sense of astonishment.

But that's not the worst of it. There's something even more strange and terrible about the body in front of me. Alex is dressed in nothing more than the thin Hawaiian shirt and shorts he was wearing last night, his feet covered in just a thin pair of socks, almost obscured by compacted snow. I wince at the thought of treading on that remorseless ice with so little protection – the pain must have been excruciating.

Definitely no need to hurry now.

I turn to Drew and Arne, hovering behind us. 'Thanks. I'll handle it from here.' As they file out of the clinic, Arne gives my shoulder a brief squeeze in a gesture of solidarity. Just before they close the door, I catch sight of Tom in the corridor, his expression pitched between fear and confusion.

I turn to Sandrine. 'Do you want to stay and help?'

The station leader nods, lips pursed, her face pale and shocked, and I wonder if she's on the verge of fainting. She wouldn't be the first to be overwhelmed by the sight of a dead body – I've witnessed it plenty of times in med school and in hospital.

'You okay?' I ask, but Sandrine ignores my question.

'Is there anything you can do?' she says, her voice quiet.

I go through the motions of checking for signs of life, feeling for a pulse, shining a light in both eyes to see if his pupils react. Then shake my head.

'He's gone.'

Sandrine sinks onto a chair. Her ice queen façade has vanished. Underneath is a small, frightened woman who is clearly out of her depth. 'How long, do you think?'

'Well, that's something we need to determine.' I examine the rest of Alex's body. His skin has a ghastly white-blue pallor, with clear signs of frostbite on his hands, nose, and toes. 'I'd say only a few hours.'

'I don't understand,' Sandrine whispers. 'He had no reason to go outside during the night.'

I quash the urge to state the obvious – even if Alex had a good reason to leave the base, his lack of clothing tells a different story.

'The cause of death is almost certainly exposure,' I conclude, hiding my own grief and panic behind a well-honed professional demeanour. 'Though I haven't the skills or resources for a full autopsy. But I have to undress him. Can you give me a hand?'

I don't really need her assistance, but I know from experience that staying busy will help her cope with the shock. Together we ease off Alex's clothes. There's a rip in the side of the shirt, I notice, as if the fabric caught on something sharp.

Was it there yesterday night, at the dinner? I don't think so.

I glance at his wrist and realise what's missing – his activity band. He must have taken it off before he left the station.

Nothing significant about that, I guess. I'm constantly reminding people to put theirs back on, after removing it for recharging.

'This is clearly an act of suicide,' Sandrine says, in the tone of someone who's come to a conclusion. Her expression has resumed that blank firmness she adopts whenever she has to deal with anything unpleasant but necessary.

Suicide? Is she right?

Did Alex, who, let's face it, was depressed or unstable – arguably both – decide to take his own life?

I try to imagine the desperation that would drive you to open the outer door, then force yourself to walk into that lethal cold dressed for a warm summer day in Honolulu. How far would you get before the freezing temperatures incapacitated you? The tower is half a kilometre away from Alpha – I'm surprised he made it all that way.

Focus, Kate. Stick to what you know.

I'm about to remove Alex's ice-encrusted socks when there's a knock on the door. Drew's face appears a second later.

'Could you check in on Caro, Kate? She's back in her cabin, but still very upset – they can't calm her down.'

I glance at Sandrine. 'Can you give me ten minutes?'

The station leader nods again. 'I have to contact UNA anyway. You go ahead. I'll catch up with you later.'

I find Caro wedged on her bed between Alice and Sonya, who cradle her as she sobs. Both women look up with relief as I walk in.

'How is she?' I mouth to Sonya, who simply lifts her eyebrows in response.

Not good then.

I consider what to do. Ideally I'd like to see Caro in my clinic, but that isn't possible with Alex's body in there.

'Do you mind if I talk to her alone?' I say to the two women, who nod and rise to their feet. Sonya takes off the beautiful knitted shawl she's wearing and drapes it around Caro's shoulders, then places a motherly hand on mine as she leaves. I must look pretty shaken myself.

I sit opposite Caro. Tears are still streaking down her cheeks. I tear off a few sheets from the roll of toilet paper someone brought into the cabin and hand them to her.

Caro dabs her eyes. I wait for her to calm down enough to speak.

'What happened to him?' she stammers, finally raising her gaze to mine.

I consider how to respond. 'We're not exactly sure. It seems likely that he . . . decided to take his own life.'

Her reaction is so sudden and fierce it makes me start with surprise.

'No!' She jumps to her feet, her expression morphing instantly from grief to rage. 'He would never do that. *Never!*' She towers over me, looking furious.

'Caro!' I stand to face her. 'Calm down. Let's sit and talk this through, okay?'

She hovers, then reluctantly sinks back onto the bed.

'Why do you say that?' I ask gently, as she fights to steady her breathing. I'm beginning to worry for the baby.

Caro exhales. Her voice, when she speaks, is more measured, but equally insistent. 'Alex would never kill himself.'

I pause. 'How can you be certain? Seems to me he's been pretty depressed.'

She fixes her eyes on mine. 'I just know, okay?' A determined jut of her chin. We remain silent for a minute or two before she speaks again.

'Kate. Please tell me . . . how long . . . ?' She stops, swallows. 'How long would it have taken?'

How long would it have taken for Alex to die? I reach for her hand and hold it in mine. 'Not long. Minutes. If that.'

She gazes up at me. 'You sure?'

'I promise. He'd have slipped into a coma very quickly.'

More silence as she takes this in, and I force myself to wonder how quickly, exactly. Five minutes? Ten? Longer?

Caro clears her throat and her next words emerge as a whisper. 'He's the father, Kate.'

I gaze at her. 'Are you certain?' I remember that moment of hesitation when I asked her last week, when she first told me she was pregnant.

She nods.

'Were you and Alex in a relationship?' I recall the many times I've seen them together. Not simply friends after all.

She nods again. 'Since the end of the summer.'

'And does . . . did he know about the baby?'

'I told him about a week ago, after the test. But I think he might have guessed anyway.'

'And how did he react?'

Caro looks up at me, her swollen eyes fierce. 'He was pleased, and relieved when I told him he was the father. He was really happy about it, but he was worried too – about me, how everyone else would react. He didn't want anybody to know, just wanted the two of us to get the hell off this station as soon as we could.'

She drops her head into her hands and emits a long, low wail. 'He asked me to marry him, Kate. A couple of days ago.'

I sit there, stunned at what I'm hearing.

'And you said yes?'

Caro nods, more tears rolling down her cheeks. When she speaks again her words echo my own thoughts: 'Does that sound like someone who's suicidal to you?'

I can't think what to say. I try to work it through logically.

Alex had everything, it seems, to live for. And yet . . . perhaps the stress of knowing he was going to be a father, the worry about his girlfriend being pregnant and perhaps giving birth so far from proper care, might that have exacerbated his mental state? Tipped him over some kind of edge?

'Do you really believe he killed himself?' Caro stares at me, daring me to affirm it.

I hesitate, then decide to change tack. 'Did you see him after he left during the film?' I ask instead.

Caro shakes her head. 'I assumed he'd gone to bed. We always sleep separately,' she adds. 'There's not enough room on these beds for two of us . . . well, three.' She gives a rueful smile, then her chin wobbles and she starts crying again. 'I should have looked in on him, Kate, but I didn't want to wake him up. He was hardly sleeping as it was. Always on the internet, checking stuff.'

'What stuff?'

'He wouldn't tell me. He just said it was to do with Jean-Luc. He . . .' She pauses. 'He was convinced his death wasn't an accident – that's all he'd say.'

'Can you remember *anything* else about last night? Or his behaviour in the last few days?' I feel a lurch of guilt. I should have pushed harder to talk to him, to get to the bottom of what was so troubling him.

Caro mulls it over. 'He said . . . it was a few days ago, when I was urging him to get more sleep, or at least go to you for some sleeping pills . . . he said he was getting closer. I asked him, getting closer to what? Alex promised he'd tell me when he had any evidence that he could take to Sandrine and demand she do something. Until then he said it was better – safer – for me if I didn't know.'

'*Safer?* Was that the word he actually used?'

'Yes. I asked him what he meant, said he was scaring me,

but he refused to say more. He told me his main priority was to deal with it, then get me off the base to have our baby.'

I chew my lip, thinking. We're interrupted by a loud rap on the door. Sandrine pokes her head around, looks at Caro, who refuses to meet her eyes.

'Are you all right?' the station leader asks her briskly. Evidently fully recovered from her shock in my surgery.

Caro makes a visible effort to pull herself together. Sandrine examines her tear-stained face, then turns to me. 'UNA wants to have a word with you, to go over things. My office in five?'

'Okay.' Behind my temples I sense the start of another headache. Along with a bone-numbing tiredness that feels like being crushed under some heavy load.

One thing is clear: this is going to be a very long day.

21

22 June

I'm on a call to UNA for over an hour, giving a preliminary report. It's obvious Sandrine has already filed it as a suicide; after all, no one strips off like that and sets off across the ice by accident.

By the time I return to my clinic, I've developed a thumping headache and a serious craving. I lock the door behind me and help myself to a hefty cocktail of medication from the supplies cupboard, then sit at my desk, feeling shaky, hyper-aware of Alex lying in the adjacent room. I need to write up a full report for UNA, but that means examining him more closely, and right now I can't face it. Though I've seen plenty of dead bodies in my career, the fact that it's someone I have spent so many months with is deeply unnerving.

As a chemical calmness slowly envelops me, I grab my note-book, turn on the camera on my phone, then get to work. I examine the body from head to foot, taking pictures and making notes of anything unusual. I've witnessed several post-mortems in medical school, but never performed one myself.

Stick to the facts, I tell myself. Record what you see.

Even so, I find myself avoiding the startled expression frozen on Alex's face. There's something so horrible about it, the confusion and fear in those rigid, frost-burnt features. My eyes flick towards them, then I have to look away.

What went through his mind in those last few moments of

his life, as the cold bit deep through his skin and shut down all his internal organs? I give an involuntary shudder, imagining him out there, dying alone in the dark.

Enough, Kate. Just do your job.

I check over his body again, noting the temperature of his skin, the continuing rigor mortis. I study the patches of frost erythema on his knees and elbows, reddish purple to violet in tone, similar to bruises.

The ice that had encrusted Alex's socks has now thawed, leaving two small puddles of water on the exam bed. I peel one off, dreading the sight of his foot. Sure enough, its covered in the livid purple and violet discolouration of frostbite.

Despite the soothing effect of the Valium, I wince again. How on earth did he endure the pain of walking almost to the tower in just a pair of socks? What level of desperation would induce someone to do that?

There are easier ways to kill yourself, after all.

Was it possible this was an accident? That Alex left wearing all his snow gear, then somehow got lost, unable to find his way back to the safety of the base? I'd heard of cases of 'para-doxical undressing' where people dying of exposure strip naked, possibly as the result of vasodilation inducing a feeling of overwhelming heat.

Was that what happened here? But surely Alice or Drew or Arne would have found his outdoor clothes somewhere nearby?

I peel off the other sock and inspect his foot, but it looks much like the first.

I close my eyes briefly, trying to ride out a wave of strain and exhaustion. When I open them again, I notice something strange. I bend to examine Alex's left ankle more closely.

What the hell?

At that moment the door opens, and Sandrine walks in. 'What are you doing?' she asks, her tone faintly accusatory.

'Come and take a look at this.' I indicate Alex's leg.

Sandrine peers at it. 'What is it?'

I lift his leg as high as I can, checking underneath. 'See, here.' I point to what appears to be a line of bruising circum-navigating his ankle. Setting his leg down carefully, I check the other. There, more faintly, a similar marking that I missed before, distracted by the patches of frostbite.

'He's been tied up,' I conclude, my voice almost inaudible with shock.

Sandrine stares at me for a few seconds, open-mouthed, then shakes her head. 'It must be from his boots.'

I consider her suggestion. Would snow boots leave that kind of bruising? It's feasible, I suppose; maybe he had a pair that rubbed. I make a mental note to check in the boot room as soon as I'm done, see if I can find any footwear that might have caused these odd markings. Unless, of course, his boots are still out there somewhere, and Drew and Luuk somehow missed them.

I glance at Sandrine. 'What are you going to tell everyone here?' I ask as she heads towards the door.

She turns to face me again. 'Exactly what I told UNA. That Alex was found dead on the ice. Suspected suicide.' Sandrine's tone is curt to the point of rudeness, and she narrows her eyes at me. 'We must not fuel any more gossip and speculation, Kate. We have to get through the next four months. That is of the utmost importance.'

I don't reply. I'm not sure how to respond.

'You understand that, don't you?' she repeats.

I nod, not prepared to argue this out until I've had more time to think. 'We need to get him into a body bag and then cold storage,' I say. 'They'll have to do a post-mortem in the spring.'

'I'll send Arne and Drew to get him, and ask everybody else

to wait in the lounge – no need for the others to see this.' With that, she leaves, closing the door behind her.

I have to be certain we're not in danger.

Jean-Luc's words pop into my head. Is it possible Sandrine is wrong? That Alex's death wasn't suicide? Or an accident.

I study the marks on his ankles again, trying to work it through. If they weren't caused by his footwear, or some other innocuous explanation . . . then what would that mean?

Even assuming he was restrained, how on earth could anybody get him outside? Alex was nearly six foot, and weighed over 180 pounds – too heavy for even someone as strong as Ark to lift unaided. But the idea that two people might have conspired to do this together was too absurd to contemplate.

How might a single assailant disable Alex enough to get him outside? Knock him out? No, there would have been signs of contusion. I've checked his head thoroughly and found no evidence of a blow.

Then I flash back to when I last saw him yesterday evening. *I feel shit.* Alex standing there, swaying, as if drunk.

But did he drink that much? A few glasses of champagne, a couple of beers. I'd noticed he'd cut down recently – understandable, given Alex had learned he was to become a father.

Then I remember my unlocked clinic four days before. I'd checked the medication stocks, but it had been a cursory glance.

Is it possible . . .

Grabbing my keys, I unlock the nearest cupboard, the one with the benzodiazepines, and count the boxes. I turn on my computer and compare the figures against the recorded stock – minus what I've taken myself these last few weeks.

I do the same with the antihistamines, and anything else I can think of that might cause drowsiness. Nothing appears to be missing.

So much for that theory.

I slump onto my office chair. Despite my earlier dose of medication, I feel a dark cloud descend. This is my fault. If Alex killed himself, then I should have stopped him, should have realised how far his state of mind had deteriorated. Insisted on antidepressants, or at least persuaded him to talk to one of the psychiatrists at UNA.

And if he didn't kill himself . . . then I should have listened. Should have done something sooner.

Either way I failed him.

22

2 July

'Whose idea was it to hold the ceremony here?'

Arne stamps his feet as we stand, shivering, in the cold storage room in Beta that's been cleared for the funeral. Against the far wall, resting on a canteen table, is the makeshift coffin Ark and Drew put together from spare pallets in the storeroom, a posy of Sonya's beautiful crochet flowers arranged on top. The sole decoration in this dispiriting location.

'Sandrine's worried about, um, deterioration if we bring him inside,' I whisper glancing round at the assembled crew, all dressed in whatever formal clothes they had to hand. 'He has to stay below freezing until we can ship him out.'

Arne purses his lips but doesn't reply. A moment later, our station leader clears her throat then starts intoning a eulogy from a printed sheet. It's thorough, if uninspired, praising Alex's hard work and dedication, his commitment to the station, to UNA, to the project.

'His family told me he always had an interest in Antarctica, even as a child,' she says. 'He grew up reading about Scott and Amundsen, Shackleton, all the great explorers. It was his life-long ambition to come out here, to experience it all for himself.'

Jesus, I think, remembering Alex these last few months. That dream turned a bit sour on him.

'According to the writer Thomas Pynchon,' Sandrine continues, 'everyone has an Antarctica. On one level or another, we all come here for answers. Not just for science, for the climate, but to discover what lies inside ourselves – and others.'

Arne cocks an eyebrow in my direction, and I suppress an insane urge to giggle at Sandrine's unexpected swerve into philosophy. Or perhaps it's simply tiredness – most of us have slept even less in the ten days since Alex's body was discovered on the ice.

'He was a good man.' Sandrine gives Caro a meaningful glance. 'And would have made a great father. I hope those who love him can take comfort in this, that part of Alex will always live on here, and that he died in the place that meant so much to him.'

The station leader lowers the printed sheet and takes a deep breath. 'Do you want to say anything?' she asks Caro.

Caro shakes her head, swiping at her tears with a tissue.

Thank God, I think, relieved. None of us – particularly Caro – should be standing out here any longer. Already the cold is penetrating my boots and jacket, creeping into my limbs. An unwelcome reminder of how Alex actually died.

After an awkward two minutes of silence around the coffin, we trudge back to the canteen and the buffet lunch Rajiv has laid out for the wake. No alcohol, I notice. Just as well. Why add intoxication to the heady mix of gossip and speculation that has permeated the base since Alex's death?

Indeed, I spot Drew, Rob, and Luuk huddled together in the corner, Tom hovering nearby, appearing slightly lost – I make a mental note to check in on him soon. Drew looks particularly tired, I notice. All this turmoil has clearly taken its toll: bringing in the body, making up the coffin, helping clear out the storeroom for the funeral – he's worked harder than anyone.

Only Luuk seems his normal self, casual, almost unconcerned by the seriousness of the occasion. Though he's toned down the supercilious smirk a notch or too. And brushed his hair.

'Here.' Arne appears beside me, proffering a plate of food. 'Eat, before you collapse.'

I take it obediently. Start on a samosa.

'So, how are you?' he asks. 'I've been wanting to catch up, but you're always busy. Or I am.'

'Just been dealing with stuff.' What with having to provide extensive reports for the UNA medical team, taking care of Caro, not to mention coping with my own shock and grief and abiding sense that I let Alex down, I've barely spoken to anyone since it happened. 'I haven't been feeling that sociable. Sorry.'

'No need to apologise,' Arne mutters, with a quick glance around to make sure we're not being overheard. 'Two deaths. The rest of the midwinter celebrations cancelled. People are starting to believe the station is cursed.'

'Cursed? I thought we were all scientific rationalists here.'

'Not everybody,' he grimaces. 'Besides, since when does that rule out superstition?'

I consider this. Ark has been particularly sombre, muttering to himself in Russian. Rajiv and Alice also seem pretty shaken by recent events, both quieter than usual. Only Sonya retains her steadfast composure, refusing to participate in gossip or conjecture.

'Do you have any theories?' Arne studies me in a way that makes me feel curiously exposed. 'About Alex?'

'Not really,' I reply, dodging the question. Much as I want to open up, to talk to someone and try to make sense of this, I can't risk inflaming the situation any further.

And certainly not here.

Arne raises an eyebrow again. Clearly I'm not very convincing.

I relent, lowering my voice and turning away so no one can read my lips. 'I don't know, Arne. I have no idea what to believe. Sandrine's interviewed everyone. Nobody saw or heard from him after he left the lounge that night. God only knows what happened.'

I've gone over and over it in my mind. Was Caro right when she said Alex would never have committed suicide? Who knows. And those marks on his ankles might have an innocent cause, though an examination of all his footwear hasn't cast any light one way or the other.

Arne sighs. I sense he wants to say something further, but I've had enough. Right now I'm desperate for a couple of pills and a few hours' respite from all this tension.

'I should go check on Caro,' I say, seizing on the excuse – though Alice and Sonya have barely left her side since Alex's death.

'Is she in her room?'

I nod. 'She needed to rest. And warm up. Doctor's orders.'

Abandoning the rest of my meal, I call in at the clinic, swallow a couple of tramadol and throw down a few diazepam as a chaser, then go to knock on the door to Caro's cabin.

'Come in,' says a weak voice.

She's lying on her bunk, still in the black skirt and top she wore for the funeral.

I sit beside her. 'How are you doing?'

Her eyes immediately well with tears. 'Don't ask. Okay?'

She has her hands inside her top, palms pressed flat against her belly. 'Is the baby kicking?'

'Loads this morning. Feels like an internal football match.' She smiles briefly, then her voice chokes. 'I can't believe he never got to feel it too.'

I touch her cheek. There's nothing I can say to that.

Caro rolls onto her side, closing her eyes. 'I don't think I can do this on my own,' she sobs.

'You don't have to. You've got me, and Alice and Sonya. Then when you're home, you'll have all your friends and family.'

She grunts an acknowledgement.

'Have you told them?' I ask. 'Your family?'

'I spoke to them a few days ago.'

'About the baby? Or Alex?'

'Both.'

'What did they say?'

Caro shrugs. 'They're frantic, they want me home. I had to explain again why that wasn't possible.' She sits, pulling down her T-shirt. 'Mum started crying, and then we got cut off. I should try again tonight but I'm not sure I can face it – you know how sometimes it's easier coping with things alone?' Caro glances at me for confirmation. 'You can just about handle your own stuff, but somehow dealing with other people's reactions makes it all worse.'

I nod, absorbing the truth of this. Remembering my own craving for isolation after the accident, how difficult I found it being around my sister, my colleagues, my friends, enduring the constant burden of their sympathy and concern. They meant well, I knew that. They simply cared.

But there were times when it made me want to scream.

'I should give you a check-over,' I say. 'Make sure everything's fine with both of you.'

'It's not though, is it, Kate?' Fresh tears start rolling down Caro's cheeks. 'What are we going to do about Alex?'

I consider pretending I don't understand, but that wouldn't be fair. 'I don't know,' I admit.

'I tried talking to Sandrine. I told her Alex would never kill himself. I told her someone must have done this to him.'

'And what did she say?'

'Nothing, basically. Just that there'd be a full investigation as soon as UNA could get a team out here.' Caro shakes her head again in disgust. 'But what are we supposed to do in the meantime? Whoever killed him is still here. How can we be sure any of us is safe?'

'But Caro . . .' I sigh, voicing the question that's plagued me all week. 'Why would anyone kill Alex?'

'Isn't it obvious?' She stares at me as if I'm slow on the uptake. 'He knew things, Kate. He was digging into Jean-Luc's death. Hell, half the station heard him shouting at you that night in the lounge – everybody was talking about what he said.'

Oh Jesus. Why on earth did I tackle Alex out in the open like that? If Caro is right, if I hadn't gone to him, hadn't asked those questions about Jean-Luc, he might still be alive today. Tears of shame and guilt prick my own eyes, and I turn away, mortified.

'And meanwhile no one's doing anything,' Caro continues, oblivious to my distress. 'Has anyone actually checked the area where they found his body? Did they look for marks in the snow? For clues?'

'Drew and Luuk went back there.' I clear my throat, trying to pull myself together. 'I'll ask them.' Should I mention the bruising on Alex's ankles? I wonder. That rip in his shirt? No. The last thing I want to do is work Caro up any more.

'And what about his activity band?' she asks. 'What was on that?'

'He wasn't wearing it. We don't know where it is.'

'But you can check the data anyway, can't you?'

'I'm trying,' I say. Indeed, I accessed the file yesterday, but couldn't make head nor tail of it. I'll have to get Tom or Rob to help me. But I'll need to be careful; if Sandrine gets wind of me digging around behind her back, I can well imagine her reaction.

Caro leans over and grabs my hand, gripping it tightly in hers. 'I've got to do this, Kate. I have to do it for Alex, but I can't do it on my own. I need your help. Promise you'll help me find out what happened to him?'

I gaze at her, hesitating. Then push down my misgivings. 'I'll chase up the data tomorrow, and talk to Drew or Luuk. But you have to promise me something in return, okay? That you won't go around trying to deal with this yourself. That you'll put your health first.'

She nods, but I squeeze her hand to emphasise my point. 'I'm serious. You've been under a lot of stress, Caro, and it's no good for you or the baby. You must keep that at the fore-front of your mind, because the last thing Alex would want is something bad to happen to either of you. Do you understand?'

Caro hesitates, seems about to object. Then a slump in her shoulders shows me she's relented. 'All right. But tell me the minute you find anything, won't you?'

I nod, at the same time wondering if that's a promise I'm prepared to keep. I daren't risk upsetting Caro further.

Cross that bridge when you come to it, I decide, as I give her a hug and leave.

23

3 July

I spend the rest of the day in bed, lights dimmed, floored by another killer headache that barely recedes even after a double dose of tramadol. Worse than the pain, however, is the accompanying slump in mood. It feels as if I've been living in this claustrophobic little bubble for ever, my previous life dropping away like a dream, leaving a creeping conviction that I may never get out of this place alive.

Irrational, sure. But hard to shake off.

Eventually I fall asleep, and the next morning I've recovered enough to tackle the backlog of work that's accumulated in the ten days since Alex died. I should follow up on my promise to check into the data from Alex's activity band, but first I need to catch up with the weekly blood tests. I start with Alice, who always comes along willingly – none of the usual face-pulling and griping I get from some of the others.

'How are you?' I ask, as I grab the blood pressure cuff.

'Okay,' she shrugs.

The faint bruising under her eyes tells me otherwise, but I don't push her. Like any halfway decent doctor, I know you have to let people come to you, not the other way around.

She glances as the cuff. 'Can we do bloods first? I'd rather get them over with.'

'Sure.'

She sits there, seemingly a world away, as I prep a needle and syringe. 'Can I ask something?' I say, rolling up her sleeve.

Alice nods.

'Would you mind going over what happened when you found Alex?' I get an antiseptic wipe and clean the inside of her elbow.

She winces as I insert the tip of the needle into her pale skin. 'Why?'

'I need to put in a full report for the team at UNA,' I fib, hoping she won't check this out with Sandrine.

Alice turns her head away as I ease the needle into the vein. 'I thought Sandrine already did that,' she says, as I draw back the plunger and the syringe begins to fill with blood. 'The UNA report, I mean.'

'She has, but I have to make sure I've covered everything from a medical perspective.'

Her lovely face remains expressionless as I remove the needle and put a plaster over the tiny wound. Sometimes Alice is impossible to read – no way to tell what she's thinking.

Finally she sighs, coming to a decision. 'Sonya wasn't feeling great when she went to bed that night.' She rolls down her sleeve. 'Too much wine gives her a bad stomach, so I decided to launch the balloon for her.'

'You know what to do?'

'It's pretty simple. Sonya showed me, in case she couldn't do it. How to take the readings too, in the meteorology hut.'

'Isn't that kind of data collected automatically?'

'It is,' Alice confirms, 'but we do manual checks as well to make certain there are no glitches.'

I nod. Sounds reasonable. Half the things we do on the base aren't strictly necessary, but useful for maintaining some sort of routine in the constant darkness. We all find ways to keep ourselves busy.

'So what happened?' I prompt. 'How did you . . . ?' I don't want to say 'find the body'. It seems so stark, so unnecessarily clinical.

'I ran the torch around the ice. I always do.'

No need to ask why. I can relate all too well to that eerie feeling of being out in the darkness, especially when there's no moonlight. The persistent dread that you're not alone.

Silly, yes, but so is most primal fear.

'And that's when you saw him?' I ask her.

'I spotted a dark shape, near the base of the tower. I couldn't tell what it was at first. I walked a little way towards it, before I registered what . . . who . . .' She pauses, swallows. 'I tried to rouse him, then radioed for help. But no one picked up, so I had to go back. There was snow drift on him, you see. So I knew . . .' Her cheeks flush, and she clears her throat. 'I knew he'd been out there for some time and there wasn't anything I could do.'

She glances at me for confirmation that she did the right thing.

'He'd been dead for hours,' I say. 'You have nothing to blame yourself for.'

Alice's face relaxes a little. She's been afraid that I – and everyone else – have been judging her I realise. No wonder she was reluctant to talk.

'Did you notice anything else?' I ask. 'Any tracks in the snow?'

She shakes her head. 'But it was quite breezy, any tracks would have been covered quickly. I could barely see my own on the way back to the station.'

'Nothing out of the ordinary?'

Alice ponders my question as I retrieve the blood pressure monitor and attach it to her arm. 'Apart from the fact he was, you know, wearing so little.' Without warning, her face crumples and she starts crying. 'It was awful, Kate,' she sobs, 'seeing him lying there like that, virtually naked, frozen. I can't sleep for thinking about it.'

I pull off the arm cuff and hand her a tissue, mentally admonishing myself. The poor woman is traumatised, and who can blame her? I should have caught on to it sooner – made sure she was coping.

I must check up on Drew, I think. Luuk too. Retrieving the body probably shook both of them up, and the effects of trauma can take a while to emerge.

'It must have been terrible,' I say soothingly to Alice, imagining how terrifying it was to be alone out there on the ice, confronted with the dead body of a colleague. 'But honestly, Alice, there's absolutely nothing you could have done.'

She nods, takes the tissue, and wipes her eyes.

'Stop by here later, okay?' I tell her. 'I'll give you a few sleeping pills so you can get some proper rest. And if you need to talk, you know where I am.'

She gives me a grateful hug. 'Thanks, Kate.'

I find Drew in the gym, running full pelt on the treadmill, headphones in his ears. I move to the front of the machine and give him a wave.

'Kate.' He slows the pace to a walk and returns my smile. 'You okay?'

I nod. 'Can we talk?'

'Sure.' He turns off the treadmill and dismounts, breathing hard as he towels down his forehead and neck. I marvel again at what good shape he's in despite his evident exhaustion; while many of us are looking distinctly frayed around the edges, Drew still appears as healthy and fit as the day I met him.

'What can I do for you?' He takes a long slug of water from his flask. Stands there, appraising me while I run through the same routine as with Alice. But Drew has nothing to add to her account.

'You didn't see anything unusual? Even when you went back out later with Luuk?'

He shakes his head. 'Why are you asking?'

'Just trying to build up a picture, a timeline. When a body is that . . . frozen, it can be hard to pinpoint the time of death. If you'd noticed any unusual tracks, we might be able to work out from the level of snow drift, how much they were covered, approximately when he went out there.'

'That figures. I should have checked when we reached Alex. I mean, we – Luuk and I – all we were thinking was to get him inside asap. In case there was something that could be done. I should have thought of it though. I'm sorry.'

'Of course. Don't blame yourself.' I nod, then take a breath. 'So do you have any theories about what happened?'

He shrugs. 'I guess I agree with Sandrine. Seems like suicide.'

I gaze at him, wondering what to say. In the face of Drew's confidence, I'm starting to think both of them are right. What if Alex was more troubled than Caro realised? What if those marks on his ankles have some completely innocent explanation?

'Why?' he asks, frowning. 'Do you disagree?'

'No,' I say a tad too quickly. 'I just want to be certain we're not overlooking anything, that's all.'

Drew regards me steadily. 'Actually, I've been wanting to talk,' he says gently. 'I'm worried about you. You all right, Kate?'

'Yes. I'm fine.'

Drew studies my face, as if he doesn't believe me. 'Don't take this the wrong way, but you seem kind of . . .' He doesn't finish the sentence.

'Kind of what?'

He shrugs. 'Overwhelmed. Like you've got the whole world on your shoulders.'

Drew's right, of course, and for a moment I'm tempted to open up and share my misgivings over what happened to Alex. I am desperate to talk to someone other than Caro, to work out whether her suspicions are justified or if she's mistaken.

He takes a step forward. For a second I'm sure Drew's about to try to kiss me again, but he simply peers into my eyes. 'Listen, you can talk to me any time. Remember that.'

He pauses, rubs the stubble on his cheek as he grasps for the words. 'I . . . I really don't want what happened between us to get in the way of our friendship. I don't want you feeling you have to keep your distance. I understand totally why you didn't want things to go any further. You were right. Relationships in this place,' Drew gestures around him to indicate the whole station, 'are a really bad idea. I get that, Kate. But we all need people to confide in – that's all I'm saying.'

He wraps an arm around my shoulder and squeezes me into a hug. I don't pull away. I'm grateful for what he said, for reassuring me that we're still friends.

'Thanks, Drew.' My voice breaks a little as he releases me. 'I really appreciate that.'

A big grin cracks his face. 'No worries, kiddo,' he says, ruffling my hair. 'Any time.'

24

3 July

'You got any particular reason for wanting to see this?'

Rob glances around, as he sits at my screen in the clinic. While he's dressed in his usual uniform of tight black T-shirt and jeans, I notice he's stopped bleaching his hair and dark roots are beginning to show.

'Due diligence,' I say ambiguously. 'I have to submit a medical report to UNA about Alex's state of mind in the run-up to his death.'

This isn't entirely true – I've already debriefed at length to the psychiatrist in Brussels, Johan Hanner. It was an excruciating interview. I couldn't shake off the sense that I'd failed, that if I'd intervened earlier or more forcefully, Alex would still be alive.

If Hanner came to any conclusions, he wasn't sharing them with me. Nor have I heard back from the medical team about the pictures I'd sent of those obscure marks on Alex's ankles.

'Right . . .' Rob clicks on what appears to be some kind of map . . . a series of coloured dots set against a flat plan of the base. The dots zigzag backwards and forwards all over the place. Impossible to work out what's going on.

'This shows all the available data on Alex's movements for his last twenty-four hours,' Rob explains. 'What do you want to know?'

Isn't it obvious? I bite back my irritation. 'Can you narrow down the time frame to that evening?'

Rob taps on the keyboard. Most of the dots disappear. I peer at the screen, trying to make sense of the rest. 'Are these tracks?'

He nods.

'Is there any way of knowing when they occurred?'

'One sec.' Rob clicks a few more things and time stamps hover over each dot. 'Here he was from 7.24 p.m. to 10.41 p.m., first the canteen, then the lounge.

'And then?'

Rob studies the data. 'Looks like he went to his cabin and stayed there.'

'Can you check his heart rate?'

Rob brings up another screen. I study the graph. Alex's pulse rate drops, shortly after returning to his room, most likely indicating he's fallen asleep. Then spikes again suddenly a couple of hours later – but only for a few minutes.

I frown, puzzled. 'What's the latest data point you have for him?'

'2.53 a.m.'

'And nothing after that?'

Rob shakes his head. 'That's the final record from his band. Or at least when it last synced with the main system.'

'How often does it do that?'

'They're set to upload every two hours – or as soon as it can connect with the station intranet.'

'So if we can find his band, it might have unsynced data?'

'It's certainly possible.' Rob swivels in the chair to look at me. 'I hear he wasn't wearing it when he was brought in.'

'No, he wasn't,' I confirm. No point lying about it.

'What do you think he did with it?'

I consider this. To be honest, I haven't given the lost activity band enough thought, too caught up with the immediate after-math of Alex's death.

So what happened to it? I ask myself now. If Sandrine is right, and he committed suicide, why would Alex bother to remove it? Even if someone realised he was missing, there was little chance they'd go to all this trouble to track him down.

Besides, asks a voice in my head, who falls asleep shortly before they kill themselves? Surely anyone that distressed would find rest impossible?

Caro's right. Nothing adds up – at least in Sandrine's version of events.

I gaze at my computer. What if somebody removed Alex's band and destroyed it, precisely because they didn't want any proof of whatever occurred in those last minutes of his life? I think of Alex's torn shirt, the ligature marks on his ankles – all evidence of some sort of struggle, which might well have shown up in the data.

Like the sudden spike in his heart rate – consistent with someone entering his room and unexpectedly rousing him from sleep.

Cette pauvre fille.

That poor girl. Jean-Luc's words fill my head. What was it Alex said, that night I tackled him in the canteen. That the doctor was upset about some woman who lost her life on the ice.

Three people, I think, who've died out there. Three people with question marks over their deaths. Antarctica is a dangerous place, no doubt about it. But this seems to be adding up to a whole lot more than coincidence.

'Anything else you want me to do?' Rob's voice pulls me back.

I inhale, releasing my breath, trying to hide my mounting unease. 'What about that night . . . could you access the data for everyone, see if there's anything unusual?'

'Unusual how?' Rob frowns.

'I don't know. I just want to check.'

He sighs, clearly wondering where I'm going with all this. 'Okay, but some people remove their activity bands at night, so you won't get much in the way of data there.'

Rob's right. Despite urging everyone to keep them on for the sake of the sleep data, compliance has pretty much dropped through the floor. I can't blame them. The plastic bands can irritate the skin, and people are always complaining they make their wrists sweat.

'Sure. But would you mind having a look?'

Rob clicks his way into yet another screen, studying it carefully. I wait as patiently as I can. It's been three hours since my last dose, and the urge for a top-up is getting harder to ignore, a growing itch I'm desperate to scratch.

'What is it?' I prompt after a minute. Rob is gazing at the screen with an air of confusion.

Reluctantly he twists it into my view. I recognise the same flat plan as earlier, zoomed in on the sleeping quarters. 'This is Alex's room again, at 2.15 a.m. You can see the signal for his tracker here.' Rob points to a clump of dots concentrated on the bunks in the corner of the cabin. 'If we scroll forwards several minutes, you'll notice a second signal.'

I feel my own pulse start to race as another series of dots appears in the corridor. A moment later they centre right in Alex's room.

'Whoever it was stayed for . . .' Rob clicks the screen shot forwards slightly. 'Three minutes and thirteen seconds.'

My breath catches. 'Who was it?' I ask.

Rob looks strangely embarrassed. I watch him hesitate, on the brink of indecision, and I wait for him to refuse, to tell me I'm crossing an ethical line.

But finally he answers. Just one word. A name.

'Luuk.'

25

3 July

It takes an age to track Luuk down. In the end, Sonya tips me off, after I've hunted all over the station, including every workshop and storeroom in Beta.

'You tried the igloo?' she asks, as I catch her emerging from the boot room.

'The igloo?' I echo. 'Why would he be in there?'

Sonya shrugs. 'A hunch.'

'Thanks,' I say, heart sinking. 'I'll take a look.'

'You want me to come with you?'

I consider her offer. It would make sense. Not simply because I'm scared of venturing out by myself into the dark, but because confronting Luuk alone in a remote location away from the base might not be the best idea in the world.

'It's okay. I know the way.'

Sonya's gaze lingers. 'You shouldn't go out there on your own, Kate.'

I stare back at her. What does she mean? Is she referring to the outside? Or is she suggesting Luuk might really present some kind of danger?

'I'll be fine,' I assure her, endeavouring to sound more confident than I feel. 'I won't be long. And you know where I'm going.'

'Okay,' she says, heading off towards the canteen. 'But don't forget to take one of the walkie-talkies out with you.'

*   *   *

I call into my clinic after kitting up in my thermals, help myself to a sizeable dose of Valium to calm my nerves. All the same, as I pull on my outdoor gear in the boot room, I'm swamped by feelings of dread. I've avoided going anywhere outside on my own since that incident with the aurora, and the closer I get to stepping back into that darkness, the more anxious I feel.

I can't dispel that image of Alex. The look frozen on his face.

Gritting my teeth. I stuff a walkie-talkie into my goose-down jacket. I grab one of the larger flashlights, then squeeze a smaller torch into my pocket for good measure; if I lose one, I'll have the other for backup.

Bracing myself for the shock of cold air, I open the door and carefully descend the steps to the ice. It's only when I reach the bottom that I realise I'm not actually certain how to get to the igloo. At least not in the dark. Drew and I usually do the snow samples just beyond the western perimeter of the station, but the igloo lies somewhere between the meteorology hut and Gamma. In daylight I'd have no problem finding it, but in pitch blackness?

I stand there, heart picking up speed, shining my torch out into the darkness. There's no moonlight, just black space. This is stupid. I should go back inside and tell Sonya I've changed my mind, that I'd like her to come with me. Or ask Arne or Drew to give me a lift on a skidoo.

But I need to talk to Luuk alone, with no danger of being overheard. The last thing I want to do is add fuel to the perpetual game of Chinese whispers that pervades the station, exacerbated now by Alex's mysterious death.

I hesitate, cursing myself. Why didn't I learn how to drive a skidoo? Arne offered to teach me, Drew too, but I always made excuses; truth is they make me nervous. I've heard too many stories of snowmobiles overturning, trapping their riders underneath.

Being imprisoned for two hours in an upturned car was enough for one lifetime.

Steeling myself, I set off in what I'm praying is the right direction, using the guide ropes to steer towards Gamma. The urge to turn around and hurry back to safety increases with every fumbling step. Even the sound of my own breathing, louder as I leave the vicinity of the base, unnerves me.

I feel as if I am venturing into the void.

After a few minutes I pause, trying to steady my ragged breathing, and slow my racing heart. I inhale deeply, forcing myself to calm down. But I can't stand still for long. Already the cold is penetrating my thick layers of clothing, making my skin tingle and my muscles ache. I try not to think about Alex being out here virtually naked, and focus instead on Luuk.

Why was he in Alex's cabin that night? And why not admit it to Sandrine, when she interviewed everyone last week? The very fact that he's prepared to lie – or at the least hide the truth – is undoubtedly a red flag.

You could always take this to Sandrine yourself, says a voice in my head. Let her deal with it. Leave her to question Luuk again.

But I don't trust her, I realise, flashing back to when we examined Alex's body; her rush to the conclusion of suicide, despite those strange marks on his ankles. My sense is that our station leader wanted to wrap the whole thing up neatly and quickly, that more than anything she abhors loose ends.

And this is most definitely a loose end.

Suddenly my hand hits empty space as I run out of guide rope. I stop again, peering into the dense blackness beyond my torch beam, trying to stay calm.

You can do this, says my inner cheerleader. What was it Roosevelt said? You have nothing to fear except fear itself.

I take another deep breath and strike out in what I hope is the right direction, ice crystals crunching beneath my boots. Enclosed in the tight hood of my parka, the noise of my pulse pounding in my ears, the jagged sound of each exhale as I propel myself into the night, is almost deafening.

But the further I go, the more terrified I become. I can't shake off a persistent nameless dread that something lurks in the surrounding darkness. That I'm not alone. I constantly fight the urge to spin around and check behind me.

'Get a grip!' I hiss to myself, out loud this time, my hand aching from clutching my torch so tightly. Like Ark said, the monsters are only in your head.

They're not real.

To my immense relief, I finally spot a white dome looming in the distance. I hurry towards it, stumbling on the uneven ground. As I reach the igloo, I see one of the skidoos parked outside, a faint light glowing through the large blocks of ice that make up the walls. Several red jackets lie on the ground, looking eerily like patches of blood against the white of the snow.

I pause again, feeling another sudden, irrational surge of apprehension. Anyone might be in there. And what if they resent the intrusion?

Don't be ridiculous, Kate.

I switch off my torch and approach the arched entranceway. Pushing on the makeshift wooden door, I stand gawping at the spectacle before me: Luuk and Ark, both stripped naked to the waist, sprawled on what looks like a pair of sun loungers. A fierce heat blasts from two paraffin heaters running at full tilt in the tiny space, only a small hole in the roof to vent the fumes. A couple of kerosene lamps provide a cosy orange glow.

'What the fuck?' Luuk stares at me aghast, quickly dropping something onto the ice and crushing it under the heel of his boot. It doesn't take a genius to work out what it was. The stench of marijuana hangs heavy in the air, thicker even than the smell of paraffin.

'Kate,' beams Ark, as I remove my goggles. 'How nice you join us.' He grimaces as a large drop of water drips from the ceiling, hitting him on the nose.

'Actually,' I say, voice stammering with cold and surprise, 'I was after Luuk.'

Ark raises an eyebrow. 'You lucky then – I leave anyway.' He heaves himself to his feet and pulls on his thermal top, picking up a torch from beside his chair. 'Have a seat.' He gestures towards the lounger as he squeezes past me. 'I walk to base,' he says to Luuk.

Luuk doesn't move, just scowls in my direction as Ark disappears into the night. I can't see his pupils, but I'm guessing he's pretty high.

I hesitate. Should I return with Ark? Postpone my talk with Luuk until he's back at Alpha?

No, I decide. Now or never.

'What's this about?' he asks with a wary expression.

'I wanted to ask you something.'

'Couldn't it wait? Seems a fuck of a lot of effort, coming out here.'

'No, it couldn't. I need to go over a few things before I close my report to UNA.'

Luuk narrows his eyes at me, waiting for me to go on.

'You went with Drew to check the area where Alex was found, didn't you?'

He nods.

'Did you notice anything?'

'Such as?' No mistaking the hostility in his tone.

'Such as any clues as to how he died.'

'Nothing at all. We checked everywhere, even around the tower.'

'So you couldn't see his tracks in the snow?'

Luuk shrugs in that offhand way of his. 'Lots of tracks around there, Kate. People go out to Omega all the time.'

He has a point. I draw a deep breath and press on. 'I was going through the activity band data earlier . . .' I pause, watching his expression carefully, but nothing alters, 'and I noticed you were in the vicinity of Alex's room that night.'

'That night. You mean the night he died?'

I nod. 'Around two in the morning. We can't be certain of the exact time of death, but you may well have been the last person to see him alive.'

Luuk digests this, his face blank. I wait for him to speak, but there's nothing.

'So I'm wondering, how was he? When you saw him.'

A small smile plays across Luuk's lips, gone in an instant. 'Don't you mean, Kate, that you're wondering what I was doing there?'

'That too,' I admit.

Luuk leans back in the lounger. 'Why don't you sit down,' he says, rubbing his face as he thinks.

'I'd rather stand.' In truth, the heat inside the igloo is so cloying I'm reluctant to venture any deeper. Plus I want to stay close to the exit.

Just in case.

'Okay,' Luuk sighs. 'Straight up, I went to his cabin to borrow his vape pen. I couldn't find mine and I needed a smoke. Also, I was concerned about him. He seemed really out of it when he went to bed; I wanted to make sure he was okay.'

'How long were you in his room?'

'Don't you already know?' he sneers. 'From the data?'

I don't reply. Simply wait for him to speak.

'It occurs to me, Kate, to ask how, exactly, any of this is your business? How is this relevant to your medical report?'

I take off a glove and wipe sweat from my forehead. 'I'm the station doctor, Luuk. Alex is dead, and I'm trying to piece together why. How is that not my business?'

He regards me for a moment. 'I was there about five minutes, okay. He didn't answer the door when I knocked, so I opened it, called his name. Alex barely responded, just grunted. He was completely out of it – I assumed he'd taken something, sleeping pills perhaps.' Luuk looks at me inquiringly but I don't respond; Alex had consistently refused medication. 'So I had a good look around, found his vaper in a drawer.'

'You took it?'

'Yeah.' Luuk shrugs again. 'I figured he wouldn't mind. I've done him enough favours on that score.'

'Such as?'

'Sharing my stash, that kind of thing.' His expression is challenging, as if goading me to recite UNA policy on illegal drugs.

'I'm not here to judge, Luuk. But equally I'm not convinced that giving Alex marijuana was doing him a favour.'

'Why?'

I sigh. 'Alex seemed troubled by things. You might even say paranoid.'

Luuk snorts. 'And you blame the drugs?'

'Chances are it didn't help.'

Anger flashes across Luuk's face, and his jaw tightens with emotion. 'Let's get this clear. Are you actually *accusing* me of anything, Kate?'

I consider this. *Am I accusing him of anything?* I'm not sure.

'I just want to understand what happened to Alex, that's all. I owe him that much. We *all* owe him that much.'

Luuk's eyes flick to the ceiling of ice right above our heads.

Suddenly his shoulders slump. 'I don't know,' he says quietly. 'I've no clue what to think, but I can't believe smoking a bit of skunk is what killed him. Besides, he hadn't done it for ages. Jean-Luc didn't approve, and Alex thought our late doctor was God, basically.' He sighs. 'Struck me as a shame; if anything, the weed helped mellow him out. He had some pretty strange ideas.'

'Such as?'

'That there was someone dangerous on the station. Someone we couldn't trust. He claimed Jean-Luc was on to them.'

'He talked to you about that?' I frown with surprise.

'A bit. Until Jean-Luc convinced him I was a health risk. We were quite friendly before that.'

'Did Alex say anything else? About what Jean-Luc was investigating?'

Luuk shakes his head. 'I tried to tease it out of him a few times when we were alone, before he went all abstinent on us, but he clammed up.' He leans forward and scratches his beard. 'To be truthful, I didn't think that much about it. People say some pretty stupid stuff when they're high, you learn not to take it too seriously. Plus Alex was . . . well . . . all that crap about Jean-Luc being murdered. You saw what he was like – he wasn't right in the head.'

'So what do you think happened to him then? Alex, I mean.'

Luuk ponders my question. 'I have absolutely no idea. Maybe he simply lost it. Decided he'd had enough. He wouldn't be the first, for sure – this place can drive you seriously fucking crazy.'

With that he gets to his feet. 'I'll give you a lift back to Alpha.'

'It's fine. I know the way.'

Luuk raises an eyebrow. 'Like after the aurora? Don't be silly, Kate.'

I ignore the jibe, wondering what I can do to prolong this conversation. I can't help feeling there's something Luuk is hiding. That I've not been asking the right questions. Including one lurking in the back of my mind.

Has Luuk ever been in my room as well?

Don't go there, Kate, warns a voice in my head. No point in antagonising him further. Plus his explanation for being in Alex's cabin seems plausible enough.

'Okay,' I say, admitting defeat. 'Let's go.'

26

4 July

'Kate, can I speak to you?'

Sandrine's face appears at her door as I walk past her office, on the way to Skype my sister. How the hell does she do that? I wonder, as I follow her inside. There's no way she can see who's in the corridor from her desk.

Does she recognise our footsteps? Some lingering scent? Or perhaps there's a hidden camera out there?

Don't be silly, Kate. That really is paranoid.

Sliding behind her desk, Sandrine eyeballs me. 'This is becoming something of a habit, isn't it?'

'What is?'

'These conversations. Me having to ask you what exactly you're doing. I heard you've been talking to several members of my team.'

How on earth does she know that? I feel a small, childish twinge of betrayal. Did Luuk or Alice say anything? *Drew?*

'Do you want to explain to me why?' Sandrine prompts.

'I have to make sure I've got a full picture of the circumstances of Alex's death.' I return her icy stare. 'As the station doctor, it's my responsibility to ensure I've investigated every possibility – especially given there won't be an autopsy for months.'

This is a stand-off, I realise. One colleague challenging another's authority, and her hostile expression tells me Sandrine's as aware of this as I am.

'Your job as station doctor is to treat the living, not stir up rumours about the dead.'

'It is my job,' I say slowly, 'to be responsible for the welfare of everyone here. I need to make sure I haven't overlooked anything. I'm being thorough, Sandrine.'

'Why did you send those pictures to UNA? Of Alex. We didn't agree to that.'

'Those marks on his ankles, you mean?' Too much ice in my tone, but I don't care. I'm swept along in an upsurge of anger and frustration. 'You dismissed them, Sandrine. You simply assumed his death was suicide. You haven't made any effort—'

'Don't you think, if UNA had any concerns, you'd have heard back by now?' the station leader cuts in.

I pause, considering. 'I need to be certain,' I add, knowing I've lost the argument.

Sandrine inhales, is about to respond when her radio beeps. She listens for a few seconds, then speaks into the microphone. 'I'll be there in a moment.'

She glances at me. 'I have to go. We'll discuss this further, Kate, but in the meantime, I want you to keep your speculations to yourself. No more stirring things up, am I clear?'

She reaches into the cupboard behind her desk and grabs a set of keys, then sweeps past me.

I stand there, feeling stung. Out of nowhere the past slams up to meet me: Ben and I arguing in the car. The woods, the rain.

'You're breaking up with me.' A statement, not a question. One he doesn't contradict.

The pain. The humiliation. How did I not see this coming?

Not now, Kate, I tell myself firmly, taking a deep breath. Not now.

I turn to leave. Then hesitate. Glancing at the cupboard

behind Sandrine's desk, I notice that in her hurry she's left it open. Inside are all the master keys to the base.

I check the door, listening. No footsteps or voices.

I go behind the desk and search for the locker keys. There, hanging by a ring, is one with 'JL – Locker 9' pencilled on the tab. I snatch it off the hook and put it in my pocket.

How long have I got? I've no idea who radioed Sandrine or why, but clearly it's urgent enough to require her immediate attention. Hopefully she'll be some time.

I quickly formulate a plan as I hurry towards the lockers in Beta. I locate number nine and open it. Leaving the door slightly ajar, I rush back to Sandrine's office and knock gently.

Silence.

I go inside and return the key to the cabinet, heart racing at the thought of her walking in and catching me in the act.

Back in the safety of my clinic, I lock the door behind me and lean against it, trying to get my breathing under control.

Shit. *What did I just do?*

Never in my whole life have I done something this dodgy – unless you include writing all those prescriptions for myself after the accident.

There's no doubt in my mind that I've crossed a line. Asking a few questions of the other winterers is one thing, stealing keys and breaking into a private space entirely another.

And it's not as if I'm immune from discovery. If anyone notices that open locker, they'll report it to Sandrine, and she'll guess immediately it was me. I glance at the activity band on my wrist, thinking of the diagram Rob showed me of Alex's movements in the station; the same could just as easily be done for me.

How could I possibly explain myself?

I'm not even sure I can explain it *to* myself. It was pure impulse – I saw an opportunity and seized it.

Suddenly I'm overwhelmed by a crippling attack of anxiety. What the hell am I doing in this place? I think, as my legs buckle and I sink to the floor.

The world spins. Trees and road and sodden earth. Mayhem followed by silence.

I squeeze my eyes shut, force it all back down. I have to pull myself together.

Then, as now, what's done is done.

No going back.

27

5 July

I wait until three in the morning before leaving my cabin. Not that it guarantees much. These days you can encounter anyone in the dead of night, given half the crew is now leading a bizarre, nocturnal existence.

I'll have to take my chances; if I bump into somebody, at least they won't find it odd that I'm up and about.

Retrieving the tiny flashlight from my bedside drawer, I down enough medication to calm my nerves but leave me alert, then venture towards Beta, taking the rabbit warren of corridors that leads to the equipment store. My hand reaches automatically for the switch, but I think better of it – why risk somebody seeing the light under the door?

I use my torch instead to navigate to the locker containing Jean-Luc's belongings. Find, to my relief, it's still open.

So far, so good.

Shining my light inside, I see several large black plastic bags stacked at the bottom. I wonder again why this stuff wasn't returned after Jean-Luc died. What possible reason would Sandrine have for hanging on to it?

The same one, I guess, that prompted her to keep that letter.

I open the nearest and take a closer look, the clothes inside releasing a faint odour of expensive aftershave. My discomfort grows. This feels wrong, an invasion of a dead man's privacy. God knows Jean-Luc had little dignity in death, suspended head first in the ice, and now, here I am, poking around his things. Should I really be doing it?

I pause, picturing the doctor's face in those videos. His tense, anxious concern for everyone's safety.

What would Jean-Luc want me to do?

Exactly this, I decide, forcing myself on. I check inside the other bag. More clothes, and two books, both in French, one novel and a slim volume of poetry. A hair brush and various toiletries, but no sign of a notebook, or anything Jean-Luc might have used as a journal.

I peer at the shelf above. Find a jumble of personal belongings, including several unopened packets of mints and an assortment of pens. I spot a photo frame and lift it down, shining my torch on the front. A picture of the doctor with a pretty woman with a halo of chestnut hair, who I assume is his wife, flanked by two small boys, both beaming at the camera. Judging by Jean-Luc's dark hair and unlined complexion, this was taken some time ago, but all the same it gives me an ache of sadness. I think of that family in France, this woman widowed, his sons now fatherless. Probably still in the first ravages of grief.

I remember my own pain at losing my father. That feeling of being rudderless, cast adrift. Up until his death I hadn't appreciated how much I needed him to be here in the world, a buffer against misfortune. A steady presence in my life.

The sight of those boys renews my resolve. What I'm doing may not be right, but it's not as wrong as doing nothing at all – whatever Sandrine may think. If Alex's theory was correct, if Jean-Luc's death was no accident, then I owe it to his family to get to the truth.

Replacing the photograph on the shelf, I shine my torch around one last time to make sure I haven't missed anything. No laptop, or notebook.

I push the locker door shut, praying nobody will discover it's unlocked before I can retrieve the keys again to secure it. Then let myself out of the storeroom, creeping back to the sleeping quarters.

A moment later I turn a corner and collide into a large male body. I give a squeak of alarm, jumping backwards.

Tom peers at me through the low-level lighting that illuminates the base at night. Or rather he's looking slightly to the side of me, eyes refusing to meet mine, making him seem furtive and shifty. 'Sorry,' he mumbles.

'You okay?'

'I was going to the canteen. For a sandwich.' He finally meets my gaze. 'Where are you going?'

Heat rises to my cheeks. 'The soap's run out in our bathroom,' I improvise. 'I went to get some from the store.'

Tom looks confused. 'So what happened?'

'Sorry?'

'The soap.' He gestures at my empty hands. 'You haven't got any.'

I gawp back at him, mind blank. 'I remembered I had some in my room.'

'Okay.' Without another word, Tom heads off towards the canteen.

I stand there, feeling panicky and stupid, imagining Ben's reaction had he been here. I picture the way he'd roll his eyes whenever I did something foolish – or pretty much anything he disagreed with.

Silly Kate.

I wait until I'm sure Tom isn't coming back, then hurry to the sleeping quarters. Skirting past my own room, I slip into Alex's, shutting the door quietly behind me, turning on my little torch instead of the overhead light. I stand there, heart pounding despite the Valium.

What am I so afraid of? I ask myself. Not just Tom returning or another winterer catching me in the act.

It's more than that. Something is very wrong here, I realise. No . . . worse.

Someone is very wrong here.

All at once my doubts and misgivings fall away, and I'm filled with the conviction that everything Alex told me was true. Too many things are starting to add up. The missing notebook and laptop. Jean-Luc's disappearing video logs. The bruises on Alex's ankles.

Somebody stole Jean-Luc's computer and diary, and it doesn't make sense that it was one of the summer staff. The laptop maybe, but why on earth would anybody take his journal? There's only one explanation – the thief wasn't concerned with their value, but with what they might reveal.

And whoever it is, they're on this station, amongst us, right now.

Staring me in the face, another, more chilling conclusion: if Sandrine knows I've been digging around, asking questions, examining the data on the activity bands, then there's a good chance this person . . . *this killer* . . . knows too.

I've put myself in grave danger.

I lower myself onto the chair by the desk, gripped by indecision and panic, facing a stark choice: either I shut up and sit tight until the first plane arrives and carries me home to safety – or I push on and hope that I can uncover the truth before it's too late.

Before anyone else gets hurt.

Oh God. I feel caught in some waking nightmare, my whole existence taking on the texture of a bad dream.

At that moment, as if my fear and confusion conjured them into, I hear footsteps in the corridor. I freeze, heart in throat, listening. What if someone heard me? What if Tom realised I was lying about the soap and has come looking for me?

I force myself to move, switching off my torch and squeezing into the gap between the wall and the door jamb – if somebody walks in, there's a chance they won't see me.

I wait, petrified, breath held, legs trembling, as the footsteps approach the doorway, but they pass on without pause. A second or two later, the telltale click of the bathroom light and the whirr of the extractor fan. I release my breath slowly, but don't move until I hear whoever it is return to their cabin.

Get a move on, I urge myself, before somebody does discover you.

I turn my torch back on and shine it around the room. It looks like nobody has touched the place since Alex died. I study the rumpled bed, the clothes slung across the bunk above, the empty coffee mugs on the tiny bedside table. On his desk, a clutter of objects: a stick deodorant, various magazines and books, a bunch of keys on a ring, a little teddy bear wearing a T-shirt with 'I love Galway' printed on the front.

No photographs, thank goodness – Alex stored all of those on his phone.

His phone. Though useless for making or receiving calls, we still use our mobiles to take pictures, listen to music, play video games or puzzles. I saw Alex on his dozens of times.

So where is it?

Carefully, quietly, I open the drawers in his bedside table and desk. Go through their contents as quickly as I can. Nothing. I check the wardrobe – no sign of it anywhere. I make a mental note to ask Caro tomorrow. Or Sandrine, perhaps. No trace of his vape pen either. Luuk must still have it.

What else could I have missed? I glance around, but staying here any longer may push my luck to breaking point. So I switch off my torch and leave, closing the door softly behind me.

* * *

I don't go back to bed – I'm way too wired for sleep – so divert instead to my clinic. Sinking into the chair by my desk, head in hands, I try to think through the thick fog of tiredness. But my thoughts swirl around like snow in a blizzard, refusing to settle.

It's no different to making a diagnosis, I decide. Survey the evidence you have. To what conclusion is it pointing?

What do I actually know?

Alex believed Jean-Luc was killed deliberately, by someone tampering with his equipment. Which could have been anybody on that expedition.

What else? That Alex's death was no suicide. Somebody lured or forced him outside in the dark of midwinter. After a struggle, they tied him up and left him to freeze to death on the ice – which would have taken only a matter of minutes, given the sub-zero temperatures and how little Alex was wearing.

I close my eyes, visualising the scene. Allow myself to be sucked into the vortex of his terror, as Alex lay there, in those last few minutes. No one to hear any shouts for help, his desperate attempts not to succumb to that monstrous cold.

Did his *murderer* stand there, watching him die, waiting to untie him again and remove any trace of their crime? Did they gag him? Or listen to his pleas for mercy?

Oh Jesus . . . My throat constricts with emotion. It doesn't bear thinking about.

Who could have done such a thing?

And *how*? Alex was a tall, strong guy, outdoor fit, and would have put up a hell of a fight.

I sit up straight, trying to steady my breathing. Where does the evidence point, Kate?

Think.

But all that fills my mind is the craving for something more to take the edge off, to calm myself down. I get up and unlock the cabinet, survey my stock. Picking up a packet of tramadol, I open it up and pop a couple of pills from the blister pack, then replace it in the box and reseal it. That way it won't be so obvious I've been helping myself.

I pause. *It won't be so obvious . . .*

I pull out the first pack of sedatives and open it up. Checking that none of the little bubbles has been perforated, I work my way slowly through the next few boxes, but find nothing amiss.

Forget it, Kate. You're wasting your time.

But I know I won't rest until I've gone through the lot, so I push myself to continue, opening each packet and checking inside. A couple of dozen later and I've still found nothing. My head thumps with exhaustion and I'm desperate to go back to bed, but I press on, moving on to the sleeping pills.

No sign of tampering in the first couple of dozen packets, but when I remove the next, I can see the sticker seal has been peeled off then carefully stuck back into place. I open it up, pulling out the patient information leaflet wrapped around the pill sachet. My heart stops and my hand starts to tremble.

Two of the blisters have been ruptured, their contents removed.

Fuck.

I check the five remaining boxes. Each has two pills missing, the blister pack replaced inside the leaflet and the seal stuck back down so nobody giving it a perfunctory glance would notice anything wrong. Wouldn't register, either, that the box was lighter than usual.

I lay the six sachets on my desk, staring at them. Twelve pills missing in total – 180 milligrams. More than enough to render someone of Alex's body weight unconscious – or at the very least extremely drowsy.

I think back to that evening, watching *The Thing* together

after our midwinter supper. Remember Alex's slurred words, his staggering gait as he returned to his room.

Did somebody slip the pills into his drink . . . or into his food? These things, as I well know, have barely any flavour at all, and stay in your system for hours.

Don't jump to conclusions, Kate. Perhaps another winterer, worn down by fatigue and sleeplessness, broke into the clinic and helped themselves? But why would they? I ask myself again, remembering the stash stolen from my cabin. Everyone knows I'll prescribe what people need.

I sit back in my chair, rubbing my aching forehead. Could it really be true? Did someone drug Alex, then drag or lure him out onto the ice?

It just doesn't seem possible.

And yet . . .

One small shred of comfort, I realise. If I'm right, then Alex didn't suffer as much as I feared – there's a fair chance he'd barely been aware of anything.

So what the hell am I going to do? I stare down at the packets lined up on my desk.

But there's no time to formulate an answer. A second later, I hear a sound out in the corridor. I spin around, frozen to the spot, eyes wide with terror as the door handle turns, and someone enters the room.

28

5 July

'What are you doing?'

Arne stands in the doorway, his gaze fixed on the heap of medication on my desk. For a moment or two neither of us speaks, then he raises his eyes to mine. 'What's going on?' he asks again.

I stare back at him, speechless with surprise.

'What's happening, Kate?' Steel in his voice as he asks a third time, and something in his expression prompts a cold rush of fear.

Arne. *Could it be Arne?*

Why not? It could be anyone.

With a swift movement he strides towards my desk. I flinch away, but he doesn't touch me. Just picks up one of the sachets and reads the label. For an instant, time freezes: Arne absorbing the import of what he's caught me doing, me considering my next move.

I leap from my chair, making for the door, but I'm not fast enough. Arne grabs my arm and pulls me back. I try to wrench away, but he holds me firm.

'Leave me alone!' I yelp, and with that Arne abruptly lets go. I stand there, breathing hard, wondering whether to run or scream for help.

Then I register the look on his face. He seems bewildered.

'Kate? What's the matter?' Arne's voice is agitated, anxious rather than angry. 'Did you take any of those pills?'

His gaze flicks to the sachets on the desk then back to me. I stare at him, trying to decide what to do. What to say.

'Kate, please, tell me. Did you just swallow those drugs?'

He's scared, I realise – or doing a damn good impression of it. I clear my throat. 'No,' I say, firmly. 'I haven't taken any of them.'

Not tonight, anyway.

'You sure?' His expression hovers between relief and disbelief. 'You're not lying to me? Because if you are, Kate, I'll wake Sandrine right now and we'll make you vomit them up.'

For one moment I have the urge to laugh. How would they do that, I wonder?

'Listen, it's not what . . .' I inhale, forcing myself to sound calmer. 'Not what this looks like.'

Because I can see now exactly how this appears. Me, here, in the middle of the night, surrounded by a heap of dangerous medication. 'I am *not* trying to kill myself,' I say emphatically. 'I promise.'

Arne eyes me suspiciously. 'So what's going on?' He sifts through the sachets. 'Why have all of these got some missing? That's not how you prescribe them, is it?'

I rub my forehead. 'No, it's not.'

'So what are you doing?'

I sigh, try to buy myself more time. 'It's a long story,' I say, hoping he'll leave it at that. Knowing, of course, that he won't.

Arne sits in the desk chair. 'Well, we've got all night.' He checks the clock on the wall. 'Or at least the rest of it.'

'What are you doing up anyway?' I ask.

'I couldn't sleep. I was heading to the canteen to make a drink, and saw the light under your door.'

It sounds plausible, but there's no way of knowing whether that's true or not.

'Look,' Arne adds, making an effort to soften his tone. 'Let me get you one too, then come to my cabin. So we can talk.'

I consider his request. 'I should go back to bed. I've a lot to do tomorrow.'

Arne shakes his head. 'I'm not letting you out of my sight for the next couple of hours. Not until I'm absolutely sure you . . .' he glances at the pills again '. . . you haven't done anything silly.'

For the first time in what feels like for ever, my lips twitch into a smile. This man is far from stupid, and his concern seems genuine.

Seems, echoes a warning voice.

'Okay. I'll have a cup of tea,' I concede, gathering up the medication and locking it back in the cabinet. 'But let's drink it in my cabin.'

'Deal.' He gets up and moves towards the door. 'And then you can explain exactly what is going on.'

29

5 July

'Here.' Arne places the mug of tea beside my bed. 'I made decaf. So you'll be able to sleep.'

'Thanks.'

'Right, tell me,' he says, settling on the chair. 'What were you doing with all those pills?'

I study his face, searching for clues. Can I trust this man? Common sense dictates I should proceed with caution; on the other hand, I'm desperate to talk to somebody about how I think Alex died. And Arne is here, now.

'I was sorting them out. Jean-Luc left things in a bit of a mess.'

Arne looks doubtful, but doesn't push me any further. Just sits there, gauging my expression, obviously wondering if he can trust me either. 'Does this have anything to do with Alex's death?'

'Why do you ask that?' I'm unable to hide my surprise.

He falls silent. Stares into his mug as if searching for an answer.

'Do you believe it was suicide?' he asks finally.

I hesitate, considering how to respond. 'Sandrine seems pretty clear,' I reply evasively. 'That's what she's told UNA.'

'So I gathered.' Arne pulls a face.

'Don't you believe her?'

'Sandrine? Our revered leader?' he says in an uncharacteristically sarcastic tone.

I frown at him in surprise. 'You don't like her, then?'

Arne doesn't answer, and picks at something on his jeans. He's fully dressed, I notice. Which is odd, come to think of it – didn't he say he'd got up to get a drink because he couldn't sleep? Why not just pull on a dressing gown?

'Arne?' I prompt.

'It's not that I dislike her.' He sighs, rubs his cheek – he clearly hasn't shaved for a few days. 'Actually, I had more of a problem with Jean-Luc.'

I frown. 'I don't understand.'

'You don't know?' he raises an eyebrow at me. 'About him and Sandrine?'

I stare at him. 'What do you mean? Are you saying that they were lovers?'

Arne nods, and I try to digest what he's just revealed. *Sandrine and Jean-Luc were having an affair?*

'But he was married,' I blurt, then feel foolish. After all, it's part of ice station culture for people to pair up for the duration – ice husband or wife, as they're called – then return to their families. What happens in Antarctica stays in Antarctica, at least in theory.

But Jean-Luc and Sandrine? I sift through a mix of emotions. Shock. Disappointment in my predecessor, who I'd taken for a committed family man. Embarrassment too – I am, it seems, always the last to know.

'Why didn't you tell me this before?' I ask Arne, feeling genuinely hurt.

He gazes at me. For a second I sense something in his look, something unspoken, but the moment passes.

'I . . .' he hesitates. 'I'm not sure. I'm sorry. I guess I didn't want to stir things up. I hate all the gossip and backbiting that goes on in this place.'

Or was it simply that Arne didn't trust me? My chest feels

tight with disappointment, and I realise I care very much what this man thinks about me.

'Was that why you had a problem with him?' I ask, pushing the feeling down. 'Not only the drugs, but because Jean-Luc was unfaithful?'

Arne shifts in his seat, trying to get more comfortable. 'Yeah. My dad carried on an affair for years behind my mother's back. I guess I'm not keen on people who want to have all the cake.'

'Have all the cake?' I echo. 'You mean have their cake and eat it?'

'Yes. I felt it was unfair on Sandrine, too, and it had a destabilising effect on the whole base. Their relationship was an open secret during the summer, but we all had to pretend we didn't know.'

I think about this. Jesus, Sandrine must have been devastated when Jean-Luc died. How on earth had she managed to keep going? Despite everything, I feel a flicker of sympathy for the station leader.

'Thing is,' Arne continues, 'Sandrine didn't want their relationship to end when they went back home. She was very jealous of his wife, apparently. Even threatened to contact her and tell her what was going on.'

'Really?' I gape at him, trying to take this all in. But was this affair really true, or merely station gossip? I make a mental note to ask Caro about it in the morning, along with the whereabouts of Alex's phone. But it fits with what Jean-Luc said in his video, the casual way he referred to her as Sandy. I've never heard anyone else call her that.

I picture Jean-Luc's belongings, crammed in that locker in Beta. Is that why Sandrine's hanging on to them? Is she afraid they might somehow give away her secret?

Or is she simply reluctant to let them go, that last part of him. It could also explain why his laptop and computer went missing – she must have known either might contain evidence of their affair. Same for that letter, the one he wrote to his wife.

In the event of my death.

Did Jean-Luc know his life was in danger? I wonder. Did he realise the killer might go after him?

'Sandrine was on that trip to the crevasse, wasn't she?' I check with Arne.

He nods. 'Most of us were. It was kind of a team exercise for those staying over the winter. A . . . what do you call it – binding experience?'

'A bonding experience. And none of the summer crew went?'

Arne shakes his head.

I try to work this through, but my head aches with exhaustion. I lean back and close my eyes. What feels like a moment later, the touch of a hand on my cheek.

Arne is staring down at me. 'I'll leave you to sleep,' he says. 'Now I'm certain you're okay.' He picks up the mugs and heads for the door. 'Goodnight.'

I stay in bed, but sleep eludes me. My head is too full of questions, of possible connections. Not least of all how someone broke into my clinic and the meds cabinet without leaving any trace.

The same way I did, I decide.

They got hold of the master keys somehow.

I try going through it all again from the beginning, sticking to what I can be sure of: Jean-Luc dies on the ice, and Alex is convinced it was murder. His laptop and notebook disappear. Alex insists Sandrine investigate, and she refuses. Then someone deletes Jean-Luc's video files, and Alex dies, after being drugged and tied up on the ice.

I've no proof, however, that their two deaths are connected.

Jean-Luc's might simply have been an accident, a fault with his equipment. Someone might have killed Alex for a totally different reason.

I think back to what Caro told me, that Alex believed the doctor's death was related to some woman who died out here in Antarctica. I remind myself to check into it online, see if I can pin down more details.

As I reach for the sleeping pills I've hidden under my mattress, another explanation occurs to me. Is it possible *Sandrine* sabotaged Jean-Luc's equipment? Out of jealousy, perhaps, or anger that he refused to end his marriage. Then took his laptop and notebook to hide any evidence of their relationship?

I chew the pills, then swallow them. As I wait for sleep to kick in, an image of the station leader fills my mind. The anger in her small wiry frame as she confronted me yesterday. No, it's preposterous to believe Sandrine killed Alex – there's simply no way she could manhandle someone of his size and body-weight, drugged or otherwise.

Despite her obvious contempt for me, I feel a lingering sympathy for her after Arne's revelation. No doubt about it, Sandrine's had a rough ride on this mission. I should put aside our differences, I think. Tell her about those missing sleeping pills, insist she reports Alex's death as suspicious.

And if she doesn't believe me? Refuses to act?

I could contact UNA myself, tell them it's possible there's a killer in our midst. But what on earth would they do about it, even assuming they believed me? It's not like they can send in the police – as station leader, Sandrine is, in effect, our only law enforcement.

But at the very least I should warn the others. Though that carries an even bigger risk, I realise – alerting the killer to the threat of exposure. Who knows what that might lead to?

Oh God. I groan and bury my head in the pillow, feeling a

mix of panic and despair. I recall Arne's alarm when he thought I'd overdosed. Remember, too, his kindness that time I got lost on the ice.

He'd voiced his own suspicions about Alex's death tonight, hadn't he? But I'd been too cautious to take it further. I'm desperate to confide in somebody, to discuss what we should do. I badly need another head to help make sense of this mess.

But can I trust Arne?

More to the point, can I trust anyone?

30

5 July

I wake feeling awful, hungover from anxiety and lack of proper sleep, my eyes achy and my mind muggy and slow. I brew a strong black coffee and take it to my clinic, resisting the siren call of the medicine cabinet – helping myself right now would be a really bad idea, after Arne caught me with those pills last night.

Steeling myself, I fire up my computer and bring up the video logs, having come to a decision in the night. But the moment I navigate to Alex's file and click it open, I already know that I'll find it empty.

Sure enough, all his videos have gone. Whoever stole the drugs from my clinic evidently took the opportunity to delete any evidence Alex might leave behind.

I feel a lurch of anger and disappointment. For a second or two I contemplate going straight to Sandrine, insisting she take a look at the empty file, but it's pointless: the computer records will show that the person who deleted those video logs was me. If I'm going to get her onside, I need something more convincing.

Instead I log onto the internet and check reported deaths in Antarctica. For such a dangerous place, there have been surprisingly few over the years, and even fewer are women. Most notable is Yvonne Halliday, the climate scientist at Mawson whose snowmobile accident made all the newspapers. A female technician called, improbably, Wanda, who died of suspected blood poisoning on a British base. Much less information is available, oddly, on Naomi Perez, the twenty-eight-year-old admin assistant found dead on the ice two years ago, not far from Scott's Discovery Hut at McMurdo. I'm overcome by a wave of sadness as I study the face shot of Perez in the news story. Pretty, with long brown hair tumbling from beneath a thick knitted beanie.

Could this be Jean-Luc's '*pauvre fille*'?

His poor girl?

No suggestion, though, that the incident was anything other than an accident. The cause of death was exposure – it was assumed she got lost in the darkness, failed to find her way back to the safety of the station before succumbing to the sub-zero temperatures.

I flash back to that overwhelming panic when I found myself alone and disoriented after the aurora. I can well imagine how terrified she must have been as the cold closed in on her, freezing the blood in her veins.

A horrible way to die, alone in that merciless night.

I check for other recent deaths in Antarctica, waiting minutes for each search to load on our impossibly slow internet. Two men in an explosion at one of the Argentinian bases. A guy who died in a fire in the generator hut at a Russian research station. A cook crushed by pack snow at McMurdo. Another two men in an aircraft accident on a German base.

I give up, feeling stymied. But what was I hoping to find?

Gulping down the rest of my coffee, I consider returning to the canteen for more, but know it'll make me wired and jittery. Instead, I navigate to the files containing the medical records; I'd glanced through them when I arrived, but it's pretty much a given that everyone here is in a state of rude health. The odd broken limb or bout of gastroenteritis in their history. Nothing of any consequence.

But in the absence of better ideas, I decide to take a closer look. I check for Jean-Luc's first, hoping they'll tell me which of the seventy Antarctic ice stations he'd spent time at. But like his video logs, his health records seem to have been removed from the system.

Is that suspicious? I'm not sure. Maybe it's protocol in the event of someone's death.

Alex's are still here, however. I go through them again, alert for anything unusual. But there's nothing, apart from a case of chickenpox when he was seven. Up until his death, Alex seems to have been exceptionally fit and active.

Who next? My mind immediately turns to Arne. I open up his records and read them from the beginning. An ear infection as a baby. A broken wrist in his teens. A bout of food poisoning in his twenties. A case of contact dermatitis, during his stint at McMurdo. Nothing particularly significant about that, but the date catches my eye – six months before the death of Naomi Perez.

A knot in my stomach as I gaze at the entry.

Could this be coincidence?

It doesn't mean anything, I tell myself firmly. Arne has talked openly about spending time on the US base, after all. Luuk too. And quite a few of the summer team, I seem to recall. Plus several of the winterers have been to Concordia as well, though I can't remember who; after a while I tuned out all the stories of various high jinks and adventures at other stations, suspecting most were highly embellished or even fictional.

I hunt through the medical records for the rest of the base, but turn up nothing. Massaging my forehead, I try to work it through. How could I pin down what it was that so concerned Jean-Luc? And why he wanted those DNA tests.

Only two ways I can think of: ask Sandrine outright, or try to find out from his personnel file. But I can't access that area of the IT systems, and she keeps the hard copies in her office under lock and key.

Hell. I remember I need to get hold of that key again, to close up the locker in Beta. I'll have to figure out some way of getting back into Sandrine's office when my mind's less foggy – perhaps I'll get a chance to peek into that filing cabinet at the same time.

Really, Kate?

I take a deep breath, wondering when I became the sort of person who seriously considers breaking into someone's office and stealing keys and sensitive personal information.

How can I possibly justify any of this?

But what's the alternative? Risk this situation escalating further? Wait out the rest of the winter, hoping for the best?

I glance at the time and decide to check in on Caro. But there's no response when I knock on her door. I give her a minute, then poke my head inside. She's lying on the bed, beginning to stir.

'Sorry. Didn't mean to wake you.'

'Hey, Kate.' Caro sits up and rubs her eyes. 'It's okay. I overslept.'

'Can we do an antenatal check? We could make it later if you like.'

'No, let's do it now.' She gets up and follows me back to the clinic, climbing on the scales without me even having to ask. I note down the reading, reassured to see that despite all the pain and drama since Alex died, she's gained nearly two pounds. Next I measure her uterus – exactly where it should be. I check her blood pressure – not in the danger zone, but slightly on the high side of normal. Given the circumstances, that's probably to be expected.

I get out my stethoscope and listen to the baby's heartbeat. Nothing amiss there.

'Everything seems fine,' I assure Caro, making notes on the antenatal record sheet UNA emailed over. 'You're both doing really well.'

She musters a wan smile.

'How are you?' I ask. 'In yourself.'

Caro shrugs. 'Shit.'

Her honesty touches me. 'It'll get easier,' I say gently.

'You reckon? At best I'm going to return home a single mother.'

There's no answer to this. 'Does Alex's family know? About the baby, I mean.'

I guess it fell to Sandrine – or perhaps someone from UNA – to inform them of his death. What a pall it will cast over his sister's marriage, I think, feeling awful for everyone.

'Not yet. Alex was planning to speak to them; he wanted to make sure everything would be all right first.'

'Are you going to tell them?'

'I was debating whether to send an email,' Caro says. 'Or call them. I can't make up my mind.'

'Perhaps an email would be better. It will give them time to digest the news before you talk to them.'

'I just don't know what to say . . . I can't work out if it'll help or make things worse.'

'I'm sure it will help. They'll want to have a relationship with their grandchild.'

'Their second grandchild – Louise is due before me.'

'Is that Alex's sister?'

Caro nods. 'He talked so often about them I feel I know them already.'

'Did he tell them about you?'

'Yeah. His mother asked if I knew how to do the haka – she thought it might scare the rabbits away from her veg patch.'

I grin. 'She sounds nice. Funny.'

'She does.' Caro stares wistfully at the window. There's a faint light outside, from a nearly full moon. Then she turns back to me. 'Did you find his activity band yet?'

I shake my head. 'But I did check into the data.'

'And?'

'And nothing much . . . It stopped recording at 2.53 a.m. that morning.'

A pained expression crosses Caro's features. Her shoulders tense as she fights down her emotions. 'Have you found out anything else?'

I consider telling her about Luuk's visit to Alex's room, and the missing sleeping pills, but decide against it. No need to add any more stress and worry to Caro's already vulnerable state of mind.

'Nothing concrete, but like I promised you, I'm working on it.'

She stares at me, clearly assessing whether I'm bullshitting her or not.

'Actually, I was going to ask if you have Alex's phone,' I say. 'Or know where it is.'

Caro shakes her head. 'I've looked everywhere for it. I assume Sandrine took it.'

'Possibly. I'll find out.'

'Why are you asking? Do you think it's important?'

'I doubt it,' I sigh. 'I just wondered who has it.'

'So you believe me now? That his death wasn't an accident.' Caro's gaze is steady and direct. She's a lot stronger than I've given her credit for, I realise; she may be young and in an awful predicament, but she's tough.

All the same, I decide to play this down. 'Let's just say I don't disbelieve you, all right? I want to make certain we get to the bottom of it.'

'Let me guess, Sandrine isn't exactly being super helpful.'

'No, she isn't,' I admit. 'On which subject . . . did you ever hear anything about her and Jean-Luc?'

'About their affair, you mean?'

So it's true. 'Yes. I only found out about it yesterday.'

'Who told you?'

'Arne.'

Caro sighs. 'Sandrine may be a complete bitch, but she was obviously devastated by what happened to Jean-Luc. She barely spoke for days, and hasn't been the same since.'

'In what way?'

Caro shrugs again. 'She didn't use to be so . . . unyielding.'

'How come you didn't go with them? On that expedition, I mean.'

'I didn't fancy it. Five days out on the ice, and climbing's not my thing. Scared of heights.' She looks at me and laughs. 'Pathetic, isn't it? Alex said he'd help me get over it.'

I offer a sympathetic smile. 'Not pathetic at all. I'm scared of the dark, actually.'

'Really?'

I nod. 'Always have been. I still have to sleep with the light on.'

'Jeez.' Caro whistles. 'No wonder you were shitting yourself when they found you out on the ice with no torch.'

I grimace, not simply with embarrassment, but with the knowledge that either Drew or Arne told everyone what a state I was in.

'Yeah, silly, isn't it?'

'We all have something. Alex was terrified of snakes. Said that was why we were made for each other – wherever we lived, we'd be okay. No snakes in Ireland or New Zealand.'

She falls silent again. We sit there for a minute or so, both thinking, no doubt, of that lost future, the one where Caro and Alex get to live happily ever after.

I know all too well how much that hurts.

'I'd better go,' Caro sighs. 'I promised Ark I'd take another look at the boiler feed. Luuk swears there's nothing wrong with the electrics, but I need to make sure he's checked them properly.'

'Don't you trust him?' I ask.

Caro pulls a face. 'I do – when he's not high.'

I think back to the igloo, my conversation with Luuk. He'd seemed pretty together to me, despite the joint they'd been smoking. But then I haven't known him as long as Caro.

'Has he given Alex's vaper back?' it occurs to me to ask. Perhaps Caro has it somewhere in safekeeping.

'His what?' She looks puzzled.

'His vape pen. Luuk said he borrowed it.'

Caro frowns. 'Alex never owned a vape pen. Like I said, he didn't smoke a lot – even before Jean-Luc talked him out of it.'

I stare at her, confused. 'Are you certain?'

'Of course I'm certain. Why?'

'No reason,' I mutter. I make a pretence of checking the time on the wall clock. 'I'm sorry, I have to go. I've just remembered I have to see someone.'

Caro gives me another puzzled look as she gets to her feet. 'You sure you're okay, Kate? You seem kind of jittery again.'

'I'm fine,' I lie, willing her to leave. 'I'll catch up with you later.'

The moment she's gone I unlock the cabinet and help myself to a cocktail of meds. My hand is shaking, I notice, either from withdrawal or shock.

Luuk lied to me. He lied about his reasons for being in Alex's room.

And I have absolutely no idea what to do about it.

31

5 July

I find Arne in the garage workshop, bending over one of the skidoos. I stand for a minute, watching him work, the efficiency and assurance in his movements. There's something so . . . solid . . . so reassuring about him.

I'm ambushed by a rush of emotion, a raw and naked surge of attraction I can no longer deny. On its heels a sense of panic. I don't want to feel this way about anyone, especially not here.

Especially not after Ben.

At that moment Arne turns, sees me, his face breaking into a broad smile.

'Hey.' He nods at my down-filled jacket. 'You been outside?'

I shake my head. 'Too chilly in here for me.' Though the garage is heated, it's still a sharp contrast to the balmy atmosphere of Alpha. Arne, on the other hand, is only wearing a short-sleeved black T-shirt and old jeans. I guess you get used to the cold in Iceland.

He gestures about the place. 'Welcome to my domain. You've not spent much time in here, have you?'

I shake my head again. 'Drew showed me around when I first arrived.'

'Well, it's not very exciting. Especially if you aren't into engines.' He studies my face. 'So how are you today? You look as if you didn't get much sleep last night.'

'Not really.' I pause, unsure how to proceed. 'Listen, I need to talk to you.'

Arne puts down the wrench he's holding. Leans against the workbench, his gaze assessing. 'Fire away.'

'I found out something the other day . . . Actually, that's not quite true. I've been doing a bit of digging into what happened to Alex. There's a few things surrounding his death I'm not happy about.'

Arne raises an eyebrow, but waits for me to continue.

'I checked the activity band data for that night and it showed someone in his room not long before he died.' I inhale slowly, trying to gather my thoughts. Should I tell all this to Arne? I wonder again.

Can I really trust him?

'You going to let me know who, Kate?'

I throw caution to the wind. 'Luuk.'

'Luuk? You sure?'

'The data doesn't lie,' I shrug. 'Besides, he admitted it.'

Arne frowns. 'You mean you've spoken to him about it? When?'

'A few days ago.'

'And what did he say?'

'He said he went to check Alex was all right. And to borrow his vape pen.' I pause again, then go on. 'The thing is, Alex never owned one – not according to Caro.'

Arne mulls this over for a minute. 'So Luuk lied?'

'Apparently.'

'Have you asked him why?'

'Not yet. I'm not sure what to do. I should talk to Sandrine, probably, but . . .' I trail off, letting Arne read between the lines.

He releases a long slow whistle. 'Jesus. I don't know what to say. So you believe Luuk had something to do with Alex's death? But how? Are you now saying you don't think it was suicide, Kate?'

I sidestep the question again. Ask him another instead. 'You were at McMurdo, weren't you?'

Arne nods.

'When, exactly?'

'A few years ago. For about three months. Why are you asking?'

'Did you know a woman called Naomi Perez?'

Arne doesn't speak for a moment, his expression inscrutable. 'The girl they found on the ice? No. I left several weeks before that.'

I feel an ache of relief. But is he telling the truth?

God, what's happening to me? I wonder, almost dizzy with confusion. Since when did I become so distrustful of . . . well, pretty much everyone?

'Kate.' Arne clears his throat. 'I don't understand where you're going with all this. Do you think her death was suspicious? She got lost, I heard.'

'No, I . . .' I swallow. Regroup. 'I don't know. It just seemed a coincidence, that's all, you being there around the same time as her.'

Arne shrugs. 'It's a big station. Over a thousand staff, and not only Americans. Lots of people keen to spend time in Antarctica do a stint at McMurdo – it's a great way to get the experience before applying for some of the smaller bases. In my case they had a really good training programme on maintaining vehicles in sub-zero temperatures. A few of us have worked there.'

'Like who?'

'Sonya, for one.' Arne's eyes flick to the ceiling as he thinks. 'Jean-Luc, and Luuk too, I think.'

'Jean-Luc? Are you certain?'

Arne nods. 'We talked about it a few times. He overlapped

with me by a few weeks, though we never met. He joked about it being a shame I was so healthy.'

'Okay.' I churn this over in my mind. So Naomi Perez was the girl Jean-Luc referred to in his video log.

'Kate?'

I look up to see Arne frowning at me. 'Level with me. Are you saying there's something going on here? Why are you so interested in McMurdo anyway?'

I gaze back at him. If ever there were a moment to open up to Arne it's this one. It's now or never – either I trust him or I walk away. I hesitate a second longer then take the plunge. 'I'm not sure,' I admit, 'but I don't believe Jean-Luc's death was an accident. Nor Alex's.'

Arne stays silent, waiting for me to elaborate.

'Those pills . . . the boxes were hidden at the back of the cupboard. Somebody removed several from each packet, and took pains to disguise it. And I reckon whoever did that gave them to Alex.'

I take another deep breath, force myself on. 'I think he was drugged, Arne, so he could be taken out onto the ice without a struggle. There were marks on his ankles, probably from being tied up until he froze to death. Then the killer removed the evidence so it looked like suicide.'

Still no response, but Arne is studying me with an intense expression.

'There are other things,' I continue. 'Jean-Luc made a video log, saying he was worried there was someone dangerous on the station. Then his videos disappeared. Simply vanished from the system. Alex's have gone too – I checked this morning.'

'You watched Jean-Luc's video logs?' The lines on Arne's forehead deepen. 'I thought those were supposed to be private?'

Heat rises to my cheeks. 'Yeah,' I say sheepishly. 'I probably shouldn't have done that.'

'No, you shouldn't.'

I drop my gaze, feeling wrong-footed. This is not going how I hoped.

'You're right,' I admit. 'But I was trying to work out what was going on with Alex, whether there was any truth in the things he was saying.'

Arne sighs, running a hand through his hair. 'So why would this person, if he exists, kill Alex? Are you implying that whoever it was murdered Jean-Luc too?'

'I think so. I reckon whoever killed Jean-Luc overheard my argument with Alex, just before midwinter. So they knew he was digging into all this.'

'All what?'

'What happened to Jean-Luc.'

'Okay . . .' Arne looks confused. 'But I still don't understand what this has to do with that woman at McMurdo.'

'According to Alex, Jean-Luc believed someone died out here in Antarctica, and that it wasn't an accident. And Jean-Luc said in his video there might be somebody dangerous on the base. If it were true, and that person found out, it would be a motive, wouldn't it, to get rid of Jean-Luc? Alex too, if he was getting close to the truth.'

Arne's attention is fixed on my face the entire time I'm speaking. 'Kate, do you have any idea how insane this all sounds?'

I blink at him, feeling mortified. Regretting coming here, telling him all of this.

Not clever, Kate. Not very clever at all.

'I'm sorry. I thought you wanted to help.' I turn away, but a hand pulls me back.

'Kate,' Arne's tone is conciliatory. 'Please . . . I didn't mean to sound critical. It's . . .' He falters. 'It's a lot to take in, all right?'

I nod. Swipe away the tear that has leaked onto my scarred cheek.

'Do you have proof of any of this?' Arne asks. 'Apart from the activity data?'

I shake my head. 'Not really. Only some photos of the marks on Alex's ankles.'

'Did you write any of it down? Those things Jean-Luc said?'

I shake my head again. 'I was going to. It was in French, and I wanted to be certain I'd understood it all correctly. I planned to show Sandrine, but when I went back to watch it again, someone had deleted all his video logs from the system.'

'In French?' Arne bites his lip. 'Is it possible you misheard? You're not fluent, are you?'

'Not fluent, no. But I'm pretty confident that's what he said. That he had to be certain we weren't in danger. Something like that.'

'So you've no evidence then, without that video? Nothing concrete.'

'No. Apart from the photographs of Alex's ankles. And the missing medication, I guess.'

Arne gives me a look, and the penny finally drops. He knows. He knows about me. He must have guessed when those pills dropped out of my pocket.

Oh shit. And now he doesn't believe me. He thinks I'm covering up my own habit.

I blink at him, trying to think what to say, but he beats me to it. 'Kate, what exactly do you want me to do?'

I stand there, wavering. I don't know. I've absolutely no clue how to deal with any of this. Suddenly the stress and my exhaustion, my worries about Caro, about my conflict with Sandrine, about everything, completely overwhelm me.

'I . . .' My voice cracks. I burst into tears.

'Kate, come here.' Arne folds me into a hug, then reaches into his pocket to retrieve a packet of tissues.

I wipe my eyes, inhaling deeply, my breathing still ragged with emotion. He takes the tissue from my hand and dabs my cheek. Then, unexpectedly, leans in and kisses me.

Our lips touch briefly, only a second or two before I come to my senses and pull away.

'Sorry,' he mutters. 'Inappropriate. It's just that I've been wanting to do that for ages. And yeah, I get it, now is hardly the time.'

'It's fine.' I sift through my confused emotions. How do I really feel about Arne? What does this mean?

'Shit,' he exclaims, turning away. 'This place. It's really fucking getting to me.'

I clear my throat. 'It's getting to all of us, Arne. Maybe Ark is right and this station is cursed.'

'Listen.' He turns back to me. 'Forget that just happened, all right? I like you, that's all. And I hate seeing you so upset.' He sighs again. 'I'll email Kristin, get her to confirm when I left McMurdo – to put your mind at rest.'

'Okay.' I linger, undecided. What I really want him to do is pull me to him and kiss me again. Properly this time.

But I'm a doctor, a professional. I've already made one mistake with Drew, and can't run the risk of another.

'I'd better go.' I hand him the rest of his tissues.

'Yeah, I should finish up here too.' He picks up his wrench, giving me a rueful smile as I walk away.

I take a different route back to Alpha, through the opposite end of the garage workshop, aiming for the door that leads into one of the smaller storerooms. It's not until I approach a large industrial shelving unit housing spare vehicle parts that I spot the flash of silver on the ground, beside a heavy plastic box containing various ropes and chains.

I bend down and pick it up, holding the piece of metal to the light to see it more clearly. My stomach turns cold as I realise what I'm looking at – Alex's activity band. Or rather, the electronic data recorder that sits at its centre, crushed almost beyond recognition.

What on earth is it doing here?

I glance behind me, but Arne is bent once again over the skidoo.

My heart begins to race. Did he see me?

I stuff the little piece of metal into my pocket, and get the hell out of there before he looks up.

32

5 July

Fuck.

I lock myself in the clinic, and study the little data unit in my hand, trying to sift through the implications. Could there be an innocent explanation for it being in the garage? Might Alex have lost it, somehow, before he went missing that night?

But that doesn't make sense. There was no one in Beta on midwinter eve – we were all in the canteen and lounge.

Besides, where's the plastic wrist strap that goes with it?

I examine the data recorder closely. It's completely flattened – no way to tell whether deliberately or by accident. Could it have been run over by one of the vehicles? But there's no room even for a quad bike in that storage area, and nobody could do this much damage by merely stepping on it.

But if someone did this deliberately, took a hammer to it maybe, why not simply dispose of it in one of the waste bins? Or bury it in the snow?

Why be so careless with such a vital piece of evidence?

I fight the urge to go back and confront Arne, remembering that kiss, the sensation of his hands on my neck as he tipped my face to his. I desperately want to believe he had nothing to do with Alex's death, but how to explain this piece of metal in his workshop?

One positive. Even Sandrine can't ignore this. I finally have something concrete to show her, some leverage to insist she contact UNA and ask for help.

But what kind of help? There's no way onto this station and no way out – not for several months yet.

Whatever happens, we'll have to deal with it ourselves.

I knock on Sandrine's door, feeling unaccountably nervous, like a young intern facing a gruelling interview. I should have brought somebody as backup, but who can I trust now besides Caro? Half an hour ago, I might have included Arne on that list, but not any more.

I knock again, but there's no answer. I put an ear to the door, wondering if Sandrine is on a video call on her computer – she and I have the only direct links to UNA on the base – but hear only silence. On impulse I try the handle and, to my surprise, the door swings open. Glancing up and down the corridor, I quickly slip inside.

I move fast, making straight for the key cupboard and removing the locker key. I'm about to leave when I spot the drawer in the nearby metal filing cabinet is ajar – clearly Sandrine left in a hurry.

Alert for the sound of anyone approaching, I open it up and scan the neat row of files. Thankfully UNA believes in hard copies as physical backups – presumably in case of power failure. There's a folder for each member of the station.

I find Arne's and pull it out, flicking through pages of interview notes and psychometric test results, looking for anything that might confirm when he worked at McMurdo.

Bingo. His résumé.

I'm quickly scanning through it when I hear a voice behind me.

'Kate? What are you doing?'

I swing around to see Alice frowning at me. I gaze at her

helplessly, trying to formulate a way to deny the obvious. 'I
. . . oh God, Alice, I can see this looks bad, but—'

'But what, Kate?' My stomach sinks as Sandrine appears
beside her, expression morphing from shock to fury.

Oh shit. I am completely fucked.

'I'll deal with this,' Sandrine says curtly to Alice. 'Can you
alert a couple of the men? I saw Drew and Luuk in the lounge
a few minutes ago.'

Alice nods and leaves, giving me a desperate look before
closing the door behind her. Sandrine stares at me, not speaking.
She glances from the file in my hands to the locker key beside
me.

Make that double-fucked, I think. Why on earth did I take
such a stupid risk?

But that's easy to answer. Because I didn't want to believe
Arne is behind everything that's been happening on the station
– so much for not letting emotion cloud my judgement.

'Sandrine, can we just talk?' I try to keep a pleading tone
from my voice. Putting the file down on her desk, I remove
Alex's activity monitor from my pocket. 'I found this. I came
here to show you and—'

'And you decided to help yourself to my keys and confidential documents,' Sandrine cuts in, spinning the file to read the
label.

'Just look,' I insist, placing the data unit in front of her. 'I
found this in the garage workshop.'

Sandrine picks up the piece of crushed metal and examines
it carefully. For a moment or two I feel hopeful that we can
resolve this.

'Where was it?'

'Near one of the shelving units. I can show you the exact
spot.'

'No need.' She puts it back on her desk.

'It's Alex's activity monitor,' I explain, thinking she's missed the point.

'I'm aware of what it is.'

'So why do you think it's been deliberately destroyed, Sandrine? Why is it in that workshop?'

She regards me coolly. 'I'm not going to get into this with you again, Kate. We don't even know it's his.'

'Of course we do,' I splutter. 'Check the data. Nobody else's is missing.'

Sandrine says nothing.

'Ask yourself why he would remove it, go to these lengths to destroy it, if he were suicidal? And why dump it there? Why not take it off and leave it in his cabin?'

More silence.

'That's not all,' I continue, my frustration building. Why is this woman so intractable? 'Somebody stole a dozen sleeping pills from my clinic, Sandrine. *Sleeping pills*. Think about that. Consider how they could be used to get someone outside without a struggle.'

The station leader gives me a long hard stare. 'Interesting you should bring that up, Kate. I was planning to talk to you about that very subject.' She pauses, assessing the effect of her words. I wait for her to continue.

'I've received information that you've been helping yourself to the base medication, Kate. Beyond your capacity as a doctor, I mean.'

'Who?' I blurt, heat rising to my cheeks. 'Who told you that? Whoever stole those pills, probably. To cover their tracks. To set me up.

Sandrine ignores my question. 'I took it upon myself earlier to check our existing stock of medication, and there are a number of anomal—'

'Check?' I ask, aghast. 'How do you mean, check?'

'I've counted the supplies of certain drugs, Kate, and verified them against your prescribing notes. The two do not match up. Not even remotely.'

'You've been in my clinic?' I stammer. 'Without my permission? *When?*' Jesus, was it *Sandrine* who took those pills from my room?

The station leader raises a contemptuous eyebrow. 'I hardly think you're in a position to criticise, are you?'

I close my mouth. Checkmate.

'Would you like to explain what has happened to all that medication, Kate?'

'I told you. Someone took it.'

'So you say. But from what I hear, it's you that has the problem with drugs, Doctor North.'

Fuck. She knows.

She's known all along.

I blink furiously. Do not *cry*, Kate. Don't you fucking dare.

'And yet you're asking – no, *demanding* – that I trust your judgement now,' Sandrine's voice is firm and steady. 'You are completely unprofessional. Worse than that, you're a liability. You've done nothing but stir up trouble from the moment—'

'Oh, and I suppose sleeping with Jean-Luc, threatening to tell his family about your affair, I guess that's not fucking *unprofessional*, is it?'

Sandrine's face reddens, as if I've just reached across her desk and slapped her. Her mouth opens as if to speak, then closes again.

'He knew, Sandrine. Jean-Luc knew there was somebody on the base who posed a danger to everyone, and he wanted you to help him prove it. And I think Alex was tracking this person down, and that's why he's dead as well. And you,' I nod at the file on her desk, then at the filing cabinet, 'you're the only one who can help us find out who—'

I'm interrupted by a loud knock on the door. We both turn to see Drew, Luuk right behind him.

'Can you leave us alone for a while?' I say. 'I need to talk to—'

'No,' Sandrine cuts in. 'I've heard enough wild accusations for one day. Please escort Kate to her cabin,' she says, addressing Luuk and Drew, then turns back to me. 'As acting magistrate on this base I am ordering you to remain in the confines of your room until further notice. If you don't agree to stay there, I will have you detained in a locked area. Do you understand?'

'You have to be kidding me!' I gasp, astounded. 'You can't be serious.'

'I am most definitely serious. You pose a danger to everybody on this station. I will be contacting UNA for advice on what to do with you. Meanwhile, I want you to hand over the keys to your clinic and the medicine cabinet.'

I look at Drew and Luuk, but they won't meet my eyes. 'Do you agree with this?' I appeal to Drew. 'Are you just going to let her do this?'

'She's the station leader, Kate.' He shrugs. 'It's her decision.'

I turn to Sandrine. 'So you're locking me up, without any kind of discussion. You're simply going to ignore what's happening here? Why, Sandrine? What have you got to lose by taking this situation seriously?'

'I have *nothing* to lose,' she snaps. 'I am doing what I consider to be best for everyone on this base.'

'And to hell with the consequences,' I spit back at her. 'You know damn well Jean-Luc was worried about what was going on here. And now Alex is dead. And you're concerned about fucking *morale*? At what point are you going to start worrying about whether or not we're safe—' I stop mid-sentence, realising the trap I'm about to walk into.

Be careful, Kate, I warn myself. Not in front of the others.

'Take her away,' Sandrine says in a clipped tone, turning her back to me as she returns Arne's file to the cabinet. I see her examining the locker key, putting two and two together.

Drew pulls a 'leave it' face at me and nods at the door. I slam my clinic keys on Sandrine's desk then march back towards my cabin, Drew and Luuk trailing in my wake.

'What was that about?' Drew grabs my arm once we get there. 'Kate, what on earth is going on?'

I wrench myself away. Glare at him furiously.

'I'm sorry,' he murmurs. 'I wanted to do something, really, but I can't directly go against—'

'Forget it,' I snap, then run into my room, wedging my desk chair under the handle to secure the door. Sinking onto my bed, I bury my head in the pillow and give way to a tidal wave of anger and humiliation.

33

5 July

'Kate?' Caro's voice. 'It's me, and Alice. You going to let us in?'

I ignore them both. I feel so wretched, so humiliated, I don't want to talk to anyone. Plus I haven't had any pills for over twelve hours now and I'm beginning to feel horrible. Not simply the craving – though that's bad enough – but sweats and chills, plus strange aches in my muscles.

Withdrawal symptoms from the opiates in the painkillers.

I just pray I don't fall victim to the usual vomiting and diarrhoea. I'm well aware from the addicts coming into A&E that going cold turkey is very hard on the body.

'We've brought you some supper. Kate, please open the door.'

I drag myself from my bed. Remove the chair and let them in.

Alice makes a sympathetic grimace, setting a sandwich and a bottle of water on my desk while Caro enfolds me in a tight embrace. Releasing me, she widens her eyes – don't say anything in front of Alice.

'You okay?' Alice hovers, clearly embarrassed, which stings even more. I can well imagine the whispered conversations around the base as news of my confinement spread. What does Arne think? I wonder. Certainly he hasn't attempted to see me; I've been alone in here for hours, and no sign of him.

Is that suspicious? Impossible to know.

'Am I okay?' I hold Alice's gaze. 'Not really.' No point pretending otherwise.

'This whole situation is ridiculous,' Caro says fiercely. 'Some of us are going to talk to Sandrine tomorrow, when she's calmed down.'

Alice chews her lip, watching me as I digest Caro's words. *Some of us.* So there are others who believe I deserve this?

'Is there anything more you need?' Alice offers. 'Books, something else from the kitchen?' She's clearly desperate to get away. I'm hurt and disappointed – I'd counted her as a friend.

'Some painkillers would be nice,' I quip, then regret it when I see her mortified expression. 'I'm fine,' I lie, 'but thanks.'

'Do you want me to take you to the bathroom?'

'I'm fine,' I repeat, irritated by Alice's officiousness. Does she honestly think I'll do a runner if allowed to go to the loo on my own? 'But I do need to give Caro a check-up. Do you reckon she'll be safe with me?'

Alice turns a bright shade of pink then nods and leaves the room, shutting the door behind her.

Caro's eyes brim with tears of sympathy. I resist the impulse to hug her again. I shouldn't get her any more involved, or cause her more stress.

Though I already have. I've already added to the general air of tension on the station. *At what point are you going to start worrying about whether we're safe?* My words to Sandrine ring in my ears – what are the chances neither Luuk nor Drew passed them on?

Stupid, Kate. Really fucking stupid.

'What happened?' asks Caro. 'Why has Sandrine done this?'

I sink back onto the bed, considering how much to tell her. I have to make an active effort to control the shivers taking over my body.

She sits beside me. 'This is about Alex, isn't it?'

'Yes. Well, partly.' I'm too exhausted and emotionally numb

to lie to her. I collapse onto my pillow, pull my duvet around me. 'I found his activity monitor in the garage – or what was left of it. It was crushed – deliberately, it seems. I took it to show Sandrine and then I . . . I did something very silly. She caught me checking out one of her personnel files.'

'You found Alex's activity band?' Caro gapes at me, clearly shocked. 'But what was it doing in the garage?'

'You tell me.'

She considers this. 'You think this has something to do with Arne?'

'I don't know. Maybe.'

She sits in silence for a while. Then winces.

'You all right?'

Caro nods. 'Just another kick. Gets me square in the bladder, every time.'

We both smile. For a second or so we're simply two women, enjoying the miracle of pregnancy, contemplating the little life inside her.

'I don't believe this had anything to do with Arne,' Caro says quietly.

'How do you know?' I gaze at her, trying to read her expression.

She shrugs. 'I just don't think so. He's furious about what happened to you. I heard him shouting at Sandrine earlier. I thought you should be aware of that.'

I swallow. 'Thanks.' Despite everything, despite my suspicions, my heart lifts a little at her words.

Caro studies my face, her expression sympathetic. She knows, I realise. She knows how I feel about Arne.

Oh shit – am I that easy to read? And if Caro's noticed, have others? *Has Drew?*

A sharp pang of guilt adds to my physical discomfort. Despite what happened in Sandrine's office, I still count Drew as a friend – I really don't want to hurt him, even inadvertently.

'That's why Arne hasn't come to see you,' Caro continues. 'Sandrine threatened to have both of you locked up, if he tried.'

'Did she?' I raise my eyebrows in surprise, wondering precisely what he said to make her react like that.

God, what a mess. I've played this all wrong. I should have gone straight to Sandrine back when I first watched Jean-Luc's video. Should have owned up, and related exactly what he said. He clearly talked to her, told her his suspicions. They were lovers after all, and presumably friends.

Because if Jean-Luc and Alex were right, if there's a killer on the base, here, now, then Sandrine's the only person who can narrow that down. She must know exactly when Jean-Luc was at McMurdo. Or if he's worked anywhere else, for that matter – after all, I can't be sure Naomi Perez was the woman the late doctor was referring to. Perhaps there have been deaths on other bases that haven't been reported.

Either way, Sandrine's the key to all of this. But the chances of getting her to talk to me look slim to zero.

'Do you happen to know when Jean-Luc was at McMurdo?' I ask, trying to sound casual – the less I involve Caro the better.

'No idea,' she says. 'But Arne might know – he was there too, I think.'

'You got any idea who else?'

Caro thinks. 'Tom, maybe? Or Luuk. I'm not sure. Why are you asking?'

I sigh. 'Just trying to figure out some stuff. Leave it to me, okay?' I give her a meaningful, don't-push-it look.

Caro falls silent. We sit there, both lost in our own thoughts, until she turns to me, her voice anxious, almost wavering. 'Kate, is it true you took all those pills?'

I close my eyes. The scar on my face itches and burns, and

I have to resist the urge to scratch it. All the familiar old pains reasserting themselves now the chemicals are clearing from my bloodstream.

'Kate?' Caro asks again.

I open my eyes and endure her scrutiny. 'What has Sandrine said?'

'That you've been abusing station medication. That you have a drug problem. Is it true?'

'Pretty much,' I admit. 'The car accident left me with some bad injuries. I was put on strong meds for several weeks afterwards. It started off being about the physical pain and then . . . well, it became something else.'

Caro regards me steadily, not even blinking.

'I'm sorry,' I say. 'I've let you down. I've let all of you down – Sandrine, everyone. You're right to be angry with me.'

Caro inhales. Looks over at the window for a moment, then turns back to me. 'You haven't let me down. Or any of us. It happens to lots of people.'

She lets her eyes linger on my scar, something she's previously been careful not to do. 'You did your best, Kate, and life dealt you a shitty hand.' Caro reaches across and gives my fingers a squeeze. 'You've got to stop now though – you know that, don't you? That stuff will kill you otherwise.'

I nod.

She hauls herself to her feet, grimacing a little as she stands. 'Promise me you won't let that happen, okay? That you'll stop taking those pills. I need you, Kate. I can't get through this without you.'

I gaze back at her and say the words, praying that this time I really mean them.

'I promise.'

'Promise me, too, that you'll tell me when you find out who did this to Alex?'

I nod again, touched by her faith in me. Caro believes I can sort this out. I can't bring the man she loves back from the dead, but I can make sure the truth comes to light.

But how on earth will I manage that now, confined to this room?

I've no doubt Sandrine meant every word she said. Were I to step outside without her permission, even go to the bathroom unaccompanied, she'll have me locked up.

34

6 July

I'm trapped, suffocating.

Panic floods my mind and body. At the edge of consciousness, the ticking sound of a cooling engine. Somewhere, beyond, the high-pitched bark of a fox.

You have to get out, urges a voice in my head. *You have to get out now.*

But I can't breathe. I try to scream, but there's something covering my mouth. I thrash, blindly, hands clawing at the air in panic, trying to escape.

'Kate!' someone hisses in my ear. '*Kate, wake up!*'

I open my eyes, see a figure kneeling by my bed, silhouetted against my night light.

'It's me,' Arne whispers, removing his hand from my mouth. 'I'm sorry, you were shouting in your sleep. I was afraid you'd wake the whole station.'

I blink at him, at once terrified and relieved. I'm okay, I try to reassure myself. I'm here, now, not back there in that overturned car.

Waiting to die.

'What are you doing here?' I croak, my throat dry.

'I had to see if you were okay.'

I pull myself into a sitting position, only to be assaulted by a powerful wave of nausea. I feel awful, almost feverish, like a bad dose of flu, only that's impossible in the closed

272

environment of the base. Merely another fresh hell of withdrawal.

'I heard what happened with Sandrine.' Arne keeps his voice low. 'I told her it's a breach of her authority to do this.'

'Thanks.' I close my eyes briefly, trying to ride out the queasiness – it's like altitude sickness all over again. My injured knee aches too, nearly as badly as in the weeks following the accident.

Arne squints at me, concerned. 'You all right?'

I nod.

'What happened, Kate? What set Sandrine off like that? She said you stole a locker key and were snooping through her filing cabinet, that you've taken a load of drugs. She's claiming you're a danger to everyone here. Why would she think that?'

I prop a pillow up and lean back on it, wondering how to play this. 'I told her about the missing pills, what I thought happened to Alex.'

'What did she do?'

'She called me a drug addict. As well as a thief.'

'Shit.' Arne raises his eyebrows. 'She really went off the deep end then.'

'You could say that.'

'So is any of it true? About you having an addiction?'

I gaze at him, wondering what I'll say next. Trying to work out the implications. 'Most of it.'

'Those pills I found you with . . .' Arne lets the sentence trail off.

'No, I didn't touch those. I was checking what was missing. But I have been taking others. A few at a time, when my own disappeared.'

'Disappeared?'

'Someone took them from my room. A couple of months ago.'

'Okay.' I watch Arne digest this. 'I'm sorry, Kate. Really. It must be very hard.' He doesn't ask anything else, I notice – and I'm grateful for that.

'But I showed Sandrine something I found just after I left you.' I say the words then pause, a tightness in my chest. Why am I doing this? Why take the risk?

Because I have to know. Because I need to see Arne's reaction.

'What was it?' he asks.

'Alex's activity monitor. Or rather, what was left of it.'

He frowns again. 'His activity monitor? Where did you find that?'

I pause, then force myself to say it. 'In your garage workshop.'

A long silence as he absorbs the impact of my words. I study his expression. He looks genuinely stunned, even confused.

'You're kidding,' he says eventually.

'It was under one of the storage shelves, not far from where you were working. It's been totally crushed.' I keep my eyes fixed on his face, see a deepening flush.

Arne looks away. Neither of us speaks for several minutes.

'You think it was me, don't you?' he murmurs, breaking the silence.

I say nothing, simply wait to see what will happen next.

Arne gets to his feet, hands clenching with some inner turmoil. Then suddenly he drops back onto his knees again and grabs my shoulders. 'Kate, you have to believe me.' He peers into my eyes. 'I promise you, I had nothing to do with what happened to Alex or Jean-Luc.'

'Did you email your ex?' I ask quietly.

He releases me. Straightens up and rubs his face. 'I'm sorry. It completely slipped my mind. I found out about you, then got into that argument with Sandrine. I totally forgot.' There's frustration in his expression, but I sense it's directed more at himself than me.

I believe him, I realise, with a mix of surrender and relief. Perhaps I shouldn't, but I do. And I long for him to hold me again, to pretend that we are anywhere but here, in this place.

Suddenly, as if I've unconsciously given him a signal, he reaches out and pulls me towards him. We kiss, at first tenderly and slowly, then more urgently. Desire fills me, pushing everything else to the margins.

I want this, I think. I *need* this.

I'm so sick of being alone.

But, as abruptly as it began, Arne pulls away. 'Not like this,' he whispers. 'Not here, okay?'

I'm crushed with disappointment, but he's right – this isn't a good idea.

'Listen, I'll tackle Sandrine again tomorrow,' he says. 'Sonya's on her case too – she's threatening to report her to UNA if she doesn't release you. You're entitled to some kind of hearing, Kate, to defend yourself.'

Defend myself how? Am I simply going to announce to everyone what I told Sandrine? Tell them I think Jean-Luc and Alex were murdered?

What would be worse, I wonder. If they believed me?

Or if they didn't?

'Do *you* believe me?' I ask Arne, as he gets to his feet. I tilt my head so I can look straight into his eyes. 'That someone killed Jean-Luc and Alex?'

Arne runs a hand through his hair. I watch him searching for the right words. And in his hesitation I read everything I need to know.

Caro and I are in this alone.

35

6 July

It takes an age to get back to sleep after Arne leaves. I spend half the night tossing and turning, alternately in the grip of sweats then shivers. I'm ragged with exhaustion when I hear another tap on my door in the morning.

'Come in,' I croak, assuming it's Alice or Caro with breakfast. Not that I've touched the sandwich they brought yesterday – appetite, it seems, is the first casualty of opiate withdrawal.

To my surprise, Sandrine enters my room. Instinctively I brace myself. What now? Has she found out about Arne's visit in the night? Is she going to lock the pair of us up in Beta?

Presumably not together.

'Can we talk?' she asks, and amazingly her tone has none of its usual brusqueness.

'Okay,' I reply warily, feeling stupidly self-conscious in my pyjamas. Hardly a dignified way to hold what will no doubt be a serious conversation. 'Have a seat.' I nod at the chair by my desk.

'Not here,' Sandrine says. 'Can you meet me in the library?'

I squint at her, bemused. 'You sure you trust me not to do a runner?'

The station leader gives me a steady look. 'I'll see you there in ten minutes.'

I lie there for a moment after she's gone, pondering this turn of events. What is Sandrine up to? Is this some sort of trap?

Will I be put under house arrest the moment I step out of this room?

Only one way to find out. I haul myself out of bed and examine my clothes. In all the upheaval of the last few days I haven't had a chance to put on a wash and I'm all out of clean laundry. I pull on a pair of rather grubby sweat pants and a black T-shirt. They'll have to do, I decide, but all the same I run a brush through my hair and check myself in the mirror.

Ugh. I look gruesome, my scar more obvious than ever. I feel horrible too, hollow and shaky, the fever and nausea replaced by a constant nagging craving for some kind of pharmacological relief.

How long will this last? I wonder. Days? Weeks?

The rest of my life?

I drag myself to the library, my bad knee objecting to every step, sending sharp signals of distress. I find Sandrine sitting in an armchair, two mugs on the table. She hands one to me as I shut the door and sit opposite.

'Black, no sugar. Is that right?'

I nod, amazed she's aware how I take my coffee. Seems I consistently underestimate this woman.

'Why here?' I nod at the shelves, filled with paperback thrillers and old copies of *New Scientist* and *National Geographic*. 'What's wrong with your office – or my cabin?'

Sandrine does an offhand little shrug, in that way only the French can pull off. 'I thought it might be better to meet on neutral territory.'

Or perhaps she doesn't want to be overheard. Hardly anybody uses this room besides Sonya.

I take a sip of my coffee, deciding to let Sandrine take the lead and get to whatever point she's brought me here to make. Knowing she'll go straight to it – this woman doesn't do small talk.

'I think we need to bury the . . .' she pauses, searching for the right word.

'Hatchet?' I offer.

'Yes, make peace.'

'Okay,' I say cautiously, puzzled by this sudden change of heart. 'So what does that involve?'

'I let you return to active duty, and you agree to leave this situation to me.'

I consider this. 'What situation, exactly?'

Sandrine sighs. 'The one you've been investigating. For my part I'm willing to concede that things have got rather out of hand. You're the station doctor, Kate. Caro is pregnant and needs regular care, so you and I need to come to some sort of truce.'

Truce. Interesting choice of word. Is Sandrine admitting she might be at fault? I'm sceptical, but let her continue.

'Did you take those missing drugs?' Sandrine holds her gaze directly on mine.

'Some of them,' I admit. No point in lying any more.

Something relaxes in the station leader's face. 'Thank you for being honest. Can you tell me why?'

I inhale, let my breath out slowly. 'Because I . . . because I have a problem. With pills. Since the accident.'

'The car accident?'

I nod.

'It is very difficult,' she says carefully, her gaze drifting away, 'when something hits you out of the blue like that. It can be devastating.'

The station leader turns back, clears her throat. 'I loved him, Kate. I loved Jean-Luc, but I couldn't openly grieve his death. The only way I could cope was to keep going.'

She closes her eyes for a second or two, fighting to get her emotions under control. 'I'm aware I have not handled my feelings in the best way. It has been hard, seeing him replaced, life going on without him. Very difficult indeed.'

So it wasn't entirely personal, I realise, her antipathy to me. Resenting his replacement was her way of grieving her lover. I think again of Jean-Luc's things in that locker – perhaps, simply, Sandrine was reluctant to let them go. I'm tempted to ask her about them, and that letter, but right now I don't want to jeopardise this unexpected détente between us.

'Jean-Luc would have liked you.' She takes a deep breath and looks me full in the face. 'You are both very determined people.'

'Determined? I guess I'll take that as a compliment.'

'It was one of the reasons he and I clashed. We had a big argument a day or so before he died – something I now regret bitterly.'

'Over those DNA samples?'

Sandrine's face stiffens. 'How do you know about those?'

'I watched his video log,' I confess. In for a penny. I ready myself for an indignant lecture, but it doesn't come.

'So you're aware, then, of what Jean-Luc wanted me to do?'

'Not entirely,' I hedge. 'Just that he asked you to cross-check some DNA samples.'

Sandrine sighs. I can see her weighing up how much to tell me. 'As you know, UNA has them on file for each winterer. Jean-Luc wanted to compare them with those taken from Naomi Perez, a woman who died at McMurdo. Or more specifically, her foetus.'

'*Her foetus?*' I stare at her, aghast. '*She was pregnant?*'

'Yes. He wanted to find out if there was a match with anyone on the base.'

I frown. 'You mean if it was possible that someone here was the father?'

Sandrine nods. 'I refused. I knew UNA wouldn't contact the

US Antarctic Program and request those samples without good reason, and it seemed to me that Jean-Luc didn't have one. Not sufficient reason anyway. Besides, what would it prove, even if it turned out that someone here did father that baby? Certainly not murder.'

'So he suspected somebody on the station was linked to her death,' I confirm. 'Why would he think that?'

Another shrug. 'He wouldn't tell me. A matter of patient confidentiality, apparently. That's also why I refused. UNA would require solid reasons for that sort of investigation, and Jean-Luc couldn't give me any. Just a hunch, he said.'

Just a hunch. So Jean-Luc didn't have proof. Then again, I know from experience how much doctors rely on hunches, especially in diagnosis. You learn to trust your instincts, when you might need to dig deeper.

'So what are you going to do?' I ask. 'About this situation. About Jean-Luc and Alex.'

Sandrine rubs her temple. Underneath her neat make-up she looks exhausted. 'I'm not sure. My main priority is simply to get us all safely through this winter.'

'Mine too,' I add. 'I very much do not want anyone else to get hurt. Or worse.'

She looks at me. 'Do you really believe Alex's death wasn't suicide?'

I hesitate. 'I can't be absolutely certain, but there are too many things that don't add up.'

To my astonishment she nods. 'Then I'll make a deal with you – you agree to leave this with me, and I'll allow you to go about your work unhindered. But without relying on any more drugs. I've taken the precaution of removing the offending medication from your clinic and locking it up in Beta. If anyone needs it, they'll have to request it from me.'

I swallow. 'Okay.'

Sandrine's expression softens. 'You've got to come off this stuff sooner or later, Kate – and it strikes me this place is as good as any. Do you think you can manage that?'

'I guess I'll have to. Though right now I feel like shit.'

The station leader allows herself a small smile. 'I'm sure you do.'

Fair punishment, I conclude. I know, too, that this woman is doing me a favour – unlike rehab or some recovery programme, you can't check out of Antarctica.

Where better to face your demons? Or monsters, as Ark prefers to call them.

'So you'll tell UNA what's going on?' I confirm, wondering whether to mention Luuk's lie about the vape pen. Decide against it. Any more 'wild accusations' might make her change her mind.

To my immense relief the station leader nods again. 'Leave it with me,' she says, glancing at her watch. 'In the meantime, let's get some breakfast.'

36

7 July

Something's wrong.

I wake with a start, gazing around in confusion as yesterday comes crashing back: that unexpected reconciliation with Sandrine, the guarded welcome from the rest of the crew – thankful, at least, to see me back on duty. And my own relief that Sandrine was onside. That finally she was going to do something about Alex's death.

So why this feeling of dread? I lie there, dazed, waiting for my eyes to adjust to the twilight of the cabin. Is this another side effect of withdrawal? The creeping horrors?

And then I realise. The room is pitch black. The night light is off. In panic, I grope for the switch, flick it a few times.

Nothing.

The bulb has blown, I tell myself, trying to stay calm. I feel in my drawer for my torch, then remember it's on my desk. I get out of bed and fumble my way through the darkness towards the switch by the door.

Fuck! A flash of pain as I stub my toe on the leg of my chair. I grit my teeth, waiting for it to subside, then stumble towards the far wall and turn on the main light.

Nothing happens.

Heart beating faster, I try the switch again, but I'm still surrounded by absolute blackness, unable to see even my hand before my face. A surge of irrational terror makes me whimper out loud. I consider screaming, calling for help, but I'm finding it hard to breathe.

I force myself to inhale and exhale a few times, steady and slow. Then feel my way back to the desk, fumbling for the torch. As my fingers make contact with the metal, it clatters to the floor.

Shit, shit, *shit*.

Dropping to my hands and knees I search all around me, but I can't find it anywhere. I crawl towards the window and open the blind, hoping for a little moonlight, but it's as dark outside as in.

I stand there, shivering with fear and cold. Neither light working can only mean one thing – and that thing is much, much worse than my fear of the dark.

The power is out.

Perhaps it's only this part of the station, I pray, dropping to the floor again and feeling around for my torch. Where is it? Steeling myself, I force my fingers under the bunk, gripped by some primitive childish terror of what might lurk underneath.

Nothing, Kate, I mutter out loud. Grow up.

Finally the tips of my fingers make contact with the smooth edge of my torch, right up against the far wall. I push my arm in as far as it will go and manage to pull it towards me, hoping it didn't break in the fall.

Hands shaking, I turn it on, feeling almost faint with relief as light illuminates my little room. Pulling on my dressing gown, I venture into the corridor. A second later I collide with someone. I give an involuntary yelp of fright and swing my torch upwards, get a terrifying glimpse of a ghoulish face peering down at me.

'Kate,' Drew grabs my arm. 'I was just coming to see if you're okay.'

'Jesus, you scared me,' I gasp. 'What the hell's going on?'

'Power cut,' says a voice behind us. Luuk, accompanied by Alice, her face pale with fright.

'Power cut?' I echo. 'Is it the generator?'

'Ark and Arne have gone to check,' says Drew.

'How long's it been down?'

'About twenty minutes,' Luuk replies.

'Where's Sandrine?'

'We just went to look for her.' Alice's voice is tight with anxiety. 'She's not in her cabin.'

'Give me a moment.' I go back into my room and start to get dressed, but a wave of dizziness forces me to pause. Oh God. What I wouldn't give right now for a couple of hydrocodone. And some Valium to chase them down.

I push the thought away and struggle into my leggings, searching around for a pair of socks. I'm almost done when Alice bursts in, her lovely face rigid with shock. Then I see she's trembling. She opens her mouth to speak but nothing comes out.

'What's the matter?' My own panic rises up again. 'Alice, what's going on?'

She shakes her head, as if she can't bear to put it into words. 'Come with me,' she croaks, heading out of the door.

Grabbing my torch, I follow her up the corridor to Sandrine's office, hearing voices arguing as we approach. A small crowd stands inside – Tom, Rob, and Sonya.

'What's going on?' I ask.

They all turn to me, their faces wearing the same expression of disbelief and horror as Alice. Rob swings his flashlight across the room. At first I can't take in what I'm seeing, can't make sense of the patches of light and deep shadow.

Then I realise.

There's a body splayed on the floor, just visible behind the desk. And it's not moving.

Sandrine.

Oh fuck. I drop down beside her. As I put a hand to her neck to check for a pulse, I catch sight of a dark patch on the carpet by her head.

'Can you give me more light?' I say urgently.

Blood glows red in the beam of several flashlights. It's oozing from the back of her skull, forming a small pool by her left cheek. No pulse that I can detect, though her skin is still warm.

I shine my own torch straight into her open eyes. No pupil response at all. My chest tightens with shock and disbelief.

She's dead.

Lifting her head, I examine the back. Find a large swelling, the skin broken, skull dented beneath. It appears someone hit her very hard – and recently.

Definitely not an accident. Nor suicide.

Oh God. Poor Sandrine. I'm hit by a wave of sadness and horror, not just for her but for all of us.

What on earth will we do now?

'I'm sorry.' I get to my feet. 'There's nothing I can do.'

Alice starts sobbing, but no one contradicts me. It's pretty obvious Sandrine is past the point of resuscitation. 'Who found her?' I ask.

'I did.' Tom's voice is quiet. Even in the constantly shifting light of the torch beams, I can see he looks pale and shocked. He glances around at everyone, as if waiting to be accused of something.

'How long ago?' I ask.

'Just now. She wasn't in her cabin, so I came to check in here.'

'Where are the others?'

'Drew's gone to check in with Ark and Arne,' Luuk says. 'Rajiv's in the kitchen checking the refrigerators.' He grimaces. 'Like we need to worry about the food staying cold.'

'What about Caro?'

'I told her to stay in her cabin,' says Sonya. 'Safer there than out here.'

We stand in silence for a few moments, trying to take this all in. Sandrine dead and the power down – could this be coincidence?

It seems unlikely.

'What are we going to do, Kate?' Alice echoes my own thoughts. All eyes turn to mine, as if in the absence of a station leader, authority has somehow devolved to me.

'I don't know,' I admit.

Rob clears his throat. 'Do you think she was murdered?'

I hesitate. What should I say? 'I can't be certain, but it appears she was hit with a blunt instrument.'

'Perhaps she fell,' Tom suggests, his focus slightly to the right of me in that odd way of his, as if eye contact causes him physical pain. 'She could have hit her head on her desk.'

I gaze back at Tom. *Could it be him?* He found her after all. But he looks so distressed it's difficult to believe.

'Maybe,' I say. 'I'm a doctor, not a detective. But it seems unlikely.' I glance at the others. They appear paralysed, too traumatised to process what any of this means.

'What are we going to do?' Alice repeats, a rising note of panic in her voice.

No one responds.

'First we need to get the power back on,' I say, in the absence of anybody else taking the lead. 'Then we can contact UNA, discuss what to do.'

'What about the emergency sat phone?' Rob suggests.

'Where's that kept?'

'In here.' He crosses to a cupboard, opens the door and shines a light inside. 'What the hell . . . it's gone.'

'Gone?' Alice wails. 'Gone where?'

'Perhaps one of the others has it.' Sonya is clearly making

an effort to keep her voice steady and calm. 'Maybe Ark or Arne took it with them.'

'That doesn't make sense,' Luuk interjects. 'If they'd come in here to fetch it, they would have seen Sandrine. You reckon they'd simply go off and leave her?'

No reply from anyone.

'So what shall we do with . . . ?' Tom's voice chokes. He can't bring himself to continue, simply nods in the direction of Sandrine's prone body.

'We shouldn't touch anything for now,' I say, trying to think through the fog in my head. 'At the very least, we should take photos before we move her, but for that we need better light, which means restoring the power. Then UNA can tell us what to do.'

And what on earth might that be?

Dealing with Sandrine's body is one thing, but what could the team in Geneva possibly suggest for managing an unidentified murderer in our midst? Tell us to barricade ourselves in our cabins for a months until they can send out a rescue plane? Or gather in the lounge perhaps, where we can all eye each other suspiciously, like Agatha Christie characters transposed to an Antarctic wilderness?

I glance at the open laptop on Sandrine's desk, its screen black. On impulse, I touch the mousepad and the computer flickers into life. Still some battery power then. I stare at the log-in, wondering what our station leader was doing right before she was attacked.

Is it possible she was in contact with UNA? That they know we're in trouble?

It's a forlorn hope, but something to hang on to. They might not be able to do anything directly, but just the thought that somebody out there in the wider world is aware of our predicament would make me feel a whole lot better right now.

'I'm going to see what's happening with the others.' Sonya heads for the door.

'No,' I say quickly. 'Nobody should go anywhere alone. The four of you go together, and check on Caro and Rajiv first. Rob and I will find out what's happening with the generator. Let's all meet back in the lounge.'

Sonya nods. 'We'll need some paraffin stoves. And the kerosene lamps.'

'We could collect some duvets too, take them into the lounge,' Alice adds. 'They'll help keep us warm.'

They're right. Already, ominously, there's a chill in the air – without power, none of the heating systems are working. I feel another frisson of alarm. What if there's something serious wrong with the generator? How long before the kerosene for the stoves runs out and we all freeze to death?

Don't be silly, I reassure myself, remembering the backup generator in the outhouse behind Beta. If Ark can't get the main one going, we can switch to emergency power.

'What about the walkie-talkies?' Tom asks. 'We could use them to stay in touch with one another.'

'Good plan. Rob and I will pick some up from the boot room. I'll find Arne and ask him to collect the lamps and stoves.' I stand there, trying to work out what else we should do. 'Conserve the torch batteries,' I add. 'Only use one, and for as little time as possible.'

With that, everybody files out of Sandrine's office, leaving me alone with Rob. He gazes down at the body, then back at me.

'Kate?' he asks, keeping his voice low. 'Shouldn't one of us go and get the gun?'

I swing my gaze up to his. 'Gun? What gun?'

'It's locked up in Beta. A pistol.'

'A pistol?' I frown. 'What for? There are no polar bears or anything out here.'

He shrugs. 'Guess someone thought it was a good idea.'

Did UNA envisage a situation like this? It seems absurd. Then again, I guess they provided that gun for a reason.

Rob crosses to the key cupboard and opens the door. Stands there, peering inside.

'What's up?' I ask, but the look of dismay on his face as he turns back to me says everything.

'The gun locker key isn't there,' Rob confirms. 'Somebody's already taken it.'

We stare at each other, both thinking the same thing: someone on this station, *someone we know*, someone we've lived with all these months, shared food and wine and conversation with, has killed Sandrine and taken the sat phone – and now they have access to a lethal weapon.

It's only then I remember the filing cabinet. I go over and pull on the handle, but it's locked. I shine my torch into the key cupboard again, but can't see any that might fit.

Maybe Sandrine hid them, after she caught me snooping inside. Decided to put them somewhere safe. I cringe at the irony. Getting in that filing cabinet might turn out to be the only way to deal with the danger that's stalking us on this station.

But right now there's a more urgent problem.

'Come on,' I say, turning back to Rob. 'We should go and check where the gun's kept. Perhaps it's still there.'

37

7 July

'Shit.' Rob shines his torch into the empty space in the gun locker.

'Yeah,' I agree. 'Shit.'

'We're really screwed, aren't we?' He drops his torch to his side, and turns to me. The laddish bravado he normally adopts around Luuk has completely fallen away, and Rob looks plain scared.

I shiver, wondering how to respond. Decide on honesty. 'I reckon that just about sums it up, yes.'

We stand in the eerie gloom, the darkness almost palpable, pressing in on us as inexorably as the lethal cold that's slowly invading our protective little bubble.

'Do you have any idea who's doing this?' he asks.

'Not yet.' If I could access those personnel files in Sandrine's office, ascertain exactly who was at McMurdo at the same time as Jean-Luc and Naomi, I might have a clue. But caution prevents me saying as much to Rob – better to do that alone.

'We should check on Ark,' he suggests. 'It's getting pretty cold around here.'

But even if I discover who's doing this, I wonder gloomily as I follow Rob along the dark corridors, what good will that do? Whoever it is, they have the gun, and presumably ample ammunition.

How can any of us defend ourselves against that?

*   *   *

We find Ark alone in the generator room, down on one knee, working on the machine in front of him, a couple of torches rigged up to illuminate the area. No sign of Drew or Arne.

'You discovered what's wrong?' I ask.

'Cooling fan broken.' He points to a piece of metal that means nothing to me.

Rob frowns. 'How would that happen?'

'Not right question,' Ark says. 'Who, not how.'

I stare back at him, horrified. 'You mean somebody did this *deliberately*?'

'Only explanation.' Ark studies the generator, his expression despondent, as if someone has assaulted his favourite child. 'Whoever did this knew what they were doing. It . . . how do you say . . . completely fucked.'

I stand there, trying to take this in. Someone deliberately sabotaged our power supply – the thing that makes life in this frozen hellhole possible. Why would anybody in their right mind do that?

To stop us contacting UNA for help, maybe. Or to keep us preoccupied with basic survival.

Or perhaps, more simply, whoever did this isn't in their right mind at all.

'Can you mend it?' I ask Ark.

'Not easy. We need backup going.'

'Is it undamaged?'

'No idea. Drew and Arne gone to check. You take care of others, okay? Make sure they safe.'

But how, I want to ask? How to keep them safe if I don't know who to protect them from?

'You got any idea how long it might take to get the emergency generator going?' I ask instead. With heat and light, it will be much easier to defend ourselves.

Ark heaves himself to his feet, groaning as he straightens his back. 'That depends on what we find.'

I nod, try a different tack. 'Can we survive without electricity?'

Ark scratches his beard and squints down at me. 'Many problems, Kate. No heat, no light, and most bad is, no water.'

Jesus. I never thought of that. 'Can't we get snow from outside?'

'Of course. But we must melt, not so easy when below zero in here too. We have fuel stoves, yes, but we need them for food and heat.' Ark offers me a gallows-humour smile. 'Look on bright side, Kate – whoever kill Sandrine perhaps get us first.'

'I don't suppose you've any idea . . . ?' I let the question hang. It's obvious what I mean.

Ark raises an eyebrow. 'If I did, they be dead already.'

'The gun has gone,' I tell him.

His expression clouds further. '*Blyad*,' he mutters in Russian. It needs no translation, and I put a hand on his arm, grateful for his honesty. To my surprise Ark enfolds me in a bearish hug for a second or two, then releases me.

'Good girl.' He grins at my startled reaction. 'I always have best feeling about you.'

I hurry back to Alpha, Rob in my wake. Both of us silent as the implications of our situation start to hit home. We're trapped on the ice without heat or power, and possibly little water, with a killer who has a gun.

Hard to see how this could end well.

I'll check everyone's okay, I decide, then hunt for that key for the filing cabinet; if I can't find it, I'll have to get someone to jemmy it open.

But who? asks a small voice in my head. If one of us is the killer, who can I trust to help me?

Suddenly a bright torch beam flashes in the corridor, and Alice looms out of the darkness. 'It's Caro,' she says, sounding breathless. 'She tripped in the dark.'

My stomach gives a little flip of alarm. 'Is she okay?'

'She says she is, but I thought you'd better look her over. She fell pretty hard.'

I take a deep, steadying breath, then hurry to the lounge, where Sonya, Luuk, and Rajiv are all huddled under duvets and sleeping bags. Rajiv isn't wearing his turban, I notice, long dark hair tumbling around his shoulders – clearly he left his cabin in a rush and didn't want to return. I turn to Caro, lying on one of the sofas, and shine my torch on her face. She smiles up at me.

'What happened?' I crouch in front of her, observing her tear-stained cheeks.

'I tripped over a chair leg in the canteen and fell onto the corner of a table.' She shakes her head, as if marvelling at her own stupidity.

'When did this happen?'

'About ten minutes ago,' says Alice. 'I was on my way to find you. Is Ark going to get the power back on?'

'Not yet,' I hedge, wondering whether to mention the missing gun. Should I warn everyone? Or will that make matters worse?

After all, someone here right now could have taken that pistol, stashed it away in the dark – the last thing I want to do is provoke them into using it.

Focus, Kate, I urge myself. Deal with the emergency at hand. 'You in any pain?' I ask Caro.

'Not really. Just a bit winded.'

'Have you felt the baby move since?'

Caro nods. 'A couple of kicks.'

'I really should examine you in the surgery.'

'I'm fine,' Caro insists. 'No need for any fuss.' She smiles at Alice, who's gazing down at her, frowning with concern.

'Give me fifteen minutes – we'll do a proper check over then, okay? There are some things I have to do first.' I glance around. 'Where's Tom?'

'In the comms room,' Sonya says. 'He's trying to set up the portable high frequency radio. To see if we can get in touch with one of the other stations.'

'Is he on his own?'

Sonya nods. 'I told him not to go alone, but he wouldn't listen. Someone should check in on him.'

'I will,' I say.

'You want me to go with you?' Rob asks.

I shake my head. 'I'll find Arne. We can do it together,' I say, seizing on the excuse to go alone, then head out of the door before anyone can argue.

38

7 July

The station leader's office is pitch black and deathly cold.
Literally, I think despondently, staring at the body on the floor.
Someone has covered Sandrine with a sheet, trying to give her
a little dignity in death, but the effect is to render the scene
even more gruesome.

Who killed her – and why?

There's an awful conclusion I don't want to face. If Jean-Luc
died for attempting to expose a killer on the station, it seems
likely Alex and Sandrine were murdered for the same reason.
And in Sandrine's case, I was the one who persuaded her to
contact UNA.

I swallow down a wave of guilt and sorrow, clutching the
torch in my hands. Would she be alive now if I hadn't pushed
this so hard?

Enough, Kate. Tackle the most immediate danger – and that
means finding out who's doing this. You've got to get inside
that filing cabinet. It's the only way to establish who might have
been at McMurdo without actually asking everyone, which I
can't help thinking would be a grave mistake – whoever's behind
this will clearly do anything to keep their identity hidden.

I check through the keys in the cupboard again, then try the
drawers in Sandrine's desk, but they contain nothing more than
a neat assortment of stationery, and a single photograph tucked
into the back of a notebook.

I study it in the light of my torch. It's a snapshot of Sandrine and Jean-Luc, together on the ice, both grinning in the bright sunshine. A lump rises to my throat. She was a woman, alone, trying to cope in an impossible situation. And she lost the person she loved.

I can relate to that.

But now she's dead. Jean-Luc and Alex too. It's too much to comprehend, too much to bear. I'm overwhelmed by a surge of longing for a good hefty dose of medication, a chemical buffer from all this horror and chaos.

You could find where Sandrine put the pills she removed from the clinic, argues a tempting voice. They'll be in one of the locked cabinets in Beta.

But no. I glance down at her body, recalling my promise the last time we spoke – somehow her death makes me all the more reluctant to break it.

Dragging my attention back to the keys for the filing cabinet, I quickly search the rest of Sandrine's office – inside the lever arch files on the shelf, behind the books in the small bookcase in the corner. I even lift the chairs and look on the underside of the desk to make certain she hasn't secured them out of sight.

No sign of them anywhere. They must be in her room, I decide, but right now I should check on Tom. More than anything I want to track down Arne – I haven't seen him since the power went out; I'm desperate to find him, to make sure he's okay, and discuss what we should do.

I recall the sensation of his lips on mine, the feel of him so close to me, the reassuring warmth of his presence, and for a moment the heaviness in my heart lifts a little.

If anything happened to him, I'm not sure I could bear it.

* * *

Tom is huddled over a large red box on his desk, looking clumsy and awkward in his thick down jacket. It's even colder in Beta than the main building, and I see him struggling to hold the tiny screwdriver in his gloved hand as he works on the delicate electronics by torchlight.

'Any joy?' I ask.

'Not so far.' He shoots a quick glance in my direction. 'It's not working. I'm trying to figure out why.'

'Can't Rob help? He's the comms expert after all.'

Tom raises his eyes and allows himself an almost imperceptible smile. 'That doesn't mean he knows how to dismantle a radio. I used to make my own, when I was a kid. At least I have some clue what I am looking at.'

'All the same, Tom, you shouldn't be here on your own.'

He shrugs. 'I can't stand the atmosphere in the lounge, everyone so suspicious of each other – I had to get away.'

They hate me.

Tom's words that time he came to my clinic ring in my ears. His admission that he sees and hears things that aren't there. I watch him work on the machine in front of him, wondering. Is it possible that I was right, that Tom isn't well? That his illness might have progressed into full-blown paranoia?

And what might that make someone do?

All of a sudden, he puts down his screwdriver and sighs. Actually looks me square in the face. 'Do you have any idea who's doing this, Kate? Who killed Sandrine? Sabotaged the generator?'

I shake my head. 'Do you?'

'No. But if we can radio another base, we can at least communicate with UNA and tell them what is happening.'

'If you can't get it working,' I nod at the machine on the workbench, 'do you know how long it might take UNA to gather there's something seriously wrong?'

Tom shrugs again. 'Not long. A few hours maybe. They might assume we have comms problems, but they'll try to reach us on the sat phone. They've probably realised by now that we've got something going on.'

I stand there taking this in. 'Let me know if you get anywhere, won't you?' I say. 'But really, I'd be happier if you returned to the lounge. It's dangerous to be here on your own.'

Tom blinks at me. 'I could say the same to you.'

There's a brief moment of silence before it's punctuated by the distant sound of shouting. I stick my head out into the corridor, then hear it again. Alice, calling my name, her voice sounding urgent. Anxious.

I grab my torch and run towards her, my knee protesting with sharp flares of pain every time I put weight on it. I catch up with Alice in the covered walkway connecting Beta to the main building.

'Oh, thank goodness,' she gasps, trying to draw breath. 'Caro . . . she's started bleeding. *Down there*,' Alice mimes, pointing between her legs.

Fuck, I think, hurrying back to the lounge.

Could things get any worse?

39

7 July

By the time we arrive in the lounge, Caro is getting to her feet, face wincing with pain. Behind her, my torch picks up a large stain on the sofa, the fabric soaked red with blood. The sight is so reminiscent of Sandrine, still lying on her office floor, that I succumb to a rush of blind panic.

I can't do this.

I can't deal with this all on my own.

Despite Ark's endorsement, I don't feel up to the job. I'm frightened and exhausted, ill-equipped to cope with yet another unfolding emergency.

You've no choice, I tell myself fiercely, fighting to regain control of my emotions. *Who else is there?*

I take a deep breath and force myself to sound calm. 'Let's get you into the surgery.' I glance around at the others. 'Can you give Caro a bit of assistance?'

Rob and Sonya lift Caro's arms around their shoulders, and start slowly walking her towards the clinic, Alice leading the way with her torch. I follow behind, mind racing through all the possible diagnoses – none of them good.

'I think she's haemorrhaging,' Sonya whispers, as we help Caro onto the exam bed in the surgery.

I nod, handing her my torch, and turn to Rob. 'Can you find a couple of the fuel stoves?' The air in the clinic feels wintry – despite the insulation, we're fast losing all residual heat.

Sonya trains the torch beam on Caro while I examine her. There's blood all over the crotch of her blue leggings; as I ease them off, she grimaces, clearly in a lot of pain.

'Where does it hurt?' I grab an absorbent pad from the cupboard and place it between her legs.

'Down here.' She puts a hand on the base of her abdomen.

I press gently on her stomach, watching her face. Her eyes water at even the slightest pressure from my fingertips.

How many weeks is she now? I do a quick mental calculation. Anywhere between twenty-seven and thirty-one – hell, she isn't due yet for at least a couple of months.

I pick up my stethoscope and place it on Caro's stomach, listening for the baby's heartbeat. Nothing.

Keeping my expression deadpan, I try again, positioning the cup on a different part of her abdomen.

'Is everything okay?' Caro asks weakly.

'One sec.' I try a third position and listen carefully. To my relief I pick up the faint sound of a heartbeat. Eyeing the second hand on the clock on the wall, I count the beats in six seconds. Around 18 or 19. That's over 180 beats per minute.

Too fast. A clear sign of foetal distress.

I quickly attach a cuff to Caro's arm to check her blood pressure. Fifty-five over forty.

Hell. That's way too low.

The diagnosis seems clear. Placental abruption, probably caused by her fall.

But what to do? My mind blanks with anxiety and a desperate ragged fatigue from sleeplessness and withdrawal. I need an ultrasound machine, a foetal heart monitor, and advice from an expert at UNA. None of which are available.

I'm on my own.

'Is the baby okay?' asks Caro again, anxiously.

'Strong heartbeat,' I reply, trying to sound as reassuring

as possible. I check the pad between her legs, already soaked with fresh blood. If she carries on haemorrhaging at this rate, Caro and her baby could die within hours – if not sooner.

I turn my back on Sonya and Alice, on their worried expressions, their faith that this is a situation I can handle, and consider the options before me: only one I can think of, and that's an impossibly tall order without power or proper medical support.

Plus I have absolutely no experience in the field.

I stand there, head spinning. What should I do?

Think, Kate. *Think.*

'Can you and Alice go and find Drew?' I say quietly to Rob, who's just returned with two stoves and several kerosene lamps and set them up in opposite corners of the room. 'Use one of the walkie-talkies to track him down. Tell him I need him to assist.' I widen my eyes at them so they read the urgency without my having to state it in front of Caro.

Sonya regards me gravely as they hurry out – she's well aware that she and Drew are the two winterers trained to assist me in any surgical procedure. 'Are we going to operate?' she mouths.

I nod, trying to look decisive and confident, but I can tell Sonya isn't fooled. I beckon her to follow me into the clinic, closing the door to the surgery so Caro can't overhear. 'We need to do an emergency caesarean,' I say quickly.

Sonya's eyes widen. 'Is that the only option? That's pretty risky, isn't it? Given the circumstances.'

'Not as risky as letting her bleed to death. And no, we haven't any choice.'

'But how can we give her a general anaesthetic?' she asks, looking perplexed. 'We can't ventilate her without any power.'

'We'll have to use Entonox and local anaesthesia.'

After a brief pause, Sonya nods. 'Okay.'

'Can you set up an IV line?' I ask her. 'Remember how I showed you?'

'I'm on it.' She retrieves a bag of saline from the cupboard. I go into the clinic and hunt through the medical manuals on the shelf above my desk, the hard copies that UNA included as a backup. I scan the notes on placental abruption.

It's not pretty. High risk of maternal and foetal death without swift intervention. I need to act fast.

This is insane, wails another part of my brain. You don't have the experience, or anything you need.

'You all right?' Sonya asks, as she inserts the needle into a vein on Caro's left hand.

'Yes,' I lie.

'You can do this,' she says firmly, as if reading my mind.

You can do this, I repeat to myself in my head, trying to believe it. You're an experienced ER doctor – you know what to do.

Without medical support? Diagnostics? Power and light?

'What's happening?' moans Caro, catching something in my expression.

I bend over her. 'Listen, I'm pretty sure your fall caused part of your placenta to dislodge from the wall of the uterus, and that's why you're bleeding. So, I'm going to give you an anaesthetic and deliver the baby. Okay?'

Caro stares at me for a second or two, then nods weakly. She looks out of it, I think, wondering how much blood she's already lost. If I don't get a move on, she could go into shock.

A moment later the door swings open and Drew appears. 'Alice said you needed me.'

'Caro's hurt herself. I have to operate. I need you and Sonya to assist.'

A flash of alarm crosses his face. 'What do you want me to do?'

'First, can you go and find where Sandrine has locked up the painkillers and analgesics. They're somewhere in Beta.'

'I know where they are.'

'You do?' I raise an eyebrow at Drew but don't pursue it. No time to get into that now. 'Bring everything. And some better torches – more than anything we need light.'

He nods and disappears. I turn to Sonya. 'You ready?'

I grab a bottle of antibacterial gel and clean my hands as best I can without running water, donning surgical gloves and a gown before going back into the surgery. 'Caro, have you ever had gas and air?'

'No,' she whispers, her voice noticeably weaker.

I drag over the cylinder and hand her the mask. 'In a minute I'll give you some drugs to take away the pain, but if you need more help, you put this over your face and breathe deeply. Do you think you can do that?'

Caro nods, then closes her eyes. I note she isn't asking me for any details of what I'm about to do. Too out of it to care – or simply too scared.

Just as well. Ignorance is bliss – or at least more bearable.

As I prep her stomach with alcohol and antiseptic wipes, Drew returns with Luuk, each carrying a large torch attached to a telescopic stand. They arrange them on both sides of the surgery bed, beams trained on Caro's stomach, then Drew hands me a carrier bag stuffed with medication.

Luuk's eyes widen as he sees the blood-soaked pad between Caro's legs. 'She going to be okay?'

'Right as rain,' I say briskly. 'Please make sure everyone who isn't working on getting the power back up stays in the lounge. I can't cope with any more casualties.'

Luuk dives out of the room without further prompting. I'm guessing he's not good with the sight of blood.

'Drew, can you gown up, then monitor Caro's blood pressure and pulse, and give me readings whenever I ask?'

'Sure.'

'Sonya, I need you to swab while I work, so I can see what I'm doing.'

She swallows. For once she seems to have dropped her stoic demeanour and looks genuinely anxious.

I root through the bag of meds and find a bottle of Fentanyl. Ignoring the surge of longing it sparks in my brain, I load it into a syringe. 'Right, Caro,' I say, careful to keep my voice steady. 'This should completely eliminate the pain. But if you feel anything at all, start breathing deeply with the mask covering your face. Drew, you might have to hold it for her.'

'You done this before?' His eyes fix on mine.

'Dozens of times,' I lie, knowing Caro can hear us. Truth is I observed a couple of caesareans during my training, but have never actually performed one. Slowly, carefully, I inject Caro with the powerful painkiller, then open the sterile packet containing the scalpel. Cup the icy metal in my palm.

It's still freezing in here, the little stoves struggling to combat the rapidly encroaching cold. Another reason to act fast.

I grip the scalpel and mentally draw the line for the incision. Then stand there, hesitating.

'Kate?' Sonya asks, looking at my hand. 'You sure you're all right?

I glance down, see my fingers are trembling. I close my eyes briefly and take several deep slow breaths. Take some of those pills, whispers a voice in my brain. Just to steady your nerves.

No.

On the next inhale, I make a neat transverse incision low into the pubic line, all the while alert for a cry or moan of pain.

Thankfully there's nothing.

'Sonya, could you swab please? Drew, check her BP and pulse – you'll have to do it manually.'

As Sonya deals with the blood, I work my way down to the uterus and make another careful lateral incision.

'BP is fifty-five over forty,' announces Drew. 'Pulse one hundred and five.'

No change. Though neither, of course, tell me anything about the condition of the baby.

A sudden rush of fluid as I rupture the amniotic sac, gushing everywhere. Sonya grabs some towels and mops it up as best she can.

I take a pair of surgical clamps and pass them to her. 'I need you to hold the incision open while I work.'

As she gets them in position, I reach into Caro's uterus, feeling for the dome of the baby's head. There. Small, but reassuringly warm. Cradling it in my palm, I slide in my other hand and pull gently.

A moment of resistance, then a second later the tiny infant emerges from Caro's stomach.

'Jesus,' Drew gasps, eyes wide. 'Why is it that colour?'

'It's the vernix,' explains Sonya. 'Standard for pre-term babies.' We all gaze at the diminutive white bundle in my hands. It looks like a tiny lifeless ghost.

A tiny *female* ghost.

'Is she breathing?' Sonya whispers.

I shake my head, pushing the tip of my little finger into her mouth to ensure her airway isn't blocked. Even under the vernix, I can see her skin is blue with lack of oxygen. I need a Ambu resus bag, I think desperately. I have to get her breathing, fast.

'Get the oxygen,' I urge Drew, 'and another mask.'

He brings me both. I prise open the baby's mouth and carefully blow inside, then hold the oxygen mask over her, hoping this will work.

It doesn't. I try again, but to no avail.

Oh God, I find myself praying. *Please*.

'Give her to me.' Sonya reaches out. 'You deal with Caro.'

I pass her the tiny bundle and watch as Sonya breathes into her mouth a few more times, then expertly turns her over and pats her between the shoulders. Miraculously there's an almost inaudible snuffle, and the little arms stiffen and move.

Tears in my eyes as I turn back to her mother, readying myself. Gently, carefully, I begin to pull on the umbilical cord, silently uttering another prayer that the placenta will come away freely; if the uterus can't contract and cut off the blood flow, Caro could bleed out in a matter of minutes.

For a moment or two nothing happens, then the afterbirth slithers out into my hands. I grab one of the torches and examine it carefully – thankfully it seems intact.

'Drew, could you give me a hand?' I nod at the swabs as I find a needle and sutures and set to work closing up the wound in Caro's stomach. 'How's the little one?' I ask Sonya.

'She's doing okay.'

'Can you clamp the cord, then cut it? I'll—'

A sudden moan from Caro, who seems to be rousing from her semi-conscious state. 'Press the Entonox mask over her face,' I tell Drew quickly, then address Caro directly. 'Hang on in there, sweetheart, it's nearly over. Long deep breaths, okay?'

I work as fast as I can, thankful I know what I'm doing now. With so much practice in A&E, I could sew up a wound in my sleep. As I tie off the last stitches and apply the dressing, I beckon Sonya over.

'I need to look over the baby. I want you to massage the top of the uterus like this, to encourage it to contract – that will help stop the bleeding.' I give her a quick demonstration, then check the pads between Caro's legs. Both sodden, but the blood flow appears to be easing.

Far from out of the woods yet, but it's a good sign.

Taking the baby from Sonya, I pull back the towel to examine her. Her skin is now tinged with pink, and she seems – despite her prematurity – to be breathing on her own. Perhaps Caro was a little further along than either of us realised. I marvel for a second or two at her perfect little features, her tiny limbs, then cover her up against the cold.

'Keep her on oxygen for the time being,' I tell Sonya, as I hand her back, 'and make sure she's warm.'

I return my attention to Caro. The blood loss is definitely decreasing, I note with relief. I squeeze her hand and she opens her eyes and blinks blearily at me over the top of the Entonox mask.

'It's over,' I say, taking it from her. 'I'll give you some morphine to help with the pain, but it'll make you drowsy, and I thought you might like to see your baby first.'

Caro blinks at me as if my words make no sense, then seems to wake up as the gas and air clears her system. 'Yes,' she croaks, trying to pull herself upright, but I put a hand firmly on her chest to stop her. 'No, don't move, not yet.'

I fetch a couple of pillows and ease them under her head, then take the baby from Sonya and lay her in Caro's arms.

'Oh my God,' she gasps, her voice croaky. 'It's so small.' She looks up at me. 'Is it a boy or a girl?'

'A girl.'

Caro gazes at her, a single tear rolling down her cheek. I leave them together for a minute before gently removing the baby and injecting Caro with a good dose of diamorphine. With any luck, that should get her through the next few hours.

'Can I hold her?' Drew asks.

I look at him, surprised, as Sonya hands over the little bundle. We both watch him study the baby's diminutive face with an expression of tenderness I've never seen on him before. Clearly witnessing a birth has brought out Drew's paternal side, made him rethink that whole no-children thing.

'She needs oxygen,' Sonya says, taking the baby from Drew's arms. He seems almost reluctant to let go of her.

'Could you possibly find another stove,' I ask him. 'And a clean duvet. We need to keep them both warm.'

He nods, and disappears. Sonya and I exchange a look, smiling, as the door closes behind him. Who knew Drew was such a softie?

I give Caro some broad-spectrum antibiotics, and we watch her drift into a hazy sleep. As long as she doesn't get an infection, she should be fine.

'Can you manage in here for a while?' I ask Sonya. 'I want to check again how Ark is getting on, make sure everyone else is all right.'

'Do we need to feed her?' Sonya nods at the baby. 'I don't imagine Caro will be up to it for a while.'

'I'll get Rajiv to bring you some powdered milk.'

Sonya frowns. 'Will that be okay?'

'It'll have to be – he sure as hell doesn't have any baby formula. We can warm it on one of the stoves and offer it to her in a syringe, but get Caro to put her to the breast when she wakes up. Chances are the baby's too small to have a strong sucking reflex, but it's worth a try.'

I fetch a few more phials of morphine, plus clean needles and syringes, then leave them on the counter. 'You remember how to administer injections?' I ask Sonya.

'Yes.'

'Give her another dose if she needs it. No more than 20 ml every four hours.'

Sonya frowns at me again. 'Why can't you give it to her?'

'I've got to deal with the power issue,' I hedge, not wanting to admit I don't trust myself around these narcotics. Or my fear that something – or rather someone – might prevent my return to the clinic. 'I'll send Alice and Rob with the milk and bottled water. Lock the door behind me, won't you?'

Sonya nods. Glances at Caro, then back at me. 'That was amazing, Kate. You saved both their lives. You've never done a caesarean before, have you? Despite what you said.'

'No,' I admit. 'Never.'

Sonya's gaze lingers on mine, but there's approval in it.

'You are very brave.' She lifts a hand and cups my face. 'I'm not sure we can get through this without you, Kate, so be careful out there. No playing the hero, okay?'

40

7 July

Back in the lounge, I find Alice and Rajiv taking refuge under
the duvets while Luuk and Rob, dressed in their outdoor gear,
fiddle with a couple of the smaller stoves that seem to be
making little impression on the plummeting temperatures. I'm
relieved to see Tom is with them.

'Is she all right?' Alice asks. I can tell immediately that she's
been crying.

I nod. 'Reckon so.'

'Drew said Caro had a girl.' Suddenly Tom's face lights up
into a rare smile.

'Yes.'

'That's very early on, though, isn't it?' he asks. 'Will she
live?'

'Do you mean Caro, or the baby?'

'Both, I suppose.'

Everyone is staring at me, waiting on my answer. I decide
honesty is the only option. 'I'm pretty sure Caro will be okay.
The bleeding seems to be under control. It's touch-and-go with
the baby though – she's very premature. In a proper antenatal
unit, her chances would be excellent, but here . . .' I stop. No
need to say any more.

'I'll pray for them both,' Tom says quietly.

I gaze at him, surprised. I never realised that Tom, like his father, is religious. I assumed it was something he'd rejected, along with his father's homophobia.

'Thanks,' I say simply. 'They're going to need all the help they can get.'

I turn to Rajiv, who's retrieved his turban and wound it back onto his head. Black, I notice, wondering if that's a comment on our situation. 'Can you spare some powdered milk?'

'Of course. Would you like me to fetch it from the kitchen?'

'Please. But take Alice, will you? And be careful.'

'Then can we go and see them?' Alice asks hopefully, making a visible effort to pull herself together.

'Caro's sleeping, but you and Rajiv can take the milk to Sonya. Can you bring her a small saucepan and some bottled water too?'

'We're already running pretty low on water.' Rajiv looks worried. 'All the pipes are beginning to freeze.'

'Rob and I were about to go out and collect some snow,' Luuk chips in. 'Plus more fuel for the stoves.'

That leaves nobody to accompany me to Beta, but I really need to find Arne.

I'll just have to take my chances, I decide. Stay watchful and alert. 'Have you got a spare walkie-talkie I can use?' I ask Luuk.

'We haven't even got one ourselves. Half the handsets seem to be missing, plus the batteries are dead on a couple of others. Drew, Arne and Ark have the only ones working.'

Fuck, I think, as I hurry to the comms room in Beta. That's all we need.

No sign of Ark in the generator room – I'm guessing he's out on the ice helping to retrieve the backup, but I can't contact him without a walkie-talkie. I check the cupboard in the boot room where they're stored, but as Luuk said, the only remaining handsets have flat batteries.

Shit. I pull on my down trousers and jacket, wondering whether to go outside and search for Ark and the others. But that means venturing into that darkness alone, with no way of calling for help if I run into trouble.

No playing the hero.

I remember Sonya's words, her injunction to keep myself safe. She's right, I decide. Too risky – even if I am desperate to find Arne.

Better to return to the clinic, check on Caro and the baby, and wait for the others to come inside. I take the shortcut through Beta, almost reaching the connecting walkway when I hear a crash emanating from one of the storerooms.

What the hell was that?

I retrace my steps, swinging my torch beam around the supply room. To my surprise, I see someone crouching on the floor. He turns as he spots my flashlight.

Arne.

A rush of relief. 'You okay?'

'Tripped over something,' he groans, his voice full of pain. 'Smashed my fucking toe.'

I walk over. Shine my light on his booted foot. 'Let's get you into the warm, then I'll take a proper look.'

Arne shakes his head. 'Give me a minute.' He reaches down and retrieves his own torch from where he dropped it on the ground. Checks it's still working.

'I hear Caro had her baby,' he says.

I nod. 'A little girl.'

He hops over, gives me a hug. 'I also heard you saved both their lives, Kate.'

Still too early to be sure of that, I think, but don't say so. 'What are you doing in here anyway?'

'Getting some silicone lubricant for Ark. He's trying to repair the spare generator.' Suddenly his torch blinks out. He bangs it a few times but it refuses to come back on. 'Great.'

'You mean the backup has been sabotaged as well?' I ask, appalled.

Arne nods. 'Whoever did it made a damn good job of it too.'

Oh God. I shudder, reeling from the impact of this news. No chance of power any time soon. What on earth are we going to do?

Why would anyone disable the power? I wonder again. Is it an attempt to kill us all? Or is the idea to keep us too busy and preoccupied with pure survival to present any kind of threat.

Impossible to fathom.

Arne puts weight on his toe, wincing.

'I'll get the lubricant,' I offer, shivering despite my outdoor gear. The temperature in here has to be well below freezing. 'Where is it?

'By the cleaning agents.' He points to a box in the corner of the room.

I walk over and pick up one of the canisters and hand it to Arne.

'Thanks.' He stuffs it into his jacket. It's only then I spot something poking out from his left pocket. I lift my torch for a better look. Then reach across and remove it before Arne can stop me.

It takes a second or two to register what I'm holding. A chunky black phone, with a short stubby antenna.

The sat phone.

What the fuck? I swing my gaze to Arne. 'You took the sat phone?'

'I was about to tell you,' he says. 'I found it in the vehicle bay. It was just sitting on a workbench. God knows how none of us noticed it before.'

I fix him with a cold stare. 'You didn't remove this from Sandrine's office then?'

Arne returns my look, his expression indignant. 'I did not, Kate. Why would I do that? I was going to bring it to Rob or Tom once I'd given Ark the lube.'

'Why?'

He takes it from my hands and presses a button. 'See for yourself. It's not working, though the batteries are okay. I thought maybe one of them could fix it.'

I frown, confused. Has the sat phone been sabotaged too? Or is there some innocent explanation?

More to the point, can I believe Arne's excuse for why I've just found it in his pocket?

I stand there, trying to think. Trying to make sense of it all.

'The gun has gone,' I say to Arne, studying his reaction.

He narrows his eyes at me. 'What gun?'

'The one that was locked up in Beta. Someone took the key, and now it's disappeared.'

Arne appears horrified. 'You're kidding. I didn't even know we had one on the base.'

'Me neither.' I inhale, watching the vapour in my breath coalesce in my torch beam. It's getting colder in here by the minute.

I hover, gripped by indecision, teeth beginning to chatter. What should I do? More than anything I want to turn to Arne, to ask for help, but I've no longer any idea whether I can trust him.

I glance over. He's staring into the distance, lost in thought. What's going on in his head? I wonder. What exactly is he planning?

I've been a fool, I realise, remembering the activity band. I accepted Arne's assurance that he had nothing to do with it simply because I wanted to believe him. I trusted him because I'd been blinded by my own feelings.

Same as back then. Same as with Ben.

I make up my mind. This is down to me.

'I have to go,' I say abruptly, leaving before he can stop me.

41

7 July

'It's me,' I hiss through the clinic door. 'Let me in.'

Sonya opens it a moment later. I lock the door behind me and peer at the baby swaddled in a duvet in her arms. A tiny face peeks out. So small and fragile, but her colour is good.

'How are they both?' I ask.

'Fine,' Sonya replies. 'I've been keeping this one on regular oxygen, plus I gave her a bit of milk in a pipette – she didn't seem interested though. Caro's still drowsy. BP normal. The bleeding has pretty much stopped.'

I receive this update with a mix of emotions. The little one will have to take some milk or water soon or we'll be in dangerous territory. But the news that Caro seems past the worst is welcome – with any luck we can get her out of here soon.

But what about that filing cabinet? I remind myself – we urgently need to find out who the hell is doing this, and the only clue lies in those files.

'What's the matter?' Sonya catches my expression in the soft light of the kerosene lamps.

'I think we should leave,' I say. 'Now.'

She frowns at me. 'And go where?'

'Gamma. You'll be safer over there.' I'll get them both installed in the summer camp, I decide, then come back and find a way into that cabinet.

'Why?' Sonya looks puzzled. 'What's going on, Kate? Has someone else been hurt?'

'Not yet, but . . .' I gaze at her, wondering what to say. I'm aware Caro might be listening, and the last thing I want is to cause her any more stress.

'I found Arne with this.' I pull the sat phone out of my pocket and show it to Sonya.

She gazes at it, puzzled. 'What was Arne doing with it?'

'He said he came across it on a workbench in the garage.'

'But you don't believe him?' Sonya frowns again.

'Thing is . . .' I lower my voice to a near whisper. 'That's not all. I also discovered Alex's activity monitor under one of the garage shelving units, before Sandrine died. It had been deliberately crushed.'

Sonya blinks at me, speechless, rocking the tiny scrap of life in her arms as she tries to take this all in.

'And you think . . .' She stops, shakes her head. 'No, I don't believe it. Not Arne.'

I gauge her reaction in the flickering light of the gas lamps.

'Seriously, Kate, Arne would never do this. Never.'

Cradling the baby in one arm, Sonya reaches over and pats my hand for emphasis. Something in her expression tells me that she, too, is aware how I feel about him. Clearly everyone knows something's going on between the station doctor and the vehicle mechanic.

No secrets in this place.

But is Sonya right about Arne, her solid belief that he's one of the good guys? After all, everybody seems to like and trust him. Except, perhaps, Jean-Luc . . . for the first time I wonder if Arne's account of the rift between them was true. 'Listen, you need—' Her words are cut short by a noise. Loud and sharp.

The unmistakable sound of a gunshot.

Sonya's eyes widen. 'Was that a *gun*?'

'The station pistol.' I spin around, trying to determine where the sound came from.

'Fuck,' Sonya says, after a moment or two – the only time I've ever heard this dignified lady swear.

Please God, I pray silently. Please don't let anyone else be hurt.

'What's going on?' asks a groggy voice behind us. 'What was that?'

'Nothing.' I go to Caro, put a hand to her skin to see if there's any heat there. Her temperature seems normal, thankfully. 'How are you feeling?'

'Sore,' she groans. 'It hurts everywhere. But okay.'

'Do you think you can get up and dressed?' I try to keep my voice calm and casual.

'Why?' Caro winces as she lifts her head to focus on me. 'What's happening?'

'I'm not entirely sure,' I admit. 'But it might be a good idea to move out of here.' I am determined now to get Caro and the baby somewhere safer – that shot sounded terrifyingly close.

I turn to Sonya. 'I need to go and see what just happened. You stay with Caro, give her some more pain relief if she needs it, then help her get dressed.'

Sonya stares at me as if I'm mad. 'You can't go out there, Kate. It's too dangerous.'

'No choice,' I say. 'I have to make sure no one is hurt. Don't let anybody in till I come back, and pack everything you need to evacuate.'

'Kate—' Sonya calls after me, bewildered.

But I'm gone.

42

7 July

The corridor is empty. And bitterly cold, the temperature now well below zero. A horrible image fills my mind as I stand, hesitating, outside the clinic. Our torch batteries going flat, one by one, the fuel for the stoves and kerosene lamps running low. The ice station engulfed in darkness, the freezing night creeping into every corner.

What will get us first? I wonder.

The killer, or the cold?

Taking a deep breath, I do the one thing I least want to do. Turn off my torch. I shiver in the claustrophobic blackness, heart racing, fighting the urge to switch it back on. The dark feels like something alive, something menacing.

It could contain anything, I think.

Anyone.

Get a grip, Kate. I focus on the route to the lounge, drawing a mental map in my head, then grope towards the far wall. Using my fingertips to guide me, I edge my way along the corridor, counting off the doorways, pushing down a sick dread that somebody might pounce at any moment.

Would I hear them coming?

My hand hits empty space. I turn left towards the lounge. What if you did encounter the killer? asks another part of my mind. What exactly would you do?

Hit them with your torch?

Emma Haughton

A second later, my foot twists on something and I crash to the floor, hands flailing to absorb the impact. My knee screams with a pain so bad I think I'm about to pass out. I lie there, in the darkness, waiting for the agony to subside. As I put out my hands to get up, my fingers close on a small round ball.

I pick it up, feeling the indentations on the surface. Jesus. I nearly broke my neck on one of Sandrine's fucking golf balls.

Her parting shot. I almost laugh with the absurdity of it.

Shoving it in my pocket, I heave myself to my feet and that's when I hear it. An audible crackle, accompanied by a momentary flash of static, just up ahead.

I freeze, heart in mouth.

Oh God. *There's someone here, with me, in the dark.*

I peer into the surrounding blackness, listening, trying not to breathe or make any sound. Not daring to move, in case I give myself away with some static of my own.

Time slows and stretches. I wait for another crack of the gun, the impact of the bullet. The thump of my heartbeat fills my head, so loud, it seems to me, that I'm afraid whoever is out there can hear it too.

Suddenly there's a scream, not far away.

Alice.

Throwing caution to the wind, I switch my torch back on and race in the direction of the lounge, ignoring the protests from my knee. As I round the corner, I spot her and Rajiv squatting over someone on the floor.

'Kate!' Alice exclaims as I run towards them. 'Quick!'

I kneel down next to the body. A rush of relief as I see Tom's eyes are open, staring at me with an expression of astonishment.

'Jesus,' I gasp. 'What happened?'

'I've been shot in the leg.' He groans. 'It hurts like fuck.'

I swing my torch to his jeans. A large bloodstain blooms across Tom's left thigh, expanding as I watch. My thoughts blank with fear and exhaustion. This is impossible, my mind insists.

This can't be happening.

'Kate?' Alice's voice is tremulous with distress. 'What should we do?'

'We'll take him into the lounge,' I say, pulling myself together. 'Can you ask Sonya for antiseptic wipes, plus some of the morphine I put out for Caro? You'll have to go on your own, so be careful.'

She nods, disappearing into the darkness. Rajiv and I manage to get Tom to his feet and help him limp down the corridor to the lounge. I hurry to clear a space on the floor. Looking around for something to cut his trouser leg, I spot Sonya's knitting basket. I root inside, find the tiny pair of rainbow-coloured scissors she uses to snip the ends of her yarn.

'Where's Rob?' I ask, as I hack my way through the thick denim of Tom's jeans.

'He went outside to get some more snow.'

'On his own?' I grit my teeth with frustration.

Rajiv shrugs. 'It's impossible, Kate. Besides, whoever is doing this has a gun. We can't protect one another from that.'

Fair point, I concede, finally exposing the upper part of Tom's leg. 'Pass me that box of tissues,' I say to Rajiv, using a handful to swab away the blood. I shine my light on the clean round hole just to the side of his femur. Tom groans as I lift his leg into the air and check for an exit wound on the other side.

'You're in luck,' I tell him. 'The bullet passed clean through, missed the bone and the femoral artery. I'll disinfect the wound and dress it, then give you some pain relief, plus antibiotics to minimise the risk of infection. You should be fine.'

He swallows, nods, his face deathly pale.

'What happened? Do you remember?'

'I . . .' he stammers, sounding shaky with shock. 'It was my fault.'

I stare at him. 'What do you mean?'

Tom's eyes brim with tears. 'It was me,' he whispers. 'I took the gun. Because I was scared. I kept hearing things . . . people outside my room . . . and then she . . . Sandrine . . .' His voice breaks. 'So I took the key when I found her, then got it from Beta.'

'So you shot yourself?' I frown at him. Was this some kind of botched suicide attempt?

'Not exactly.' Tom groans. 'Someone came at me, out of the dark, and tried to snatch it away. The gun went off in the struggle.'

'So you didn't see who it was?' Rajiv asks.

Tom shakes his head. 'I dropped my torch. I couldn't see a thing.'

'Can't you remember anything about them?' Rajiv sounds frustrated, and scared. 'Not even how he smelled? Didn't he make a noise?'

Tom shrugs helplessly. 'It was all too fast.'

'Have you still got the gun?' I ask.

He shakes his head again. 'He was too strong.'

Everyone's assuming it's a man, I notice. But they're almost certainly right. It's impossible for this to be Caro or Sonya, and it seems unlikely any of it could be down to Alice.

At that moment she returns with the medical supplies, cheeks red with exertion, as if she ran all the way. She stares in horror at Tom's leg while I grab the dressing and bind the wound tightly to stop the bleeding, then help him onto the couch.

'Keep your leg still. I'll give you something for the pain.' I turn to Rajiv. 'Is there any water?'

He fetches a bottle with an inch left at the bottom. Helping Tom into a sitting position, I get him to swallow the antibiotics while I prep the syringe. Slowly, carefully, I suck up some of the morphine, hands trembling with shock and a rush of longing for that beautiful clear liquid. It would be so easy, too easy, to pocket the rest and help myself while everyone is distracted.

Just a little. Just enough to smooth the edge from all this horror.

'Here, take this.' I hand Alice the morphine phial. 'Remind me or Sonya to give him another dose in four hours.'

'Is he okay?' asks a voice behind me.

Arne.

I swing around. He looks out of breath, as if he's been running too. 'Yes,' I tell him. 'It's only a flesh wound.'

He peers down at Tom, then turns back to me. 'What did you do with the sat phone?'

'It's in the clinic.'

'You've found the phone?' Alice asks, her expression hopeful.

'It's not working.' Arne rubs his head, eyes scanning the lounge. He seems distraught. Exhausted. 'Christ, this is insane. We have to do something!'

'Like what?' Rajiv asks. 'What can we do?'

We stand there in silence for a moment.

'Get the others,' I decide. 'We need everybody here – except Sonya, who can stay with Caro. But everyone else. And find some more stoves.'

'Why?' asks Arne. 'What's your plan?'

I look him full in the face. 'One of us did this. One of us attacked Tom, and killed Sandrine. Alex too. So we all stay in here, together.'

Arne, Alice, and Rajiv stare back at me.

'It's the only way,' I insist. 'The only way we can stay safe.'

'But what about the gun?' Rajiv sounds bewildered. 'How will we be safe if one of us has a gun?'

'We search one another,' I say simply. 'Then we just watch each other and wait.'

43

7 July

It's an eerie scene. Nine of us in full outdoor gear, swaddled under duvets, trying to keep warm. Tom slumped on the sofa beside me, leg outstretched, his skin pale with shock. The air claggy with the smell of paraffin, as four little stoves struggle against the vicious cold seeping in through the outside walls and up through the floor.

No one is speaking, all of us stunned by recent events. Nor does anybody seem interested in the packets of biscuits, nuts, crisps, and trail mix Rajiv brought in from the store-room, in an attempt to keep us all fed. I gaze around at our faces, hollow-eyed and ghastly in the dim yellow light of the kerosene lamps. We resemble the walking dead, I think grue-somely.

Ark's monsters come to life.

But we're no longer in immediate danger. Arne and Drew checked everyone as they entered the lounge, then Ark and Rob frisked them both in turn. Wherever the killer stashed that pistol, it's not in here. I've searched every nook and cranny to make sure, even running my hand down the back of the chairs and sofas.

We're safe – at least for now.

The silence deepens as we eye one another surreptitiously, each thinking exactly the same thing.

Which of us is the killer?

Who murdered Alex and Sandrine, and possibly Jean-Luc too? Who took that gun from Tom?

I study my fellow winterers one by one. Ark looks disgruntled, anxious to get back to his beloved generator, his outdoor jacket and trousers covered in grease stains. Alice, barely visible under her duvet, huddles on a sofa, features tense with anxiety and exhaustion – none of us has managed more than a few hours' sleep in the last twenty-four. Next to her Rajiv looks wistful and sombre, as if he'd rather be anywhere but here.

On the opposite side of the room, Rob and Luuk nurse bottles of beer, defying my suggestion that we all keep a clear head. Luuk gives every appearance of being slightly bored by the whole situation, while Rob's eyes dart around the room, never settling on anyone for more than a second.

Only Drew and Arne seem much like themselves – Arne gazing up at the ceiling, lost in thought, while Drew studies everyone as carefully as me, his expression blank as we briefly cross gazes.

Which one of you did this?

Think, Kate, I urge myself, as my mind starts to drift. What do you know? I try to work it through logically. I can safely rule out Alice, along with Caro and Sonya – none of them could have manhandled someone of Alex's bulk out on the ice. Or, for that matter, overpowered Tom.

And the killer isn't acting impulsively, I realise. This situation has been well thought out – whoever murdered Sandrine sabotaged the power either just before or afterwards, in an effort to distract us and prevent contact with UNA.

Nor does it seem the killer is doing this for kicks, otherwise Tom would be dead. Sandrine must have represented a threat in some manner – probably because she was about to expose him.

What else can I be sure of? I wrack my exhausted mind for

answers. I know Luuk lied about the reason for being in Alex's room. That both Alex's activity monitor and the sat phone were found in the vicinity of Arne's garage. That Sandrine confirmed Alex's story about Jean-Luc's suspicions, and the link with that woman's death at McMurdo.

But, try as I might, I can't make sense of it all. The facts don't seem to bring me any closer to a definitive conclusion. And there's no way at the moment I can get to the contents of that filing cabinet.

Not alone.

'So what are we going to do?' Drew breaks the uneasy silence. 'Anyone gonna own up to this shit?'

'Well, it's not me,' says Rob firmly, taking another swig of beer.

'Nor me,' adds Rajiv, while Alice and Luuk nod their heads in agreement.

Everyone looks around accusingly at each other, prompting Ark into a sudden bark of a laugh. 'Who is killer raise hand,' he demands, gazing about expectantly.

This is insane. Impossible to believe that whoever murdered Alex and Sandrine is just sitting here, calmly, pretending innocence.

Even the idea of it is sickening.

Unthinkable.

I close my eyes, considering my next move. Should I mention the connection with the death of Naomi Perez at McMurdo? Suggest several of us break into that filing cabinet together?

But that would mean dividing the group, exposing us all to danger. No way the murderer would simply stand by and wait for his identity to be revealed.

It's not a risk I'm willing to take.

'Whoever did this, we can safely assume they aren't about to admit it.' Arne's voice cuts through the simmering atmosphere of mutual suspicion. 'So all we can do is stay safe until help arrives.'

'What help?' asks Rob. 'It's next to impossible to fly a plane out here under these conditions. Arne's found the sat phone, but even if I can get it working, it won't be much use. UNA will know by now that we're in trouble – the problem is, there's nothing they can do.'

'Surely they'll have to do *something*,' wails Alice, close to tears again. 'They'll have to at least try.'

Drew shakes his head. 'Flying in the middle of winter has almost never been attempted, in the whole history of Antarctica. So many things can go wrong – the huge distances, the constant darkness, the temperature – the fuel might freeze, or the plane itself – steel becomes very brittle in these temperatures and can break. Not to mention the weather, visibility, the altitude, the lack of a proper runway. Plus the pilots would need to refuel en route. And we've no runway lights, no way for them to make a safe landing.'

I mull this over. 'Might they try though? Even if they can only get a small plane out here for Caro and the baby.'

A forlorn hope, I know, remembering the Russian doctor who had to remove his own appendix; the American physician who was forced to biopsy and treat her own breast cancer for months before she could be evacuated.

'They might,' Arne agrees, 'but they would never risk it without contacting us first and finding out exactly what's wrong.'

'So we need a plan,' I insist. 'We have to assess the resources we've got, and how we can make them last until then.'

Rajiv nods. 'Kate's right. We should put our heads together.'

'Food, water, heat – we need generators,' Ark says sullenly. 'I should be there fixing, not in here having nice chat.'

'How long do you think it might take you?' Drew asks him.

Ark shrugs. 'Hard to say. Have to find way to mend cooling fan. Days, maybe week.'

'Have we got enough kerosene to keep going that long?' Rajiv asks. 'It takes a lot of fuel simply to heat snow for water.'

Ark shakes his head. 'Not enough.'

'What about the diesel for the generators?' Alice chips in. 'Can't we use that?'

'Many problems,' Ark says gloomily. 'Diesel not evaporate like kerosene, is hard to burn and very dirty. Lots of bad chemicals. Plus there is problem of carbon dioxide – ventilation system no longer work without electricity. We need fresh air with open flame or else we die slowly.'

Shit. I think of Caro and the baby, still shut up in the clinic with two heaters blasting away. I didn't consider that. All the more reason to get them out of there soon, I decide; one thing you can say about Gamma, it's well ventilated.

A loud wail from the opposite sofa makes me start. 'I just want to get home to my daughter,' Alice sobs, collapsing onto Rajiv's shoulder. 'I don't want to die in this place.'

'You're not going to die,' says Arne calmly. 'None of us are.'

'So how are we going to survive, like this, for the rest of the winter?' demands Rob. 'Not to mention that someone has access to a gun and possibly intends to pick us off, one by one.'

'We don't know that,' Rajiv snaps. 'We've no idea what happened to Sandrine. We can't even be sure she was murdered. And Tom isn't dead, are you?'

All eyes settle on Tom. He blinks back without replying.

'Besides, there's no sense in killing all of us,' Drew points out. 'Murder everyone and you can't go on the run, can you? You'd just have to wait for the police to fly in and arrest you.'

Tom clears his throat. 'Unless you could make it look like an accident,' he croaks. 'And that you were the sole survivor.

After all, there'd be nobody left to contradict you, and plenty of time to destroy any evidence to the contrary.'

Everyone falls silent as they absorb the impact of Tom's words. Jesus, is that the killer's end game? His 'get out of jail free' card?

Murder all of us, then proceed with a leisurely cover-up?

'That's not going to happen,' I say firmly, pulling the duvet more tightly around me. 'And in the meantime, we have to prioritise keeping safe and warm until UNA can find a way to intervene. I suggest we make a list of what we need to do, and that we operate in groups of three – no one left on their own, for obvious reasons.'

'And who made you de facto leader?' Luuk finally finds his voice, throwing me a challenging look. 'Why all of a sudden are you giving the orders? Seems to me it wasn't long ago you were confined to your room for breaching pretty much every rule on the base.'

'Luuk, I've no desire to be the one in charge – by all means—'

'Come to think of it,' he cuts in. 'Most of this kicked off when you arrived. Ever since you got here there's been nothing but trouble. You stirred things up with Alex, then you came after me—'

'That's not what happened,' I reply indignantly. 'I simply tried to talk to Alex – and to you, for that matter.'

'Felt more like a fucking interrogation from my end,' glowers Luuk.

'Back off.' Drew gets to his feet, but I hold up a hand to stop him. I take a deep breath, hesitating.

Gloves off, I decide. 'I simply asked you, Luuk, why you were in Alex's cabin right before he died.'

An audible intake of breath from several people in the room. Alice's eyes widen in Luuk's direction.

'And I told you why.' Luuk glares back at me.

I hold my nerve. 'And that was a lie, Luuk. You said you went to borrow Alex's vape pen, but Alex never owned one – not according to Caro.'

He stares at me, open-mouthed. Clearly blindsided by my accusation.

'What the fuck, Luuk?' Arne turns to him. 'What were you doing in there?'

Luuk swallows. I watch him desperately trying to decide what to say next. 'Okay, I lied,' he admits. 'That wasn't the real reason I was there.'

'So what was the real reason?' Drew demands.

All eyes fix on Luuk, who visibly squirms under the scrutiny. Probably wishing he hadn't started this. 'Some of my stash went missing – Alex was one of the few people who knew where I hid it. I thought I'd take the opportunity to speak to him.'

'Your drugs, you mean?' Alice says.

Luuk ignores her.

'So what did Alex say?' I ask.

'Nothing,' Luuk shrugs. 'Like I told you before, he was totally out of it. I could barely get a word out of him. So I had a quick look around his room, then left.'

I study him. Is Luuk telling the truth this time? Impossible to tell. 'When were you at McMurdo?' I ask instead.

He turns and frowns at me. 'What the hell kind of a question is that?'

'A simple one, Luuk. With a simple answer.' I can see Arne watching me out of the corner of his eye; he knows, of course, exactly why I'm asking.

Luuk snorts. 'Christ, you're a prize bitch, aren't you? No wonder Sandrine didn't trust you – and now she's dead. Bit of a coincidence, that, isn't it?'

Before I can say anything in my defence, Arne leaps up.

Bounding over to Luuk's chair, he drags him upright by the collar of his jacket. 'What the fuck do you mean by that?' he yells in his face, shaking him.

Alice gives a yelp of alarm as the two men start to struggle, Luuk managing to free himself from Arne's grasp and aim a punch at his head. Arne retaliates by hitting him in the jaw, then kicking his legs out from under him. As Luuk stumbles and falls, he catches one of the stoves, bringing it crashing to the floor.

'*Chyort!*' yells Ark, as kerosene spills onto the carpet, a rivulet of flame in its wake. He scrambles to his feet and rights the stove, grabbing the nearest duvet to smother the flames. All the while uttering a steady stream of Russian invective that needs no translation.

'Fucking morons,' he shouts at Luuk and Arne once he's extinguished the fire. 'You want to burn whole station? Finish us fast?'

Arne looks abashed. He lifts both hands in a gesture of apology. 'Sorry. You're right. All this is just getting to me.'

But Luuk is having none of it. 'Screw you all,' he says, picking himself off the floor and rubbing his jaw. 'I'm not taking any more of this shit. I'm going to look for that fucking gun.' He picks up one of the spare torches and slams out of the room.

Moments later, Drew gets up and follows him.

My stomach churns in a spiral of panic as the rest of us stare after them. This is all going wrong, I think. Horribly, horribly wrong.

Only one thing is clear – none of us is safe on this station.

44

7 July

'You have any idea how to drive one of these?' Sonya asks, as I examine the nearest skidoo.

I shake my head.

'I'll do it,' murmurs Caro, voice groggy. She's dressed in outdoor gear, the waist of her down-filled trousers widened with string to allow for her injured stomach and the dressings on her wound. The baby is tucked deep inside her jacket, supported by a makeshift sling Sonya fashioned out of a sheet. I'm praying they'll both stay warm enough for the journey to Gamma.

'You're in no condition to drive,' I say. 'Doctor's orders.'

Caro's face twitches with pain as we help her onto the passenger seat, draping her in a duvet for extra warmth. With all the food and medical supplies, it's clear there's no room for anyone else.

'You should take her,' I say to Sonya.

'No.' She shakes her head vigorously. 'Caro needs you more. If something were to happen, I wouldn't know what to do.'

I hesitate. She's right. Caro is far from out of the woods, even without the stress of the transfer to the summer camp. But I'm still not happy about leaving Sonya here, and all the other snowmobiles are out on the ice, probably by the emergency generator hut.

'Go,' she urges. 'I'll follow as soon as I can find a spare skidoo.'

I haven't got a better idea, so climb onto the driver's seat. I insert the keys I found in the vehicle bay cupboard, then hesitate, wondering what to do next.

'Make sure it's in neutral, then press the ignition button to turn on the engine,' says Caro. 'You'll need to let it warm up a bit.'

She sounds exhausted. Despite dosing her up with painkillers, I'm well aware of the toll even this short journey must be taking. She should be lying down, recovering, not venturing into the coldest and most hostile environment on earth.

But the alternative, leaving her trapped on the base with a killer wielding a gun, doesn't bear thinking about.

Checking the gears, I push the button and the motor comes to life. I wait an anxious minute or two for the engine to warm up. Can I really do this?

'Now turn the thumb throttle,' Caro prompts.

I do as she says and the skidoo lurches forwards, making Caro gasp with pain. 'Sorry,' I say, raising my voice above the sound of the engine.

'Ease it gently,' she replies, and I try again, and this time the skidoo glides across the tracking towards the doorway. Seconds later we're out on the ice, the cold hitting us like a slap in the face as I tentatively pick up speed and turn in the direction of the summer camp, making sure to avoid the ropes that mark out the walkways.

'You okay?' I shout back to Caro, who's clutching my waist with one arm and holding onto the skidoo with the other, but my voice is lost in the wind that's whipping the snow into flurries and reducing visibility to a few metres. A second later my goggles freeze over. I lift a gloved hand and swipe it across the lenses, clearing my vision enough to keep going.

I'm about a hundred metres from Alpha when it dawns on me what an incredibly stupid move this is. I can barely see where I'm going, and with no experience at driving a skidoo over the uneven ice, we're in constant danger of overbalancing.

I should turn around, return to the base. Find somewhere secure for Caro and her newborn.

But where? As we crawl across the ice, as slowly as I dare without stalling the engine, I have to admit to myself that nowhere is safe from someone with a gun. Especially not Gamma, given it's basically a couple of glorified tents. Our only hope is the killer won't bother with us out there, that once Sonya arrives to care for Caro, I can go back to Alpha and deal with the situation before anyone else gets hurt.

Because out here, teeth gritted against the wind, ice crystals swirling around us, I'm forced again to consider the killer's end game – and mine. He knows, clearly, there's little chance of getting off this station without being apprehended. Sandrine's murder has changed everything – whenever UNA gets here, none of us will be allowed home before her killer has been identified.

I have to find out who it is, and talk to him, I decide. Reason with him. Persuade him the best thing to do is give himself up now, rather than face a worse outcome later.

With a rush of relief, I see the Gamma tents loom out of the darkness. A second later, the skidoo comes to an abrupt halt that almost pitches me over the handlebars. 'You all right?' I shout to Caro, reassured to feel her arm still around my waist.

'What happened?' she yells back into the wind.

'I don't know.'

'Press the ignition button again.'

I press it, but nothing happens. What the hell is wrong? I try again, suppressing a moan of frustration when the engine doesn't respond. 'It's dead,' I say, immediately regretting my choice of words.

A silence as Caro thinks. 'It's probably the cold,' she replies, voice flat. 'These things aren't designed to operate in temperatures below minus thirty. We should have warmed up the engine a bit longer.'

I sit there for a moment, panicking. What now?

Caro answers the question by climbing awkwardly off the skidoo. 'We'll have to walk.' She grabs a torch and shines it into the darkness, but without the bright beam of the headlights we can no longer see the camp.

Just keep heading in the same direction, I tell myself, trying to stay calm. It can't be much further.

'Do you think you can make it?' I ask Caro, worried about her condition. She should be in bed, not trudging across the ice in sub-zero temperatures. I should have planned this more carefully, considered the risks.

What the hell was I thinking?

'Let's go.' Caro starts to walk in the direction we were heading. But she's moving so slowly, with such evident pain and exhaustion, that I catch up with her in a few strides, even with the weight of the bags I'm carrying. I sling her arm over my shoulder, and we advance side-by-side, step by strenuous step, the cold piercing our clothing, creeping into our flesh, into our bones. We keep our faces down, sheltering from the wind, watching out for pitfalls in the snow.

Our progress is agonisingly slow, my bad knee flaring with pain at every step. Fear starts to get the better of me.

We're not going to make it, I think. All three of us are going to die out here, and it will be entirely my fault.

Caro stumbles on a ridge in the snow and we both lurch forwards, torch flying from my grasp. Thankfully it doesn't go out, and as I crawl to retrieve it, I see we're only thirty metres or so from the main tent. Clutching the torch firmly, I pick up the bags, and help Caro to her feet. We shuffle our way across the ice; I'm almost tearful with relief as we finally reach the entrance.

The place is as cold as a morgue. Colder. I steer Caro into a little cabin at the rear of the main dorm and sit her down on one of the beds. As the emergency evacuation point, the whole of Gamma is equipped with everything we need to survive, and it doesn't take long to find a couple of stoves and kerosene lamps and light them. I retrieve several sleeping bags from the cupboards and drape them around Caro and the baby.

'Is she okay?' I peer at the downy crown of head just visible inside Caro's jacket.

'I think so. I can feel her moving now and then.'

'We'll try feeding her again, as soon as it warms up in here.'

Caro nods and lies back on the bed, closing her eyes. She looks utterly depleted, and I feel a terrible weight of responsibility.

Can I do this?

Can I keep them safe, warm, alive, until Sonya gets here?

I lie on the bed opposite, shivering, and listen to the hiss of the stoves and kerosene lamps, the wind buffeting the side of the tent, for once grateful for the icy draught that flows into the cabin – we won't suffocate anyway. As the temperature in the little room starts to lift, as warmth relaxes my muscles and my teeth stop chattering, I drift into an exhausted sleep.

45

7 July

I come to with a jolt, suddenly alert. Take a few moments to
remember where I am and how I got here. I glance over at
Caro, asleep on the camp bed opposite, the baby still cocooned
in her jacket.

How long since we arrived? And hour? Two?

I reach in my pocket for my phone to check the time, but
realise it's missing. Hell. I must have lost it when we fell on
the ice.

Where on earth is Sonya? I listen, alert for the sound of an
approaching skidoo, but hear nothing outside beyond the low
moan of the wind.

Maybe she thought better of it? Or perhaps she couldn't
find a spare vehicle. I try not to dwell on worse alternatives:
the killer cornering Sonya somewhere in Beta, wielding a gun
. . . the killer attacking Arne . . .

Arne.

I remember how he leapt to my defence when Luuk started
accusing me in the lounge, and I feel a sharp pang of guilt and
anxiety. Try as I might, I cannot convince myself that Arne
has anything to do with all this.

But I didn't tell him I was coming here. I didn't tell anyone.
Just went straight to the clinic, checked Caro was well enough
for the journey, then we made our way to the garage, all the
while praying we didn't bump into any of the rest of the crew.

How long till Arne realises we're missing? More to the point, how long before the killer notices too? Will he decide to come after us? After all, it won't take much effort to work out where we are; it's not as if we could hide away in the igloo, or Sonya's meteorology hut.

At best, all I've achieved is to buy us a little time, I realise, with a dragging feeling of dread. And time is no defence against a man with a gun, and the rest of the winter to use it.

Stop.

I shut down that train of thought before it spirals out of control, and get up to check the fuel levels in the stoves. Beside me, Caro stirs and wakes. I search through the bag of medicine Sonya packed and find the morphine.

'Do you need another dose?' I ask, figuring enough time has passed to minimise any risk.

Caro nods. Watches quietly as I insert the needle into the phial and suck ten millilitres into the syringe. I help her sit and remove her jacket, her face contorting with pain at the effort of movement. Keeping the baby swaddled under the duvet, she pulls up her sleeve and extends her arm.

'All done,' I say, then turn my attention to the bundle on the bed, relieved to hear a small snuffling sound from the tiny infant.

I feel a tug of tenderness. It's a miracle she's still alive. Caro too. All the odds stacked against them.

'Shall I try feeding her?' Caro blinks at me, her skin pink in the soft light cast by the kerosene lamps. I touch her forehead, glad to find no sign of fever.

'She may not have developed a strong sucking reflex yet. But give it a go – if she can take a little colostrum that will be the best thing for her.'

'Colostrum?' Caro looks confused.

'Your first milk. It provides condensed nutrients for newborns. Antibodies too.'

'But is it safe? After the . . .' she nods at the half-used phial of morphine.

'A small amount will get into your milk, yes, but not enough to affect her. It's more important to control your pain or you won't be able to feed her anyway.'

Caro pulls up her T-shirt and exposes a breast, wincing as she tries to position the baby without putting pressure on her stomach. She hesitates, looking uncertain.

'Nuzzle her mouth near your nipple,' I suggest, trying to recall my stint on the maternity ward. 'She'll work out the rest.'

I watch as Caro lifts her daughter to her breast, a smile breaking out on both our faces as the baby roots for a second or two, then opens her mouth and latches on. She sucks for a full minute, then her eyes close and she falls back to sleep.

We both sit in silence, watching her breathe. This precious scrap in a place hostile to life of any kind. It's at once awe-inspiring and terrifying, and again I feel that terrible burden of responsibility bearing down on me.

'Talk to me,' Caro says in a near whisper, sounding small and scared. Clearly she's finding this as overwhelming as I am. 'Anything to take my mind off . . . well . . . everything.'

Everything. That one word sums up our predicament. The three of us alone, vulnerable, defenceless. Somewhere out there, a killer with a gun. Around us a vast wilderness of darkness and cold.

And nobody coming to the rescue.

I try to think of something that might take her mind off it all – mine too – but Caro gets there first. 'Tell me about the accident.'

'What accident?' I frown, confused.

'The one that happened to you.' She lies back on the bed, pulling the duvet over herself and the baby. 'It was a car crash, wasn't it?'

That accident. My chest contracts as I remember what I'd give anything to forget.

'It was.' I sigh, struggling to focus through the fog of my exhaustion and withdrawal. 'But you don't really want to hear—'

'Yes, I do,' Caro cuts in. 'I really do. You saved my life, Kate. I want to know what's gone on in yours, what's made you so unhappy. And I don't mean just what happened to your face, because it's obvious this thing is more than skin deep.'

'Obvious?' I frown again. 'How?'

Caro thinks. 'It's like . . . I'm not sure how to put it . . . it's as if it's always there, as if it never leaves you. Only sometimes, I get a glimpse of how you must have been before.'

Jesus, am I really such an open book?

'You never talk about it,' she explains, 'and it's clear you don't want people to ask. Like it's . . . unmentionable. It's obvious you're not over it.'

I gaze at her. I guess she's right. 'Okay.' I inhale, steadying myself. 'What do you want to know?'

'Were you on your own? When it happened?'

I shake my head. 'I was with my fiancé, actually.'

Caro's face registers surprise. 'You were engaged?'

'Yes.' An image of Ben rises up in my mind. How he looked that night when we left the hospital after our respective shifts – hollow-eyed, exhausted, a fresh crop of stubble on his cheeks. We barely spoke as we walked to the car.

'You want me to drive?' I offered, knowing Ben had just spent six hours in theatre performing a particularly tricky bypass.

He nodded, remaining silent as I steered out of the hospital car park and onto the streets of Bristol. I assumed the operation hadn't gone well, that perhaps the patient hadn't survived, but I didn't ask. That was one of our rules. We never discussed work, never brought it home with us – the only way to manage it was not to give it space in your head.

'So what happened?' Caro prompts.

I inhale. 'Do you want the short version or the long one?'

'The long one. I reckon we could be here for a while.' She offers a rueful smile.

'I was driving,' I tell her. 'Ben was really tired. He was a heart surgeon, so often in theatre for hours at a time . . .' I stop, not sure how to say all this out loud. It feels formidable . . . impossible. I send Caro a helpless look, but she simply waits for me to continue.

I take another deep breath and surrender to the gravitational pull of the past. I describe everything in all the detail I can remember – which is far more than I've ever let on to anyone else. How Ben's silence endured through all my attempts at small talk. I thought he was listening to the news on the radio, the endless political turmoil of Brexit and the Middle East, but suddenly he reached out and switched it off.

'You okay?' I glanced at him as I took the turning towards Leigh Woods, the back route home. A bit longer, but less busy than the motorway. Plus I sensed there was something Ben needed to get off his chest. Perhaps he'd had another run-in with his ambitious colleague Deepak.

'Kate,' he said, swallowing. 'I need to tell you something. The thing is . . . I've been offered a new job.'

'Hey,' I exclaimed, delighted. 'That's fantastic! Consultant surgeon?' I glanced over again, expecting him to return my smile, but he kept staring out through the windscreen as if mesmerised, though at that time of night there was little to see.

'Actually no,' he said, after a pause. 'It's a position in a different hospital.'

I took my eyes off the road for a second to look at him again. There was something in his expression I couldn't fathom, and I felt the first twinge of foreboding. 'Which hospital?'

'In Michigan. The Holland.'

'Michigan?' I blurted. '*You mean in America?*'

'Unless there's another one I'm not aware of.'

I gripped the steering wheel, trying to take this in. Since when had Ben been looking for jobs abroad? And why the hell hadn't he said anything to me? I felt a shiver of anger. Did he simply assume I'd tag along, put my own career on hold and trail after him?

Christ, I thought we were beyond that kind of patriarchal shit. I gritted my teeth and tried to keep my voice measured. 'I didn't know you were looking abroad. In fact, I didn't know you were looking for a new job at all.'

Ben grimaced, scratched the stubble on his chin. 'Yeah. I should have told you.'

'*You think?*' I replied, unable to contain the sarcasm in my tone.

A minute passed in relative silence. Just the low hum of the Mercedes' engine. A few drops of rain pattering on the windscreen.

'Are you going to accept it?' I asked, feeling at once hollowed out and desperate. 'When would we go? After the wedding?' But that wasn't for another six months yet. We hadn't even planned it properly, beyond deciding we'd have the reception in his parents' garden in Cheshire.

Ben didn't reply. I kept a tight grip on the steering wheel, making a conscious effort to slow around the sharp bends as we entered the woods.

'Listen, Kate . . .' Ben spoke quietly, faltering. 'I . . .' He rubbed his forehead. I glanced at him again. He seemed weary in a way that went beyond the stress of a long and difficult operation. And all of a sudden I knew what was coming was bad.

Very bad.

'Kate.' Caro's voice pulls me back to the present. 'What did he say?'

I realise I've stopped talking, have wandered off somewhere in my mind. I sigh, forcing myself on. 'Ben told me he was going to accept it – and that he'd be leaving as soon as he'd worked his notice.'

Caro's expression turns to shock, my own emotions reflected on her face. 'What the fuck? He expected you to just drop everything and go with him?'

I clear my throat so I can continue, picturing Ben's features as I focus on what he actually said. 'I'm leaving at the beginning of March. I've already booked the flight.'

'You're kidding me.' I gaped at him, astounded.

He shook his head, still refusing to meet my gaze. He chose this moment deliberately, I realised, so I had to keep my eyes on the road and he wouldn't have to look me full in the face. A pain rose into my throat, threatening to choke me. A tight, suffocating sensation.

'What about me, Ben? What about the wedding?'

He swallowed again. Working himself up. 'Actually, there's another thing I need to tell you.'

The moment the words left his mouth I knew what was coming. 'There's someone else, isn't there?' I whispered, voice barely audible above the engine.

But Ben heard me. 'Yes.'

I should have pulled over, I say out loud to Caro in that tiny cabin surrounded by the endless hostile night. I should have stopped the car so we could talk.

But I kept on driving, tears smearing my vision. 'Are you going to tell me who she is?' I asked Ben.

'Does it matter?'

'Of course it fucking does!' The car veered into the other lane as I glared at him. Ben made a grab for the steering wheel. 'For fuck's sake, Kate, pull over. Let me drive.'

But I didn't. I wouldn't. I carried on clutching the steering wheel to prevent myself from hitting him, to stop the fury welling inside me from spilling out and engulfing both of us. 'Who is it?' I repeated, louder.

'No one you know.'

'A nurse?'

He snorted. 'Yeah, right. Like I'm that much of a cliché, Kate. Actually she's a junior doctor. Paediatrics.'

I sifted through my mind, trying to remember all the doctors in that department, but the hospital was large and staff turnover high. It was impossible to keep up with everyone. 'Does she know you're engaged? That you're getting married?'

Ben shook his head again. 'We're not getting married, Kate. That's precisely what I'm trying to tell you.'

All at once the tears arrived, streaming down my cheeks. Ben turned away, embarrassed, staring out of the passenger window at the silhouettes of trees, their winter-bare branches glowing eerily against a nearly full moon.

'Why?' I swiped the tears with the back of my hand. '*Why?*'

'I can't give you a reason, Kate. It doesn't work like that.'

'Then fucking try, okay? I need to know.'

He closed his eyes and rubbed his forehead, thinking. 'She . . . it's . . . *fresh*, Kate. I don't know. Exciting. Spontaneous. Everything about us – you and me – is so predictable, so earnest. All we do is work and eat and sleep. We barely even screw any more, let alone have any fun.'

He looked at me properly for the first time since getting in the car, his expression pleading now, begging me to understand.

'You're leaving me.' A statement, not a question, but still I waited for him to contradict it. 'Shit!' I slammed a fist down on the steering column when he didn't. '*Shit.*'

'Kate, slow down!' In my tears his face was blurry, but I could see his eyes wide with alarm. 'Pull over, okay?'

I kept going.

'Seriously, you're driving way too fast.'

'Fuck off, Ben.'

It was at that moment the fox appeared, darting out of the trees into the road. It froze, eyes glinting in the headlights, confused by the sudden glare. Staring right at me, as if trying to communicate something.

I swerved to avoid it. And everything changed for ever.

'Kate?' Caro studies me with a concerned expression. 'Kate, I'm so sorry.'

I'm crying, I realise. Great convulsive sobs.

'Are you okay?' she repeats.

I clear my throat again. 'Not really.'

Caro looks at me long and hard. 'It wasn't your fault, you know.'

I shake my head and turn away. 'Apparently I was doing at least sixty,' I tell her. 'Ben was killed instantly when we hit the tree. I broke my leg, ruptured my spleen, and my face was lacerated by a branch that came through the windscreen.' Instinctively my fingers find my scar, trace its line across my cheek.

My mark.

A permanent reminder of my guilt.

'Shit,' Caro whispers, taking all this in. '*He died?*'

'It took several hours for the emergency services to cut us out of the car,' I continue, voice cracking with the pressure of memories finally allowed to surface. 'I passed out for a while, then came round in the ambulance. We were rushed back to the same emergency room where I worked.'

I glance at Caro in the twilight of the kerosene lamps. 'That was almost the worst thing, seeing the faces of my colleagues. That's when I realised that Ben was dead, from their expressions, the pity and sympathy in their voices.'

Caro's gaze doesn't waver. 'You do know it wasn't your fault, don't you?' she repeats.

I shake my head again vehemently. 'But that's not true, is it? At best, I was careless. I should have pulled over. At worst . . .' I stop. Better not to go there.

That way madness lies.

'At worst what?' Caro is gentle, coaxing. '*Kate, tell me.*'

I squeeze my eyes shut. Force myself to voice my worst fear, the thing that haunts me, day and night. The pain I'll do anything to numb. 'What if it wasn't an accident?' I whisper. 'What if I made it happen? Deliberately.'

Caro frowns. 'What do you mean?'

I swallow again, swipe away more tears. 'Sometimes, when I can't sleep, when I'm lying there awake, I start thinking, you know, if I intended it to happen.'

'*If you intended it to happen?*' Her frown deepens. 'To hurt yourself and Ben, you mean?'

I nod, recalling those bright eyes in the headlights. Sometimes I wonder if I imagined it, that fox. Was it really there? Or did I conjure it up afterwards to absolve myself? To give myself an excuse for what happened.

I clear my throat again. 'The worst of it is, I'll never know, will I?'

Caro shuffles forward, pain fleeting across her face, and reaches for my hand. 'Kate, listen to me.' Her fingers squeeze mine. '*I know*, okay? I'm absolutely certain that you would never deliberately hurt anyone, however angry or upset you were. You simply don't have it in you.'

I stare at her, disbelieving. Suddenly the baby gives a little mewl, her face twisting, and Caro releases my hand to check her. There's a minute or so of almost soundless crying before she falls back to sleep.

Wind, I decide. That tiny digestive system kicking into action.

I gaze at Caro. 'Have you thought what you'll call her?'

'Yes.'

'You going to tell me?'

'Do you even need to ask?' Caro smiles. 'I'm calling her Kate.'

My eyes widen and I have to swallow again before I can speak. 'I'm honoured. Thank you.'

'Kate Louise,' Caro adds. 'Louise, after Alex's sister. I thought about Alexandra, but it seemed a bit . . . well . . . too much.'

'Kate Louise. That's a beautiful name.'

I study the pair of them for a moment, then get to my feet. 'You two should get more rest. If you need more pain meds, let me know.'

Caro looks nervous. 'Where are you going?'

'Not far,' I reassure her. 'Just to collect some snow. I'll heat it on the stove for fresh water. Then I'll find some food, and check we've got more fuel.'

Caro lays her head down on the pillow. 'I meant what I said, Kate,' she murmurs. 'You have nothing to forgive yourself for. You have to let this go.'

I hold her gaze for a few seconds, then nod. 'I promise I'll try.'

Taking one of the torches, I venture out into the freezing cold of the main tent – it must be minus twenty or thirty in here. I hunt in the kitchen for containers I can load with snow, but everything is too small. I check all the cupboards, but find nothing bigger than a saucepan.

Surely there's a plastic bin or bowl around here somewhere? I open the door to the storage space under the sink – nothing of use, but as I'm about to close it up again I see a glimpse of metal behind the U-bend.

Bending down, I shine my torch inside. Something silvery reflects the light back at me. I reach in and pull the object from its hiding place, hardly believing what I'm looking at.

A laptop.

Expensive, by the look of it, slim and sleek. I get down on my hands and knees and shine my torch deeper into the cupboard to check for anything else. In its beam, I see a maroon-covered notebook, and a small object in a black case. I reach in, easing them around the pipework that kept them hidden from view. The smaller one turns out to be a phone in a flip case – Alex's mobile, I realise, remembering him playing video games on it in the lounge.

I pull off my gloves, open up the notebook, and shine my torch on its pages. Small neat handwriting in French, executed with a fountain pen.

No doubt about it.

I've found Jean-Luc's journal.

46

7 July

I stare, shivering, at the journal, my fingers already so numb with cold that I can barely hold it. Though I'm desperate to read what's inside, I daren't return to the heated cabin, loath to disturb Caro and the baby.

Besides, I need to focus on this alone and undistracted.

So I grab a sleeping bag and wrap it around me as I squat on one of the beds in the main dorm, using my torch to scan the pages of close-written French script. To my surprise, I can understand most of it – Jean-Luc was old school, his language devoid of slang or difficult idioms.

As with the videos, all the earlier entries reveal his excitement, his delight at being once again in Antarctica.

A flagship project! Such an honour to be here! I feel so much joy at being on the ice again, in this beautiful, pristine environment. It speaks to my heart like nothing else.

I flip through the pages, noting the date of each entry. Sure enough, as we approach the weeks before his death, the tone shifts. This is a different Jean-Luc. Sombre and serious. Worried.

I never felt easy about N's death. Why was a young woman wandering outside in the dark on her own? I cannot forget those tears frozen on her cheeks, the rips in her clothing. How to explain them? I had a feeling there was more to it, but a visiting doctor's feelings don't carry much weight on a large US base.

I scan further, heart in mouth. Lots of stuff about the experiments. Calls home to his wife Nicole, reports on how the children were getting on at school. Then finally I find what I'm looking for.

I struggle now to recall A's exact words when I mentioned N's death to him. Stupid of me not to have noted them down at the time. 'Such a tragedy. Especially as she was pregnant.' Something like that, but I recall better the sensation it gave me, how my skin went cold. That sixth sense I have sometimes when a situation feels wrong.

How does he know that, I asked myself? How did he know she was pregnant?

I'd read all the reports from the medical team – she was barely eight weeks and apparently none of her friends on the base were aware of her condition. Yet when I first asked A if he knew her at McMurdo, he claimed it was only in passing.

Jean-Luc's words begin to blur and swim.

'A'.

Since Alex is dead and Ark has never set foot on the American base – he's made several jokes about how he'd never get clearance – that single initial can only stand for . . . Arne.

Oh God, it's him, I think, tears choking my throat.

It's been Arne all along.

Pain in my heart as sharp as ice, and it takes all my strength not to wail with anguish as I force myself to read on. I find a paragraph written a week or so later – just a few days before that fateful expedition to the crevasse.

S and I have had a huge row about the DNA checks. I worry we were overheard – people are always eavesdropping in this place. She refuses to ask UNA. Says it's pointless, no one there will agree to request the samples from N's baby, not after her death was ruled an accident.

I told her I disagreed, that it had to be worth a shot. She called me paranoid. Paranoid! Sometimes that woman infuriates me. So inflexible.

Now I'm unsure what to do. Perhaps S is right, and I'm reading too much into this. But I have a hunch about A, and I have learned to listen to gut instinct. I've met his type before. Plausible. Never betraying his true nature.

Nevertheless, I cannot insist she request those checks. I suppose I could ask UNA myself, explain my reasons, but sooner or later it would get back to S, and she's already being difficult about our personal situation. I can't risk angering her further. I must wait until we return from the expedition, then try again to convince her.

Mon dieu, quel gâchis.

My God, what a mess, I translate in my head, flicking through the last couple of pages. Nothing of note, just more ruminations about his relationship with his wife. Intimacies that I skim through, uncomfortable, as if I'm somehow intruding.

Pulling my gloves back on, I sit, shivering harder now, trying to take this all in.

So Arne had a relationship with 'N' – Naomi Perez. That baby must have been his. But why kill her? I remember how fondly he talked about his ex's child – Margret, wasn't it? He seemed to like kids – or so he made out to me.

Then again, what reason do I have to trust anything he said? *Plausible* – that was how Jean-Luc describes him. Never showing his real nature.

It's true. Arne is very plausible, very convincing. I've been utterly taken in – even to the point of falling for him. *Everyone was taken in*, I remind myself, recalling Sonya's reaction when I spoke to her in the clinic. Caro coming to his defence too, back when I told her where I'd found Alex's activity monitor.

I stare at the notebook in my hands, the laptop and phone beside me. What should I do with them? They're valuable evidence, after all, proof that Jean-Luc's death was no accident.

Nor Alex's.

I think of Arne gaining access to my clinic, taking those sleeping pills, and remember Drew's comment when I arrived on the base, about Sandrine losing her keys. Arne must have stolen them from her office – after all, I managed the same while her back was turned.

With those master keys, Arne could gain entry to any part of the station. He could help himself to whatever he liked in the clinic, and access the medical files to delete Jean-Luc and Alex's videos. He must have got wind that I was digging around, looking into what happened to my predecessor; after all, plenty of people heard my argument with Alex that night in the canteen.

One of the best men I've ever known has been murdered, and instead of helping me find out who the hell did this, you want to stick me on fucking antidepressants!

Alex's words reverberate in my head, making me wretched with guilt. He was right all along. Had I believed him, had I acted sooner, maybe he – and Sandrine – would still be alive now.

Beneath the guilt, a rising sense of anger at Arne's betrayal. At my own stupidity. I trusted him. I believed he cared about me.

Had started, perhaps, to love me.

But it was all an act. I've been played, deceived. Arne exploited my naivety, my need to be loved, to be reaffirmed after what happened with Ben.

What a fool I've been.

At that moment I hear a noise, coming from somewhere outside. The sound of an approaching skidoo.

Sonya. Thank goodness.

I glance at the little collection of objects on the bed, wondering whether to leave them out to show her. But some sixth sense, shared with Jean-Luc, warns me to be cautious. I get up quickly and lift the mattress, sliding them underneath. Then head towards the exit as the buzz of the engine grows louder and finally stops.

I hover by the door, waiting to greet Sonya, flooded with relief to have someone here to help me look after Caro. Someone I can confide in, discuss what we should do next.

But when the door opens, there's no sign of my friend. Or of anyone else.

Arne has come alone.

47

7 July

'Kate.' Arne takes a few steps towards me, sounding out of breath. 'Thank God. I saw the abandoned skidoo and thought you hadn't made it.'

I stand there, rooted to the spot. My mouth opens but my words stall, as if frozen by the blast of cold air that followed him in.

'Kate?' He removes his goggles, frowning at me. 'Is everything okay? Are Caro and the baby all right? I've been so worried about you.'

I stare at him.

Plausible. Yes, that's exactly the word.

Despite all I know Arne's done, is capable of, I still feel the tug of him. Part of me desperately wants to be convinced by this role he's playing, longs to be sucked into it, to pretend everything is exactly as he would have me believe. It would be so easy to go along with it, to surrender to wherever it took me.

Then I remember Caro and her tiny daughter – above all, I have to keep them safe.

'I was about to collect some snow for water.' I force myself to sound casual. 'Caro needs a drink. Can you help?'

Arne gazes at me with an inscrutable expression, as if he's trying to figure something out. 'Kate, it's all kicking off back at base. We—'

'Tell me outside. They're both asleep.'

I return to the kitchen and pick up the saucepan. Glancing around to check Arne isn't watching, I quickly open the cutlery drawer, select the largest knife I can find and stuff it inside my jacket.

'Christ, it's freezing in here,' says Arne as I rejoin him. 'Where are Caro and the baby?'

'In one of the rear cabins.'

I edge towards the door, but he grabs my arm. 'Listen, we have to talk—'

'Let's do it outside. I don't want to wake them.'

Arne releases me, following me into the night. I march away from the camp as fast as I can, clutching the saucepan in one hand, my torch in the other. I need to draw him as far from Caro and the baby as possible.

And then what? I ask myself, teeth chattering in the unbearable cold. What exactly are you planning to do, Kate?

Stab him?

I remember how Arne hit Luuk in the lounge, the deft and decisive way he overpowered him. Anyway, how would my kitchen knife be a match for his gun?

I grit my teeth and carry on.

'Hey,' Arne calls after me, 'why so far? The snow here is as good as anywhere.'

I stop. Gaze around. We're about fifty metres from the camp. I turn to face him, dropping the saucepan and reaching inside my jacket for the knife. 'I know what you did to Naomi Perez,' I say flatly. 'And that you killed Jean-Luc and Alex. And Sandrine.'

I shine my torch beam on his face to gauge his reaction. Arne looks completely stunned. There are several moments of silence as he takes in what I've just said.

'What are you talking about, Kate?' He takes a step closer, then stops as he spots the knife in my hand.

'You can't be serious.' He stares at it, horrified. 'Kate, tell me you're joking. You can't possibly believe I would do anything like that.'

I study the confusion in his features. It's so convincing I almost fall for it. Almost drop the knife onto the snow and go to him.

'Listen to me, Kate.' Arne moves towards me and I back away, maintaining the distance between us. 'I can prove it,' he says, his tone urgent, 'I can prove I had nothing to do with that woman's death. I emailed Kristin before the power went down and she sent—'

'*Stop lying!*' I shout, brandishing the knife to keep him away. 'There's no point. I don't believe a single word you say.'

Arne frowns, miming bewilderment. Suddenly he lurches forward, knocking the knife from my hand.

'Kate, for fuck's sake,' he yells, grabbing my arm. 'You have to—'

A loud crack reverberates through the darkness.

I stand there, uncomprehending, gazing right into Arne's eyes in that split second before he crumples before me. Instinctively I drop the torch and try to catch him, but he's too heavy. He falls onto the ice with a heavy thump.

I stare down at him, frozen with shock and surprise.

What the fuck just happened?

Someone shot him, I realise, mind reeling with disbelief.

That sound was a gunshot.

Arne is lying face down in the snow. I kneel beside him, whimpering with panic, trying to heave him onto his back, but I can't grip properly in these bulky gloves. I take them off and try again.

Behind me, the crunch of ice as someone approaches. I spin around, shining my torch into the endless night. See a figure looming towards me, features obscured by the high rim of his jacket and wide goggles, a large fur hat covering his hair.

All I know is it's a man, obvious by his bulk and stance.

In his hand, a small black pistol.

'You all right, Kate?' Drew sounds concerned.

'Yes . . .' I turn back to Arne, and feel inside his necker for a pulse. Detect the faint beat of his heart.

He's still alive.

'Quickly,' I say pulling my gloves back on. 'We have to get him inside.'

But Drew doesn't move. Just stands there, staring down at the pair of us.

'Help me,' I urge, 'or he'll bleed to death.' I frown up at Drew, but he's shaking his head.

'He was going to kill you, Kate, like all the others.'

'None of that matters,' I insist. 'I'll treat him, then we'll put him somewhere safe, where he can't hurt anyone else. We'll let the police deal with this. We can't simply leave him to die.' Already the snow around his temple is staining red – the bullet must have hit his skull.

But Drew still doesn't move.

'Drew,' I urge, desperate, 'for Christ's sake, help—'

'Shut up,' he snaps. 'I need to think.'

I frown at him, bewildered. There's something wrong here. He's just shot someone, and yet Drew's acting as if . . . as if it's nothing.

And why has he got the gun? Did he find it in the station? *Or did he know where it was hidden all along?*

The ground beneath me tilts and spins, and suddenly I'm back there, emerging from that little plane after my long journey to Antarctica. A man extending his hand in greeting.

'Andrew,' he says. 'But everyone calls me Drew.'

Andrew.

'A'.

'Y-you,' I stammer, trembling with shock and the sudden, certain conviction I'm right.

'Me what?' he asks.

'You were at McMurdo, weren't you? When that woman died. Naomi Perez.'

Drew tilts his head. Though I can't see his eyes, I'm aware all his attention is fixed on me. 'What sort of question is that?'

There's a hardness in his tone now, a change in his manner I can't put a finger on. As if he's dropped some kind of act.

Plausible. Never betraying his real nature.

My predecessor's words ring in my head as I scramble to my feet and find my voice. 'You killed Naomi, didn't you? And Jean-Luc, when he started to become suspicious. Alex and Sandrine too.'

I wait for Drew's indignant reaction, his shocked denial. But nothing happens. We stand there in the dark, the almost perfect silence, only the faint sound of our breath freezing, the tiny ice crystals tinkling as they fall to the ground.

An eternity before he speaks.

'I wish you hadn't said that, Kate. I really do.'

Drew grabs my arm, glancing down at Arne's body. 'Forget him,' he says. 'He's not worth it.'

I wrench away, suddenly furious. Oblivious to the danger I'm in. 'Why?' I spit into his masked face. 'Why did you do it? Why did you do any of it?'

Drew doesn't respond. After all, what could he possibly say? All pretence between us is now over. There's no rational explanation for his actions. The answer lies deep within his soul – as obscure, probably, to himself as to me.

'Let's take a walk.' Drew grasps my arm again and drags me across the ice. I try to resist, but it's impossible – he's so much bigger and stronger than I am.

'What are you going to do?' I ask instead. 'How are you going to explain any of this?'

'Oh, that's easy,' he replies, his voice terrifyingly matter-of-fact. 'I came across Arne here,' he gestures back at the body behind us, already covered with a light smattering of snow, 'about to attack you. I managed to wrest the gun from him, but accidentally shot him in the struggle. Sounds plausible to me.'

Plausible. I glare at him in revulsion. 'So you put that activity band in the garage? To point the finger at Arne?'

Drew grins but says nothing.

'And what about me?' I ask quietly, bracing myself for the answer. 'What are you planning to tell everyone about me?'

He stops, turns. Shrugs. 'You ran off in a panic, dropped your torch and got lost in the darkness. I searched for you everywhere, but found you too late. Your little body collapsed into the snow, in a foetal crouch perhaps, a desperate attempt to keep warm. Poor terrified Kate.'

I reach up with my free hand and rip away his goggles. I want to see him. And I want him to know I see the person inside.

'It was you, wasn't it, who took my torch? While I was watching the aurora.'

Drew grunts, reaches down to retrieve his goggles, checking them over to make sure they're not broken. 'You pissed me off, Kate, messing me around like you did. So it occurred to me, why not teach you a lesson?'

'Like taking those pills from my room?'

Drew grins again but doesn't bother to confirm it.

'And you broke into my clinic, didn't you? To steal those pills and delete Jean-Luc's video logs.'

He sniffs, replacing his goggles. 'Careless of me not to think of them sooner.'

'Careless of you too, not to remember to lock the clinic door after you left.' The thought is oddly reassuring. He's not as clever as he assumes. Even if by some miracle Drew gets away with everything that's happened out here on the ice, sooner or later he'll slip up and betray himself.

Gripping my arm again, Drew drags me along in his wake, deeper into the night. I imagine him pulling off my protective clothes, holding me down until the cold invades every part of me.

The same as he did with Naomi – and Alex.

And I find I don't even care, not really. I'm too exhausted. Too overwhelmed by the futility of it all. By my own failure to see what was right under my nose until it was too late.

'Promise me something,' I say, stumbling on the snow. 'You won't hurt Caro, will you? Or her baby?'

His fingers dig tighter into my arm. 'I would never hurt that child.' His voice is fierce as he spins me to face him again, shining his torch into my eyes. 'She didn't tell you?'

I blink, half blinded. 'Who? Caro?' I stammer. 'I don't understand.'

'She isn't Alex's child,' he hisses. 'That little girl is *mine*.'

'Yours?' I repeat, incredulous.

Then I recall Caro's hesitation when I asked her about the father, back when she first revealed her pregnancy. I hadn't pushed her to explain – it was her business after all. When she told me later that Alex fathered her baby, I didn't think to question it further.

'So Caro never mentioned our fling?' Drew snorts. 'Before she fell for that Irish moron.'

I hear the hatred in his tone. Is he secretly in love with her, I wonder? Is that what Alex's death was really about? Was Drew's motive simply jealousy?

'And what about Naomi?' I ask, hoping to divert Drew from

what he's intending to do. At least buy myself a bit more time. 'Why did you kill her, if it wasn't because she was pregnant?'

He pauses. Releases my arm. 'Naomi was a bitch. Shouting and threatening to sue me for child support. I didn't believe her about the pregnancy. I thought she was simply fucking with me.'

'So that's why you mentioned it to Jean-Luc. You wanted to find out if it was true?'

'Yeah. Pretty stupid, in hindsight, but I had to know. I felt shit about it, you see. Not about Naomi, but my child. I don't believe in hurting innocent kids.'

I shiver, wondering what horrors lurk in his past – probably enough to fill a whole psychiatric textbook. While genetics plays a large part in psychopathy, it takes a pretty fucked-up childhood to turn someone into a cold-blooded killer.

And I come to a decision. I won't tell him I know he's not the father of Caro's baby. I have the blood type of everyone on the base off by heart, in case I ever have to set up a person-to-person transfusion requiring compatible volunteers. Caro's blood type is O, and the baby's is A – I tested her right after she was born, using one of the kits in the clinic. It's biologically impossible that Drew – blood type B – is little Kate's father.

But if believing that will protect Caro and her child, then I'm not about to put Drew straight.

'Anyway, I reckon here'll do.' He swings his torch around. The beam skims across the desolate ice, cutting through the surrounding blackness for a few seconds. There's no moonlight, but I'm no longer scared of the dark. No thoughts now of monsters lurking in the shadows, ready to pounce.

I've got a real live human one beside me, possessed by his own demons – and they're much scarier than anything out there.

'Two ways this goes down,' Drew says to me. 'You fight, Kate, and make this worse for yourself. Or you simply embrace it. It's faster that way, more peaceful.'

He's right. So I don't struggle as he removes my hat and gloves and jacket. Offer no resistance when he pushes me onto the ice and yanks off my down-filled trousers.

He strips me almost bare, then leans over me. 'This is your fault,' he says, sounding disgruntled. 'You could have avoided this, Kate, could have kept your head down and your nose out of my business.'

'Fuck off, Drew,' I gasp. Already my jaw is stiff and I'm finding it hard to breathe as my body reacts to the lethal cold. I wait for him to hit me, kick me perhaps, but he's too clever to leave a mark – not this time. Alex might have needed restraining, but Drew knows I'm no match for his superior strength.

'Don't be scared,' he bends and whispers into my ear. 'I'll be close by, so you won't be alone. Best not to struggle or kick up a fuss – they say it's just like going to sleep.'

Like hell it is, I think, remembering that death-mask grimace on Alex's face. Suddenly I'm filled with panic and desolation and regret, but I force myself not to cry out, not to plead or beg as Drew extinguishes the torch, plunging us both into blackness.

Just for a minute or so, the clouds clear, and I glimpse countless stars refracted through my freezing breath, dissolving into haloes of gold. Somewhere, impossibly far away, a meteor streaks across the sky, plunging down to earth.

Thank you, I say silently, to a god I don't believe in. Glad, in some part of me, that the last thing I will ever see is so much beauty.

As the clouds return, I squeeze my eyes closed, feel frozen

tears seal them shut. Grief washes over me now – not only for myself, but for Alex and Jean-Luc and Sandrine too.

But most of all for Arne.

He came to help me. To save me. And he died believing that I hated him, that I feared him. That I'd written him off as a monster.

I'm sorry, Arne. *I'm so so sorry.*

I send it out as a prayer into the darkness, along with three words I never had a chance to say to him.

Something I never thought I'd feel for anyone again.

Instinctively my body contracts into a tight ball in an effort to stay warm. But I'm shivering so hard now I can hardly breathe, and there's no longer any sensation in my hands or feet as the capillaries in my skin constrict, and my heart diverts blood to my vital organs in a frantic attempt to keep me alive. The cold is so deep, so penetrating, so all-encompassing, that it feels like fire. I recall again those accounts of people stripping off as they die of exposure, believing themselves to be overheating.

Fireworks start to fill my dying brain, my own internal aurora. Beyond them, a gathering dark of a different kind, creeping towards me, inch by inch. In it, inevitably, my fox. It pads up to me, climbing on my chest and staring down with those wild and beautiful eyes.

'Kate,' it says, in a voice at once close and far away.

A vixen.

My little brown vixen.

'Kate,' she bends and nudges my cheek with her muzzle. 'Wake up.'

I sense her warm animal breath on my skin, her wet nose brushing ice crystals from my hair, from my cheeks, from my eyelids.

'For God's sake, Kate, open your fucking eyes and look at me!'

Instantly my fox vanishes into the night. A sensation of weightlessness as I'm dragged upwards and shaken hard.

I summon all my remaining strength and force my frozen lids apart. Blink into the bright light trained on my face.

'Shit.' Caro emits a great gulping sob. 'Look what he's done to you!'

She disappears for a moment, returning with my clothes. Quickly, clumsily, she forces my jacket over my rigid arms. Laying me back briefly on the ice, she drags my trousers over my shaking legs.

'Caro?' I croak, barely able to speak, to formulate a thought. Where am I? How did I get here?

Then I remember.

'Drew,' I rasp, desperately. 'Caro, Drew is—'

'I know.' Grunting with the effort, she heaves me into a sitting position. 'I heard everything that bastard said to you.' She chokes on another sob. 'I'm sorry I couldn't help you sooner, but you have to move slowly if you don't want an animal like that to hear you coming.'

She swings her torch and I peer through its narrow beam. Spot a plumbing wrench lying a few metres away. Beyond it, Drew's prone body. Just as I'm beginning to think he's dead, his leg moves, followed by a dull moan half muffled by snow.

'One second.' Caro props her torch on a ridge of ice, then gets back to her feet, clutching her stomach in pain. I watch, shaking with cold, with adrenaline, while she returns to Drew. She removes several thick plastic ties from her jacket pocket, the kind I've seen her use countless times on loose pipes or cables in Beta. Expertly she secures his ankles and hands, trussing him like a steer, face wincing as she moves.

I guess she's had plenty of practice, I think, recalling her childhood on that New Zealand cattle farm.

Then I remember something else.

Something far more important. And far more urgent.

'Arne,' I call out hoarsely to Caro, filled with an all-consuming panic. 'We have to find Arne.'

48

12 July

'Is everything ready?' Luuk asks, clomping into the clinic in his snow gear.

I glance around, making sure. 'As ready as we'll ever be.' I push down another surge of anxiety, only too aware of the approaching danger. The odds stacked against us.

'You coming, Kate? Sonya?' Luuk looks from one of us to the other.

I hesitate. I should stay here, make certain Arne is comfortable. The pain where the bullet shattered the side of his temple is still troubling him, though thankfully there seems minimal damage to his brain. Plus I need to replace the dressings for his frostbite.

But I also know that if this doesn't go right, I'll have even bigger problems on my hands.

'You go,' Sonya says to me. 'I'll stay here and make sure he's okay.'

'How long will we be?' I ask Luuk.

'Not long,' he replies. 'Half an hour max? We really could use your help if you can manage it. Tom's busy with the radio, so there's only six of us.'

I check on Arne. He's on the exam bed, sleeping off another dose of morphine.

'Go.' Caro gives me an encouraging smile from the armchair where she's nursing little Kate, who's proving stronger than

anyone could have hoped. No harm came to her, thank goodness, from being left swaddled up in that cabin in Gamma
while Caro went outside to investigate the source of the
gunshot. She's as tough as her mother, I decide.

I hurry to the boot room and kit up, adding an extra balaclava and hat for good measure. Then stand there, heart racing,
gripped by another rush of fear.

You can do this, I insist to myself, trying not to think of
my recent ordeal on the ice, that vice-like deathly cold. I want
desperately to be there, to help make this happen, but I'm too
afraid.

I close my eyes and steady my breathing. Remember Caro's
strength and courage, says a voice in my head.

Arne's too.

If they can do it, so can you.

Taking a deep breath and checking the remaining battery
life in my torch, I open the door and go outside, joining the
others on the ice.

'Right.' Luuk hands us each a length of wood wound tightly
with cloth, giving off a strong smell of gasoline. Plus a cigarette
lighter each – God knows where he found all of them. 'I'll take
the two drums at the top. Ark, you take the next two, then
Rob, Rajiv, Alice, and finally Kate. Everybody clear on what
to do?'

All five of us nod.

'I'll use this flashlight as the signal, okay?'

We all nod again.

'Anyone religious here?' Luuk asks finally.

Ark shrugs. 'Does Russian Orthodox count?'

'That'll do. Start praying, and make sure God is paying
attention.' He glances around at all of us. 'Good luck.'

We exchange nervous looks, then trudge across the snow to
take up our positions. I find I'm praying too, well aware of

everything that could go wrong. We're going to need all the help we can get.

The odds are stacked against us – and those odds are huge.

Enough, I tell myself, as I stand in the darkness by one of the large fuel drums Ark and Luuk have dragged out onto the ice.

Thankfully the wind has dropped since Caro and I took refuge in Gamma, and we're surrounded now by stillness. I stamp my feet to keep warm, listening for any break in the silence, hear nothing but Alice coughing fifty metres away. I take slow steady breaths, trying not to think about the cold, about what happened out here during that terrifying episode five days ago.

And everything that came after. Finding Arne near dead on the ice, half frozen and losing blood from the wound in his head. How it took three people – Ark, Luuk, and Rob – to drag Drew back to Beta and lock him up in one of the store-rooms. The anxious hours by Arne's side, waiting for him to regain consciousness, hoping against hope that any injury to his brain wasn't too extensive.

My joy and relief when he finally opened his eyes and murmured my name. A miracle.

Two miracles, I think, remembering little Kate.

Now we just need a third.

I strain my ears but there's still nothing. So I distract myself by studying the heavens above me. No clouds tonight, and I can see billions of tiny pinpricks of light, those countless stars and galaxies, and the bright opalescent band of the Milky Way. It's beautiful, and I drink it in – this may be the clearest view I'll have of the night sky for the rest of my life.

I've just managed to locate the Southern Cross when I see Luuk's torch flash on and off three times.

The signal.

Fumbling, heart thumping, I pull off my glove and remove the cigarette lighter from my pocket. My hand is shaking so much I can barely hold it, and it takes several attempts to light the end of my torch. The flames leap out, illuminating the surrounding ice with an eerie orange glow that reminds me of the aurora.

I dip it quickly into the barrel, jumping aside as the fuel explodes with a whoosh and flare of red. I hurry across to the other side, and ignite the second barrel. Standing back, I gaze up towards the others, marvelling at the two parallel lines of fire before me.

Please God, I pray, more sincerely now.

Please let this work.

In the distance a sound, a faint buzz like an insect. I listen, wondering if I'm mistaken.

Did I imagine it?

Slowly, inexorably, the noise grows louder, developing into the distinct drone of an engine. I squint into the sky, scanning the area north of our makeshift runway, pulse racing with an equal mix of fear and excitement.

There!

Alice whoops as she spots it too, an array of lights, some blinking, some static, low on the horizon. My heart lifts as the Twin Otter angles into view, the lights growing bigger and brighter as it veers slightly to the left and lines up with the runway.

I clench my fists to contain my emotion.

Please let them make it. Please.

The high-pitched whine of the engines, its two whirring propellers, increases to a roar as the plane loses height, heading for the ice. I cover my ears with my hands, holding my breath, as I watch it drop ever closer to the ground.

Please.

For a moment I think it won't make the landing, that the little aircraft will surge back into the air, but a second later its wheels hit the ice, bouncing several times, sending up a spray of snow crystals that sparkle in the orange light. The Twin Otter races towards me, its engines screaming as it decelerates fast, finally coming to a halt a few metres from where I'm standing.

They made it.

They actually fucking made it!

A chorus of cheers as everyone hurries to meet the pilot already descending from the cockpit. Several passengers emerge from the side doors, two in army uniform, carrying formidable-looking guns. Raising a hand to greet us, they proceed immediately to unload supplies from the rear of the plane.

A third passenger joins the pilots as they approach, smiling broadly and shaking all our hands. 'Goodness,' the man says in a soft Canadian accent, 'I have to admit that was a bit hairy.'

To my embarrassment, I burst into tears, overwhelmed with relief and elation and gratitude. They've made it. These men all risked their lives to make this journey in the dead of winter – a journey so formidable, so fraught with danger, it's rarely ever been attempted.

The Canadian puts a comforting arm around my shoulder, and studies my face in the flickering light of the burning barrels.

'I'm guessing you're Kate.'

I nod, wiping away tears with my gloved hand before they freeze.

'I'm Jon, the replacement doctor. I hear you've been quite the hero.'

We don't have long. The pilots have to keep the engines running to stop the oil and fuel from freezing. Jon, Ark, and the two soldiers help wheel Arne out on a trolley and load him into the aircraft, Caro and her baby taking the seat by the window.

I linger on the ice, saying goodbye. Ark envelops me in one of his bear hugs, clearly unwilling to let me go, his shoulders tight with emotion. Alice is openly crying, Tom beside her, supporting himself with the crutches I'd found in my clinic.

'Take care of that leg,' I tell him, squeezing his arm. 'Not too much exertion until it's fully healed.'

He nods, and Sonya grabs something from her jacket pocket and drapes it around my neck. A beautiful scarf, in the same wintry colours as my lovely socks.

'See you soon,' she says, pressing her lips together and blinking hard.

I climb almost reluctantly into the seat between Arne and Caro. Despite everything, I find I'm sorry to be going. Leaving these people, after all we've been through together, is proving a great deal harder than I anticipated.

But they're in safe hands now. The base has a new doctor, and the soldiers will take care of Drew until everyone can be flown out safely in September. Ark has managed to repair the generator, and Tom's leg is healing nicely – he's adamant he wants to see out the rest of the winter with the others. Even Luuk has been transformed by the unfolding horror on the station, picking up the slack left by Arne and Drew.

I check on Arne, who manages a weak smile and gives me a thumbs up. But Caro senses how nervous I am. She glances down at little Kate, cradled inside her jacket, then grabs my hand.

'It's going to be all right,' she whispers, and gives my hand a reassuring squeeze – she knows how much I hate flying, let alone in these conditions.

'Final check,' says Mike, the lead pilot. 'Everybody strapped in safely?'

We murmur our assent.

'Next stop, Chile,' quips Sam, the co-pilot, and I clutch

Caro's hand tightly as the plane taxis around and lines back up on the runway.

Seconds later we start sliding forwards. I stare out of the window, my fear almost drowned out by the noise of the engines as we pick up speed, the ice transformed into a steady blur of white.

A small, barely perceptible lift, and suddenly we're airborne.

I crane my neck around as the Twin Otter begins to circle. I can just make out the others on the ground, shimmering in the light of the burning barrels, waving goodbye.

Instinctively I raise my hand and wave back, though of course they can't see me. Then I watch, mesmerised, as the lights of the ice station grow smaller and smaller, finally fading completely as we fly into the boundless Antarctic night.

Acknowledgements

It can be a long journey to get to THE END, so a huge thank you to everyone who's helped me along the way. Big gratitude to my agent Mark 'Stan' Stanton and Julie Fergusson, editor Jo Dickinson, along with Sorcha Rose, Melis Dagoglu, Charlotte Webb, Helen Parham and all the fantastic team at Hodder.

I'm also indebted to all my lovely writer pals on Facebook, but particularly Caroline Green and Julie-Ann Corrigan for beta reading, with honourable mentions to Susi Holliday, Essie Fox, Roz Watkins and Amanda Jennings for their help and support.

As always, thanks to Marie Adams, for keeping me sane. And I'm ever grateful to my friends and family, particularly James Ridley and Hetty Rees-Haughton for battling their way through a very early draft. Not forgetting a special mention for my father, Bob Haughton, who I hope will be tickled pink to see his own name in print right here.

More generally, I owe an enormous debt to all the brave souls who've spent months out in Antarctica and detailed their fascinating experiences on blogs and videos. Thank you, I couldn't have done this without you. Please forgive any liberties with time, place, customs and so on, in service of the plot. I hope your stay on the ice was considerably less fraught!

Last, but not least, thank you to everyone who has taken the time and trouble to read this story. I hope you enjoyed it.

Emma

THRILLINGLY GOOD BOOKS
FROM CRIMINALLY
GOOD WRITERS

CRIME FILES BRINGS YOU THE LATEST RELEASES FROM
TOP CRIME AND THRILLER AUTHORS.

SIGN UP ONLINE FOR OUR MONTHLY NEWSLETTER AND BE THE FIRST
TO KNOW ABOUT OUR COMPETITIONS, NEW BOOKS AND MORE.